The Shadow in the Glass

JJA Harwood is an author, editor and blogger. She grew up in Norfolk, read History at the University of Warwick and eventually found her way to London, which is still something of a shock for somebody used to so many fields.

When not writing, she can be found learning languages, cooking with more enthusiasm than skill, wandering off into clearly haunted houses and making friends with stray cats. *The Shadow In The Glass* is her debut novel.

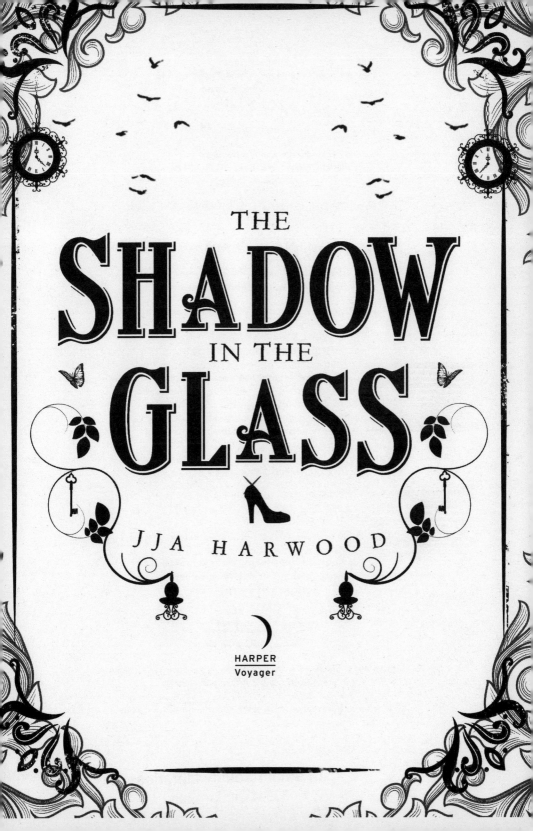

THE
SHADOW
IN THE
GLASS

JJA HARWOOD

HARPER
Voyager

Harper*Voyager*
An imprint of HarperCollins*Publishers* Ltd
1 London Bridge Street
London SE1 9GF

www.harpercollins.co.uk

HarperCollins*Publishers*
1st Floor, Watermarque Building, Ringsend Road
Dublin 4, Ireland

First published by HarperCollins*Publishers* Ltd 2021
2

A catalogue record for this book is available from the British Library

ISBN: 978-0-00-836809-8 (HB)
ISBN: 978-0-00-836810-4 (TPB)

Set in Sabon LT Std by Palimpsest Book Production Limited,
Falkirk, Stirlingshire

Printed and bound in the UK by
CPI Group (UK) Ltd, Croydon CR0 4YY

MIX
Paper from
responsible sources
FSC
www.fsc.org **FSC® C007454**

To Rosie, Jess, Georgie and Wei, for all their support and encouragement. This is, technically, all their fault.

PART ONE

If anyone caught her, Eleanor would be dismissed on the spot.

The house clicked and creaked as it settled into sleep, the heat of the last days of August quietly slipping into the night. Eleanor was the only one awake. On silent feet, she was as insubstantial as a flame. She could drift past cold fireplaces and dust sheets looming like glaciers and all she would leave behind was the faintest stirring in the air.

Candlelight shimmered on the walls as she crept into the library. The dark spines of the books were rows of windows, waiting for the shutters to be pulled back. Open one, and she would know the secrets of Ottoman palaces; open another, and she would gaze across deserts. Granborough House would fade away. Eleanor smiled. Some things were worth risking dismissal for, especially with the master out of the house for the evening.

Eleanor set down her candle and surveyed her subjects. Damp equatorial rainforests, steaming in the heat. Versailles, glittering in the dark like an Earthbound star. Verona – Juliet on her balcony, sighing into the darkness. It was a perfect night for poetry: she could stretch out her legs and whisper sonnets into the slow, hot silence. But she would cry, and Mrs Fielding would be able to tell the next morning. Better to keep her face blank, in case the housekeeper grew curious.

Eleanor locked the door, slipping the library key back up her sleeve. She'd stolen the key from Mrs Pembroke's house-keeping chatelaine. Even though the mistress of the house had been dead for more than three years, shame still crawled under Eleanor's skin when she went through Mrs Pembroke's things. Not that Mrs Pembroke would have minded. She had spent the last few months of her life propped up on pillows, telling Eleanor how to care for everything she would inherit from Mrs Pembroke's will.

The weight of the key against Eleanor's forearm felt like shackles. Mrs Pembroke never would have wanted Eleanor to creep around the house like a thief, just for something to read.

The lady of the house had not wanted Eleanor to be a housemaid at all. Versailles, Verona, perhaps even the rainforest – these were all places Eleanor might have visited, if only Mrs Pembroke had lived. A lump crawled into Eleanor's throat. Mrs Pembroke had been planning to take her on a tour of Europe when Eleanor was old enough to enter Society. Suddenly it seemed cruel to have so many travelogues spread out in front of her, when she'd once been so close to seeing the places all these men had written of.

Eleanor gave herself a little shake. She'd told herself not to get upset.

She lifted *The Fairy Ring* off the shelves and felt better the moment it was in her hand. Her own fingerprints from years ago marked the table of contents – smaller, of course, than they were now – the corner of the back cover was fraying slightly, from all the times she'd plucked at it as she read.

Settling into her favourite chair with that book in her

hands, the lump in her throat melted away. At seventeen, she knew she ought to have grown out of such things, but it was difficult to set aside a world where trees grew delicate gold and silver branches and strange creatures lurked in cool, clear water. She lost herself on narrow paths twisting through dark woods, yearned to spin straw into gold, and envied the twelve brothers who had been changed into swans. It seemed like a fine thing to be a clean white bird that might fly anywhere it liked.

She put the book back when the clock struck midnight, making sure to replace it exactly where she found it. The chimes were quiet, but the sound dropped through to the pit of Eleanor's stomach like a leaden weight. An old memory struggled to the surface of her thoughts – she was nine years old and curled into a ball, back pressed against the leg of an iron bed as a cheaper, harsher clock tolled midnight – but she shook it off. It wouldn't do to think of her own mother now, she'd make herself upset again. Somewhere outside a hansom cab rattled over the cobblestones; she flinched, heart pounding, and almost knocked her candle over. Mr Pembroke was supposed to be dining at his club tonight. What if he'd changed his mind and come back early?

Eleanor listened at the door, forcing her nerves into submission. Nothing from downstairs. If she was quick, no one would even guess that she'd left her room. She crept back up the servants' staircase and slipped into her little room, trying not to wilt at the sight of the bare boards, the skeletal iron bedframe, her useless scrap of curtain hanging limp over the window. She crawled into bed, ignoring the smell of mildew from the blankets and holding the memory of the fairy stories like hands cupped around a tiny flame. When she slept, she dreamed of vast wings carrying her away, and she could not tell if they were her own.

It was hard to believe in fairy tales when you woke up to the smell of damp. Eleanor's shoulders felt like a bag of rocks and her knees were already aching. Nothing felt magical in her little garret. Her chest of drawers was small, cheap and splintery; her jug and washbasin were chipped. The sloping roof came too close to her head and damp mottled the walls and ceiling. She might have been sleeping at the bottom of a well.

Eleanor pulled on her uniform – a hard-wearing brown wool dress, which still scratched no matter how many times she washed it – remembering the steady beat of wings she'd dreamed about. She'd tell Aoife about it later, and they'd list all the places they'd fly away to while they polished the silver.

As she did every day, Eleanor checked her money drawer before she left her room. She didn't open the drawer properly, just dragged it out a few inches so that the purse lurched forward, coins clinking. It was a silly habit, but hope rekindled in her chest at the sound. She had almost twenty-five pounds now: nearly enough to rent clean and pretty rooms for a few months, but she would need to find a way to live after that. She wouldn't be emptying other people's chamber pots for much longer.

She crept along the corridor and knocked on Leah's door.

Without her stays Leah's stomach stuck out like a hillock among the valleys of sheets. Her dark hair was spread out across the pillow, long limbs sticking out from under the blankets. She twitched in her sleep, eyelids fluttering, wincing as the baby shifted. The rest of the maids had been pretending not to notice while Eleanor helped Leah let out the waistline of her uniform. Anger flashed through Eleanor like lightning. Eleanor would've pretended for the full nine months and feigned surprise when the baby came, but it was not up to her. It was up to Mrs Fielding, and everyone knew that the moment Leah could no longer hide her condition, Mrs Fielding would dismiss Leah without a reference. Leah knew it too. Her carpetbag had been packed for weeks, just in case.

Eleanor cleared her throat. 'Leah?'

Leah started awake, her eyes flying open. 'God above, Ella! I thought you were—'

'I don't think he's back yet,' said Eleanor, closing the door behind her. 'I wondered if you'd like some help getting dressed.'

Leah flushed. 'I'm only showing a little.'

Eleanor kept her voice gentle. 'More than a little, these days.'

Leah eased herself out of bed and got to her feet, and when she was standing Eleanor felt a flutter of hope. Her friend had always been full-figured, and when she drew herself upright perhaps Mrs Fielding would think that Leah had only put on weight. Of course, there were other signs too – dark circles under Leah's eyes from all the sleepless nights, a slight thinning in her face thanks to the morning sickness – but all the maids were tired, and Leah could always say she'd eaten something that disagreed with her. Perhaps Leah wouldn't have to leave *just* yet. Perhaps things would be different this time.

There was no mirror in this room, which was as small and shabby as Eleanor's, so Leah shook out a stocking and tried to wind it around her waist, to see how much she'd grown.

The ends only just met. She threw the stocking aside, hands shaking. Eleanor picked it up and smoothed it flat, folding it up so she didn't have to look at Leah's face. It took longer than it should; a slow, desperate frustration made her clumsy.

'Mrs Fielding might not have—'

Leah gave a hollow laugh. 'If *you* noticed weeks ago, Little Nell, then there's no hope for me at all.'

The old nickname had a sting to it, like a needle slid under Eleanor's fingernail. She fought to keep her composure. 'You never thought about...about bringing on your time a little early? There are women who can—'

Leah stared at her, her grey eyes full of disbelief. 'I could never! Where did you hear about something like that?'

Eleanor flushed. Leah hadn't been the first maid to fall pregnant at Granborough House. 'Oh, of course, I couldn't either,' she gabbled. 'But you don't seem very happy and I thought I'd—'

'Of course I'm not happy!' Leah snapped.

Eleanor reached out a hand, but Leah batted her away.

'You'd better get on.'

Eleanor went downstairs, leaving Leah to wrestle with her stays. The vast basement kitchen of Granborough House was still and dark; the street-level window splashed a thin slice of light across the floor. Eleanor filled the coal scuttle and lit the kitchen range after three attempts, before the rest of the servants came in. The coal smoke stung her eyes, but she stared at the flames until tears were streaming down her face.

Fetching the first lot of water was always the worst part of Eleanor's morning. The iron bucket smacked into her shins as she walked up the steps to their little slice of garden. Grey light oozed over the high walls. The herb garden, the trees and the old coach house were vague shapes in the gloom. As she went to the pump at the end of their overgrown strip of grass, the broken windows of the abandoned coach house glittered.

The trough underneath the pump was full of water and a fine layer of dead flies. She wrenched the handle. The pump made a horrible sucking noise and spat water all over her skirts. Beyond the wall hansoms rattled past, fast and sharp. The houses around them were only just beginning to stir to life. Eleanor could hear doors opening, buckets clanking, the subtle sounds of chimney after chimney warming up along the street. Mayfair was still quiet, but she could already hear the racket when she turned her head towards Marylebone. Slow rumbling announced the arrival of the costermongers' carts, already laden down. From far off came a cry of 'Coffee! Hot coffee!' – Speakers' Corner, she guessed. The costermongers always got there early, selling pigs' trotters to zealots so concerned with their souls that they forgot what they put in their bodies. But that was the best way to eat the costermongers' wares. The fruit-seller at the corner of Wigmore Street had been boiling his oranges, and that wouldn't be the worst of it.

She hauled the bucket back inside.

By the time she was done most of the maids were huddled around the kitchen table. Skinny, frizzy-haired Lizzie was yawning into her bowl of porridge. Leah was still absent. Aoife smiled at Eleanor, bleary-eyed. Daisy, their last remaining kitchen maid, was hunched over the stove, the muscles in her strong brown arms flexing as she stirred the heavy porridge pot. As Daisy ladled out another bowl, Aoife caught Daisy's eye and blushed. Eleanor could've sworn she had seen Daisy wink.

'Where's Leah?' Eleanor asked. 'Is she still dressing?'

Aoife tore her eyes away from Daisy, blushing. 'I've not seen her.'

Eleanor handed an empty bowl to Daisy. 'Well, we ought to set something aside for her. She'll need her strength.'

Lizzie, the head housemaid, rolled her eyes. 'Oh, spare me your moralizing, Ella. It's her own silly fault she's eating for two.'

Eleanor whirled around, her temper flaring. 'It is *not* her fault and you know it.'

Lizzie smirked. 'There's a lot of things I know, Miss Eleanor.'

Leah clattered into the kitchen and Lizzie fell silent. Leah hadn't managed her stays properly; her dress bulged and sagged where they hadn't quite fastened. It made her stomach seem larger than ever, and her eyes were very red. Still, she grabbed the porridge that Eleanor had set aside for her and wolfed it down.

'You took your bloody time,' Lizzie muttered, looking away.

Leah set aside her bowl and gave Lizzie a long, cool look. 'You didn't. There's hardly any porridge left. Tell me, does food taste better when you take it from someone else?'

Lizzie flushed and slammed her spoon onto the table. 'You watch how you speak to me!'

Mrs Fielding swept into the room before the argument could properly ignite, already immaculate despite the early hour. Her black dress had been brushed to a shine and her brown hair, greying slightly, was twisted into a savagely tight bun. Mrs Banbury, the cook, slouched in after her, short and stocky, her grey-streaked hair sagging down her neck. Both of them already looked hot and tired.

'Still eating, girls?' Mrs Fielding asked, rubbing an old scar on her neck. 'Come along, we've lots to do.'

Lizzie simpered at Mrs Fielding. 'We've just finished, Mrs F.' She turned back to the table. 'Ella, you can clear this lot away now.'

Mrs Fielding nodded. Looking over them all, her eyes landed on Leah, took in the bump, and they all saw the decision settle into place. Eleanor watched her jaw clench, the tip of the scar twitching, and knew that there was nothing she could do or say to make Mrs Fielding change her mind.

Tonight, Eleanor would go to the library again. She would read until her eyes ached. She would drown herself in words, sink into the vanilla-smell of the binding, replace her blood with ink. She'd feast on other worlds and make herself anew. A fresh, clean, charming thing with a story from every continent, safe in a world where good, kind girls would not be abandoned…

'Get to work, girls,' Mrs Fielding snapped, staring at Leah.

Eleanor had been told to wash the kitchen floor when Mrs Fielding led Leah out of the kitchen, past the abandoned laundry room and into the housekeeper's private rooms. Eleanor clattered around the kitchen as she fetched her supplies. Three buckets: soapy water, clean water, and water and vinegar, and enough rags and sponges to make a patchwork quilt. She scrubbed each flagstone carefully, first with soap, then water, then the vinegar mixture, until her hands were red and stinging and a fine web of tiny cracks was bleeding across her knuckles. She wished that the sound of cloth on stone could drown out Leah's pleading.

It wasn't supposed to be like this.

Eleanor knew she shouldn't have expected any better. Eleanor's mother had been Mrs Pembroke's servant since they were both teenagers, and they had still confided in each other long after Eleanor's mother left Mrs Pembroke's employ. Eleanor had vague memories from when she was small of playing on the floor between the two women as they planned out her future. Mrs Pembroke had promised Eleanor a good character reference for her first job, and hoped that she'd care for Mrs Pembroke's own daughter, in her own grand house, when the time came. But when she was eight, Eleanor's mother fell ill, and all those plans had been eclipsed by a long year of nursing that Eleanor remembered only in snatches: sweeping the floor with a broom as big as she was, helping her mother sit up against the big iron bedframe, spooning broth into her mother's mouth. When her mother died, followed by Eleanor's father not long after, Mrs Pembroke had taken Eleanor in. Everyone expected her to train Eleanor up as a housemaid, give her a good reference and send her on her way.

Instead, she had treated Eleanor like a daughter.

When Eleanor woke up screaming in the night, it was Mrs Pembroke who came running through the bedroom door. Mrs Pembroke took Eleanor into the library every morning and had patiently taught her French, arithmetic and a little piano, without the help of a governess. Mrs Pembroke even helped Eleanor dress, brushing out Eleanor's long blonde hair and making her giggle by twisting it into silly shapes. Eleanor never wondered at the close attention: Mrs Pembroke had always wanted another little girl, and often said so. For a few shining years she had been 'Miss Eleanor', dressing in silks and satins, and the world where she'd had to change the sheets with her mother still lying in the bed was far, far behind her.

Eleanor was going to be a lady. She was going to be beautiful, and soft, and safe. Her life should have been an endless carousel of parties, trips abroad, and problems so gentle they would not hurt at all. Mrs Pembroke had even taught her how to waltz with her son, Charles. He was only a little older, blue-eyed and gangly and with a straggly moustache he was inexplicably proud of. When he was home from school, Mrs Pembroke would have the footmen clear a space in the drawing room so that Eleanor and Charles could plod around mechanically, staring at each other's feet. Charles's face had always been bright red, clearly mortified at being asked to dance with a girl four whole years his junior, but he'd taken one look at his mother's misty eyes and danced with Eleanor anyway.

Then, Mrs Pembroke died.

The smell of the vinegar made Eleanor's eyes water, dragging her out of her reverie and back to the present day.

Leah came out of Mrs Fielding's rooms and vanished up the servants' staircase. Moments later she was back, her red carpetbag in hand, and stalking towards the back door. Mrs Fielding watched her leave, her face utterly blank.

Eleanor ran after her.

'Leah!'

Leah whirled around with one hand already on the gate. Her grey eyes were lit with nervous energy, and there was a tightness to her expression that made Eleanor take a step back. Hansoms clattered past on the road, broughams glided after them. The look on Leah's heart-shaped face was so strange, Eleanor was half afraid she might try and throw herself under one. She couldn't let her leave like this.

'Don't go,' Eleanor said.

Leah's face twisted. 'I don't have a bloody choice!'

'You could sneak back up to my room when she's not looking. I'd bring you food. Or the coach house! No one ever goes in there!'

'Oh, for Christ's sake, Ella!'

Eleanor fiddled with her apron. She wasn't going to cry, she told herself. It would only make things worse. 'I'm sorry.'

'No. I…I didn't…' Leah pressed a hand to her mouth. When she took it away, her eyes were hard again. She set down her bag and grabbed both of Eleanor's hands.

'Don't let him touch you,' she hissed. 'Not for anything. He comes near you, you just…hit him. Kick him. Smack him over the head with the poker! You do what you need to, you hear?'

Eleanor nodded, clinging to Leah's hands. 'Will you write to me?'

Leah let go of her hands and picked up the bag once more. 'You know I never learned. Remember what I said. And tell Aoife, too. You'll have to keep an eye on her, now I can't.'

'I won't let anything happen to her.'

Leah was blinking fast. 'God,' she muttered. 'I wish I'd never come here. It never used to be like this.'

'No,' Eleanor said, feeling older and lonelier than ever. 'It didn't.'

Eleanor emptied her buckets in the garden. Sudsy water splashed up her skirts. Sunlight fell hard on her face. If she wasn't careful, she would burn. She watched the dirty water splash across the grass with her fists clenched, pinned in place. She had to get herself under control before Mrs Fielding saw.

Leah was right.

A few years ago, Granborough House had been a different place. There'd been footmen, laundrymaids, a coach in the

14

coach house instead of beggars the constables had to run off every winter morning. Eleanor had dug her toes into perfectly brushed carpets, watched her reflection in every gleaming surface, and lingered next to warm fireplaces. When Charles was home on his school holidays they would sit on plump chairs in the library and practise their French together – if he stayed still long enough. But after Mrs Pembroke's death the footmen left. The coach was sold; the coachman dismissed. The butler left, shortly followed by the valet, each hiding a crate of fine wines in their luggage. The carpets faded, the shining surfaces dulled, more and more fireplaces stood empty and cold. Charles stopped coming home. Then one morning, Mrs Fielding had shaken her awake at five o'clock and told her that now, she had to earn her keep. It didn't matter that Mr Pembroke was Eleanor's legal guardian, and ought to treat her like his own child. She'd been relegated from 'Miss Eleanor' to plain old Ella, her own name used to remind her of her place. She'd been fourteen, and she'd watched her future crumble.

She forced her temper back into place and brought the buckets in. Lizzie was rummaging for rags in one of the cupboards; Eleanor resisted the urge to bash the buckets against her bony knees when she put them away. Daisy was peeling carrots and talking about the public house she wanted to open with her brother, who had become a sailor in the West Indies like their father; Mrs Banbury was sweating over the iron range, standing on an old housemaid's box to help her reach the pans. The cook had a rash all up her neck that blossomed in the heat, and every so often her hand would creep up and scratch it. Aoife was waiting at the kitchen table, a letter clutched in her hand. She started forward when she saw Eleanor.

'I've a letter from home! Oh, miss, will you read it for me?'

Eleanor smiled. 'There's no need to call me "miss", Aoife.'

Daisy rolled her eyes as Aoife blushed. 'Too bloody right there ain't.'

'Save your gossip for Sunday, girls. That mutton here yet?' Mrs Banbury called over her shoulder. Lizzie straightened up at once, eyes snapping to the tradesmen's entrance.

Daisy yelled back. 'Ain't the boy been, Mrs B?'

'Jesus wept! You should know, you dozy girl!'

'Been doing the carrots, Mrs B!' She waved one to prove her point.

Mrs Banbury swore and caught sight of Eleanor.

'Be a dove, Ella, and run and fetch the master's mutton. That bloody boy's not been.'

'It's only noon,' Lizzie said quickly, 'he'll come yet.'

Mrs Banbury fixed her with a sharp look. 'I've no time for "yet". If it's not here by one that's dinner ruined. Go on, Ella. Get your basket.'

'Now?' Eleanor asked. 'Might I wait until Aoife's ready to collect the laundry, and we could go together?'

'No, now,' Mrs Banbury snapped.

'Without a—'

She caught herself, but it was too late. She was already shrivelling under the weight of her own embarrassment. Daisy widened her eyes at Aoife and twirled a bunch of carrots in her hand like a parasol, mouthing 'Without a chaperone?'

Lizzie snorted with laughter. 'As if *Miss* Eleanor would sully herself by going to the butcher's on her own! I'll go, Mrs B. She'll have a fit of the vapours otherwise.'

'Back to work!' Mrs Banbury snapped at Lizzie, ignoring

16

her glare. She turned back and sighed before she patted Eleanor's arm. 'God above, child,' she said, more quietly, 'you won't be snatched the second you step outside our door. Go on, now. Go.'

Eleanor found her old wide-brimmed hat, turned up her collar and slipped on a pair of gloves before she went outside. Ladies were like lilies, pale and lovely. She would be too, if she could help it. A veil would be better, but it would never work with her dark dress. She rather liked the thought of gliding through the streets like a ghost, the world set in shadow around her. But people might think she was in mourning (or worse, a Catholic), and the veil would only become one more thing to wash.

The heat was like a slap. Her damp dress steamed in the sun. Their street was quiet, the row of gentlemen's town-houses blindingly white in the sunlight. The only movement came from a large ginger cat stretched out on the pavement, twitching its tail. Eleanor turned towards Marylebone – the Mayfair butchers were far too expensive for them now – and the noise pressed in on her. Brown dust stuck to her skirts, twirled around horses' hooves, climbed up the legs of passers-by. Children crowded around a Punch and Judy show, sticky with sweets and sweat. Cabs and carriages rattled past, windows cranked wide open. Horses snuffled hopefully at trays of apples. Costermongers sold ginger beer and straw-berry ices, red-faced from shouting in the sun. Milkmaids fought their way through the crowds, pails sloshing. As one passed by Eleanor caught a whiff of rancid milk, and saw a fine layer of brown dust and dead bugs floating on its surface.

Elbows jammed into her sides. Her feet skittered on the dust. A child tipped up her empty basket, then ran away swearing when nothing fell out. Horses snorted in her ears, cab drivers cracked their whips over her head, and there was shouting on all sides.

'Apples! Fresh apples!'

'Billy! You come back here this *instant*!'

'Strawberry ices! Lovely strawberry ices! Penny for the babby, missus, and one for you besides—'

'All aboard for Piccadilly! You, sir, you going down Piccadilly?'

Eleanor darted out of the way of an omnibus. Someone trod on her skirts. A hand reached for her purse and she slapped it away. Another hand reached for her bottom; she smacked that one with her basket. Dogs growled at her, a piper blew his whistle in her ear, flies whirled around her head and finally, she reached the butcher's, pummelled and sweating. Not even the sight of the pig carcasses strung up in the window could dampen her relief.

She ducked inside, trying to ignore the smell of meat that hadn't been kept out of the sun. The butcher's boy – a young man of about twenty with dark hair and a long, thin face – straightened up and wiped his bloody hands on his apron. Eleanor had seen him hanging around the tradesmen's entrance to Granborough House, waiting for Lizzie and looking apologetic. They'd been walking out together for almost a year, but if the arguments Eleanor had overheard were anything to go by, Lizzie was wasting her time.

'Granborough House delivery, please.'

'It gets *delivered*, you know.' He looked up and raised his eyebrows. 'You're a Granborough House girl?' he said. His

18

eyes flickered down to her waist. 'Ain't seen you before. You new?'

'No. I've been there a few years.'

He laughed at that, disbelief echoing all around the shop. 'You never have! How'd a pretty thing like you last that long? The old man gone blind?'

Eleanor thought of Leah and hopelessness settled on her like a shroud. She pretended she hadn't heard. 'The Granborough House delivery, please.'

'All right, all right. Didn't mean nothing by it.'

He handed her a large parcel wrapped in waxed paper. When she tried to take it he didn't let go. 'Will you be there when I make my next delivery?'

'I shall be working. Thank you.'

She yanked the parcel out of his hands and stuffed it into the basket. He grinned, showing a missing canine tooth. 'I'll pop up and see you, how about that?'

'Perhaps not. Do let me know if you have a message you'd like me to give to Lizzie. She's your sweetheart, isn't she?'

His grin faded slightly. 'Well, I wouldn't say sweetheart, not as such...'

'I think *she* would.'

Eleanor stepped back into the crowds, mouth set in a tight line.

Lizzie was hanging around the servants' entrance when Eleanor got back. She watched Eleanor hang up her hat and take off her gloves while chewing on a ragged thumbnail.

'Thank the Lord,' said Lizzie, 'Miss Eleanor has survived a visit to the outside world without a chaperone and returned to us safe and sound. We're all bloody delighted.'

19

Eleanor took a deep breath. 'It's sweet of you to say so, Lizzie,' she said, her tone calm and measured.

'Such a pity there was nobody about to carry your sedan chair.'

'Yes.'

Eleanor picked up her housemaid's box. The wide wooden box, shaped more like a basket, was laden down with old rags, tins of polish and an enormous feather duster. Eleanor could feel Lizzie glaring at her as she hung it on her arm, and daydreamed about clipping her round the head with it.

'Well?' Lizzie snapped.

Eleanor put on her most innocent expression, the one that Lizzie had always hated. 'Excuse me?'

A muscle worked in Lizzie's jaw. 'What did he say?'

Eleanor thought of the way Lizzie had smirked when she'd talked about Lea, and a savage glee uncurled in the pit of her stomach. She kept it from showing on her face. There'd be no more smirking if she had anything to say about it.

'I'm sorry, who do you mean?'

'You *know* who I bloody well mean! Bertie! Does he have a message for me?'

'Is he the tall fellow, with the dark hair? He asked if I was new.'

Lizzie's hand jerked away from her mouth. Blood welled up on the side of her nail. 'What d'you mean by that?'

Eleanor kept her eyes wide and earnest, but inside, she was crowing. 'He only wanted to know if he'd seen me before. I let him know that he had not.'

Leaving Lizzie fretting, Eleanor slapped the dust off her skirts and climbed the stairs on sleeper's legs. The second-floor landing was dark and quiet, a long, thin carpet muffling her footsteps as she crept down the empty corridor. Untouched dust sheets and closed shutters gave the air a still, heavy taste, but at least it was cooler.

Five minutes in the library was all she needed. Five minutes to bask in the smell of old books and let all the anger ebb away. She ducked inside. It looked smaller in the day, but the sunlight picked out the bright threads in the old Persian carpet and the gold names on all the spines. It was a treasure chest, and all the jewels were hers. She went to the nearest bookcase and pulled an old travelogue off the shelves. Just five minutes.

The door opened behind her. Eleanor whirled around.

Mr Pembroke stood in the doorway.

She couldn't help it. She backed away before she could stop herself. There was no way she could slip past him; he was a big man made bigger by better dinners than she could ever afford. How someone like him had ever married a lady as generous and kind as Mrs Pembroke was completely beyond Eleanor. She supposed he might have been handsome, once, but now sweat plastered his dark hair to his forehead, his face was puffy and jowly, and his eyes glistened like rotten fruit when he looked at her. Even in the day she could smell the brandy on him.

Her hands balled into fists. How dare he, she thought, how *dare* he show his face? Leah had been dismissed that morning, with *his* child in her belly. Leah, who had given her a silly nickname and taught her how to turn Lizzie's sharpness against her, had been dismissed without a reference, unmarried, and with a baby she didn't want. Leah wouldn't be able to get another job now, and no decent landlady would rent rooms to an unwed mother. Her money would run out, she'd have nowhere to stay, and if anything went wrong with the baby she'd never be able to afford a doctor. God knew where Leah was going to go, or what she was going to do. Mr Pembroke didn't care. He'd strolled towards the library, large hands in the pockets of his shiny silk waistcoat. His frog eyes were as carefree as a child's, he was humming a tune, and the force of her own hatred felt like it was going to set her blood alight.

The whistling stopped when he saw her.

'Ah,' he said. 'Ella.'

She forced herself to curtsey. He was still the master of the house; she could not afford to be careless. If Eleanor was thrown out without a reference, she'd have nowhere to go either. His collar was spotlessly white, his silk cravat gleaming, his dark suit brushed and pressed. Leah had done it all the day before. She had insisted on picking up his laundry and laying out his clothes in the hope of catching him in his room. It could've been the last afternoon Eleanor and Leah spent together, if Leah hadn't tried to beg some money for his child. But the coward hadn't come home last night, and now Leah was gone.

'What are you doing with that book?'

'It...it was out of place, sir,' Eleanor lied, forcing her tone back towards humility. 'I was only putting it back.'

'Well, don't let me stop you.'

He nodded towards the bookshelves and kept standing in the doorway. Eleanor turned around and shoved the book back into place, shame crawling under her skin. She could *feel* him watching her.

'Tell me, Ella,' he said slowly, when she turned back around. 'How old are you?'

'Seventeen, sir.'

22

He raised his eyebrows as though she hadn't been living in his house for just over seven years. 'How you've grown.'

Eleanor said nothing. She wanted, desperately, to wash her hands.

Mr Pembroke strode towards an armchair and sat down. 'Do you know, I can still remember when you used to sit on my lap. Come here. Indulge an old man.'

He patted his knee. Eleanor clutched her housemaid's box like a shield. Her entire body seemed to be filled up with disgust and fear, like coal smoke staining everything it touched. *Don't let him touch you*, Leah had said. She hadn't expected it would start this soon, not when her friend hadn't even been gone for a full day.

The thought of Leah stopped her from being swept away on a tide of revulsion. Eleanor thought fast. She wasn't going to end up like her.

'I confess I don't remember that, sir,' she said, shuffling towards the door as much as she dared. 'I'm sure you had more important things to attend to than amusing children. I mainly remember your wife from that time.'

Even after three years, a brief spasm of grief twisted across his face. Eleanor felt it too, but hers came with a vicious thrill of triumph. Even in death, Mrs Pembroke could protect her.

'She was such a generous woman,' Eleanor continued as she backed further away, watching two high spots of colour appear on Mr Pembroke's flabby cheeks, 'and so kind. She was a second mother to me. And so keenly aware of a lady's duties. I don't think I've ever met anyone who took such good care of her servants. I shall always remember her example. I try to act as though she would wish me to every day—'

Mr Pembroke got to his feet and stumbled to the door. 'I – yes, yes. That will be all.'

He lurched out of the room, eyes bright and jaw clenched. Eleanor counted to five, and then scurried over to the door and locked it, heart rattling in her chest. She leant against the door, holding it shut.

She'd been telling the truth. She couldn't remember much about Mr Pembroke from her childhood. He had been a distant and forbidding presence, and the only real memories she had were of him screaming at Charles in the school holidays about his marks, which had never been good enough. It was only after Mrs Pembroke had died, and Eleanor had been relegated to the wrong side of the green baize door, that she had learned what he was really like.

She stared at the back of the chair he had been sitting in and shuddered. She'd need to clean it if she ever wanted to feel safe in here again. But, she reminded herself, she had learned something valuable. Mr Pembroke still missed his wife, and if she had to make that knowledge her shield then that was what she was going to do.

She needed all the armour she could get.

Residual fear was still bubbling in the pit of Eleanor's stomach when the sun went down. The heat strangled her as she climbed the servants' staircase, flies buzzing over her head. The library would calm her – but even that was tainted by the memory of Mr Pembroke standing in it.

Eleanor flung open the door to her room and opened the window as wide as it would go. Through the glass, a forest of rooftops and chimneypots crowded around a slice of sky. On a clear morning she could see the vague shape of Hyde

Park, but now the smoke from the chimneys and the heat haze had transformed it into a green smudge on the horizon. She stripped off her dress and corset, both of which were too small, and splashed her face with cold water. She could feel her damp chemise drying on her skin, sticky in the heat.

'Ella? Are you awake?'

Aoife was standing in the doorway, clutching her letter in her hand. She blushed when she saw Eleanor in her underthings. 'Oh, Lord, you're in your shimmy! I'm sorry, I'll come back later...'

Eleanor grabbed her shawl and threw it around her shoulders. The wool was scratchy and hot. 'Here. Shall you mind me in this?'

Aoife still looked embarrassed, so Eleanor asked her to wait outside while she put her clothes back on, even though she felt like she was choking with every button she fastened. Aoife came back in as soon as she was finished and handed Eleanor her letter.

'Oh, it's from your mother!' said Eleanor, scanning down the page.

Aoife made a quick, nervous gesture. 'You've to tell me the news before you read it out loud. It's better if I know before you read.'

Eleanor smiled. 'I always do. She says she's well, and so are Mary and her little ones, and so's Patrick, although she says she's not heard from him since he set sail.'

'Is that normal?'

'I think so. I suppose he won't get a chance to post any letters until he puts into port. Ask Daisy, she'll know. Anyway, she says that Michael – I'm sorry, Micheál – is keeping well and that the warm weather is helping his chest, and that he sends his love.'

25

Aoife sagged against Eleanor's bedpost. 'Good. Did she say if Micheál needs anything?'

Eleanor scanned through the letter again. It was clearly written by an Englishman; she could tell from the way Aoife pronounced her family's names that whoever had written it had written down the closest equivalent. Aoife's own name was written as Eve, though Eleanor had never told her. She didn't want to put any more distance between Aoife and her family by rechristening her.

'He's quite all right.'

Aoife let out a sigh of relief and sat down at the foot of Eleanor's bed, resting her chin on her knees. 'Good. You can read it now.'

Eleanor sat down too and began to read the letter properly. Aoife laughed at her mother's jokes, gasped at all the village gossip, and flushed every time Eleanor read a leading question about boys. But despite her smiles, there was a wistfulness in her eyes that made Eleanor wonder. If her brother had not been sick, would Aoife have come to London at all?

Aoife gave a happy sigh when Eleanor finished reading the letter. 'Thank you, Ella. Can we write a reply?'

'Of course. What do you want to say?'

Aoife seemed to shrink into herself. 'I...I don't know. I don't think I want her to know about today.'

Eleanor remembered Leah clutching the garden gate and felt something twist inside her. 'No. I imagine not.'

Aoife stared at her bare feet, poking out from the hem of her dress. 'I wish I'd something fine to tell her about. London's not how I thought it'd be at all. I thought there'd be ladies in fine dresses and trips to the Crystal Palace. Exciting things.'

'Well,' said Eleanor, forcing some brightness back into her voice, 'let's think of some.'

Aoife stared at her. 'And lie to my mam?'

'Not *lie*,' Eleanor soothed, 'she's your mother, she'll know you're only being silly. Besides, the world is always so much nicer written down.'

'She will?'

'Of course! Tell her…tell her the other day you met a Mughal prince in the street, and he offered you a pearl as big as your head as thanks for directing him to Buckingham Palace. Only you did not take it, of course, because you are a smart girl who knows that the only payment worth having is diamonds.'

Aoife gave a small smile. 'I'd not be smart if I turned down a pearl as big as my head.'

'Tell her a rare and brilliant tropical bird escaped from the home of a distinguished professor,' said Eleanor, warming to her theme, 'and all the pigeons and sparrows and crows in our square are dunking themselves in paints of every colour out of sheer envy.'

Aoife giggled. 'But Ella, they'd never fly!'

'All right. Tell her I've run off with a handsome Russian boyar named Sergei – no, *two* boyars, and they both arrived on the same night and everyone was just *mortified*. I've told them both I will marry the man who lets me hold the sun in the palm of my hand, and they're both pulling out their moustaches trying to accomplish it.'

'Which one will you choose?' said Aoife, laughing.

Eleanor pulled a thoughtful face. 'I suppose that depends. Which one is taller?'

Aoife tried to give a scandalized gasp but laughed halfway through. 'After you put them to all that trouble?'

'Of course! It's a poor man who can't solve my riddle by holding up a hand,' she said. She held out her hand palm up and shuffled into Aoife's line of sight. Eleanor tilted her hand so it sat flush with the rooves of the house opposite, and through the dirty, darkened glass of her window, the sun set in her outstretched fingers.

The next morning, Eleanor felt Leah's absence like a missing tooth. She stood in the doorway of her friend's room, staring at the stripped bed and empty drawers, still half-open from where Leah had packed in a hurry. She should have done more, Eleanor thought. She should have given Leah her wages, or smuggled her back upstairs – but it was too late for that now. She didn't even know where Leah slept last night. Hindsight could not help her.

Daisy opened her bedroom door as Eleanor walked past, the tight black curls she had inherited from her West Indian mother springy without their pins. Her dark eyes flicked to Leah's bedroom door and back.

'She'll be all right,' Daisy said.

Eleanor sighed. 'Do you think so?'

'It'll be hard,' Daisy yawned, 'but she'll get through it. Listen, Ella, be a dove and get some water going on the stove. My hair's not behaving; I'll never hear the end of it from Mrs Fielding if I don't fix it.'

Eleanor nodded and went downstairs. Even Lizzie was quiet. She avoided Leah's place at the kitchen table and ate her porridge in silence, her eyes darting between Eleanor and Aoife. There was a calculating cast to Lizzie's face that Eleanor mistrusted and, not for the first time, she wondered how Lizzie had lasted for the eight years she'd been at Granborough House.

With Leah gone there was even more work to divide among

the girls. Eleanor spent the morning running up and down stairs: down to the garden to empty the slops bucket, up to the drawing room to rid it of dust and dead flies, down to the cellar where she found Aoife sobbing over Leah, her face streaked with tears and coal dust. Eleanor led her out to the pump, got her to wash her face and hands, and brought Daisy to comfort her. She left the two of them standing in the shadow of the coach house with their arms around each other. She cobbled together a lunch of bread and cheese with her back to the door, trying to pretend she hadn't seen the quick kiss Daisy had buried in Aoife's hair.

They came back inside fifteen minutes later, still a little tearful, and there was a knock at the tradesmen's entrance. Aoife was wiping her eyes and Daisy had been collared by Mrs Banbury again, so Eleanor put down her lunch, brushed away crumbs and answered it.

It was the butcher's boy. He looked taller when he wasn't behind his counter. 'Afternoon, Goldilocks,' he said, grinning. 'You got your order for this week?'

'You'll have to speak to Mrs Banbury about that. Shall I fetch her for you?'

He winked. 'Best not.'

Eleanor took a step back and raised her voice, so the others would notice. 'I can't speak for the kitchen staff. Excuse me.'

She turned away and he caught her sleeve. She thought of Mr Pembroke and the finger-shaped bruises she'd seen on Leah's arm and tugged her hand away, fast. 'Mrs Banbury!'

The butcher's boy whipped his hands away into the air as the cook whirled around. 'All right, all right! Didn't mean to give you a fright. I thought, nice girl like you, she oughtn't to be by herself...'

There was a sound from somewhere over Eleanor's shoulder.

29

She turned around and saw Lizzie standing in the kitchen, a carpet beater hanging limply in her hand. The butcher's boy darted out of the door up the steps into the garden. Lizzie ran after him, yelling, 'You come back here, Bertie! Just you come back here!'

Mrs Banbury ushered a stunned Eleanor over to the kitchen table. 'You all right there, pet?'

'I didn't mean any trouble.'

Daisy snorted and sliced the top off an onion. 'Shouldn't have been having it off with the butcher's boy then, should you, Miss Eleanor?'

'You mind your tongue!' Mrs Banbury snapped.

Eleanor sat down. 'Having what off?'

They went quiet, exchanged a significant look, and Eleanor finally realized what they meant.

She gasped. 'You think *I* would—'

'No,' snapped Mrs Banbury, glaring at Daisy, 'we don't. And we'll say no more about it.'

'They...they have an understanding! I would *never*—'

Daisy grinned. '...work out where to put it?'

Mrs Banbury slammed a pot onto the range. 'I *said*, we'll say no more about it!'

Daisy rolled her eyes. Eleanor peered at the steps that led into the garden, worried.

'Do you think I should go and explain?'

'Never you mind them,' said Mrs Banbury. 'They'll sort things out themselves.'

Eleanor got out of the kitchen before Lizzie came back.

Eleanor was hiding in the dining room with the window cracked open, listening. She could not tell if Lizzie's shouting

30

had stopped over the noise of pipers, costermongers, cart-horses and dogs barking in the street. She glanced at the clock; half an hour had passed. Surely Lizzie and her sweetheart would've reconciled by now.

She swept down the dining-room table and began to polish it. Fretting would not make Lizzie calm down any faster, she reasoned, and she needed to look busy in case anyone found her. Besides, the dining room still smelled of yesterday's dinner. The hot, dark room and the smell of poached salmon clinging to the crimson curtains reminded her of Jonah, sitting in the belly of the whale.

The furniture polish was sharp enough to hide some of the smell of old fish. The rag glided across the table, smooth as ice. A vague, dark outline emerged, and for a while she thought her eyes were playing tricks on her until she recognized her own reflection.

The door opened and closed again with a snap. Eleanor looked up and saw Lizzie gripping the back of a chair, her knuckles white. Her face was raw with anger. Panic curled itself around Eleanor and squeezed. She'd never seen Lizzie like this.

'Lizzie!' Eleanor said. 'Are you quite all—'

'Don't,' she muttered. 'Don't you dare.'

'I only—'

'Don't you say a bleeding word! You've done enough damage already!'

'Lizzie, I never meant to cause any—'

She laughed. It sounded hollow. 'Oh, you didn't mean to, did you? Lord in Heaven, how many times have I heard you make that excuse!'

Eleanor frowned. 'I don't understand.'

'No,' Lizzie spat, 'of course you don't. You don't think I remember what you was like when you first came here? You were some wild little urchin best left to the workhouse! We tried – Lord, how we tried to be kind to you. You were an animal!'

'*What?*'

'Kicking and screaming and scratching and biting like a bloody monkey! Left half of us with black eyes and tore Mrs F's neck half open! And when you was done you'd blink up at the mistress and tell her *you didn't mean to.*'

Lizzie was shaking. Her grip on the chair was so tight it rattled against the floor.

'Well, you never had me fooled. You meant it, all right. Just like you meant *this.*'

Eleanor threw down her cloth. 'I never meant any such—'

'You knew me and Bertie was walking out together. You see this?'

She reached into the collar of her dress and slapped something onto the table. It was a ring, hanging from a fine gold chain.

'D'you know what I had to do to get this? How many times I had to simper at his daft old ma, how many times I turned a blind eye to his sprees? I've put up with damn near everything to get out of this place, and I'll not have you take it from me!'

'I hardly think *I'm* responsible for your sweetheart's—'

Lizzie kicked the chair out of her way. Before Eleanor could run she was in front of her and drawing back her hand. The slap, when it came, was brutal.

'Don't you talk back to me! High and mighty Miss Eleanor, putting on airs and graces like the Queen of bloody Sheba!'

Eleanor darted away from her. 'Calm down, *please*—'

'You hold your tongue! You think you're better than me because a dead woman told you you're special?'

'Lizzie!'

'Well, she ain't here, is she? And there's nothing else standing between you and *him*.'

Eleanor went cold. 'It's just as likely to be you!' she snapped.

Lizzie smirked. 'How d'you think I've lasted here, Miss Eleanor? All it takes is a word in the right ear. As long as there's another girl here, I'm safe.'

Eleanor couldn't move. She thought of Leah, and all the girls before her who'd left Granborough House in disgrace. Lizzie had sent all those girls – sent her *friend* – to Mr Pembroke. She'd seen the tears, seen the bruises, and still she sent them to him. Horror crawled up Eleanor's throat, choking her.

Still smirking, Lizzie lowered her hand.

'Bertie'll come back in a few days,' she said, her voice low and insidious, 'and I'll forgive him, like I always do. But it'll be too late for you then. The master'll have his claws into you by the end of the week. I'll make sure of it.'

She stalked out of the room. Blood pounded in Eleanor's ears. She tried to pull out a chair to sit down but missed, her hands were shaking so badly. Soon, Eleanor would be trapped on a dark and humiliating path she could not escape from. Mr Pembroke would break her, and Lizzie would let him do it.

Eleanor's chest was tight. Her breath came in short, sharp gasps.

She couldn't let it happen.

* * *

'Ella? Are you in here?'

Eleanor jumped out of her chair, stumbling on unsteady legs. She wiped her eyes. The others couldn't see her like this – pale and puffy-eyed and wrung out like an old dishcloth. If Lizzie knew it was this easy to frighten her, she'd have won already.

Aoife came into the library, a feather duster wedged under one arm, a dustpan and brush clutched in one hand. She gasped when she saw Eleanor.

'Your face!'

Eleanor's hand fluttered over her throbbing cheek. Her fingers still trembled. Lizzie's slap had left one side of her face red and swollen – the benefit of all her years of service, Eleanor thought, bitterly. That butcher's boy didn't know what he was letting himself in for.

Aoife set down her things and started looking around the shelves. 'Have you anything cool in here?'

'I'm quite well, Aoife,' said Eleanor, her voice thick.

'You're not,' said Aoife. She picked up the scoop from the fireplace and wiped the flat side on her apron. 'It's a bit mucky, but it'll do.'

Eleanor pressed the cool metal against her cheek. It stung, but soon the throbbing subsided. 'Thank you.'

Aoife bit her lip, her eyes wide and troubled. 'Was it Lizzie? I saw her tearing up the stairs after she had that row.'

Eleanor nodded.

'But it weren't even your fault! Speak to Mrs Fielding, she—'

'She didn't see any of it,' Eleanor said, suddenly weary, 'and Lizzie's been here since she was fifteen. It'd be her word against mine.'

'I'll speak for you!'

'You didn't see any of it either, Aoife.'

'But it's not fair!'

Surrounded by bookcases towering over her head, Aoife looked tiny. The sunlight picked out all the freckles on her face and shone on the curve of her cheek, still quite round. She had never looked more like a child.

Eleanor tried to smile. 'I'll be all right. Just give me all the heavy tasks for a few months. Then I shall be as strong as she is, and she won't dare touch me.'

Aoife gave a little laugh. 'Daisy says she cracked her one before she was made head housemaid, and Lizzie's never bothered her since.'

'There! One good hit is all I need.'

'Anyway, she'll not try it again any time soon. Mrs Fielding docked her pay for rowing with her young man. She'll mind her ways now, or she'll be dismissed.'

Eleanor did not correct her. Mrs Fielding wouldn't do anything. It would take months to replace a maid as experienced as Lizzie. Mr Pembroke had made a name for himself below stairs as the worst lecher in London, and the pay was nowhere near high enough for a sensible maid to overlook that. Besides, Lizzie could do far worse than hit her. The realization coiled around Eleanor like a snake. She had already done it to Leah, and she would do it to Aoife after Eleanor had gone.

'Here,' Aoife said, 'Lizzie's gone to pick up the laundry now. Come down to the kitchen and see if Mrs Banbury can spare you something sweet.'

They left the library, Eleanor's legs still a little unsteady. She flinched at the creaking of every step.

* * *

35

Eleanor had the last slice of the day to herself.

Mrs Banbury took one look at Eleanor's smarting cheek and handed her a piece of honeycomb. Eleanor broke off a piece for Aoife and ate it at the kitchen table. Daisy tutted sympathetically and tapped her temple while she was chopping potatoes.

'Aim there,' she said, 'one good smack'll do it.'

All eyes turned to Mrs Banbury. The cook said nothing.

When she'd finished the honeycomb Eleanor went up to the third floor to turn down the bedrooms. With Charles away, Mr Pembroke's was the only one still in use. Eleanor listened at the door of the master bedroom, heart stuttering against her ribcage, before she went inside.

It was empty, apart from Mr Pembroke's pet canary, which chirruped and fluttered against the bars of its large, ornate cage as she came in. A little of the tension eased out of her. She remade the bed in a tangle of flapping sheets, flicked a cloth over the floor of the birdcage, crammed his shirts back into the clothes press and shoved his cravats back into their drawer. There were a few letters from Charles on his pillow, all with European postmarks, but she didn't dare stay to read them, although at the sight of Charles's familiar, rounded handwriting she was tempted. Her fear had lost its edge, but after Lizzie's threats just being in Mr Pembroke's room was enough to make her skin crawl.

She bolted out of the door as soon as she was finished and made for the servants' stairs. She clattered back down into the kitchen as all the servants but Lizzie were digging into slices of cold tongue and potatoes.

'You got that done just in time,' said Daisy, loading up a plate for Eleanor. 'His Nibs has almost finished his tea.'

Mrs Fielding laid down her knife and fork. 'You are speaking about the master of this house, Daisy. Show some respect!'

Mrs Banbury pointed her fork across the table. 'Daisy's a kitchen maid, Bertha. You leave her discipline to me.'

Mrs Fielding sniffed. 'Well, *my* girls wouldn't dare speak about the master in such a way.'

Eleanor stopped up her mouth with a large piece of potato before she said anything she'd regret. She ate quickly; Lizzie was serving Mr Pembroke's dinner and she wanted to be well out of the way by the time it was done. Eleanor's stomach churned. Even now, Lizzie would be pouring Mr Pembroke's wine and painting Eleanor's character in shades of scarlet. She could just imagine it. 'Ella, sir? She's turned out very fast...'

Eleanor pushed her plate away and rushed up the servants' staircase. It was bare and narrow and cheaply furnished, like the rest of the servants' quarters, but here, she was safe. Mr Pembroke was a gentleman; he would not follow her through the green baize door. Between the staircase, the kitchen, and the servants' dormitories in the attic, she could disappear into a cheaply plastered warren quicker than a rabbit.

Lizzie, however, was another matter.

A footstep creaked on the staircase below. Eleanor glanced over her shoulder. The door to the first-floor landing was opening, and Eleanor could already see Lizzie's shadow, laden with dishes. Before Lizzie could spot her, Eleanor darted through the door to the third-floor landing.

She stopped. The third floor held all the bedrooms, and Eleanor was outside the one that had been hers. Eleanor stared at it. She tried to tell herself she was listening for more footsteps, but all she could hear was Mrs Pembroke's voice saying,

'And this will be your room, Eleanor, dear'; all she could see was Mrs Pembroke's long-fingered hand turning the handle, a sapphire ring winking on her finger.

And what a room it had been! Eleanor couldn't remember much about the house she had lived in before coming to Granborough. There were only flashes that came to mind, now: a bucket full of coal that cracked against her shins as she carried it, lye soap stinging at her hands as she tried to scrub something out of the floorboards, an iron bedstead pressing into her back. But whatever that place had been, it was nothing compared to this room. Mrs Pembroke had opened the door to a bright, pretty room that she'd furnished just for Eleanor. There had been pale curtains at the windows, a flowered jug and basin on the washstand, and soft white sheets on the bed, where Mrs Pembroke had read her 'Rapunzel' and 'Sleeping Beauty' in a soft, melodious voice. Pastel-coloured dresses of silk and satin had sat in her clothes press, wallpaper printed with roses had hung on the walls, and a small square of carpet had sat by the side of the bed, where she used to kneel down and pray every night. The room had been soft, as gently coloured as a sunrise, all its contents more delicate than eggshells.

Eleanor's hands were trembling. She opened the door.

It was almost as she'd left it.

The windows were shuttered, the curtains limp with dust. The bed was covered in dust sheets, the hangings folded away in boxes in the attic. The washstand was still there, although the jug and basin were gone along with the carpet, leaving a pale square of wood on the floor, like a shadow. She'd been allowed to keep her linen – she was still wearing it three years later, though she'd been letting out her chemise for years – but everything else in the clothes press had been sold.

At least the wallpaper was the same, she thought.

Eleanor drifted across the floor in a daze. Here, she had tried on her first proper corset. Mrs Pembroke had laced it up herself, making sure it sat properly over her chemise and telling Eleanor not to worry if it pinched. She'd been so proud to set her stays aside and get her first real piece of women's clothing. The corset eased her shoulders back and fitted snug around her waist, and even standing there in her underthings she had felt so grown-up. She had turned to Mrs Pembroke, standing straighter than she'd ever done before, and there had been tears in Mrs Pembroke's eyes.

She was still wearing that corset. It had been too small for years.

Eleanor hugged herself, the coarse material of her uniform scratching her fingers. All the shadows seemed to press in on her.

She left with a lump in her throat and ducked back through the door to the servants' staircase, knowing what she would find in her little garret room. The walls mottled with damp. The straw mattress that rustled as she slept. The chipped jug and basin on her faded chest of drawers, the grey, scratchy blanket on her bed.

She opened her bedroom door.

The room had been torn apart.

Upended drawers lay on the floor. Her stockings had been ripped in half, huge strips of material had been torn away from the collars of her dresses, and her underthings had been completely shredded. Her sewing kit had been emptied, strewing needles everywhere. Even the blanket was covered in boot prints.

She remembered Lizzie, stalking out of the dining room hours ago, and knew what she had done.

Her breath caught. The purse.

Eleanor scrabbled through the mess. Needles skittered across the backs of her hands. It *had* to be here. Lizzie couldn't have taken it. Had she known? No. No, she couldn't have. But if she'd found the purse in her temper, and heard the clink of coins inside it...

Eleanor threw aside a bundle of stockings, panicking. She shook out every shift. She looked under the bed. She upended the empty chamber pot. She reached under the chest of drawers, tore through every pocket, and peered into a mousehole in the corner of the room.

Her money was gone.

It was all gone.

Three years' wages, stolen. She'd been saving it so carefully. She'd let down the hems of all her old dresses. She'd unpicked seams and re-used the thread. She'd never bought so much as a hot cross bun – and now, it was all gone.

Lizzie had taken it to stop her getting away from Granborough House. Eleanor got to her feet. She wasn't going to let her get away with it. She was used to the occasional slap but this – no. *No.* She wasn't going to be treated like this for the sake of Lizzie's pride.

Eleanor hurtled back down the servants' staircase and pelted through the kitchen, past the laundry room and skidded to a halt outside Mrs Fielding's rooms. She hammered on the door and did not stop until the housekeeper answered.

'Ella?' said Mrs Fielding, looking alarmed. 'Is everything all right?'

'Someone's been in my room, Mrs Fielding.'

Mrs Fielding sighed, pinching the bridge of her long nose. 'I really haven't the time to be resolving petty disputes. I have a lot to do, you know, and—'

Eleanor could feel the tears building like a thunderstorm. 'You don't understand! My wages are gone – all of them, just gone!'

Mrs Fielding's expression hardened. 'You are making a very serious accusation, Ella. Are you quite sure you've looked everywhere?'

'Of *course* I've—'

'Less of that tone!' Mrs Fielding snapped. 'Go and search your room again and do make sure to look everywhere, this time. If you can't find them, I shall help you put the matter before the master.'

Eleanor went cold. She knew exactly how that would go. Mrs Fielding would be with her, at first, but there was always something that needed Mrs Fielding's attention and she wouldn't stay for long. And when the door had closed, leaving Eleanor on the wrong side of it, she would have no choice but to listen to whatever Mr Pembroke said because she had nothing, now, there was no way she could get out. She had no relatives who would take her in, no references to get another job, no money to rent a cheap little room. If she left Granborough House she'd be sleeping in the penny doss-houses in Whitechapel and the Old Nichol, slumped over an old clothesline because it was cheaper than paying for a bed, and even then she'd be begging for the pennies, or worse.

Mrs Fielding was watching her. Her dark eyes flickered all across Eleanor's face, sharp despite the shadows and the lines beneath them. Her mouth was pressed into a thin, disapproving line, her square jaw set.

'Or perhaps you would prefer not to discuss this with the master,' she said, her voice flat. 'Telling tales at your age is hardly appropriate.'

'But I—'

'That's enough, Ella! Go to bed. I've had a long day and I don't need you to make it any longer.'

She closed the door. Eleanor stared at the wood, the varnish gone after years of scrubbing, and began to climb the servants' staircase again. She felt as if something had been scraped out of her, leaving her raw and smarting.

There was nothing she could do. Mrs Fielding didn't even believe her. If there was any justice in the world, all those stolen coins would burn like glowing coals, and Lizzie's thieving fingers would sizzle when she tried to spend them.

But they wouldn't. Lizzie had taken her money, and Eleanor had *nothing*.

She opened her bedroom door, stared into the crimson sunset and fought back the urge to scream.

The library. She needed the library.

Eleanor ran through corridors striped with moonlight, the library key clutched in her hands. She couldn't breathe through the tears. She needed her books, a comfortable chair, a lockable door. She had to get out of Granborough House somehow, even if it was only in her head.

Her feet skidded on the carpet as she ran into the library. Forcing herself not to slam the door, she locked it, leaning against the wood and sobbing silently into her hand. She couldn't be heard. She couldn't let anyone take this from her, not when she'd lost so much already.

She stalked along the shelves. Fairy tales? No – they were

for children, and she wouldn't be allowed to be a child much longer. Travelogues – what perfect torture *those* would be. A book of martyrs? She almost laughed. Her thoughts flitted from subject to subject, and every one of them felt wrong. None of them would help her forget herself tonight; she'd read them all before. *Oh God*, Eleanor thought. Would this library be the only escape she ever had?

Eleanor retched. Shaking, she leant against one of the book-cases, and slapped herself hard across the face. She couldn't lose control now. If anyone heard her, they'd tell Mr Pembroke. She wasn't going to let him take this place from her.

Eleanor pressed her forehead against the cool wood and forced herself to breathe deeply. Lizzie had robbed her, cutting her off from the easiest way out. Well, tomorrow she would search Lizzie's room, and take whatever money she found there. A mad plan sparked into life. She could steal the laudanum from the kitchen cupboard and slip a few drops into every decanter in the house. Not much – just enough to keep Mr Pembroke in a haze. If anyone caught her, she could be accused of poisoning her employer and guardian. She could be sent to prison, or hanged, if she was caught. Until now, it had never seemed worth the risk.

Eleanor was still trembling, but her breathing had slowed and her stomach was beginning to settle. The library key made deep ridges in her palm; she forced herself to set it aside. Tomorrow she would set her plan in motion. All she had to do now was get through tonight. She could make it through the next few hours.

Something caught her eye.

It was a small, unfamiliar black book, on the edge of her favourite armchair. Eleanor snatched it up at once. This was what she needed. She'd never seen the book before, and she'd read every other one within arm's reach. It had been so long since she'd had something new. It was about the size of her own hands, the leather-bound cover slightly warped with age. It fitted perfectly into her palm, cool in the stifling heat.

She eased herself into her seat, the book sliding into her lap. She kept her eyes closed, squeezing the arms of the chair until she felt less like a hunted thing. When her hands began to cramp, she opened her eyes, picked up the book and forced herself to read.

'The Tragicall Hif...History,' she began, 'of the Life and Death of Doctor Fauftus. Faustus.'

She frowned at the book. If the letter s was going to look like an f all the way through, she wasn't going to get very far. She flipped to the frontispiece. There was a squat little man in a triangular sort of outfit standing inside a magic circle, pointing a book at a creature that had been scribbled out. The ink bled into the paper, hiding the thing in a dark haze. She caught a suggestion of horns.

She settled down to read.

The rhythm of the words tugged at her like a lullaby as Faustus planned to summon his demon and dreamed of all the treasures it would bring. Eleanor knew it wasn't going to end well. She'd read enough fairy stories to know that selling your soul to the Devil rarely ended happily ever after. The just would be rewarded and the wicked would be punished, as they ought to be, but until then she'd enjoy the thrill of watching other people consume forbidden fruit. Her limbs uncurled and she leant back into the chair as the infinite possibilities of magic sprawled out before her. Her finger caught on the edge of a page as she turned it and a bead of blood welled up. She'd smeared red across the beast on the frontis-piece before she noticed it.

She put her finger in her mouth and went back a few paragraphs to reread a good bit.

'I'll have them fly to India for gold, / Ransack the ocean for Orient pearl, / And have them search all corners of the new-found world / For pleasant fruits and princely delicates.'

Eleanor closed her eyes. What would she ask for, if she had such a powerful servant at her beck and call? Gold. Diamonds. Piles and piles of jewellery, so that if she tried to wear it all at once she wouldn't be able to stand up. A magic carpet that would take her all around the world, past the palaces of India and the pyramids of Egypt. She would glide over forests and oceans, whirling beneath her in a blur of green and blue, and at night she would lie back in the sky and sleep in a nest of stars. She could draw the universe around her like a cloak with a servant like that, robing herself in rainbows and moonlight and the shine on soap bubbles and a thousand other lovely, impossible things.

When she opened her eyes, there was a woman sitting opposite her.

The woman's light brown hair was pulled back into a neat bun, threaded with silver. She was middle-aged and plump, not short, not tall. Her printed calico dress looked soft and clean. The woman would've looked perfectly ordinary if it hadn't been for her eyes. They were all black, like holes through her face.

'I do hope I'm not disturbing you,' she said, her voice gentle and almost familiar.

The key was on the arm of Eleanor's chair, where she'd left it. The door was closed. She *knew* the room had been empty when she'd locked it. She blinked, hard. The black-eyed woman still sat there.

She'd been discovered. The black-eyed woman must've been hiding in the shadows when Eleanor came in, blinded by her tears. Eleanor snatched up the key and crammed it under a cushion, heart pounding. Had Mr Pembroke placed her here? What was she going to do?

'You shouldn't be here,' Eleanor said.

'Well, dear,' the woman said, smiling pleasantly, 'you shouldn't be here either.'

All the heat leached out of Eleanor. She couldn't stop staring at the woman's flat, black eyes. They were totally empty, as though someone had poked a finger through the eyes of a painting.

'Don't be alarmed, Eleanor. I only wish to talk to you,' the woman said.

Eleanor clutched the book like a shield. 'How do you—'

'I know all sorts of things, dear child. I know that your name is Eleanor Rose Hartley. I know that you turned seventeen last month. I know what brought you here. You are right to be worried, though you know that already. Your downfall has already been set in motion.'

It was as if the black-eyed woman had cracked open her skull and rifled through her thoughts. Fear wrapped its tendrils around her. 'Did Mr Pembroke send you?' she whispered. 'I haven't done anything wrong. Not really.'

The woman sighed. 'My dear girl, surely you don't think so little of me! I have come here to help you. You need protection, Eleanor – especially now Lizzie Bartram has taken the money in your top drawer. What would you do with a child in your belly, and no way to put a roof over your head?'

Eleanor stared at the black-eyed woman. There was no way she could have known that it was Lizzie who had robbed her. She hadn't even mentioned Lizzie's name to Mrs Fielding.

In the dark, it was impossible to tell how many shadows the black-eyed woman had. Now three, now seven, now one that was far too small for her. Eleanor blinked again, trying to force herself to see properly. The black-eyed woman stayed exactly where she was, smiling comfortably in her padded armchair. Her shadows did not. Eleanor relaxed. This, she could make sense of.

'I don't believe you're real,' Eleanor said.

The woman laughed. 'Oh, dear! And I thought you'd be so pleased, after you called me. Not in the usual way,' she said, as Eleanor began to protest, 'but I'm sure you've worked that out.' The woman nodded to the book in Eleanor's hands.

Confused, Eleanor flipped through it and saw the spot of blood on the frontispiece. 'This? I don't understand. It's just a play.'

'And fairy stories are just stories, and not lessons for careful children, or escapes for girls with nowhere left to run. Nothing is ever only one thing, dear girl. If that were so, then *you* would be just a housemaid.'

Eleanor bristled. She brandished the book at the black-eyed woman. 'But this is a *play*. Actors speak these words all the time and nothing happens. Surely you don't mean to say you pop up at every production of *Faustus*.'

'Dear me, no. I should never get anything done. But you are right. Four years ago, when you were perfectly content, I should never have had the pleasure of your acquaintance even if you chanted those words in Latin by the light of a full moon. I require something a little stronger. Blood, of course, and

47

wanting. That is all magic is, at its core. And you want a great many things, do you not, Eleanor?'

Eleanor shifted in her seat and put the book down, avoiding the woman's black eyes. She was *all* wanting. Good food; a warm, soft bed; hot baths and beautiful clothes; the simple pleasure of a day with no work stretching ahead of her. Her mother, Mrs Pembroke, both of them strong and healthy and ready to gently lift her problems out of her hands. Eleanor tried to be good, she tried to be kind, but she wanted so many things that she could feel them gnawing at her from the inside.

The black-eyed woman leant forward. 'I can help you leave this place.'

'I can—'

'Leave on your own? Of course you can. But when? How? What kind of position do you think you will be in, when you leave Granborough House?'

Eleanor remembered Leah, one hand on the garden gate, that awful expression on her face. Whatever it took, she would not leave as Leah had done.

'But I can offer you so much more than those meagre wages you had saved; barely enough to scrape by for a few months. Security. Freedom. The chance to see the world. You wouldn't have to scrimp and save and dodge wandering hands for years. You could leave whenever you wanted, with whatever you wanted.'

The back of Eleanor's neck itched; she had to fight the urge to look over her shoulder. 'Are you asking me to steal something?'

The woman laughed again. 'You are a sweet little thing. No. You may be as law-abiding as you like. But you will have power. The first real power you've had in your life, I'd wager.'

Power. The word was unfamiliar, even in Eleanor's head. A dark, solid kind of word that made her think of smoke rings, blown from expensive cigars.

'What do you mean, power?'

'I'd like to propose a bargain. I will offer you seven wishes. Whatever you ask for, I shall grant you. There are few limits.'

'Wishes? I stopped believing in fairy godmothers long ago.'

The woman's eyes flashed. 'Perhaps you ought to have a little more faith.'

She snapped her fingers. The little book, balanced on Eleanor's knee, burst into flame. Eleanor jerked backwards before she realized there was no heat. Flames snapping at her fingers, Eleanor reached for the book. The second she touched it, the fire vanished. Her fingers came away clean, with no soot or ash in sight. It even felt a little damp to the touch. Rotten. A new fear lapped at the edges of her thoughts. What kind of creature could do such a thing?

Slowly, she set the book on the arm of her chair. The woman was smiling at her.

'Don't worry, dear. I never would have hurt you. But I hope you realize that I am perfectly serious. I can grant wishes. I will grant yours, if you let me.'

A horrible certainty stole over Eleanor, like frost creeping up a window pane. 'And what would you ask in return?' she said, already knowing the answer.

The woman's eyes flickered to the book. 'Perhaps I should've let you read a little further. Your soul.'

'What? No, I – no!'

'I'm not unreasonable,' the woman said mildly. 'I would

49

only collect my due if you made all seven wishes. I've no wish to cheat you, my dear.'

Eleanor stared at the book. She was half-convinced that when she looked up the black-eyed woman would be gone. A part of her hoped she would be. She knew Eleanor's secrets, true, but surely she could not be real, with her shadows squirming around her like witches' familiars. But when she looked back the black-eyed woman still sat there, still smiling, still silent.

Her soul, in exchange for seven wishes. What would she be without it? Where did she keep it? Would she even notice if it was gone? It was not like losing a finger, or an eye, or a lock of hair – she knew what she would be without them. If she bartered away her soul, what would she become?

Her soul...

'Why are you offering me this deal?'

The black-eyed woman spread her hands. 'Does it matter? Just think of it, my dear,' she said, holding out her hand, 'you'll be safe, warm, well-fed. You can leave your cares behind. Anything you want is yours. Anything.'

The black-eyed woman's hand was perfectly smooth. There were no lines on her palm, no whorls on her fingertips. Eleanor's hands were scrubbed raw, a fine web of cuts across the knuckles, skin flaking all along her fingers. They were the hands of an old woman, and Eleanor was seventeen.

Anything she wanted...

She wouldn't have to end up like Leah. She could find her, give her a place to recover. She could stop Aoife from going down that path, too. She could keep her friends safe. And not just that. A soft, warm bed. A roof that didn't leak. Hot, delicious food every night, food that wouldn't get knocked out of her hands. No more knots in her back. No more throbbing knees from scrubbing floors. No more itching uniforms. No more Mr Pembroke.

She would be a lady. A real lady, like Mrs Pembroke had wanted her to be. She'd be safe, warm, well-fed, well-dressed, and that would be only the beginning of it. She could spirit herself away to all the places she'd read about, and fly home again quicker than blinking. There would be no door left closed to her, no secret that she could not uncover, and she would be adored everywhere she went.

With her hand held out the black-eyed woman looked like a mother, waiting for her child to come to her. Eleanor took it. For a moment, the black-eyed woman's hand seemed to flicker.

'Eleanor Rose Hartley,' said the black-eyed woman, her smile vanishing, 'I will be with you always. I will give you anything you desire; you have only to ask. You may use this gift seven times, after which your soul will belong to me. Do you understand?'

The silence billowed around them.

'I understand.'

'And do you consent to it of your own free will, knowing the price you must pay?'

'I do.'

'Then, Eleanor Rose Hartley, I am your servant.'

Eleanor started awake. She was still in the library chair, head lolling against the leather. The little book was still on her lap, and her candle had almost burned down. Dirty moonlight crept through a gap in the curtains. Everything was just as she had left it, but the black-eyed woman had gone.

51

Eleanor stretched out a kink in her neck and put the book back on the shelf. She was usually careful never to fall asleep in the library; it gave her strange dreams. Tentatively, she touched the cushion of the black-eyed woman's chair. It was cold. Eleanor's shoulders slumped. It had been a dream after all.

She blew out her candle and unlocked the library door. She knew she ought to go back to her room before anyone saw her, but instead of leaving she crept towards the window. Heavy brocade curtains swept the floor, the embroidery glinting in the moonlight.

The library was at the front of the house, two storeys over the entrance hall. From the window she could see the empty street, all its colour stolen by the darkness. The moon gleamed against the velvet sky like a new shilling, shifting under a veil of smoke. Under its light Eleanor's raw, red hands looked pale and clean, her hair turned to pale gold. If anyone should pass along the street, Eleanor thought, they would see her shining at the window, like a girl made of precious stones. But there was no one outside – only a solitary cat, prowling from shadow to shadow along the street.

From somewhere deep in Granborough House, a clock chimed midnight.

Under the silver light, Eleanor could see the library as it had once been. In daylight, the carpet looked faded and cobwebs gathered in corners too high for the maids to reach, but the light of the moon brushed those details aside. The colours were softened, the cracks in the leather armchairs were hidden, the slight charring where the poker rested against the fireplace was merely a shadow. The moon showed the room as it ought to be, and it did the same for her. There was nothing weighing her down. Her hands looked clean and smooth. She caught a glimpse of her reflection in the vast mirror that hung over the fireplace and was startled by the blue of her own eyes, gleaming in the pale light. She looked like she could do anything.

She looked like a girl whose wishes might be granted.

Eleanor licked her lips.

She tried to tell herself that it was a bad idea. It had been a dream, after all. Making a wish would only get her hopes up for nothing. And if it hadn't been a dream – which, of course, it had – then she'd sold her soul. She remembered her fairy tales; a deal like that could not be broken lightly. But, an insinuating voice at the back of her mind whispered, weren't there also stories of people clever enough to cheat the Devil? Wasn't she as sharp and quick as they were? All she needed was to stop herself from making the last wish. Surely she had sense enough for that.

Eleanor drifted away from the window. She'd spent so long reading, dreaming of magic. She'd imagined herself floating above every dirty, common thing, safely wrapped in clouds or starlight. She'd never imagined herself too afraid to soar. Perhaps she was still dreaming. It might be easier if she were. But if she was, what reason did she have to fear?

She stretched out her hands in front of her, like a stage magician about to cast a spell. For a split second, she saw her mother's hands in hers – she'd had the same strong, quick fingers, the same oval-shaped nails. Eleanor screwed her eyes tight shut and shook the thought away before she could remember the iron bedstead pressing into her back. She had nothing to fear.

She would make herself a fairy tale. She would craft

something precious and wonderful out of thin air – something small, to start with. And when she could conjure beauty and hope with only a word, she would paint her life in bright and brilliant colours, and she would never even have to think about who she had been and what she had left behind.

A silence settled on the library. It was not the quiet of a city asleep, punctuated by distant sounds from music halls and hansom cabs rattling over cobblestones. This was true silence, and something in it seemed to be waiting.

Eleanor cleared her throat and closed her eyes.

'I wish,' she said, her voice sounding far too small in the quiet, 'for a pair of shoes the same colour as moonlight.'

Something changed. A moment of absolute stillness descended on Eleanor like a shroud. Dust motes hung in the air. She felt her own breath in her throat. Then a strange prickling sensation swept through her, leaving her feeling magnetic.

She opened her eyes and looked down. There were no shoes.

Eleanor held in a sigh, all her hopes curdling.

The next morning, Eleanor woke up feeling as though she had barely slept at all. There was a crick in her neck and everything ached. A slice of dark blue sky was just visible through her faded red curtains.

Eleanor groaned. Why was she so sore? She couldn't remember going back to bed; had she tripped up the servants' staircase? The steps were steep and uneven, it would have been an easy mistake to make. Or perhaps she'd sat up mending her torn things and hit the floor when she fell asleep. Her right side hurt the most. Perhaps that had been where she'd landed. Eleanor sat up, wincing as she stretched, and rubbed her eyes. If only she could—

She stopped. Something was glinting on the floor.

Eleanor peered over the edge of the bed and her mouth fell open. Her breath caught in her throat. Dancing slippers made of a lustrous silver satin, trimmed with blue silk so pale it might have been ice, sat neatly on her rough wood floor.

Eleanor stared. She had to be dreaming. Surely this wasn't real. Making a wish in a moonlit library was one thing, but surely her little room, with its bare floorboards and creeping damp, was far too ordinary for magic.

She stretched out a trembling hand. Her fingers were going to pass right through the shoes, or stick to them, and then she would know that she was dreaming. The shoes were not really there. She was still asleep, of course she was still asleep...

Her fingers met satin, soft and inviting.

Eleanor clapped a hand over her mouth. A peal of giddy laughter was rising in her chest.

The wishes were *real*.

Her hands were shaking. A grin split her face in two. Everything the black-eyed woman had promised was true. It wasn't a dream, she could have anything she wanted, she could leave Granborough House...

The future burst into life before her. She could be a lady, just as she'd once hoped. She would have servants, and a feather bed, and she could gorge herself until she was fat and happy. She would stand on Juliet's balcony, tour the palace of Versailles, climb through the ruins of Pompeii – and when she did, people would say 'Right this way, Miss Hartley', and beg for the privilege of carrying her bags. She would reshape her life into a glorious, shining jewel, and all who saw it would envy her...

But if the wishes were real, then so was the price she had paid.

Her soul was no longer her own.

She had already made one wish. It was too late now. She was already changed – but how? What had she done to herself? Unconsciously, her hand drifted up to her face; she stared at her palm, her breath coming sharp and fast. She still looked the same. She still *felt* the same – but no, she didn't. She felt like the top of her head had been sliced off and all the secrets of the universe had been tipped straight into her skull.

What had she done?

Eleanor forced herself to calm down. Of course she didn't feel the same. Things *weren't* the same – Leah had been forced out, Mr Pembroke was already circling Eleanor and she'd found out that magic was real, it was *real*, and she was the only one who knew. But, she thought, what would she be when the shock finally began to fade? Would she be herself still, or would she be a sharper, crueller thing? Or would she finally be able to see the world with clear eyes, the only person who could see its secret heart?

Last night, the black-eyed woman had said she would not take her soul until Eleanor had made her final wish. Perhaps it was not too late. She had six wishes left – no, five. She must never use the last wish: her soul was hers, and hers alone. Only now, Eleanor was one step closer to losing it.

Eleanor clutched at the slippers. Despite what she'd done, she could not contain her happiness. They were smooth and soft under her rough fingers, and even the feel of them made her grin.

She had a way out – not just for her, but for Aoife, too. But it was a door she could only go through carefully. She must plan out her wishes like a general moving troops across a battlefield; one wrong move and there would be blood. But she *had* a way out, she had it, after all these years she had it. Everything she'd dreamed of was within her grasp. All she had to do now was reach out and take it.

Eleanor hugged the shoes to her chest, the light of her secret shining under her skin.

Eleanor drifted down the servants' staircase and into the kitchen, all her thoughts alight. The shoes were bundled up in a torn petticoat and shoved into an old suitcase which she'd slid behind her chest of drawers. No one was going to take them from her.

She raked through the ashes and lit the kitchen range, and distractedly smacked her hand on the hard iron door. It stung, and three little scratches on the side of her hand opened up and began to bleed. Eleanor barely noticed. It was hard to make herself care about something so trivial when this could be the last time she ever lit the kitchen fire.

She straightened up, staring around the wide stone kitchen. This could be the last time she slid across the stone floors, sat at the rickety wooden chairs, stared out of the narrow street-level window set high into the wall. No more bending to rummage through the cleaning cupboard, no more lugging around her housemaid's box, no more choking on dust in the wine cellar. She would rise above it all, straight-backed and proud, and everyone would smile to see her restored to her proper place again.

Lizzie tried to goad her over breakfast; Eleanor barely heard it. What did she need twenty-five pounds for, when she could wish for all the money in the world? Mrs Fielding snapped at her for wasting her time the night before; Eleanor let the words wash over her. She had no need to listen to Mrs Fielding when she could use the wishes to catapult herself back to the height of Society. Mrs Banbury took her aside, and gently asked if there was anything wrong; Eleanor beamed at her, so brightly that the cook stepped back. Nothing could be wrong when Eleanor could make everything right.

When they had finished breakfast, Mrs Fielding gathered them all around the kitchen table and told them she had an announcement. Through a giddy haze, Eleanor heard that Charles would be returning home. His things were being sent ahead, and they were to prepare the house for his arrival. That punctured Eleanor's reverie. The last time she had seen Charles was at Mrs Pembroke's funeral, over three years ago. Actually, 'seen' was not quite true. Eleanor had not been allowed to attend the funeral – she had still been considered a young lady, then, and it would not have been proper for her to attend. She had been stuck in her old bedroom instead, weeping into a pillow for most of the morning. At three o'clock the front door had banged open and Charles and his father had stormed in, shouting at each other before the footman could get the door closed. Eleanor could not hear what they were saying – the echoes made it difficult to discern the words – but before long a pair of angry feet were stomping along the corridor and another door slammed.

Eleanor had wiped her eyes and counted to one hundred, wanting to be sure of the silence. Then, she'd crept along to the far end of the corridor and knocked on Charles's bedroom door. There had been shuffling and thumping sounds coming from the other side of the door. They stopped, at once. She knocked again, and still heard nothing. She went back to her room with a lump in her throat. The next morning she found a note pushed under her bedroom door, in Charles's rounded hand. He had urgent business in Oxford, the letter said, and had to set off immediately – three months before he had been due to go to university. He offered her the pick of all of the books in his room and a tin of gingerbread that he had hidden under his bed, and promised to write to her every week. Eleanor ran to say goodbye, but he had already gone.

Charles had not written. Eleanor had tried to tell herself that he was busy. But as days became weeks, and months became years, she realized he was never going to write at all. Now she was standing outside his room once again, with a housemaid's box clutched in her hands and Aoife by her side, and in a few weeks' time she was going to have to look him in the eye and stop herself from asking why he had not written to her.

Eleanor pulled herself up short. She had the wishes now. In a few weeks' time she would not be in Granborough House. She would be somewhere decadent and splendid, eating pheasant and lobster that had been cooked specially for her, and Charles would be lucky if she deigned to notice him at all.

She pushed open the door.

Charles's room looked like a junk shop.

In the three years he had been away from Granborough House, Charles had not come home once, and Eleanor envied him for it. He spent the university holidays with friends, or attaching himself to his professors' expeditions. He had been everywhere. Shooting deer in the Scottish Highlands, tangled in purple heather and green bracken. Drinking red wine on the balcony of a Venetian *palazzo*, watching the city slowly flooding. Standing in the ruins of Pompeii, the sun bleaching the stones ash-white. But every time he went to a new place, he bought all the souvenirs within arm's reach and sent them back to Granborough House before he moved on.

'Jesus, Mary and Joseph,' said Aoife, leaning her brushes against the wall. 'Where'd he get all this tat?'

Ornately worked pewter tankards were clustered around the foot of his four-poster bed. Painted scenes of ruins and fields winked up at them from china plates, several of them smashed. A cracked Venetian glass bottle lay on its side, next to a dusty stick of rock, a box of toffees, and four painted biscuit tins. Strewn across it all was a collection of cravats, handkerchiefs and scarves made of French silk, Irish linen and Indian cotton.

'What are we supposed to do with all of it?'

Eleanor picked up the handkerchiefs and began shaking them out. She had to stop herself from checking to see if there was anything for her, even after three years of silence. 'Put it away, I suppose. It's all his.'

Aoife eyed the stick of rock. 'All of it?'

Eleanor closed the door. 'Nearly all of it.'

Aoife snatched up the stick of rock and wiped the dust off with her apron. Eleanor went for the toffees. She sat on Charles's bed and offered the box to Aoife.

'We'll tell him that the mice got to it on the boat back home,' said Eleanor, picking out a fat toffee. 'He doesn't ever need to know.'

Aoife hesitated. 'You oughtn't to sit on his bed. It's not proper for us to sit on the furniture.'

60

Eleanor popped the toffee into her mouth and did not get up. Aoife was right. Servants should not sit on furniture that was reserved for their betters, but Eleanor would be damned if either Charles or his father had turned out better than her. Besides, if she was going to make herself a lady, she ought to get used to softness again.

She leant against one of the bedposts and spread out the red and gold hangings across her skirts. They suited her much better than her brown wool dress. 'If you could do anything in the world, Aoife, what would you do?'

Aoife glanced at the door. 'Would you get off the bed, Ella? What if someone should see you?'

Eleanor shook her head. 'You haven't answered my question.'

'I'd cure Micheál,' Aoife said at once. 'Now will you stop lolling about?'

'And after that?'

Aoife threw up her hands. 'I don't know! What kind of mood are you in, Ella, that you're asking all these questions? There's work to be done.'

Eleanor chose another toffee. 'There's *always* work to be done. And it's always us that must do it. Don't you think that's unfair? Why shouldn't we take a turn in soft beds and good clothes? Haven't we as much right as—'

There was a shout from further down the hall – a man's voice, incoherent and angry. Eleanor sprang off the bed at once, cramming the box of toffees under Charles's blankets. Aoife jumped and cowered back from the door.

'Is that the master?' she whispered.

'I think so. Wait,' Eleanor said, as Aoife started for the door. 'We'll go together.'

Aoife nodded and waited for Eleanor to open the door. The

two of them crept into the corridor, Aoife still clutching the stick of rock.

The door to Mr Pembroke's bedroom was open. His jacket was discarded in the hallway, his coat slumped across the wide banister of the main staircase. The shouting – no, sobbing, Eleanor realized – was coming from his room. She laid a hand on Aoife's arm and Aoife hid the stick of rock behind her back.

They shuffled towards his bedroom. The closer they got the stronger the reek of brandy became. Through the open door Eleanor could see Mr Pembroke in his shirtsleeves and a half-open waistcoat, cradling something in his hands and crying like a child.

Tentatively, she knocked on the open door. 'Sir?'

He whirled around. His brown hair was dishevelled, his eyes were bloodshot, and his face was blotchy from crying. He was standing by the birdcage, and cupped in his large hands was a small, yellow body, its head at an unnatural angle.

'Get out of my sight,' he rasped. 'Get out!'

Aoife bolted. Eleanor followed her, and the two of them hid in Charles's room, not moving, until the sound of Mr Pembroke lurching down the stairs echoed back up to them.

Eleanor leant against the door, breathing hard. Aoife came closer, her eyes huge with worry.

'Was that...'

Eleanor nodded.

Aoife put a hand over her mouth. 'That poor little bird.'

Eleanor tried to feel sorry for Mr Pembroke. But even if she screwed up her compassion and wrung out the last drops, she could not do it. The little canary had been blameless, of course, and she was sorry that it was dead. It had been a pretty thing, and listening to it sing had made cleaning Mr Pembroke's bedroom far more bearable. But when she thought of Mr Pembroke, and what he had done to Leah, she could not feel anything at the sight of his tears. He had taken too much from too many for her to want to spare him any loss.

'Yes,' said Eleanor, 'that poor bird.'

PART TWO

Eleanor sat in the dining room, the Pembroke family silver laid out in front of her. It winked and flashed as she worked the dirt free from the crests. Set against the gleaming, dark table, they looked like stars aligning themselves into constellations of her own making. She tilted a knife and a couple of spoons until she'd made Ursa Major. She'd seen it in a book once, and had spent the next few nights staring out of her attic window, looking for a shape of a bear in the stars. All she'd seen were streetlights that turned the chimney smoke orange.

Of course, she *could* make her own constellations now. She could write her name in stars, line up the planets from red to blue, or drag them closer to the Earth so that she could see their colours better. Now that she had the wishes, she could do anything.

Her hand cramped and a fork clattered to the floor. She left it there, massaging the sore spot in her palm.

Not that she would drag the planets around, of course. She had only six wishes left – no, five, she reminded herself, because she could not use the last wish if she wanted to keep her soul – and it would be silly to waste one on something as frivolous as that. She needed to plan carefully if she was going to make her dreams come true.

She was going to make herself a lady. She could whisk her friends away from Granborough House. She'd never have to even *look* at another scrubbing brush. She could travel the world, just like Charles did, and leave a string of broken hearts behind her. She might not even need the wishes after that.

The door opened, and Mr Pembroke came in.

Eleanor jumped to her feet, forks clattering across the floor. She stepped back, desperate to have something in between them. Mr Pembroke closed the door behind him, his hand slipping off the doorknob. Sunlight flared across his face, showing up all the glistening sweat. He squinted into the light as he looked at her, the hand shielding his eyes casting long, deep shadows across his pale cheeks.

'Why, Ella,' he said, his voice mild, 'I hope I didn't startle you.'

Eleanor was already scrabbling for a response that he couldn't twist when she remembered that she didn't need one. She had the wishes now. She could say what she liked, and if he tried to punish her it would slide right off her, like rainwater on a window pane. The knowledge was like strapping on armour, or picking up a sword. Still, she reasoned, better not to speak her mind yet. The last wish had taken a while to work, and a man like Mr Pembroke could do a lot of damage with a little delay.

She retreated behind a blank, chilly politeness that she could wear like a mask. 'May I help you, sir?'

He gave her an insidious smile. 'I daresay you can. Do sit down. Now, Ella, certain rumours about your character have been brought to my attention...'

A prickle of fear ran through Eleanor. Lizzie had started work already. Well, Lizzie could say what she liked. Soon

Eleanor would be so far above her that she wouldn't even notice what Lizzie thought.

'Rumours, sir? May I ask where you heard them?'

Mr Pembroke waved a hand. 'Oh, the details of such things are not important, I assure you...'

'I believe they are,' Eleanor insisted, hating how small her voice sounded. 'If you will excuse me, I am going to fetch Mrs Fielding. I should like to have her support in this matter.'

His smile faltered. 'Come now, Ella, there's no need. Mrs Fielding is a very busy woman. I'm sure that we can come to an arrangement between ourselves...'

It was already starting. She knew exactly what kind of 'arrangement' he had in mind. Fear churned through her. She had to get someone else in the room. 'On the contrary,' she said, 'if this matter is important enough for you to consider it personally, as the master of the house, then you must agree that it is my duty to make sure that Mrs Fielding is aware.'

Eleanor almost ran for the door. She was turning the handle when Mr Pembroke said, indignant, 'Your duty is whatever I tell you it is.'

Duty. It was a word she had heard a lot in Granborough House. It was a word that ground and scraped and pushed and tugged, and over the past three years it had seemed to be all that Eleanor heard. But it was not a one-way street. As master of the house, Mr Pembroke had a duty to look after his staff, to provide them with food, clothing, and a safe place to rest their heads. And he was not just her employer; he was her legal guardian. He had a duty to her more than anyone else in this house. He was supposed to take care of her. He'd promised Mrs Pembroke when she lay dying, Eleanor had *heard* him make his promise, and he had broken it.

69

Anger blazed through her. Well, he could break all the promises he wanted. It wouldn't matter. She had the wishes. She could break *him*.

'We all have our duties, sir,' she said, keeping her tone neutral as she opened the door. 'I assure you, I remember *mine*.'

The weight of the laudanum in her pocket was unfamiliar. A heavy purse waiting to be stolen. Eleanor thought of Lizzie, and her fists clenched. She wouldn't have needed to do this if Lizzie hadn't stolen her money.

Mr Pembroke had gone out. The moment he'd left, Eleanor went straight upstairs, the bottle banging against her leg. It had been easy to steal. Mrs Banbury kept the laudanum in the kitchen cupboard, and amid the clatter of the maids it was all too easy to hide a little bottle among a stack of plates. She'd palmed it in the middle of putting them back, and no one had noticed a thing. Still, she had to be careful. She could be hanged if anyone saw; they'd take her for a poisoner. Of course, now that she had the wishes she supposed it would not matter if she was arrested – she could simply wish her way out – but she'd rather not have such an unpleasant scene.

The study first. Mr Pembroke kept half his decanters there. She told herself to be sensible and only faltered when she reached the second-floor landing, and saw the study door.

Eleanor drifted closer, turning the bottle over in her pocket. The study door loomed ahead of her. She listened. Mrs Banbury and Daisy, yelling to each other in the kitchen. Aoife, singing an Irish air from the floor above. Mrs Fielding calling to Lizzie from the hallway. Nothing from the study.

Eleanor went inside.

The study looked as it always had: dark, sombre, and rather

like a lair that had been dug out underground. The walls pressed in too close, the cabinets and bookcases leant too far forward, and the portraits of long-dead Pembrokes were starting to fade to a sludgy tobacco-brown. The eyes in the portraits watched her as she wedged a chair underneath the doorknob. How had she never shrunk back from all those faces? She half-expected their eyes to flicker, or strange shadows to pass across their faces as she turned away. She almost turned their faces to the wall, but there was no time to linger.

It was done in a matter of minutes. One sip, and Mr Pembroke would drift gently off to sleep instead of putting his hands on her. He'd never notice all his crystal decanters had been opened with the amount he drank. She thought of Leah as she added the last drop of laudanum and cringed. She should have done this months ago – no, years. If only she'd thought of it then, Leah might be here still, happy and laughing while Mr Pembroke dozed in a chair.

She slipped the bottle back inside her pocket. Would it be enough? How much laudanum would it take to knock out a man like Mr Pembroke? He was far bigger than her, he drank gallons of brandy, and God knew what he did when he was off on one of his sprees. And there were other decanters, too – what if he drank from those instead?

Eleanor gave herself a shake. Now that she had the wishes, she could make sure that Mr Pembroke never found himself alone with a maid again. The laudanum was a temporary measure, so that she had time to plan. She would not need to drug the other decanters then.

Eleanor left the study and drifted towards Leah's room. She cursed herself for being too afraid to drug Mr Pembroke's decanters earlier. If only she'd thought faster, acted quicker

– but it was too late now. She'd never see Leah again. Eleanor had no idea where Leah might have gone and no means of finding her, because Leah could not read or write. London had swallowed her up, with her kind, fierce eyes and her quick laugh. Eleanor laid a hand on the door to Leah's room. How long would it be before the city spat her out?

Eleanor wiped her eyes and went back down to the kitchen to replace the laudanum. Mrs Banbury was at the range, a vast knob of butter sizzling in a pan, while Daisy cleaned out the larder. No one was looking at the cupboard she'd taken the little bottle from. She strode across the kitchen, drew the laudanum out of her pocket and—

'Ella!'

Mrs Fielding was standing behind her. Eleanor froze, the cupboard door open, the laudanum in her hand. The handle shook under her fingers. This was it, she thought, *this was it*. Any minute now Mrs Fielding would yell for the constable, shrieking about poisoners, and there was nothing she could say or do because she had been caught with the bottle in her hand...

'What on Earth are you doing with that?' Mrs Fielding asked.

Eleanor started. She hadn't been expecting a chance to explain herself. But now that she had one, all that was going around her head was *I've been caught, I've been caught, I've been caught...*

And then, it occurred to her.

She turned around, aware of the flush in her cheeks. *Good,* she thought, it would serve her.

'I...I've been caught short, Mrs Fielding.' She laid a mean-ingful hand on her abdomen. 'I thought perhaps a drop or two, for the pain...'

Mrs Fielding sighed. 'Oh, come now, Ella. I had supposed you a good deal hardier. Go and scrub the hall floor; it'll take your mind off it.'

Eleanor curtseyed and fetched a bucket, scrubbing brush and soap, clutching her triumph tight, so that it would not show.

That Sunday, Mrs Fielding took them all to church. Mr Pembroke never went, but Mrs Fielding insisted that the maids be seen in the family pew every week, so that people would not talk. It did not work. The whole parish could see the number of maids dwindling, and Mr Pembroke hovered over them all in his absence like a malevolent ghost.

They walked to church two by two, heat already rising off the cobblestones. Deeper into Mayfair, the streets were quiet, with only the creak of water pumps and windows being opened to be heard. In those streets, Sunday was sacred. But turn a corner and the shriek and rattle of the markets rang across the road, costermongers sweating over their barrows as they tried to sell people their Sunday dinners. Little girls ran from door to door, selling watercress grown on filthy flannels. Great trays of fish stank in the heat. Cheese sweated through its muslin wrapper, kidneys dripped blood quietly onto the pavement.

Eventually the church came into view. Eleanor felt a prickle of unease. She had sold her soul. Would she be able to enter holy ground? She pinched the skin of her wrist. Of course she would. The wishes weren't evil, surely.

Aoife sighed as they went through the lychgate. 'Mrs Fielding, couldn't we go to a proper church, just once?'

'None of your papacy here, Aoife!' Mrs Fielding hissed. 'People will hear you!'

Aoife rolled her eyes. 'It doesn't even smell right,' she muttered.

Eleanor stared straight ahead, ignoring the parishioners who whispered as they passed. She could feel them counting the line of maids, staring at Leah's empty place the way people peered into cages at the zoo.

'...only a matter of time, of course. Bachelors are always getting into these sorts of scrapes...'

'...but the girls weren't brought up properly. They can't help themselves...'

'You know he calls them all by their first names? Oh, yes! Well, it makes sense when you consider it. Who'd want to get into bed with a girl called Hartley?'

Eleanor stumbled. The speaker, a middle-aged woman in an arsenic-green dress, turned away with a titter when she saw the look on Eleanor's face. Eleanor curled her hands into fists. The parishioners giggled and gossiped about what went on at Granborough House as if it were the plot of an operetta. Mr Pembroke was cast as the lovable rogue, an ageing Don Juan in a smoking jacket, and the maids were buxom girls who laughed too loud and could be won over with a bawdy wink. None of them had seen the bruises.

The reverend came and found them before the service. She'd thought he might. Reverend Clarke was a small man with a voracious interest in the lives of his parishioners, particularly the young, unmarried female parishioners who kept falling pregnant at Granborough House. He had an instinct for gossip that was so unerring it might have been divine guidance. Eleanor was surprised he hadn't beaten a path to their door, when the news of Leah's dismissal got out.

Eleanor watched the reverend tease more details about Leah's departure out of Mrs Fielding, with all the tenacity of a terrier chasing a rat from its hole. Eleanor tried to listen to another conversation – Mrs Kettering's son had married a local girl he'd met in India and was bringing her home, Colonel Hardwicke's daughter would be converting to marry her Jewish sweetheart, a shoemaker's had been burgled two streets away – but the whispers about Leah tugged at her like insistent hands. Eleanor held her head high and stared into the distance, proud and fierce. She'd find a way to stop their whispering, soon.

The laundry copper at Granborough House was rusting in a big, hulking heap in a vault of a room off the kitchen. Maintaining the machinery and the three laundrymaids who'd worked it had been expensive, and when it broke Mr Pembroke had dismissed the three maids and started sending his laundry out instead of having it fixed.

Eleanor was going to pick it up. Brandy was not too expensive, she'd noticed. Neither was Mr Pembroke's subscription to his club. It was only women who seemed to be too expensive, she thought, no matter how low the cost.

A fug of heat hung over the pavements, but Eleanor pulled on her gloves and wide-brimmed hat. Even this far away from the river, she could still smell the Thames, dank and fetid under the summer sun. But in Mayfair, the doors were not propped open, the windows were not thrown wide. It would be crass to admit that the occupants of such grand houses could sweat.

They all pretended to be perfect. The other servants that Eleanor passed nodded to her politely, and enquired after her health if she looked like she might linger. But a few weeks ago, they had been just as cordial to Leah, and now it was as if she'd been lifted right out of their memories, like stitches being unpicked from a sampler. Leah might never have been there. It had been the same when Eleanor's mother had taken ill. Kind neighbours closed their doors to her, not wanting to risk consumption, even when Eleanor cried on their doorsteps.

Eleanor heard the noise and bustle of Marylebone before she met it. Away from the mausoleum streets of Mayfair, the city was teeming with people. Fruit-sellers lost in clouds of flies. A line of men wearing sandwich-boards, dripping in the heat. A woman selling coffee from a barrow, face shiny with sweat. Crossing-sweepers drooped on street corners, slumped on their brooms. Omnibuses and carts and hansoms and private carriages clattered up and down the street, and the reek of horse dung, rotting fruit and burnt coffee made Eleanor feel dizzy.

She could not wait to take herself away from all of this. The sooner she could pay other people to descend into the swell of humanity on her behalf, the better. Mrs Pembroke had never gone anywhere she had not wanted to go. She'd had people for that.

Eleanor faltered. Someone smacked into her, swearing, but she paid them no mind.

She could wish for Mrs Pembroke to come back. She could wish for her *mother* to come back. The black-eyed woman had said she could wish for anything, hadn't she?

Eleanor drifted into the shade of a plane tree, its leaves already browning. A beggar was leaning against the bark; he held out his hand, but Eleanor ignored him. She didn't have any money of her own, anyway.

Could she really bring Mrs Pembroke back? What would happen if she did? Would the world snap back into place as though she had never died, or would she reappear, whole and healthy, after everyone had mourned her for three years? Eleanor had not quite made her peace with Mrs Pembroke's death – even if Mrs Pembroke had lived for thirty more years, it would still have been too soon – but three years of grieving had taken their toll. Even if she woke up tomorrow and Mrs Pembroke was alive again, she would still feel the weight of all those years without her. Would she ever be able to look at her again? Would she ever be able to stop?

Besides, she thought, remembering the woman's flat, black eyes, wishing the dead back to life might not be a good idea. All her instincts told her that anything the black-eyed woman brought back would not be as it had been in life. She might keep them in terrible agony, forever stuck on the point of death but unable to pass on. Despite the heat, Eleanor shivered. Her own mother's death had not been easy. To be stuck, forever, in that state...

Eleanor shoved the thought away at once.

A plump woman with puffy, red-rimmed eyes and a yellowing kerchief around her neck sidled up to her. 'Pardon the intrusion, miss,' she wheedled, 'but I can see you're distressed. Is it money you're after? Only I couldn't help noticing your lovely hair, such a beautiful shine on it. I could give you three shillings for the lot, if you'd step this way...'

Eleanor recoiled and fled into the crowd. A fiddler nearly caught her in the eye with his bow. A small girl chased a hoop into her legs. Trays of sweating ices, damp ginger beer and cloudy gin were shoved under her nose. Eleanor ignored them all, barging through the crowds with her head held high. It was silly to think about such things – especially in public, where anyone might see her distress. She ought to put them out of her mind, as she always did.

But with the wishes, she'd never have to think of such things again. Poverty, hunger and illness – these did not have to trouble her now. She could drag everyone she cared about back from the brink of death and set them so far above their cares that they would not even remember what hardship looked like. She could feed the hungry, shelter the homeless, cure the sick. And she could do all of that just by wishing for money. Anything she wanted, she could take. She'd never need to be afraid again.

The street pressed in on all sides, hot and close. But Eleanor held her head high and set her shoulders back, lit with a power she was only just beginning to understand.

Everything around Eleanor seemed so small.

The laundress hadn't cleaned Mr Pembroke's suits properly; the water had been too hot, and the fine wool had shrunk. Mrs Fielding had shouted at Eleanor when she found out, because Mrs Fielding was tired and overworked and Eleanor was there to be shouted at. Eleanor could not bring herself to care. All she could think about was the wishes.

She would need to be sensible, of course; her next wish needed careful consideration. But every time Eleanor saw a gleaming landau trotting along the street, every glimpse of a dress in brilliant blue or glowing pink, every burst of song, she knew she could take it. All the fine and lovely things of the world could be hers. What did scrubbing and polishing matter when compared to that? She moved around Granborough House as if she was asleep, but she had never felt more awake.

Even when she was scrubbing the marble hall floor, the sound of the brush seemed to say *wi-shes*.

Lizzie had noticed.

She stuck out her foot when Eleanor passed, to see if she would trip. She 'accidentally' knocked Eleanor's dinner onto the floor. She engaged Mrs Fielding in a long and loud discussion about Leah's morals, or lack of them, and kept glancing at Eleanor to see if she'd crack. Eleanor said and did nothing. She only flinched when Mrs Fielding said 'of course, I wasn't surprised at all. Girls are always throwing themselves at the master.' Reality had cut through to Eleanor then in one vicious slice, and her hands were clenching before she even realized it. But she held in her anger, and went back up the servants' staircase to call Lizzie names in the privacy of her own room.

Her bed was completely drenched.

Eleanor seethed. Lizzie was trying to provoke her into doing something stupid, so that Mr Pembroke would have an excuse to take Eleanor aside for a 'private word'. The sensible thing was to ignore her, but Eleanor was so, *so* tired of being sensible. She checked her case, heart pounding, and sagged with relief when she saw that the shoes were still there. God knew what Lizzie would've done if she'd found those, especially after that poor shoemaker had been robbed.

The sun was setting in a blaze of crimson. Eleanor's little room was filled with red light. She drank it in, breathing deep until her anger stopped throbbing. By the time she had calmed down the sun had set and the house had settled back into quiet. Mayfair was silent, but at four storeys up there was no escaping the sounds of the city at night. Music halls, rattling cabs, distant shouting – they stuck to Eleanor like tar, reminding her that she was trapped in the realm of the ordinary.

It was time to escape.

Eleanor took off her boots so that they would not make a noise, and crept down to the library. The steep wooden steps of the servants' staircase did not creak underfoot; she knew how to walk silently. She eased the door to the second-floor landing open and stole into the corridor, her stockinged feet catching on the carpet. She shuffled towards the library – just five minutes, that was all she needed – and froze as a door creaked open behind her.

She turned. Lizzie was standing in the doorway to the servants' staircase, grinning, a candle clutched in her hand. 'The master wants to see you,' she hissed.

Eleanor stepped back, heart beating so fast it felt like it was rattling. No. Not now. It was too soon. She wasn't ready, she would never be ready.

Lizzie advanced, holding her candle high. 'Go on, Miss Eleanor. You're needed upstairs.'

Eleanor barged past her and darted down the servants' staircase. She had to get to the kitchen – there would be knives there, cleavers, a coal scuttle she could swing at Lizzie's head. Anything to get Lizzie to leave her be. Lizzie swore and came after her.

Eleanor burst through the kitchen door and snatched up a carving knife. She whirled around. Lizzie skidded to a halt when she saw the blade glinting in the candlelight.

'You bring that thing near me and I'll scream,' she hissed.

'Go ahead,' Eleanor spat. 'They won't hear you with baize on all the doors.'

Slowly, Lizzie set her candle down on the kitchen table. Eleanor listened for footsteps on the stairs, but heard nothing.

'Give me back my money.'

Lizzie grinned. 'Can't. Spent it.'

A dull whine was building in Eleanor's ears. The bones in her hands stood out stark as she gripped the knife. How had Lizzie spent Eleanor's future so quickly?

'You can't keep hold of that thing forever,' said Lizzie. 'Mrs Banbury'll make you give it back. And when she does, I'll be there – and so will *he*.'

'Stop it.'

Lizzie took a step forward. 'He'll lose his temper if you drag it out like this. That's what happened to Leah. But you know that, don't you, Miss Eleanor? You saw all her bruises.'

'I told you to stop it!'

'Or what?' Lizzie nodded to the knife. 'You won't use it. It'll only make things worse. Better to go to him now and get it over with.'

'Stop! For pity's sake, stop! My God, how can you stand to be like this?' Eleanor spat, tears prickling in her eyes. 'How can you throw him girl after girl and just…just…God! I wish you'd just stop, just once!'

Something changed.

For a split second, Eleanor saw everything. Dust in the air, made silver by a shaft of moonlight. The reflection of Lizzie's pale face in the blade. A beetle skittering underneath the kitchen range. Then, a strange prickling sensation swept through her body, leaving her feeling magnetic.

She'd made a wish.

She hadn't meant to do it. The wishes were valuable things, she had to spend them wisely. Only now she was one step closer to losing her soul, all because she couldn't keep a lid on her temper. Shame tugged at the edges of Eleanor's thoughts. She needed to be more careful.

Lizzie was staring at her, her throat working frantically. The knife clattered to the floor. Eleanor backed away, heading for the stairs.

'It isn't going to be me,' Lizzie hissed, the faintest tremor in her voice. 'It won't *ever* be me.'

Dawn filtered through a thin film of grease on Eleanor's window. She was tangled in her damp bedclothes. The heat was already rising – Eleanor could feel the sweat in her own hair – and still they had not yet dried. But, she thought, at least it cooled her down.

Costermongers trundled their carts through the streets below. From further afield came the sounds of animals being driven to market, but all she could see from the little window was a thin line of streetlights winking out, one by one. A trail of breadcrumbs, slowly being eaten away. She dressed and tried to stretch the ache out of her neck, still furious with herself for making a wish without meaning to. Damp cloth leached the warmth out of her limbs as she went downstairs.

She could not afford to delay any longer. She would have to make another wish – one that she'd planned for, this time. It was an easy choice to make, now that she knew Mr Pembroke had set his sights on her. She would wish for money, and put herself forever beyond his reach. But first, she wanted to see how her second wish would come true.

It was strange to think of how that might happen. Perhaps the wish would have completely transformed Lizzie's personality, and she would be sweetly apologetic and ready to make amends. But, Eleanor thought, there were some things that were *too* strange to contemplate. Lizzie would probably find herself called back home on urgent family business; after all, magic had to have *some* limits.

The kitchen was filled with the kind of heat that crawled into her mouth, laced with the heavy taste of ashes. Eleanor shook them out of the vast range's grate, picking out the cinders and cleaning the flues before laying the fire. Her fingers smarted and ash sputtered all over her skirts. The range was still warm, but it would be a while before it was hot enough for porridge; the others would not be down for some time.

Eleanor shook out her apron over the ash-bucket. The kitchen was a mess. A thin layer of dust and soil was scattered around the steps leading up to the garden. Chairs had been knocked out of place. A cupboard door stood half-open, revealing an empty bottle of cheap gin, and the tip of the coal scuttle was bent out of shape.

She rolled her eyes. It was just like Lizzie to make a mess after their confrontation, knowing that Eleanor would be the first one downstairs to clean it up. Well, she thought as she straightened the chairs, that was fine. When Lizzie saw Eleanor as a lady, she'd think twice about being so spiteful.

Eleanor put the gin bottle in the pile for Mrs Banbury; a boy would come round to collect them later for a penny or two. She set the coal scuttle back in its place and swept the soil and dust into a neat pile, obliterating the marks in the dirt with a broom. She swept the little pile into a dustpan, went out the back door and climbed the steps up to the garden, tipped the dust outside – and saw Lizzie, lying face down in the water trough.

It wasn't the first dead body Eleanor had seen.

There'd always been a few. Mrs Pembroke, of course, lying

in state like a queen. The occasional beggar frozen in the doorway of a shop, or bleeding quietly in the gutter. Her mother. When consumption had finally taken her, Alice Hartley had been the same colour as her bedsheets, despite everything Eleanor had tried. The life had been draining out of her for months, and by the end she wasn't much more than a husk that rattled as it breathed.

Lizzie hadn't looked like a husk. She'd looked worse than that. Blotchy, swollen, and—

Eleanor dug her fingernails into her arms as bile rose at the back of her throat. She wasn't going to think about that.

She'd been put in the drawing room, next to a cooling mug of hot brandy. There were policemen everywhere. Not the gangly constables who stammered if she asked the time. These policemen were quiet, hard-eyed men with hands the size of dinner plates.

The voices of the crowd bounced off the walls and buzzed around her ears. People had pressed up against the garden wall all day, hoping to get a look at the body. Even though Eleanor was on the first floor she kept expecting to see them pressed up against the drawing-room windows, trying to catch a glimpse of her, too.

The door opened. Eleanor flinched.

'Ella?' said Mrs Fielding. 'Ella, dear, the Inspector wants to talk to you.'

He was the tallest man she had ever seen. Even with his hat underneath one arm he had to duck to get through the door. His dark clothes made him look like an undertaker. His black eyes were sunken, and as she got up to greet him Eleanor thought of the black-eyed woman.

'Detective Inspector George Hatchett,' he said. 'I understand you found the body.'

Eleanor nodded.

He gave her an appraising look. 'Sit down, please. You've had quite a shock, I imagine.'

Eleanor sank back into her chair. The Inspector riffled through his notebook. He made a few notes, slowly and carefully, and Eleanor wondered what on Earth he could be writing. She hadn't even said anything.

'Well,' he said, 'let's start at the beginning. You are a housemaid here, is that correct?'

She nodded.

'And you are also Mr Pembroke's ward?'

She nodded again.

'And how long have you been living here?'

'Just over seven years.' Her voice was a cracked and whispery thing. 'Working for three.'

He raised his eyebrows. 'Is that so?'

She nodded again. He made a clucking noise with his tongue. It was so out of place that she wanted to laugh – as if a raven had started squawking like a hen – but if she started, she wasn't sure if she would cry, be sick, or keep laughing and laughing until she sank to her knees, shaking.

It was all her fault, Eleanor thought. She hadn't realized Lizzie had been so upset after they argued. Eleanor had been so angry, so scared, that she hadn't spared a thought for Lizzie. To think she'd said all those awful things right after Lizzie's sweetheart had thrown her over.

'Tell me what happened earlier this morning. In your own words.'

Lizzie could have been perched on the arm of the Inspector's chair, leaning against the window pane, or sliding her hands around Eleanor's throat. Every shadow was as dark as her hair. Every distant creak was her footstep. Whenever the air was stirred, and the tang of polish coiled through the room, it was because Lizzie had closed the door behind her. She half-expected Lizzie to appear behind the Inspector's chair and point a discoloured, accusing finger right between Eleanor's eyes.

Eleanor's dress was still damp. She couldn't say if it was from Lizzie's last act of spite or the moment when she'd found her. Either way, it felt like Lizzie's blood splashed across Eleanor's skin.

'Miss Hartley?'

What could she say? What would he *want* her to say? Would she have to account for everything she'd done, at every minute since she'd woken? Eleanor didn't think she could. When had she come downstairs? Five? She couldn't remember hearing the clock. No, it must have been earlier than that. Or later. Perhaps it wasn't five o'clock at all...

'Miss Hartley?'

'Her lips were blue,' she blurted.

The Inspector blinked at her. 'I beg your pardon?'

'We tried to pull her out of the water before you came. Mrs...Mrs Fielding said she might not have been there long. But when we turned her over her lips were blue. Is that normal?'

'It's not uncommon.'

Eleanor put her head in her hands. 'She shouldn't have done it. I knew she was dead the moment I saw her. I never wanted them to turn her over.'

'You knew? How?'

Certainty had slammed into her the minute she saw the shape in the garden. Lizzie's hands had been snarled up like

86

withered roots, half-hidden in deep gouges in the soil. She'd known as soon as she saw those frozen fingers.

The Inspector sighed. 'Have you drunk that brandy, Miss Hartley?'

Eleanor shook her head.

'I must insist that you do. When you've finished, I want you to try to remember exactly what happened when you found Miss Bartram. Anything you can tell us will be of help.'

Eleanor looked up. 'Why? She...she drowned herself, didn't she?'

'Why do you say that?'

'Well, she must have done. She argued with her sweetheart the other day. He'd...he'd taken a shine to me, you see.' Eleanor looked down at her hands. She took a gulp of brandy, enjoying the burn it gave as she swallowed. 'I did nothing to encourage him,' she added quickly, as the Inspector scribbled furiously, 'but he grabbed at me and Lizzie saw, and she was very upset. When I saw her, lying there...'

She stopped. The Inspector leant forward.

'I'm afraid that would not have been possible,' he said, gently. 'We suspect murder.'

The mug slipped through her fingers.

Murder.

He kept her in there for over an hour. By the time the interview was over his notebook was full, even though she hadn't told him everything. Then he'd helped her to her feet and told her to get something to eat, as if she were a child hankering for a biscuit.

Eleanor made it halfway down the corridor before she threw up in a plant pot.

She couldn't face eating. The thought of food when Lizzie's bloated face kept flashing through her mind was obscene. Besides, the kitchen was full of policemen, and she was sure they'd all be watching the flash of the knife as she sliced the bread, listening to the splash as she washed her hands. No. She couldn't do it.

The drawing-room door opened. Eleanor whirled around, but it was only the Inspector.

'Ah, Miss Hartley. Could you tell me where Mr Pembroke is? I need to speak with him.'

Eleanor started. 'You don't think *he* could've—'

The Inspector held up a hand. 'I understand Mr Pembroke was the last person to see Miss Bartram alive. An interview is all I need.'

'He left,' said Eleanor, licking her lips. 'He heard the noise, and when he found out what had happened he went out before you arrived.'

'Out? Do you know where?'

Eleanor shook her head. The Inspector was watching her very closely. Eleanor hadn't told him about confronting Lizzie in the kitchen, or about Lizzie's threats to throw Eleanor to Mr Pembroke. His notebook was full enough already. He hadn't just scribbled down everything she'd said. When she'd struggled to speak past the lump in her throat, he'd made notes then, his calculating eyes on her hands, her dress, her red eyes.

The Inspector lowered his voice. 'You seem nervous, Miss Hartley. Let me reassure you that everything you have told me will be kept in the strictest confidence, unless the case should come to trial.'

Eleanor's eyes flickered up and down the corridor. Mrs

Fielding was standing in the doorway to the servants' staircase, her face pale.

'Now, I must ask if there is any reason why you assumed your employer might have harmed Miss Bartram?'

It was too good an opportunity to miss, but Mrs Fielding was still standing in the doorway. If she overheard, Eleanor would be dismissed with no money and nowhere to go. Eleanor glanced towards her, and made sure the Inspector saw.

'Find the other girls,' she whispered, just loud enough for him to hear.

It was well into the afternoon before the policemen left. They paced across the kitchen in long strides, measuring the distance between the tradesmen's entrance and the corner where the kitchen coal scuttle was usually kept. They stood at the bottom of the servants' staircase and opened and shut the baize doors, shouting up the stairs to see how much sound they kept out. They searched Lizzie's room, and crowded around the water trough.

Eleanor kept well out of their way. She, Aoife and Daisy waited in the drawing room in case they were needed. Aoife couldn't stop crying, and Daisy went ashen every time she caught sight of the coal scuttle propped up against the fireplace. Eleanor couldn't look at it. When they'd turned Lizzie over, there'd been a mark on her forehead from where someone had struck her with the coal scuttle in the kitchen. Then, she must have staggered into the garden, where her attacker had drowned her.

Aoife sniffed. 'I wish they'd all go away,' she said, wiping her eyes. 'They must've found everything by now.'

'Did they say what they were looking for?' Eleanor asked.

Daisy snorted. 'They won't tell *us*. Not until they know we didn't do it, anyway.'

Aoife whimpered. 'Don't be ridiculous,' Eleanor snapped, shifting in her seat, 'they don't suspect us!'

A policeman called up the servants' staircase and all three of them jumped.

'You were in with that Inspector a long time,' Daisy muttered, her brown eyes fixed on Eleanor. 'What did he want?'

Eleanor threw up her hands. 'Of course I was in there a long time! I found her! And...it wasn't easy, you know. I was upset.'

'I'm sure you were,' said Daisy, her voice careful.

Something in her tone made Eleanor stiffen. It was as if Daisy had smoothed all the sharp edges off her words and placed them gently into the conversation. The silence in the room seemed thicker now that she had spoken.

'I *was*,' Eleanor insisted.

Eleanor was sitting between Daisy and the door. She saw Daisy's eyes flicker towards the doorknob, just once. In that same measured voice she said, 'I wasn't suggesting anything else,' and did not speak again.

By night the crowds had gone. Most of them went with the policemen when they took the body away. Some boys had spent the evening daring each other to scale the wall and stick their hand in the water trough, but that had ended when a tearful Mrs Banbury had taken a swipe at them with a carpet beater.

Eleanor had tried to take her mind off everything. When the Inspector left she'd gone back up to her airless room to finish the last of her mending. No one had stopped her. But when she'd opened the door to her own room and seen all the rips Lizzie had left in her clothes she'd stared and stared, gripping the bedpost as her chest grew tighter and tighter.

She couldn't stay here. Whoever killed Lizzie could be back at any minute. She had to get out.

Eleanor threw her mended dresses into her case and wedged it in front of the door. No one could sneak in now. Still, she had to be ready. She kicked her torn things under the bed – she couldn't bear to look at them any more – and cracked the window open to listen. Hansoms in the streets, newspaper boys calling out the evening editions, a man ranting about iniquity and sinners. Nothing from the garden. But then, they hadn't heard anything last night, had they? Someone had hit Lizzie over the head and drowned her, right outside their door, and they hadn't heard a thing. With all the baize doors closed, someone could be creeping up the stairs right now and Eleanor would never know until her bedroom door creaked open.

Eleanor hauled her bed in front of the door, the legs screeching across the floorboards. She wasn't going to let whoever killed Lizzie get her too. It must have been the butcher's boy, Eleanor thought. He and Lizzie had argued, and now she was dead. That couldn't be a coincidence.

But perhaps that wasn't the only coincidence.

Eleanor had made a wish last night. She had wished for Lizzie to stop and now Lizzie was dead. Could the black-eyed woman have…

Eleanor shoved the thought away at once. Of course she hadn't caused Lizzie's death by wishing. The wishes weren't *like* that. They were gifts, like in fairy stories, and they would make her dreams come true. They wouldn't kill people.

'Of course they couldn't,' said Eleanor, 'of course not.'
She was not sure if she was expecting a reply.

Eleanor gave up on sleep and went downstairs at four in the morning. It was still dark outside. It wasn't a problem until after she'd lit the range, when she had to go out to the water pump. Then, the night seemed to billow and swell around her, seeping underneath the doors like smoke.

Eleanor drew out a kitchen knife from the block. The handle slipped in her sweaty fingers, so she dug out a rag and wrapped it around the palm of her hand. She was *not* going to drop it, not when Lizzie's murderer could be right outside.

Bucket in one hand, knife in the other, Eleanor eased the back door open with the toe of her boot and clambered up the steps to the garden.

Snakes of mist coiled around her legs. Clammy air oozed across the back of her neck, a strangling hand. The long, low shape of the water trough was a deeper patch of darkness, the rim of a pit that waited for her. The arm of the pump glistened: an iron scaffold.

Eleanor put a lit candle on the step and whispered a prayer. She tightened her grip on the knife and stepped out.

The creak of the bucket's handle made her think of garrotte wire. Daisy said her cousin had been garrotted in the West Indies. Daisy said she still had the scar, running right across her neck. Daisy said that all the warning her cousin had got was the singing sound the wire had made, as the garrotter wound it tighter around his hands...

A rat flitted across her path. Eleanor yelped and almost dropped the knife.

She was nearly at the water trough. The long, thin shape,

slightly raised from the ground, looked exactly like a coffin. Oh, dear God, she was going to have to clean it out today. The water glistened like oil in the darkness, a foul sweetness rising from the surface, and Eleanor's stomach roiled.

She turned in a wide circle before she set down the bucket. The garden was empty – at least, she thought it was. The candle she'd put on the top step sent a thin beam of light spilling onto the grass, but as she turned back Eleanor realized that this had been a mistake. The light blinded her to what was really in the darkness.

She rammed the knife into her apron. She hauled on the arm of the pump, her hands slipping off the handle. She grabbed it again, yanked it downwards, and sloshed water into the bucket so fast that her arms went numb. The second she was done she tugged the knife back out and stared around the garden, heart pounding.

Nothing.

She picked up the bucket and lurched back to the kitchen. Almost there. She'd be safe inside soon. She'd close the door behind her, lock it tight, and wouldn't even have to look at that awful pump for the rest of the day. She could feel it over her shoulder. A sickly, cold smell drifted out of the water, marking the place where Lizzie had died. Her eyes flickered down to the bucket, and she wondered how long a body could live without drinking.

Finally, she reached the steps down to the kitchen. She set the bucket down, fumbling for a candle.

'Ella?'

Eleanor shrieked and dropped the knife. It clattered down the stairs. Someone else yelled too, and a match flared in the dark.

Eleanor snatched up her candle. Daisy and Aoife clutched each other at the bottom of the stairs, terrified, a carving knife wavering in Daisy's hand. They broke apart when they saw it was only Eleanor.

'I'm sorry,' she whispered. 'You startled me.'

Aoife shook out the match and slumped against Daisy's shoulder. In the sudden darkness, she began to cry.

'I'm sorry,' Eleanor said again, 'I was...I'm sorry.'

Mrs Fielding stood at the head of the kitchen table, her eyes ringed in shadow. The tip of her scar stood out white against her neck, just visible underneath the high collar of her dress. Eleanor couldn't stop staring at it. Surely Lizzie had been lying, to say that Eleanor had given her that scar.

'This will be a difficult time,' Mrs Fielding was saying. 'Lizzie will be very much missed. I need not say that the manner in which she died will affect us for many years to come. But I would like to reassure you all that you will be safe here. I will be asking Mr Pembroke for permission to change the locks. I've known him since he was a boy and he has your best interests at heart. He won't let any harm come to you.'

Eleanor kept her face neutral.

'We will have to make up the shortfall now that...now that Lizzie is no longer with us,' Mrs Fielding continued, blinking very fast. 'But I have reason to believe that this will not be for long. Master Charles will be arriving from Paris soon, and shortly after his return we will be able to engage more staff. Until then, I hope I may depend upon your usual patience and hard work to see us through this difficult time.'

She waited. Aoife clapped, but stopped when she saw no one was joining in.

They were dismissed. Eleanor and Aoife were sent up to the third floor to clean the bedrooms. Aoife went to change Mr Pembroke's sheets – thankfully, he was in the study on the floor below, and had not heard them coming – and Eleanor went into Mrs Pembroke's old room.

It was exactly as it had been on the day she died. It always shocked Eleanor to see it like this, when her own bedroom on the family floor had been disassembled so quickly. Mrs Pembroke's brushes were still on the dressing table. Her night-gown was still folded on the pillow. There was a candle by the bed, and a trace of smoke still lingered in the air. There was a pocket sewn into the padded headboard for a book of matches. One of them was missing.

Eleanor made sure to hide the evidence of her own secret trips into Mrs Pembroke's room. Drawers were pushed in at exactly the right angle, brushes were realigned on the dressing table. But she was not allowed to be there unless she was cleaning; Mr Pembroke was. He did not need to be careful.

Eleanor crept over to the dressing table. She'd sat here as a child and let Mrs Pembroke brush her hair. The mirror was still covered; the black gauze had been draped over the glass after Mrs Pembroke's funeral and it hadn't been touched since. She couldn't look at the bed. Three years ago, she'd seen the shape of Mrs Pembroke's body beneath the white sheets. Even now, the sight of them made her shudder.

She picked up one of the brushes instead; a few strands of red-gold hair were still trapped in the bristles. There was a letter beside it, dated a few days ago, which began 'My darling Emmeline'. Cushions on one of the chairs had been flattened. The spot was directly opposite a painting of three small girls

95

hanging over the dark fireplace. The oldest of them could not have been more than three or four years old, the youngest barely a few weeks. All three had an oddly waxy, stiff look about them. They were the Pembrokes' three daughters, and all of them had died before Eleanor came to Granborough. Mrs Pembroke had told her their names when Eleanor had first arrived – Beatrice, Eugenia and Diana – and explained that though they were gone, she still loved them, like Eleanor loved her mother.

The memory was so clear. Mrs Pembroke had leant down, taken both of Eleanor's hands in hers – the sleeves of her black crepe dress had crinkled when Mrs Pembroke had touched them – and said, 'I nursed them, just as you nursed your poor mother. You need not feel so alone,' and that was when Eleanor had cried, after months of staring into nothing.

Now, Eleanor felt strangely untethered. Here, Mr Pembroke wrote letters to his long-dead wife, and stared at the picture of his long-dead children. If he cried, she could not picture it.

She could not bear to think of him in this room. How a monster like him had married Mrs Pembroke, the best woman Eleanor had ever known, she would never understand. Eleanor turned the letter over so she wouldn't have to look at it, slapped the cushions back into shape and shoved the window open to let out the smell of smoke. She'd make it as if Mr Pembroke had never been here.

But that would be easy, she thought, with a readiness that frightened her. All she would have to do was make a wish and he'd end up like Lizzie...

Eleanor's hand slipped on the window latch and she yelped. She sliced open one of the three scratches on the side of her hand that had only just scabbed over. She bundled it up in her apron, trying not to think of Lizzie. Of course the wish hadn't done that, of course it hadn't...

There was a knock at the door and Aoife came in. 'I heard a noise. Are you well?'

'It's just a scratch. I caught it on something. Are you—'

Aoife burst into tears.

'Oh, Aoife,' Eleanor said, rushing over to her. 'What is it?'

'It's the cage,' Aoife sobbed. 'I kept looking at it all empty and then I thought of Lizzie and I just...I just...' Aoife buried her face in her hands. Eleanor rubbed her back and shushed her like a baby. 'I want my mam,' Aoife wailed.

Eleanor remembered the way Mrs Pembroke had stroked her hair after a nightmare and held her hand. Mrs Pembroke would have known just what to say, but all Eleanor had was silence and a lump in her throat.

'Are you going to tell her what happened?' she asked gently.

'I can't!' Aoife sobbed. 'She'd go mad for fretting! And with Micheál so poorly and all...she'd make me come back, Ella, and how'd we pay for the doctor then?'

'You could always look for another place.'

'Daisy tried last spring. She said Mrs Fielding wouldn't do her a reference unless the master said so and the lady wouldn't take her on without a character. How'd I get another place without that?'

Eleanor passed a shaking hand over her face. Another way out closed off.

'I didn't even *like* Lizzie!' Aoife wailed. 'She was a – but I can't even say it, now, because you're not to speak ill of the dead!'

Eleanor bit her lip. Lizzie's last taunts still rang in her head. Her grin had flickered in the candlelight as she'd spoken those words. Knowing what she'd done, what she was going to do, Eleanor was not sorry that Lizzie was dead.

But would she be sorry if she had killed her?

Eleanor pushed the thought away at once. Of course she hadn't killed Lizzie with a wish. It was stupid to think so. Besides, if that was what had happened then surely she would have known. The shoes had appeared overnight, as if by magic. If Lizzie had been killed by magic, then there should've been something magical about her death, and even the police thought it ordinary. Lizzie would have dropped dead the moment Eleanor spoke the words aloud, or vanished in a puff of smoke. That was how magic worked in stories.

Eleanor put an arm around Aoife and pulled her head against her shoulder. She stared into the covered mirror and saw her and Aoife's reflections, hazy behind black gauze – and, for a moment, a shape that might have been something else entirely. But then Eleanor blinked, and it was gone.

A feather of dirty cloud was spreading across the sky, swelling and billowing as it gained momentum. The heat off the cobblestones was pressed back down as the cloud rose, making horses irritable and giving Eleanor a dull, whining headache.

Eleanor waded through the crowds scurrying for cover, weighed down with a heavy leg of mutton in her basket and tugging her skirts away from horses' hooves. She ducked to avoid flapping canvas as a costermonger put up a shade.

Granborough House loomed ahead of her, already visible where Marylebone faded into Mayfair. The heavy clouds gathered directly above it, as though they had poured straight out of the chimneys like ink spilling from a bottle. The attic windows looked like eyes full of tears.

Eleanor considered not going back. She could sell the contents of her basket to whoever would take them, take the money and disappear into the crowd. What did she have in Granborough House that she cared for? Only memories – and Aoife, of course. With Leah gone and Daisy confined to the kitchen, Mr Pembroke would move on to Aoife, if Eleanor left. She couldn't let that happen.

Besides, she thought, as she bypassed a crossing-sweeper with a weeping sore leering at her, if she did leave, where would she go? If there was a safe place for young girls in London, she did not know where it was. There were all sorts of stories. Respectable country girls would find an advertisement for a clean, well-kept and entirely proper boarding house only to walk into a bordello, and they would not be allowed to leave. Finding a safe place to live would not be a matter of knocking on a clean and shiny door and asking nicely. And even if she did find somewhere to lay her head, who would let her in with no references to vouch for her character and no money to pay the rent?

Rain spattered against Eleanor's cheek, made grey by the soot and smoke of many chimneys. Soon, the rain was pelting against the cobblestones, rattling like pennies on the rooftops, and the street was engulfed in a mess of noise as the crowds fled from the downpour. A costermonger selling strawberry ices threw himself over his machine, shielding his wares with his stomach. Flower-sellers shrieked and ran for cover, holding their trays over their heads. A piper shoved his instrument inside his jacket and ran to a nearby church, splashing the legs of a wedding party crowded under the lychgate. The only thing that seemed to be happy was a brown butcher's dog, rolling around in the rain.

Of course, now Eleanor could rely on the wishes.

But should she? She'd lose her soul if she made them all. And besides, there was so much about the arrangement that did not seem right. The black-eyed woman's smile had been perfectly serene, her voice oddly familiar, but those eyes... Eleanor shuddered.

And now, Lizzie was dead. Eleanor had made a wish and Lizzie had died.

But surely, Eleanor told herself, that had to be coincidence. Her first wish had been so lovely – those beautiful shoes appearing just before the sunrise, like a gift from a fairy tale. Her second wish – *if* that had been how it had really come true – hadn't felt like that at all. Perhaps the black-eyed woman had had something else planned, but Lizzie had been killed before she could carry it out.

Eleanor felt herself wilting. It sounded like an excuse, even in her own head.

She headed back to Granborough House, water dripping into her collar despite her hat. The street was the colour of churned-up mud and old bird droppings. The rain bounced up from in between the cobblestones, each drop as filthy as a much-handled coin. There was so much muddy water in the street that the crossing-sweepers looked like they were trying to brush aside a river. Eleanor hurried along the pavement and pulled her shawl over her head. A hansom splashed past and she darted away from it, knocking into an old woman waiting by a hot-potato cart. The woman swore at her, but Eleanor was already gone. A street-seller called to her, holding out a cup of coffee. A damp beggar held out his hand to Eleanor, his one eye pleading. A man with a tray of 'Heathful Tonics' around his neck tried to grab her arm. There was a miserable organ grinder in the square, a shivering monkey curled up in the collar of his jacket. With every turn of the barrel organ, a fresh wail arched over the street.

An elbow caught Eleanor in the ribs. A hand brushed against her hips, and she could not tell if it was feeling for her or her purse. An umbrella sliced through the gloom, and she ducked to avoid it scratching across her eye. She huddled into her shawl and kept walking, a sick, twisting fear slowly filling her up.

Eleanor forced herself to follow through with her plan. Lizzie's death had not changed anything. She needed the money Lizzie had stolen from her. Surely Lizzie could not have spent twenty-five pounds in one go – that was almost three years' wages. She must have been lying. And if she hadn't been, Eleanor would take what Lizzie had bought and sell it on.

Of course, Eleanor thought as she climbed up the narrow servants' staircase, she could always wish for her money back. But the words 'I wish you'd just stop' kept circling around her head, dragging her thoughts back to Lizzie's pale and bloated face, and the black-eyed woman's empty eye sockets loomed in Eleanor's memory, vast and unknowable, and—

Eleanor shoved the thought away. It hadn't been like that. Of course it hadn't.

She eased the door to Lizzie's room open with the toe of her boot.

Drawers were hanging open, the sheets had been cast aside, the straw mattress had been slit open and rummaged through. Whatever the policemen had been looking for, they'd made a mess searching for it. Eleanor went inside and started looking in the chest of drawers. She reached for the first pile of stockings and drew her hand back, imagining Lizzie's work-roughened fingers carefully folding and putting her things away. Sweat trickling down her neck, she turned over Lizzie's stockings and chemises, listening for footsteps on the stairs and trying not to feel sick.

At last, she found something. Her fingers met something hard and Eleanor lunged for it. She drew out a leather purse and tore it open, heart pounding. It was empty. Eleanor's twenty-five pounds was long gone.

She turned to leave, and something caught her eye. It was a jug and basin made of patterned white porcelain, far too fine for the plain, sensible room of the head housemaid. Lizzie had been a senior servant, and had been entitled to a larger portion of tea in the mornings and the first helping of every meal, after the cook and housekeeper had served themselves. She had not been entitled to this.

Eleanor crept closer. The jug had been put under Lizzie's bed. She bent down, pulled it out, and felt a slap of recognition.

This had been hers. This had been the jug and basin set that Eleanor had used for years, which Mrs Pembroke had chosen for her specially. She'd thought it had been sold off, but all this time, Lizzie had been hiding it.

A wave of anger crashed over her. Eleanor snatched up the jug and basin and took them into her own room, her hands shaking. There was nothing that Lizzie wouldn't have taken from her. Well, now Eleanor was going to take it back, and there was nothing that Lizzie could do about it, because at long last she had stopped—

Eleanor almost dropped the jug. Her anger vanished, and a cold fear crept through her.

She had to know.

The rain had leaked through the roof at Granborough House, soaking into the maids' attic rooms. Aoife and Daisy were sprinting upstairs with all the buckets they could find, and back down again to pile up their things in the middle of the kitchen floor.

Eleanor ignored them. She retreated into her own room, where there was a large damp patch on the ceiling, but nothing had actually leaked through. She closed the door behind her and sank onto the bed. Lizzie had died after she made the second wish. And, though it had been terrible, she had got what she had asked for. Lizzie's death had stopped her torments.

Eleanor gripped the edges of her bed.

She didn't understand. Wishes were supposed to be *nice* things. They were granted by smiling fairy godmothers and left everyone living happily ever after. They couldn't leave her like this – lost in horror and disgust that was deep enough to drown in.

She remembered the woman's black eyes. Pits. Coal shafts. Empty.

Eleanor cleared her throat. The black-eyed woman had said she would be with her always. If Eleanor called her, would she come?

'We must talk. It's important.'

'What seems to be the problem, dear?'

Eleanor had been staring right at the place where she'd appeared. She'd seen nothing. One moment there was the dark shape of the dresser. Then she'd blinked, and the black-eyed woman was there, perching on the end of Eleanor's bed as if she'd come to read her a story.

'When I wished for Lizzie to stop tormenting me, she died.'

The black-eyed woman's face was perfectly still.

'Did you do that?'

The sound of the rain vanished. It still spattered against her window, but it was silent.

'Did you think your wishes would be granted with no cost?' the black-eyed woman asked, her voice silky. 'Eleanor, darling, wishes are made every day but they are seldom granted. It takes a good deal of magic to grant a wish, and magic has its price. All things do.'

Eleanor couldn't understand. The black-eyed woman had been sent to help her, hadn't she? She was supposed to smile, and be kind, and tend Eleanor's glorious future with a gentle hand. Instead, she had watered Eleanor's hopes with blood, and now they had grown into twisted, monstrous things. How could she have done something like this?

'But…but that doesn't make sense,' Eleanor insisted. 'Nobody died to grant my first wish! You must be mistaken.'

'Perhaps not a *person*, but there was a death. Even a little canary's life is enough. I cannot make magic from nothing. Think of it as lighting a fire; there must be a spark to set the blaze.'

'I do not want people to *die*!'

'Then, my dear, you must not make any more wishes.'

The black-eyed woman looked like someone's mother, or the gentler kind of schoolmistress. After Mrs Pembroke's death Eleanor had imagined countless women like her who might take her in. Distant relatives in country cottages, or honest church-goers ready to usher her in from the cold. But the black-eyed

104

woman knew that, Eleanor realized. How many nights had Eleanor lulled herself to sleep imagining a woman with her neat brown bun, her pretty flowered dress, her gentle motherly arms? And here she sat, so exactly like her daydreams that she could have sprung, Athena-like, from Eleanor's own head. Even her voice was familiar – something like her mother's, or Mrs Pembroke's. Only the eyes were different. Flat, black, cold. They were the eyes of what the black-eyed woman truly was – the thing that wanted her soul. She'd squeezed herself into the shape Eleanor's imagination had given her, with only her eyes to give her away.

Eleanor wondered what she really looked like, and pushed the thought away at once.

The black-eyed woman had killed the canary. The black-eyed woman had killed Lizzie. Her plump fingers had stretched out like eagles' talons, and hacked and slashed Eleanor's wishes into being.

'I think you should leave,' Eleanor whispered.

The black-eyed woman vanished. Eleanor hadn't felt the mattress move, nor had she felt it when the black-eyed woman sat on the foot of her bed. It was as if she'd never been there.

Eleanor had never wanted anything to be true so badly.

Eleanor did not sleep. She stared at the wall, tears pouring down her face. Lizzie was dead because of her, and that sweet little canary.

If Eleanor hadn't made any wishes, they would still be alive. How had she ever thought that anything good could come of selling her soul? How had she ever imagined that a being called by blood would ever bring any joy? She had blindly taken the black-eyed woman's deal like a child running into the woods, and now the path was lost and she was surrounded by things moving through the trees.

The butcher's boy had killed Lizzie and the canary might have – how *had* the little bird died? She couldn't remember – but the woman had set them on those paths, paths that Eleanor had laid the moment she spoke her wishes aloud. It was all Eleanor's fault.

Hers, and the black-eyed woman's.

The black-eyed woman had appeared like a glimpse of a great creature below the surface of the water. What had been a flat, empty expanse of darkness shifted and became a vast, shining flank, or a glittering tapestry of scales. Even the woman's eyes were black and still, like an immense dark lake. In making a wish carelessly, Eleanor had been trailing her fingers over the water, waiting for something to lunge towards her hand.

How could she have been so thoughtless?

If only she'd been better, Eleanor thought, clutching her head. If she'd been wiser, more careful, the kind of girl Mrs Pembroke would have wanted her to be. Mrs Pembroke would never have made such a careless mistake. She would've taken one look at the black-eyed woman and seen her for what she truly was. If Eleanor had been better, kinder, cleverer, she would not have made the deal. Mr Pembroke would not have attacked Leah. Eleanor, at the age of nine, would not have sat at the foot of the old iron bed with her hands over her ears while her mother…

Eleanor shook her head. She had to find a way out of the deal. The black-eyed woman had never mentioned anything like this. She'd lied to her. She'd never asked for power like this. There had to be a way out of the deal.

And until she found one, she would not make any more wishes.

Eleanor crept down the servants' staircase. It was gone midnight – she'd heard the chimes and flinched, as she always did – and the house was quiet. The smell of rain oozed under the gap of the door to the second-floor corridor, and over the sounds of it falling Eleanor could hear something scrabbling behind the cheaply plastered wall.

She was going to the library. There had to be something in there to help her find a way out of the deal. She couldn't sit and lament over the state of her soul; she had to take it back. It was hers, and it would not be taken from her.

She did not see the light coming through the gap under the door until it was already opening. Her heart stuttered, she shrank back, but it was too late.

Mr Pembroke was standing on the second-floor landing, a candle clutched in his hand. He was swaying on the spot, his waistcoat half-undone, a brown stain on his rumpled white shirt. But his eyes were fixed on her, and a slow, horrible smile was spreading across his face.

'Ella,' he slurred, 'what are you doing out of bed?'

Eleanor gripped the banister, just to have something to hold on to. She was in her nightdress, her hair in a sloppy plait, her feet were bare. Mr Pembroke was staring at them, his eyes bloodshot.

'I thought I heard a noise,' she said. 'I'm sorry, sir, I see that must have been you. If you'll excuse me, I—'

'No. I need to talk to you. In the study.'

Eleanor reached for the doorknob. He was clearly drunk. Maybe if she shut the door he'd forget she'd ever been there, and she could creep back to bed as if nothing had happened...

Mr Pembroke pointed a finger down the corridor. 'If you don't come into the study, you're dismissed. I'll throw you out in the clothes you stand up in.'

Eleanor stared into his dark, wet eyes, the colour an oily, glistening brown, and knew that he would do it. He would not care that he was her legal guardian, or that she had no money and no shoes on her feet. He would wash his hands of her as he had done with so many other girls before Eleanor, and move on to Aoife afterwards. She could stop him with a wish, of course – but could she really speak those words standing in front of him, and watch the light fade from his eyes?

She followed him into the corridor.

Mr Pembroke staggered into the study. Eleanor followed him inside, leaving the door open. All the portraits on the wall stared as Mr Pembroke lurched into his chair, catching his hip on the wide mahogany desk and swearing.

Eleanor's mind was racing. Without being asked, she went to the sideboard and poured him a glass of brandy from one of the decanters she'd added to earlier. She placed the glass on the green leather desk top and Mr Pembroke tossed it back in three gulps.

'Good girl,' he slurred. 'Another.'

Eleanor poured a larger glass. Mr Pembroke had to make two attempts to pick it up.

'Now,' he said, his words bleeding together, 'what's all this about a policeman?'

Eleanor stared straight ahead. 'We were all interviewed, sir.'

Mr Pembroke drained half his glass of brandy and waggled

a shaky finger at her. 'You're being deliberately unhelpful, Ella. I thought you were a good girl.'

Eleanor topped up his glass. The pupils of his eyes were tiny. She felt a flush of hope: the drug was working.

'I've heard some worrying things,' Mr Pembroke slurred, brandy slopping over the side of his glass, 'about you and young Lizzie. I'd like you to set my mind at rest. I'll have to dismiss you, you know, unless you give me a reason to let you stay.'

Even behind the desk, he was far too close. She could see every bead of sweat on his forehead. He'd loosened his collar, and there was a red mark on his flabby neck from where it had been fastened too tight. Mr Pembroke's dark, wet eyes glistened like rotting fruit. She wondered how deep the rot went.

'You know better than to listen to gossip, sir,' she said, keeping her voice light. 'Why don't you take another drink and put it out of your mind. I'm sure that—'

Mr Pembroke's hand shot out, lunging for her wrist. He missed, his cigar-stained fingers bumping into the decanter instead. Eleanor caught the bottle before it fell and poured him another glass.

'Ungrateful girl,' he muttered. 'I've fed you, clothed you and given you a respectable position for years. And now I look to your character, to know you better, and you won't oblige me! Where's your loyalty? Is an ounce of gratitude too much to—'

Anger burned through Eleanor's fear. The rot went all the way down.

Mr Pembroke picked up the glass and began to drink. Quick as a snake, Eleanor darted forward and tipped the glass up, forcing the brandy down his throat. He spluttered, the tiny pupils of his eyes struggling to focus on her as she settled back into position. The smell of urine drifted towards her and she wrinkled her nose. She'd have to clean that up tomorrow.

'What the Devil did you—'

Eleanor blinked at him. 'Me, sir? I didn't do anything.'

'You damn well spilled my—'

Eleanor started filling up his glass again. 'I assure you, sir, I haven't moved from this spot. I would never dream of doing so, without your permission. Do take another drink.'

Mr Pembroke stared at her, his head swaying slightly. 'But... but you just...'

Eleanor pushed the glass into his unresisting hand. 'You haven't finished your drink, sir.'

He rubbed his eyes, forgetting about the glass in his hand. It slipped and smashed, slopping brandy all over his shirt. Eleanor let it fall and fetched another glass, pouring out yet another drink. She forced it into Mr Pembroke's hand and lifted it to his mouth.

'I should hate to think that I have displeased you, sir,' she said. 'I'm sure I should never look myself in the eye again. But, *sir*, I would like to remind you that I am not like the other servants at Granborough House. I am your ward. You are my guardian in the eyes of the law and you cannot dismiss me so easily.'

Mr Pembroke's eyes were glassy. His tiny pupils flickered to her face, to the glass, to a point behind Eleanor's shoulder. Still he drank, as greedily as a baby. The stink of urine, old brandy and sweat rolled off him in waves. How much of this he would remember, Eleanor could not say. But a strange kind of power seemed to have settled on her. She was still afraid

110

of him, but now she wondered why she had ever listened to him.

She took the glass away and stepped back, just in case, but Mr Pembroke's head slumped forward as she moved, his eyes unfocused. He mumbled something, and Eleanor started putting the decanter away.

'I think perhaps you are a little the worse for drink, sir,' Eleanor said, shutting the decanter back in the cupboard, 'and you've let some silly ideas go to your head. I'm sure that now, you understand that there's no need to pay them any attention. But of course, you knew that you were never in any danger from me. If you did not, why, you would not have let me pour you all those drinks.'

Mr Pembroke's eyes slid in and out of focus. His hand twitched. He tried to speak. 'You—'

Eleanor gave him a perfectly polite smile, triumph burning under her skin. She didn't *need* the wishes. She might not be able to write her name in stars without them, but she could keep herself safe.

'Goodnight, sir,' she said, heading for the door. 'I think you'll find that we won't need to have this conversation again.'

The next morning, Eleanor told the others she was going to clean the library. After breakfast she clattered up the stairs with bucket and dusters while Daisy and Aoife were still rolling up their straw pallets – they were sleeping on the kitchen floor, after their rooms had been damaged in the rain. No one heard the staccato beat of Eleanor's shaking fingers against the bucket as she climbed the stairs.

The moment she was through the library door, she dropped her cleaning supplies and slammed the door behind her. The key slipped out of her fingers twice before she could get the door locked. There had to be something in here to get her out of the deal.

Ignoring the bucket still rolling on its rim, she snatched up the copy of *Faustus* and flipped through the pages, so fast that they tore. Magic circles, spells, confessions written in the margins – there had to be *something*. But there was nothing except the demon on the frontispiece, hiding under layers of old ink. Who'd scribbled it out, all those years before?

She flipped to the end – nothing there except Faustus's downfall, and her stomach swooped to read it. Would all those creeping, crawling things come for her in the end too? *No*, she thought. She couldn't let herself think such nonsense; it would not serve her. She peered down the length of the spine, in case there was something hidden there – nothing. She held the book up by a corner of the cover and waggled it, in case anything fell out. A piece of paper drifted to the floor and she seized it.

MEPHISTOPHELES: *Why, this is Hell, nor am I out of it. Think'st thou that—*

Nothing. Nothing! Eleanor threw the book across the room, tears prickling in her eyes. It smacked into a bookcase and she regretted it at once. She checked it for damage, half-expecting to see the black-eyed woman glaring at her when she turned around.

There must be something else here that could help her.

Eleanor tore through the bookshelves. She rifled through the family Bible, scanning the passages about demons and witches. She snatched up copies of *Daemonologie*, the *Malleus Maleficarum*, a record of the witch trials in the sixteenth century. Was this what the woman had made her? Had all those witches who'd been burned and hanged been as desperate and hungry as she was?

Nothing, still nothing. Eleanor sank to the floor, her hands covered in paper cuts. Little smears of blood spotted every page she'd touched. *Oh God*, she thought. What if she'd summoned something else? How many other creatures were lurking between these pages?

Eleanor listened carefully. The rain beat against the window and trickled down the chimney. Beyond the glass broughams and hackneys rolled past, their iron wheels muffled by mud. Somewhere above her head, a floorboard creaked.

She cleared her throat. 'Hello? Are you there?'

The shadows shifted. A knot in the side of one of the wooden bookcases became a pitiless black eye and the woman emerged, smiling. It was the only human thing about her face. Without that smile her face might have been a mask, waiting to be lifted off.

Eleanor held out the copy of *Faustus*. 'I don't want it.'

'That book is not yours, dear.'

'That's not what I meant!' Eleanor snapped. 'I don't want to be a part of this deal any more. You didn't tell me what the wishes would do! I didn't ask for this!'

Eleanor could hear the whine in her own voice. The woman was looking at her with an unbearably patient smile on her face, her eyes two pits.

'But you did,' the black-eyed woman said. 'You sold me your soul in exchange for seven wishes. You knew the price you must pay, and yet you paid it.'

'You didn't tell me that people were going to die! If I'd known that—'

The black-eyed woman cut across her. 'I asked for your soul. Really, my dear, what did you expect?'

113

Eleanor's fingers were stained with black dye, from where her sweating hands had gripped the book's cover. 'I want it back,' she said, in a very small voice.

'But you have already made two wishes,' the black-eyed woman said. 'The contract might have been broken earlier, but now we are bound together by laws far bigger than you or I. Repent all you like, but how am I to return your soul in parts?'

The sky darkened, the rain beating ever harder against the glass. Beneath the black-eyed woman's feet, shadows sprawled and squirmed across the floor. Eleanor scampered out of their way, heart hammering.

'What do you suppose you would be, with only five-sevenths of your soul?' the black-eyed woman mused. 'Do you think you could still laugh, for example? Perhaps all the love you have would be desiccated, leaving your heart filled with dust. Perhaps all the beauty in the world would be flattened for you, and every time you heard a nightingale's song it would be as meaningless as the shriek of a factory bell. Perhaps you wouldn't feel anything at all. A question for the philosophers, I suppose.'

The black-eyed woman came closer and patted Eleanor's hand. Her eyes had no shine. When she stood in the light those empty eyes stole it, not even leaving a glimmer. With a jolt, Eleanor realized she was not sure if the woman *had* eyes at all, or if those dark pits were holes in her skull.

'There is no turning back, dear,' the black-eyed woman said. 'You sold your soul and received your wishes. The bargain has been struck. You have only to decide how to use it.'

PART THREE

The first week of September passed in a haze of rain. The damp patch on Eleanor's ceiling was spreading, reaching out like a malevolent hand. Every time she got into bed she stared at the ceiling and imagined the black-eyed woman staring out of the deeper patch of darkness. She buried her head under her pillow and screwed up her eyes, whispering prayers that turned into a litany of *please please please* over and over again.

Mrs Fielding noticed the dark circles under her eyes and assumed Eleanor was grieving for Lizzie. Her solution was to keep Eleanor busy, and with Charles's return drawing near there was more than enough work. Eleanor wiped down the windows with vinegar and water, swept the carpets with damp tea leaves, black-leaded every grate and shook the shape back into Charles's old mattress, punching the feather bed until her arms ached and her eyes began to water. The vinegar stung the cuts on her hands, she kept flicking the tea leaves onto her dress and the black-leading was still lodged under her fingernails, no matter how hard she scrubbed.

Now, she and Aoife were in Mr Pembroke's study. Eleanor hated being there. The memory of the night she'd drugged

Mr Pembroke seemed seared into her, and she could not stop glancing at the decanters. Aoife did not notice, shaking damp tea leaves across the carpet and humming as she swept them up again, grey with dust and ash.

Aoife finished sweeping and straightened up. 'I'll go and tip this lot out,' she yawned, 'I'll not be long.'

Eleanor finished dusting one portrait and moved on to the next. It showed a man in the wig and embroidered coat of the last century, and as she climbed onto a chair to reach the top of the frame Eleanor recognized Mr Pembroke's dark, wet eyes in the painted face. She shuddered.

There were voices coming from the corridor.

'Come now, you needn't be frightened. It's such a little question.'

Eleanor heard Aoife's voice. Her stomach lurched.

'Fifteen, sir.'

'Fifteen! I ought to have known. You're such a fresh little thing. You're quite a child...'

Disgust, anger and fear churned under Eleanor's skin. She jumped down from the chair and burst through the study door. Mr Pembroke was standing a little way down the corridor, leaning over Aoife as she clutched the pan of dusty tea leaves like a shield.

Eleanor faltered. It had been more than a week since that night in the study, and she had not seen Mr Pembroke since. She had picked up his laundry, tidied the papers scattered across his desk and made his bed, and still she had not seen him. Once or twice, she could have sworn she heard footsteps suddenly stop when she passed along a corridor, but when she turned to look behind her there was never anyone there.

Nerves roiled in the pit of her stomach. Forcing him to

drink the brandy had seemed like an excellent idea at the time but now, with his bulk blocking the way to the servants' staircase, she was not so certain. How much did he remember? How much would he punish her for?

He started back when he saw Eleanor.

'Ella,' he said, his eyes flickering to her empty hands.

Eleanor forced herself to curtsey, teeth gritted. 'You'll have to excuse us, sir. We'll only be a moment, and then you may have the use of your study again. Aoife, come and give me a hand with the carpet.'

She held the door open and Aoife scurried inside. Mr Pembroke turned his gaze to Eleanor, his mouth set. He looked at her for a long time, his large hands clenching and unclenching like twitching spiders.

After a while Eleanor said, in her most careful voice, 'May I be excused, sir?'

'Ella,' he muttered, 'I...I seem to remember we had some kind of disagreement.'

Doubt was scrawled across his face and his eyes were pleading; it was a question, not a statement. Eleanor felt a thrill of triumph and kept her face blank. 'Sir?'

'You...you were...'

'Are you quite well, sir? Should I send for a doctor?'

His hands twitched again. 'A doctor? I don't need a—' He broke off, squinting at her face. 'Have your eyes always been blue?'

Eleanor fought to stay calm but inside, she was reeling. The black-eyed woman's face flashed across her memory, empty but for the grin. Had he seen her, that night in the study?

She kept her voice slow and measured, as though talking to a distressed child. 'Of course my eyes are blue, sir,' she said, watching her words pick away at his confidence, 'and they've never been anything else.'

Mr Pembroke nodded, his face very pale. He strode towards the main staircase and disappeared up it, and it sounded a little like running.

Eleanor had been dreading the arrival of Sunday morning. A distant clock chimed two and her eyes snapped open. The awful knowledge that the day had arrived coiled around her like a snake.

She knew what the woman was, now.

She was a demon. Beelzebub himself had sent her to whisper in Eleanor's ear and she'd fallen into his trap. She ought to have known better. Hadn't she sat through enough sermons? She'd made Eve's mistake and listened to temptation, when the woman's flat, black eyes should have told Eleanor all she needed to know. Her silken promises had turned to iron around Eleanor's wrists, and she'd bartered away her soul. And today, she was going to have to go to church and face what she had done.

They walked to church two by two. Eleanor kept her eyes downcast and saw only mud and rats until the shadow of the church loomed over her. The rest of the congregation filed in while Eleanor hesitated at the lychgate. The gravestones jutted out of the ground like jagged teeth, ready to tear her into pieces.

The sweat inside her gloves felt like blood dripping from her fingers. She'd sold her soul, her *soul*, and now Lizzie was dead.

'Ella!' Mrs Fielding hissed. 'Come along!'

Eleanor *was* to blame, even though the butcher's boy had

been the one to drown Lizzie. Guilt wrapped itself around her like a corset laced too tight. And, she thought, churches were holy ground – what would happen when she went through the lychgate? She'd been to church twice and nothing had happened, even though she'd already struck her bargain. But things were different, now she knew what she had done.

'Ella!'

Would the reverend be able to tell? Of course he would, she thought; he was a holy man, he would know these things. Dear Lord, what if he denounced her from the pulpit? What if he started yelling like one of Cromwell's Puritans and named her a witch? Would she be arrested? Burned at the stake? Or worse – what if she was handed over to the Inquisition? There'd never been one in England – at least, that was what she thought – but the world was so much smaller than it had been, it wouldn't take long for her to be brought to the Continent. The Inquisition were always doing unspeakable things; she'd read about them, once, and felt so sick she'd had to close the book. If the reverend knew what she'd done, would he hand her over to the Papists?

'*Ella!*'

Mrs Fielding was standing in front of her, flushed and angry. The tip of her scar was visible under the high collar of her best dress.

'A sudden headache,' Eleanor said, quickly. 'I think I'd best go home.'

Mrs Fielding grabbed Eleanor by the wrist and hauled her past the lychgate. Eleanor braced herself.

Nothing happened. The reverend was watching her, but he didn't look as if he were about to thunder fire and brimstone from a spartan pulpit. He looked bemused, and slightly too fat for his robes.

Mrs Fielding dragged Eleanor inside the church. Eleanor barely had time to remember a story she'd been told as a child – the witch had tried to enter the church and the moment she set foot inside, it *collapsed around her ears* – before she realized that nothing had happened.

Mrs Fielding rounded on her, mouth already open, but she faltered when she saw Eleanor's smile.

'I do apologize, Mrs Fielding,' she said, relief blossoming like a flower, 'I wasn't quite myself. I hope I didn't disgrace you.'

She swept into the body of the church before Mrs Fielding could say anything else and took her place in the pew. Nothing had happened. Perhaps she wasn't as unclean as she thought.

The sermon washed over her and she settled back to listen.

The marble floor glistened under a thin veil of water. Scrubbing fiercely, Eleanor could see the reflection of her face, getting redder with every swipe. A second shape flickered in the water. She blinked, and it was gone.

Someone knocked at the front door. Eleanor eased herself upright, opened it, and saw Inspector Hatchett, monolithic in the doorway. He took off his hat when he saw her. 'Good morning, Miss Hartley. Might I have a word?'

Lizzie. He must suspect that Eleanor had killed her. Why else would he have come to visit her a second time? Had someone overheard Lizzie and Eleanor arguing the night before she died?

It wasn't fair. She hadn't killed Lizzie – but of course, she had set Lizzie's death in motion when she'd made her second wish, even though she hadn't known what she was doing and the butcher's boy had been the one to drown Lizzie. But the Inspector couldn't know that, unless – Eleanor's stomach twisted in fear. Had the black-eyed woman brought him here, as recompense for Eleanor trying to escape their bargain?

The Inspector put out a hand to steady her. 'Are you quite well?'

'Have you got him?'

'I would prefer to discuss that indoors, if you please. Is there somewhere we might talk in private?'

Eleanor peered into the street. No Black Maria outside, rocking on its wheels as prisoners banged on the blacked-out windows. No burly constables lurking by the railings. Just a couple of curious beggar children and a rag-and-bone man. The Inspector wasn't here to take her away.

She led him upstairs, listening carefully. Mrs Fielding was clattering around in the cloakroom off the entrance hall, Aoife was whistling along the second-floor corridor, and Daisy and Mrs Banbury were trapped in the kitchen with meringues and soufflés. When she was sure that they would not be found, Eleanor bundled the Inspector into the morning room.

Once, this had been Mrs Pembroke's favourite room. She'd written her letters here, reviewed the menus, and let Eleanor sit on her knee while she settled the household accounts. Now the windows were shuttered, all the furniture was swathed in dust sheets, and her portrait stared across the room with sad, filmy eyes. Eleanor shut the door behind her and brushed the dust away from the painted face, very gently.

123

She lit a candle and motioned him away from the door. 'We can speak freely here.'

He followed her over to the fireplace. 'Now, Miss Hartley,' he began, 'the matter I came to question you about is some-what...delicate. But before I do, I must ask you who you were talking about when you answered the door.'

Eleanor blinked at him, surprised. 'The butcher's boy, of course. I thought that was why you'd come.'

The Inspector's mouth tightened. 'I'm afraid not. We are searching for him, but he seems to have vanished. And now, please, to the business at hand. I must beg your pardon, but these inquiries are necessary.'

Eleanor inched out of the candlelight, feeling strangely relieved. The butcher's boy had fled; he *had* killed Lizzie.

The Inspector looked visibly uncomfortable. 'I took your advice and tried to trace the former maids working at Granborough House. It seemed a number of them had been... taken advantage of.'

'Did you find Leah?' Eleanor blurted, before she could stop herself. 'Where is she staying? Can you tell me?'

'I'm afraid I was unable to trace Miss Wallace,' the Inspector said, and Eleanor slumped against the fireplace, all her hopes wilting. 'However, I found some of the others and...some of them are well.'

Leah. Martha, who'd left last year when the bump had become too large to hide. Janie, who Mrs Fielding had found with her clothes in disarray. Gertrude, who'd been dolly-mopping on the side – Mr Pembroke had found out, and he had punished her for it. Worse, she thought there were more. Girls who'd been ushered out when she was still sitting on Mrs Pembroke's knee. And now...

'I have spoken to the housekeeper,' the Inspector continued, 'but she would not discuss it with me. I assume this is what you were referring to at our last meeting, Miss Hartley?'

Eleanor nodded. The Inspector let out a long sigh and made a note.

'And – forgive me, Miss Hartley, but I must ask – do you have reason to believe that the girls were willing?'

Eleanor shook her head.

The Inspector made another note. Candlelight sharpened the grooves on his face. 'And how long has this been going on?'

'I'm not sure. Certainly since Mrs Pembroke's death, three years ago.'

More scribbling. His pencil bobbed in the light, casting strange shadows on the wall. Upstairs, a door slammed, and Eleanor flinched.

'Did you ever suspect your employer of having an inappropriate relationship with Miss Bartram?'

She shook her head. Someone was coming down the stairs. Mrs Fielding, come to look for her? Or worse – what if it was Mr Pembroke?

'One more question, please, Miss Hartley. Did you ever—'

There was a creak of a door opening further down the corridor. Eleanor blew out the candle, seized the Inspector's hand and forced him to hide. They crouched behind a chair, listening to the footsteps. Her pulse fluttered like humming-bird's wings, and the Inspector squeezed her hand.

Aoife walked past the morning-room door, whistling. Eleanor slumped against the chair, but did not get up until the sound had faded.

'I think you'd better go, Inspector,' she whispered.

'I'm grateful for everything you've told me, Miss Hartley.

If Mr Pembroke should ever behave improperly with you, or any other maid in his employ, come straight to me. I will help as much as I am able.'

Eleanor couldn't speak. There was an unexpected lump in her throat.

The Inspector seemed to understand. 'My sister was in service,' he said, his face dark. 'She told me some of the things an unscrupulous master might do.'

'Thank you,' she whispered. 'Now, wait here, and I'll see you safely out.'

At three o'clock on the day that Charles came home, Eleanor was lined up in the hall with the rest of the maids. Starch crackled in the black folds of her dress uniform. The house shone. Polish masked the scent of damp. Fires crackled in all the right grates. A leg of pork was roasting in the oven, and a pot of Julienne soup was simmering on the stove. The gleaming hall floor reflected the maids' white aprons – ghosts, floating under the surface of the water.

As they waited for Charles to arrive, Eleanor tugged on her cuffs. Her sleeves were too short; she'd not worn her dress uniform in years. Several inches of wrist showed, making her dry, red hands stand out even sharper against the white of her apron and cuffs. She knew Charles was going to notice. Oh God, what if he tried to shake her hand, which had once been so soft and delicate? One look at what three years of hot water and carbolic soap had done to her fingers and he wouldn't even touch her.

There was a clatter from the top of the stairs.

Mr Pembroke was leaning heavily on the banister. Eleanor

caught a whiff of stale sweat and brandy as he passed, and heard him stumble down the stairs. Let him fall, she thought. He deserved it.

Mrs Fielding nodded to Aoife, who stepped forward and dropped a curtsey.

'Shall I help with your jacket, sir?'

His voice was slurred. 'What? Oh, yes.'

Aoife fussed around him, re-buttoning his waistcoat and straightening his jacket. Mr Pembroke stood there, his eyes unfocused. It was only when she was tying his cravat that he noticed her. He whispered something in her ear and Aoife's hands slipped.

Eleanor seethed. God alone knew where Leah laid her head, and Eleanor couldn't begin to guess where the rest of Mr Pembroke's girls were. Some of them might have persuaded their mothers to pass the baby off as a child of their own. Some of them had probably ended up as working girls, and Eleanor could only hope their customers were kind to them. She would not let Aoife become one of them.

Aoife fled back to her place in the line. There was a sharp rap at the door; Charles had arrived.

He was not the boy she remembered.

Then, he'd been shaped like a string bean, with a mop of vaguely yellow hair and a moustache like a caterpillar crawling along his upper lip. The man who came in was taller, broad-shouldered, and his golden-brown hair was brushed smoothly into place. His full-lipped mouth was already smiling, his clothes neatly tailored to his lean body. The straggly moustache was gone, and even from this distance she could see his eyes were brilliantly blue. His mother's eyes.

He glanced around the hall. He saw her, she *knew* he saw her, but he said nothing. His expression flickered, and then he turned his eyes to his father.

And that, she thought, was it. She was *staff*. Her pride stung at the thought. She'd been relegated to the ranks of faceless housemaids, no more worthy of notice than the umbrella stand in the hall. But what had she been expecting? She hadn't heard from Charles in three years. She'd been foolish to think he might've objected to her being forced to earn her keep. Perhaps he'd known all this time, and hadn't cared. The thought punctured an old daydream and Eleanor's face grew hot. She'd been stupid to imagine that—

Charles and his father went upstairs, the rest of the maids sloped off to the kitchen and, too late, Eleanor realized she had been left with the bags.

Eleanor opened the door to the second-floor landing, listening to the voices from the study. Mrs Fielding had sent her to tell the Pembrokes that a visitor was waiting in the drawing room, but Eleanor was in no hurry. She'd heard her own name through the door to the servants' staircase and a mix of curiosity and dread had pricked up her ears.

A thin slice of light spilled into the corridor. The study door was ajar. Voices rang down the hall. She avoided the creaky floorboards and listened.

'...you swore you'd send her to school! What would Mother say if she—'

'Don't talk to me about your mother!'

'She was left in your care! You have a duty!'

'A duty I can't fulfil! You know the sacrifices we've had to make! If we can't keep a footman, we certainly can't afford to pay for her governess, or for her ballgowns, or whatever else it would take to make that drudge a lady!'

There was a slamming sound and a rattling of glass.

'She is *not* a drudge.'

Eleanor blushed, and panicked. She couldn't let them know she'd been listening. She pressed her cold fingers against her cheeks and knocked on the open door. Charles was flushed and angry, but he smoothed back his hair and smiled when she came in. His wine was still lapping at the edges of his glass. She faced Mr Pembroke, and fixed her eyes on a point above his head. If she looked into his face she would splinter, and something dreadful would ooze out through the cracks.

'There's a visitor for you in the drawing room, sir.'

Charles's smile vanished. Mr Pembroke did not appear to notice.

'A visitor? Who the Devil…hand over the card.'

Eleanor passed Mr Pembroke the visitor's card, being careful not to touch him. He squinted at it. 'Miss…Darling?'

Charles's face brightened. 'So soon! Father, you know I wrote to you about my fiancée—'

'Yes, yes. Keen, isn't she?' He laughed, and Charles went scarlet.

Mr Pembroke took another drink. 'Well, this'll solve our other little problem.' He turned back to Eleanor and forced a smile. 'Ella, as a reward for being such a good girl we've a new position for you. Miss Darling will need a lady's maid. You're to stay with her at the Langham until the wedding. There. Won't that be nice?'

He'd spoken to her in just the same way when he'd last given her a Christmas present. Only now, he was staring straight at her, a satisfied twist at the corner of his mouth. He was sending her away, like he'd sent away Leah, and clearing a path to Aoife.

Eleanor stumbled halfway through her curtsey. 'Thank you, sir.'

'Trot along down to the drawing room and introduce your-self, then. She's waiting.'

Eleanor left, reeling. Confronting Mr Pembroke hadn't done her any good. He wanted her out of the way and so he had removed her. There was no one standing between him and Aoife now except Daisy, but Aoife's work took her all over the house when Daisy was confined to the kitchen. It would be so easy for him to corner Aoife in an upstairs corridor, where Daisy could not hear her over the clatter of pans...

You're such a fresh little thing. You're quite a child...

She had to get Aoife out.

The door clicked shut behind her.

'Eleanor?'

Charles had followed her. Eleanor flushed. It had been so long since anyone called her by her real name without putting a sting in it. Her name sounded wonderful, coming from him.

'I didn't know,' he said. 'I thought when you didn't answer my letters—'

Eleanor was suddenly aware of her too-short sleeves. She put her hands behind her back. 'Begging your pardon, sir, but I haven't received any letters from you.'

'But...' He glanced at the study door, a muscle flickering in his jaw. 'You must excuse me, Eleanor. It seems my father and I have more business to discuss.'

Eleanor squeezed her hands tighter, desperate to keep her smile from showing. 'I hope I haven't caused trouble for you and the master, sir.'

Charles passed a hand over his face. When he took it away, his eyes were burning.

'Would you be so good as to allow me ten minutes with my father, in private? Afterwards, if you would meet me outside the drawing room I should very much like to introduce you to Felicity.'

'Of course, sir.'

'And call me Charles, please.'

She shouldn't. Housemaids did not call employers by their first names. Besides, she was afraid she'd stumble over her words if she opened her mouth.

Charles squared his shoulders and went into the study. He was so little like his father, Eleanor thought. His height seemed to be the only thing he had inherited from Mr Pembroke. The rest was all his mother – although surely Mrs Pembroke's eyes had not been so blue.

Eleanor had gone five paces before the shouting started again. She sprinted towards the servants' staircase and hurtled down to the kitchen, where Daisy was whisking an enormous bowl of cream and Aoife was trying to steal some.

'I need to talk to both of you,' Eleanor whispered. 'Outside.'

They followed her into the garden. Greasy fog curled around their ankles and a fine layer of coal smuts clung to the plants in Mrs Banbury's herb garden. Eleanor led them away from the door, where the clatter of horses' hooves and cart wheels would stop their voices carrying down the stairs.

'I'm being sent away – no, please, Aoife, don't interrupt,' she said, when Aoife's mouth opened. 'You need to listen. There isn't going to be anyone to look after you here—'

'She's got me!' Daisy snapped.

'And how often do you get out of the kitchen?' Eleanor

shot back. 'Aoife, you're in danger. Mr Pembroke is coming for you next – no, don't cry, please just listen. If he gets you alone, get him a drink from the decanters in the study. Make sure he finishes it. I've drugged them.'

Aoife stopped crying with a whimper. 'But...but that's...'

Daisy stared at her. 'With what?' she said, her voice loaded.

'It's laudanum,' she hissed, 'it won't kill him! He'll just get sleepy and you can slip away. And if anything goes wrong – do you remember that policeman, the tall one? He's said he'll help, if anything...happens.'

Aoife clutched at Eleanor's hand. 'You are coming back?'

'Of course I am! It's only until the wedding. You'll be all right, until then?'

Daisy put an arm around Aoife's waist. ''Course she will. She's got me.'

Eleanor threw her arms around them both. 'It won't be long,' she whispered, fighting to keep the tremor out of her voice. 'I'll be back before you know it.'

Eleanor had never seen a woman so mechanical as Miss Felicity Darling. She perched on a drawing-room chair, back ramrod-straight, her legs and arms at perfect right angles. Her feet were neatly tucked together and her face was arranged into an expression of polite disinterest. When she raised her teacup to her lips, Eleanor listened for the clicking of cogs.

Her smile clunked into place when she saw Eleanor and Charles. 'Ah, Charles, there you are! I was beginning to think you'd be cloistered up in that study forever! And who's this dear little thing?'

She spoke with a tinge of a Manchester accent she was trying to hide.

'Eleanor has kindly agreed to take on the position of lady's maid during your stay at the Langham.'

Eleanor bobbed a curtsey, but Felicity was already talking again.

'What a delightful little creature; wherever did you find her? Do come and have some tea, Charles.'

Felicity gave a sharp nod. Dismissed, Eleanor went upstairs to pack her things. It was strange to think of Charles having a fiancée. She'd never thought of him as someone who might fall in love, although now, thinking of his broad shoulders and his easy smile, it was difficult to say why. He'd just come back from Paris – was that where they had met? Had he escorted Felicity to the glittering Opéra Garnier, strolled past the old paintings in the Musée du Louvre with her on his arm, taken her hand on the banks of the Seine and smiled? Had it been as wonderful as Eleanor had imagined it might be?

She gave herself a little shake and kept on climbing the stairs, trying not to feel her boots pinching her toes, the scratchy wool of her servant's uniform. From the drawing room, she could hear Felicity laughing.

At any other time, Eleanor would have marvelled at the Langham Hotel. With its high ceilings, glittering lights and smooth, shiny surfaces it looked like a palace – but as she was carrying Felicity's luggage as they arrived, all Eleanor was concerned with were the stairs. Felicity sat at a table by the window while Eleanor dragged the cases and boxes up to her room. By the time she had lugged the last hat-box up the third flight of stairs, Felicity was halfway through a pot of Earl Grey and a plate of sandwiches.

Felicity dabbed at the corners of her mouth with a napkin. 'They do have porters here, you know.'

Eleanor blushed. Of course the hotel had porters. A real lady's maid would know that. But she'd been so eager to impress Felicity that she'd taken everything up herself. She hadn't even said anything before she'd revealed herself as an ignorant little girl. A real lady's maid would have never made such a stupid mistake.

But perhaps a real lady might have cared to let her know.

'Please accept my apologies, Miss Darling.'

Felicity gave a magnanimous nod. 'It's only to be expected. You are untrained, and quite ignorant of what I shall require of you.'

Eleanor kept her face blank. 'I shall take every opportunity to learn, miss.'

'I hope it will not take too long.'

Felicity went back to her tiny sandwiches and Eleanor looked around. It was the prettiest room she'd ever seen, with a cream bed, gilt mirrors and plush carpets. Eleanor longed to dig her toes into the carpet, to run her fingers over the silk-embroidered bedspread, to press her forehead against the smooth glass of the mirrors, cool as ice. However, there was only one bed, and it was clearly not for her. Where would she sleep?

'I have some questions for you, Hartley.'

Eleanor tried to look keen. 'Yes, miss?'

'How long have you known Charles?'

'All my life, miss.'

Felicity's gloved hands tightened in her lap. 'Do you communicate often? Communicate means—'

'I know what it means, miss,' said Eleanor, forcing a smile, 'and no, I'm afraid not. We were playmates as children but we have not spoken since he went to Oxford.'

'Do you think him a good sort of man?'

'I do.'

Felicity's eyes flickered across her face. They were a shade of grey so pale they were almost colourless. When her eyes moved, the pupil seemed to hover, like a shadow hanging there of its own accord.

'Well,' Felicity said, 'I know Charles thinks of you as his little charity project, but you must not become accustomed to this position. You are completely unacceptable, given your connection to Miss Bartram, and I will be looking for a new girl to fill the position.'

Her new mistress stirred the tea. The silver spoon clinked against the edges of the china cup. Each chink of metal on porcelain was like a pinch.

'Miss Darling,' Eleanor began, 'I—'

Felicity held up a hand. 'No maid of mine will be linked to a murder investigation. You needn't bother the Pembrokes with this information; after all, *I* am now your employer.'

Felicity plucked another sandwich from the tray and popped it into her mouth with a flourish.

'Well? Aren't you going to start unpacking?'

Eleanor gritted her teeth, curtseyed, and turned to the huge pile of luggage.

As the days went on, Eleanor fell into a routine. She brought Felicity breakfast every morning, and thought of Daisy and Aoife yawning over their porridge in the kitchen at Granborough House. When she laced Felicity into her embroidered corset, she saw Leah struggling to close her stays on

135

the morning she left Granborough House. When she mixed Felicity a brandy and water – which Felicity insisted she needed for her health – she saw the laudanum dropping into Mr Pembroke's decanter.

She never should have left. At Granborough House, she had at least been able to see Aoife. If she screamed, Eleanor would have heard, and come running. Being away was much worse. When she closed her eyes all she saw was Mr Pembroke, leaning over Aoife in the corridor. She shouldn't just have added a few drops of laudanum to the decanters; Eleanor should have yanked Mr Pembroke's head back by the hair and forced the whole bottle down his throat.

She ought to have been pleased. Being Felicity's maid had benefits. She ate better, she had new clothes for the first time in years, and she was earning more than double what she'd made as a housemaid. A better person would've been grateful. But all her comforts had been bought by Aoife's isolation, and every time she tried to enjoy them an undercurrent of guilt tugged at Eleanor's thoughts.

And then, there was Felicity.

Every evening, Felicity went into her dressing room and counted her possessions. She had a small green notebook that she carried everywhere, and every time she bought something new she added the details to her inventory. During her nightly inspection of the dressing room, she would tick it off the list, and did the same every morning.

This was because the floor of Felicity's dressing room was where Eleanor slept.

The notebook wasn't just to prevent Eleanor stealing Felicity's jewels. Felicity would inspect the quality of everything and list the trimmings she wanted for every hat and dress. If

Eleanor hadn't completed the alterations by the morning count Felicity would dock her pay.

Eleanor would have given her right eye to watch that notebook burn.

She opened Felicity's cavernous wardrobe and took out a dress in Paris green ringed with endless flounces, to be trimmed with gold braid. Eleanor would never have chosen something like that – it was far too ostentatious, and the dye was giving her a headache – but she couldn't resist holding it up against herself in the mirror. Eleanor sighed. She would've looked like a wood sprite in that dress, emerging glittering from between the trees.

Eleanor set to work. As she sewed, she thought about her wishes.

They hung over her head like stars, casting a sinister glow over everything she touched. This dress could be hers, this coat, this hat. All she needed to do was wish for it. She wouldn't have to imagine Felicity's notebook alight – she could make it happen, and watch her scream and singe her skirts. But if she did, someone would die. At six o'clock in the morning and with her stomach feeling empty enough to cave in on itself, she might have risked her own soul, but all the hunger and tiredness in the world would not make her risk someone else's life as well.

She finished trimming the first flounce and started on the next. The first light of dawn crept under the door. Eleanor would have an hour, maybe two, before Felicity got up.

Eleanor knew what she would wish for if she could guarantee no one would get hurt. She'd wanted it since the moment she saw Mrs Pembroke, smiling and secure in her fine house. As a wealthy society lady, Eleanor could see the world, keep poverty and sickness from her door, and no man would ever dream of raising a hand to her.

But from what she could work out with her past experience of the wishes, it would not be so simple. She could wish to be a lady and find herself married to a man like Mr Pembroke. Her wish would have come true, but she would be unhappy. She could wish to be rich, but she still might not find herself wealthy. Mr Pembroke was officially her guardian and controlled all of her money until she was twenty-one. It was simple enough now, because she didn't have any, but if she wished for riches he would find a way to spend them.

She bit off the thread and started on the next flounce.

Planning out her wishes was doing her no good, she told herself. She wasn't going to make any more, not when they would kill someone with a word. The risk to her soul wasn't worth the gain. Better to think of another way out. Her situation had improved. She was away from Mr Pembroke, earning better wages and eating better food. Perhaps away from the tension of Granborough House, she could come up with something. Felicity was the only drawback, but perhaps in time she would soften.

Felicity showed no signs of softening as she threw open the dressing-room door later that morning. She spread out the skirts of the green dress, turning it this way and that, her eyes flickering to a grey dress as straight and severe as a workhouse pinafore in her wardrobe. Her mouth tightened every time she looked at it.

She let the green dress fall back into the wardrobe and plucked at the grey. 'Dispose of this old rag, Hartley. It isn't fit for a pauper. Bring my hairpins.'

Felicity dressed carefully that morning. She cycled through

four dresses – peacock blue, mauve and olive, canary yellow and rhubarb pink – before she settled on a striped red-and-white walking dress. Eleanor laced her in and out of so many bodices that her fingers were numb. Next came Felicity's jewels. Fat rubies, sparkling diamonds and glowing pearls tumbled through Eleanor's hands, snake-cold and rattling. Then Eleanor dressed Felicity's hair, leaving her fingertips sticky with bandoline. Hairpins skittered through her fingers. One of them caught on the back of Felicity's head and she let out a hiss of pain.

Felicity went to the mirror and examined herself. She patted her pale hair, smoothed her skirts, stroked the glassy surface of her jewels. Eleanor washed the bandoline off her hands and tried not to think of candy canes.

Felicity beckoned her over. 'Roll up your sleeve, Hartley, and hold out your arm.'

Eleanor did as she was told. Felicity leant forward, grabbed her arm in both hands and twisted. Pain sparked across Eleanor's skin.

'Have a care with those pins,' Felicity said, shoving Eleanor away. Eleanor stumbled backwards, her arm raw and smarting. She gritted her teeth and apologized, willing away the tears filling her eyes. She should've stuck the pin in harder.

Felicity turned back to the mirror. 'Make yourself present-able.'

Eleanor rolled down her sleeve, trying not to touch her stinging arm. 'Yes, miss.'

The smell of horse manure and rain oozed through the open window of the hansom, but Eleanor did not care. They were going back to Granborough House for the first time in a week, and if she didn't have the window open she was going to be sick. How much damage could Mr Pembroke do in seven days?

The hansom rolled to a halt outside the front door, the steps gleaming white in the rain. Eleanor scrambled out of the carriage at once and had already started for the tradesmen's entrance before she remembered Felicity. Face burning, she unrolled the steps, put up an umbrella and helped Felicity to the door. Felicity gripped Eleanor's smarting arm, digging in her fingernails.

Aoife opened the door for them. Her face broke into an enormous smile when she saw Eleanor. 'You're back!'

'Quite the welcome, I'm sure,' Felicity sneered, striding into the hall and leaving Eleanor to wrestle with the umbrella. 'Run along, girl, and tell my fiancé I've arrived.'

Aoife scurried away, blushing. Felicity stared around the hall with an appraising eye, taking in the marble floors, the sweeping staircase, the mahogany banisters. 'Make a note, Hartley,' she said, staring at the wallpaper, 'I want something a little less dated in here. Scheele's green would do very – Charles!'

Charles was coming down the staircase, beaming. 'Felicity! How are you finding the Langham?'

'Oh, charming, although I miss you terribly, of course. You must have me over for dinner or I shall waste away.'

'Well, I hope tea will suffice until Thursday, at least. And you, Eleanor? I hope you've been enjoying your stay.'

'Thank you, sir,' she said.

'There's no need for you to call me sir, Eleanor.'

Felicity raised an eyebrow. 'I did not realize you ran such an informal household, Charles.'

He blushed. 'Well, ordinarily I should never dream of it. But Eleanor and I grew up together. I could never ask Eleanor to call me "sir" after I'd spent so many years pulling her pigtails. It'd be unnatural, coming from her.'

There was a glint in Felicity's eyes like the shine on a blade. 'Is that so?'

Panic began to flutter in Eleanor's chest. Barely ten minutes inside Granborough House and she was already in trouble again.

'Goodness, yes,' said Charles. 'I'm afraid I was a perfect beast towards her. She used to ask me for help with her French and I taught her the most awful phrases.'

Eleanor started. 'You did? Which ones?'

Charles went scarlet. 'I thought you knew! You were always smiling when you said them back to me – you joined in when I laughed! You must've known, surely!'

'What did you teach me to say?' Eleanor asked, unable to hold back her smile.

'I can't tell you now! You're...'

'Run along, Hartley,' said Felicity, taking Charles's arm. 'I shan't need you.'

Eleanor scurried to the servants' stairs as Charles and Felicity climbed the grand staircase to the drawing room. The moment she came through the kitchen door, Aoife threw her arms around her.

'Look at you! Give us a twirl, Ella. I've another letter from home, will you read it to me?'

Eleanor smiled, forgetting some of her fear. 'Of course, but are you all right? You haven't been...'

They both glanced at Mrs Fielding.

'I'm well,' Aoife said, although Eleanor noticed the shadows around her eyes and the way she fiddled with the cuffs of her dress. 'Will you read my letter, please?'

Eleanor spent half an hour in the kitchen, reading Aoife's letter aloud and writing a reply for her, all while being pelted with questions about Felicity and the Langham. All too soon, the drawing-room bell rang and all Eleanor's panic came flooding back.

'You remember what I said?' she asked Aoife, squeezing her hand.

Aoife nodded. Eleanor went upstairs, hailed a cab and escorted Felicity back to the Langham in a silence that made her stomach curdle.

Eleanor knew what was going to happen now.

Felicity crushed her skirts in her fingers as she climbed the stairs to her hotel room. Her arms were like bowstrings, waiting to be drawn back. When Felicity waited for Eleanor to unlock the door to her room, she stood like a hangman waiting at the gallows: silent, still, and with her face empty.

Eleanor shut the door behind her, heart beating fast.

All Felicity's packages were stacked neatly by the foot of the bed. The pillows had been plumped, the sheets had been changed. The tablecloth was clean, there was no dust along the windowsill and every surface had been buffed to a shine.

No one was coming.

'Lock the door,' Felicity said.

Eleanor locked it. She tried to reassure herself. Felicity couldn't do much damage. She was a good sight taller than Eleanor but she was still a lady. Ladies' arms were slim, their hands soft; they were meant for playing the piano and smoothing out their skirts. Eleanor had spent the past three years avoiding Lizzie, who'd lugged iron buckets full of coal up and down the stairs all day. It wouldn't hurt as much as—

Felicity slapped her.

Eleanor staggered back, her cheek throbbing. Felicity took a deep, steadying breath.

'Proverbs,' she said. 'Twenty-three fourteen.'

'I...what?'

Felicity slapped her again. Eleanor turned her head with the blow. It took the bite out of the slap, but it still stung.

'Proverbs, twenty-three fourteen,' Felicity snapped, 'recite it.'

All Eleanor could think of was 'deliver us from evil', and that would get her another slap. Then she remembered, and dread swelled up inside her.

'"Thou shalt beat him with the rod, and deliver his soul from—"'

Felicity hit her again. Her eyes were shining.

'I do this for your own good,' Felicity hissed, 'as fathers do for their children. Adultery is a sin, Hartley. Fornication is a sin. You've sinned far too much already.'

'Miss, I swear, I haven't—'

'I don't want to hear your excuses! You are my *maid*. You've no business with my fiancé! I'll have no more of this. No more, do you hear me?'

Smog seeped under the shuttered windows of the hansom. Felicity insisted they be closed; ladies were not gawped at. More likely than not, she didn't want the dye on her dress to run; today's confection was in magenta and mauve and would turn Felicity's skin the colour of a bruise if it got wet. Eleanor was beginning to feel sick. Unless Felicity opened a window,

143

ladies would end up smelling of whatever the previous passenger had left in the cab, which was likely a dead cat.

Eleanor shut her eyes and listened instead. Street-sellers. Horses. Omnibus drivers, swearing as they passed. Fiddlers. Children, whooping in delight. Mr Punch, yelling, 'that's the way to do it!' and a shout of laughter. A burst of French, and another language she did not recognize. And then, finally, the driver slowing the horses as their cab drew to a halt.

Eleanor helped Felicity out of the cab, tugging her skirts away from the filthy wheels.

'Father!'

Mr Darling stood like a stretched-out coil of paper – tall, thin, and curling in on himself from the shoulders down. To Eleanor's surprise, there was a woman on his arm. She looked nothing like Felicity. Felicity was a glittering dagger of a girl; Mrs Darling was a fat little sparrow by comparison. Mrs Darling tugged at her husband's arm. He saw Felicity. Sharp spots of colour blossomed across his worn face.

'What are you wearing?' Felicity's father's eyes narrowed.

All the shine went out of Felicity's eyes. She swallowed, hung her head, fiddled with the lace at her cuffs. 'It's perfectly respectable,' she began, 'and quite—'

'Hello there! I thought I'd never find you!'

Charles came striding out of the fog, crisp and clean in cool dove-grey. His smile faltered as his blue eyes flicked between Mr Darling glaring at his daughter, the drooping Felicity, and Eleanor, who was trying her best to blend into the background.

'I hope I'm not interrupting anything,' he said, watching Felicity with a worried look on his face.

Felicity pressed her lips together and shook her head, once. Her fists were clenched.

Charles glanced at Mr Darling, Mrs Darling, and all the people passing by who were clearly trying to eavesdrop. Then, as suddenly as striking a match, a dazzling smile spread across his face. He spread his hands wide, relaxed his shoulders and beamed at the Darlings as if there was no one else in the world he would rather see.

'Well then!' he said, good humour dripping from every syllable. 'Shall we? I've so been looking forward to seeing you both, Mr Darling, Mrs Darling. How are your boys?'

Mrs Darling began to thaw. 'Very well, thank you. Walter and Edgar were so pleased with the soldiers you sent them, and Gerald adores his new book. You received their thank-you notes, I hope?'

He steered them towards the dressmaker's, placing himself between Felicity and her father as he did so. 'I did, and very charming letters they were, too! You must congratulate the twins for me; my hand was never half so fair when I was their age.'

Felicity clung to Charles's arm. Mr Darling began to unbend; Mrs Darling beamed. Eleanor trailed after them like a shadow. Charles nodded along diplomatically with Mr Darling. He lavished praise on Felicity's brothers. He proffered his arm and steered the Darlings gently away from the grimier patches of pavement. He blunted the sharpness of their words, soothed frayed tempers, and punctured awkward silences with compliments that always managed to sound sincere. For Eleanor, who had seen him blush and stammer since the age of fourteen, it was uncanny.

Once, just once, his charming demeanour slipped. Felicity and her father were sniping at each other in a sharp hiss that carried across the street. Mr Darling jabbed a finger under his daughter's nose as they walked, and two high spots of colour

145

blazed on Felicity's cheeks as she tried to stride away. Charles saw passers-by staring after them and whispering to each other, and a flush crept into his cheeks. Eleanor felt a pang of nostalgia and pity to see him embarrassed – she hated the thought of his being uncomfortable, but he looked so like the blushing boy she remembered that she almost smiled.

He caught her eye, gave a rueful little smile and then the charm was back. 'I understand you grew up near Chatsworth,' he said, turning to Mrs Darling. 'You must tell me about it. I should love to see the Peaks in the autumn, I hear they're splendid.'

Mrs Darling, who had also noticed the argument, seized on this at once. 'They are! Jeremiah, dear Charles is thinking of visiting the Peaks, you must come and talk to him...'

Walking into the dressmaker's was like stepping into an aviary. Swathes of material glistened and flickered on the counters, hummingbird-bright. Lace fluttered in customers' fingers. Rattling buttons might have been the clicking of beaks; quiet laughter sounded a little like birdsong. In her plain dress Eleanor felt like a slug, waiting to be pecked at.

Felicity detached herself from Charles's arm and marched up to the dressmaker, barging past a group of red-eyed women looking over folds of black bombazine. The dressmaker scampered out from behind the counter to meet her.

'Miss Darling,' she said, 'what a pleasure to see you again! And you've brought your fiancé? And your mother and father! How charming...'

'She is not my mother!' Felicity hissed.

'May I interest you in something for your trousseau?' she said. 'Something in eau-de-nil, I think, would bring out your eyes most beautifully...'

'I want my order,' Felicity snapped. 'You said it would be ready this afternoon. Where is it?'

The dressmaker nodded to a couple of shop girls, who went scurrying into the back room. 'Of course,' she said, leading her towards the dressing room, 'the green silk. An excellent choice, Miss Darling...'

Mrs Darling frowned after her. 'You, maid,' she said to Eleanor, 'I take it the green silk is not her wedding dress?'

Charles's mouth fell open. Eleanor's cheeks were hot with shame.

'No, madam, but I believe it is something for her trousseau.'

'Oh, dear.'

Mr Darling's lip curled. 'Go and make her see sense, Esther. Her mother was just as frivolous; she needs a firm hand. I'll be in the cab.'

He left. Mrs Darling patted Charles's arm.

'I must say, we are glad Felicity has found such a steady young man. Do let us know if you require any advice.'

She bustled off towards the fitting room. The second she had gone, Charles turned to Eleanor.

'Eleanor, you *must* let me apologize on behalf of...'

'I'm sure Mrs Darling meant no harm.'

'But to speak to you so!'

'Please don't concern yourself with it. I've heard worse.'

Charles's face sharpened. 'What do you mean by that?'

Eleanor slipped on her servant's mask, the blank expression that served her so well. Charles noticed. When her shutters came down, his eyes flicked to the dressing room and back.

'Eleanor, is Felicity...civil towards you?'

Eleanor's cheek still stung. She ached all over from sleeping on the floor and there was a crick in her neck she couldn't

147

stretch out. Her boots rubbed, her new dress was scratchy along the seams and her corset suddenly felt like iron bands. Charles was looking at her as if he knew all of this. Eleanor blushed. It had been so much easier when they were younger, when he hadn't been tall and broad-shouldered and with lips that seemed fuller than she remembered. She could not imagine confiding in him without it feeling intimate, and he was going to be marrying another woman in a matter of weeks. But despite that, and even though they were surrounded by strangers, Eleanor wanted to tell him everything.

She licked her lips, wondering where to begin.

Then, the door to the fitting room was thrown open. Felicity emerged, tightly laced into an acid-green dress with a cuirass bodice, pleated ruffles and a luminous gold trim. Her stepmother followed, pursing her lips. Both of them were red in the face.

'Well?' Felicity snapped. 'What do you think?'

'Lovely, miss,' whispered Eleanor.

'Yes,' said Charles, his voice hard, 'it's lovely.'

Felicity glittered. Her pale hair was smoothed into elaborate curls. The swooping layers of her golden skirts were trimmed with sparkling beads. Lace frothed at her neckline, her diamonds shone orange, white and yellow, and the light itself seemed to spark and curve around her.

She looked like a candlestick.

Eleanor had spent the whole afternoon running after Felicity. Polishing her jewels, twisting up her hair, discreetly buying a pot of rouge and smuggling it back up to the hotel room. Her fingers were raw from tugging on laces, there was bandoline lodged under her fingernails, and she stank of Felicity's perfume.

148

In all the excitement Eleanor had forgotten to tell the hotel staff that Felicity wouldn't need her dinner. In fact, she'd been so forgetful that she'd told them to send it up to the room after seven o'clock, along with some ice. Felicity had slapped her for spilling oil of violets across her gown, and her cheek still hurt.

Felicity would be dining at Granborough House, sparkling at the foot of the table as the guest of honour. Eleanor had expected to accompany her – a lady always needed a chaperone – and was looking forward sloping off to the kitchen to check on Aoife. She was itching for a chance to talk to her away from Mrs Fielding, but Felicity had seen the shine in her eyes and said, 'I shan't be needing you, Hartley,' and watched Eleanor's reflection falter as she stood in front of the mirror.

Felicity's parents would be chaperoning her instead. They had been waiting for her in the lobby. About halfway down the stairs Felicity had hesitated, her gloved hands scrunching her satin skirts. Then she'd squared her shoulders and strode defiantly into the lobby.

When Eleanor got back to Felicity's room, her dinner was waiting under a gleaming silver cloche, the ice tucked discreetly behind a chair. Eleanor lifted the lid and a pair of mutton chops emerged from a cloud of fragrant steam.

She sat down and smoothed the napkin across her lap. Perhaps Felicity was right to be defiant.

Eleanor allowed herself one perfect hour.

She sat at Felicity's table, in Felicity's chair, and ate Felicity's dinner. She'd had a hot bath, using Felicity's array of soaps and lotions. She stood in front of Felicity's wardrobe in her chemise, tying up her hair in Felicity's ribbons, holding Felicity's dresses up against her reflection and stroking all the silks and satins. She'd even lain in Felicity's bed. It had felt so good to touch something soft that she did not have to mend.

But then the hour ended. Eleanor dressed herself in her own plain wool dress. She'd stacked up the dirty plates and cutlery outside someone else's door and opened the windows to let out the smell of mutton. She'd put the dresses and ribbons away, cleared away the bath things and slapped the dent out of Felicity's mattress, her eyes stinging.

To make herself feel better, she flicked open her battered suitcase and tried on the shoes she'd wished for. They fitted perfectly, although they looked a little strange peeking out from under her coarse, dark dress. Eleanor put them away. She didn't want them to be spoiled, when they had cost her so much.

Now it was ten o'clock, and Felicity would be back at any minute. Eleanor didn't even have a book to occupy her; she hadn't had a chance to raid the library at Granborough House before she left. Their absence itched and scratched at her thoughts, making her restless and jittery. All she could do was hold the ice to her cheek and wait.

It hurt less, but it still stung. Charles would never know; Felicity would keep her away from him until the mark faded. It was only a matter of time before she was dismissed; Felicity had already started looking for another lady's maid. When Eleanor was out in the cold, who could she rely on?

No one. Apart from herself. Or the black-eyed woman.

She stalked through Eleanor's thoughts, dreamlike and sharply real at the same time. The wishes she'd granted had come true. Eleanor could make another, but someone else would die if she did. It wasn't worth the risk.

Not for the first time, Eleanor realized how little she knew about the black-eyed woman. She had no idea how she had come to be trapped in the book – was it like the jinn in Aladdin's lamp? Eleanor didn't even know what she was. She'd assumed the black-eyed woman must be a demon – she had come from the pages of *Faustus*, after all, and Eleanor couldn't think of anything else interested in the buying and selling of souls – but how could that be right, if Eleanor was able to set foot on holy ground?

Eleanor was teeming with questions. She cleared her throat. The sounds of the hotel had begun to fade hours ago – footsteps on stairs, broughams and carriages pulling up to the entrance, doors opening and closing – but now, they seemed a fraction quieter. As if something was listening.

'Hello?'

Silence.

'I'd like to talk to you. Can you...come out?'

'If you insist, dear.'

Shadows shifted. The black-eyed woman stood perfectly still, in a spot where there had been nothing but darkness. The back of a chair became the swell of her skirt, the sharp edge of a corner became the line of her shawl.

She sat at the table, hands neatly folded. Something in the way she walked did not seem right. Every step was measured, even, and precise. It reminded Eleanor of Felicity on the morning they'd met. Felicity had seemed so scared of knocking something over she'd walked like a mannequin. The black-eyed woman had that same stilted air, born of endless observation. With a shiver, Eleanor wondered how long she had been watching for.

'I wanted to apologize,' Eleanor began, ignoring the prickling feeling on the back of her neck. 'I was very rude to you when we last spoke.'

The black-eyed woman gave a gracious nod. 'That's quite all right, my dear.'

'Will you tell me your name?'

She gave a smile. It was empty. 'You may call me Alice. Or, if you prefer, Emmeline.'

Eleanor flinched. Her mother's name. Mrs Pembroke's name. Hearing them from the black-eyed woman's mouth stung. The chair felt like the end of an iron bedstead, pressing into her back.

'Those aren't your names, are they?' she asked, her voice quiet.

The black-eyed woman spread her hands. 'They may as well be. I hope that, in time, you will come to think of me in the same way. I have only your best interests at heart.'

Eleanor resisted the urge to ask if the black-eyed woman *had* a heart. 'I must call you something.'

'There is no need.'

'But how am I to find you, if I want something? I don't even know where you live. You just appeared from that corner! How did you get here?'

'It's not nearly as impressive as it seems. Suffice to say that I am quite as real as you are, but that does not mean we are the same type of creature.'

'I'm not sure what you mean.'

'No, I imagine not.'

The woman's eyes were flat and still. So was her smile. Perhaps that was how she managed her disappearing trick – simply staying so still that the eye glazed over her. Mesmerists and mediums did that sort of thing. It was easier to believe that the black-eyed woman was like them than to acknowledge that she was something else entirely.

'Why did you call me?' she asked.

Staring into the woman's black eyes was like looking over the rim of a pit. Eleanor shifted and looked away. 'I thought we ought to get to know each other.'

The black-eyed woman laughed. 'My dear girl, I know you already. But if it's conversation you want, I can oblige. How are you finding your new position?'

What did she mean, *I know you already*? What was she? Eleanor adjusted the ice and wondered how best to broach the question. The woman's smile did little to soften the emptiness of her eyes. The thought of making that smile disappear made sweat prickle across the palms of Eleanor's hands. 'It hasn't quite been what I expected.'

The black-eyed woman tutted. 'It was cruel of Miss Darling to treat you so. But she is a desperate woman. I expect cruelty is her last weapon.'

Eleanor remembered Mr Darling's face. Drawn and pale, but still lit with anger at the sight of his daughter's dress.

'I fear your Charles is in for a nasty shock.'

A bead of cold water rolled down Eleanor's sleeve, like a fingernail running across her skin. 'What do you mean?'

'I'm sure Miss Darling is quite the little angel in front of Charles now, but that won't last past the honeymoon. Of course, it'll be too late for him then. She won't give him reason to let her go. Another unhappy marriage in the Pembroke family tree.'

'Another?'

'Oh, yes. There have been many, over the years.'

'Have you seen them all?'

The black-eyed woman smiled. 'I have seen many things. I will see many more.'

My dear girl, I know you already. Eleanor shivered. 'Do... do you see everything *I* do? Even when you're...elsewhere?'

'Of course. How else could I grant your wishes?'

Eleanor swallowed. Melting ice dripped through her fingers. 'When you disappear, where do you go?'

The black-eyed woman patted Eleanor's hand. 'It's a little difficult to explain. I am always with you, but I am elsewhere as well.'

'I don't understand.'

'I wouldn't expect you to, dear. Just try to think of it as moving between the gaps.'

'What gaps? How can you move between them? What... what are you?'

The black-eyed woman's face could have been carved from rock. Firelight cast strange shadows across her skin. One moment her eyes seemed as large as the sockets of a skull, the next they were sharp and small. In the flickering light, the space behind her chair was full of swooping, avian shadows.

Icy water trickled down Eleanor's wrist. Her pulse fluttered like a trapped bird and suddenly, she realized how fragile it was. It stuttered and stammered and rushed and danced, but one day it would stop, and the black-eyed woman would still be there. Eleanor's hopes and dreams meant nothing to her. Her ageless hands could change Eleanor's life, sculpting wishes out of formless dreams, but she would do so without caring. The realization moved through Eleanor like ink swirling through water, dread staining everything it touched.

The woman's smile widened.

Then, a key clicked in the lock, and she vanished. Before

Felicity opened the door, Eleanor leant forward and felt the seat of the woman's chair. It was cold, as if she had never been there.

No one had told Charles that Felicity was looking for another maid, but he could tell something was wrong. Sometimes Eleanor would catch him looking at her. He always turned away, but she caught glimpses of the crease between his brows, or the tightness in his jaw. Eleanor thought about taking him aside and telling him the truth, but soon realized that this would backfire. He could do nothing but speak to Felicity, and that would only paint a target on Eleanor's back. Still, in the quiet moments before Felicity awoke Eleanor would imagine him uncovering the truth and smile to herself. Eleanor knew he would defend her. He always had.

Once, he'd helped Eleanor down from the carriage. He'd held out his hand and she'd raised her head, put her shoulders back and, for a moment, the world seemed infinite. Felicity saw. Eleanor didn't care. Charles's fingers had been so warm, so gentle, that she hadn't wanted to let them go. He might have been leading her onto a dance floor, and for a moment Eleanor wondered what it would feel like if he took her in his arms. She'd paid for it later. Felicity had pinched her arm so hard all Eleanor's bruises had purple crescents in the middle. Eleanor would have to keep Felicity's fingernails well-trimmed.

She wondered if her replacement would be so foresighted.

Felicity conducted the interviews while Eleanor worked in the dressing room. They were nervous, eager girls – and they were girls, not women. Some of them were almost children. What had Felicity been thinking? Fourteen-year-old country girls wouldn't know which end of a lady was which. Ask them to tell the difference between real and imitation lace and they'd tell you cloth couldn't play pretend.

Now, Felicity sat discussing their faults with a frothy-looking friend. Eleanor was in the dressing room with the door propped open, addressing a stack of envelopes.

'Of course it's no use having an uneducated maid,' Felicity drawled, '*quite* the embarrassment. But too much education can be just as bad. Half the girls I've seen have traipsed mud all round my rooms, and the other half witter on about all sorts of silly things. A lady's maid should know when to be silent, don't you agree?'

The sharp rattle of cups on saucers was not enough to drown them out. Nor was the scratching of Eleanor's pen. Nor was the grinding of her teeth. Neither one of them knew what it *really* meant to be a lady. If Eleanor was in their place, she would never be so indiscreet. She would be perfect, glorious, kind, and she would look on their dirty, pinched faces and smile.

Felicity had lowered her voice. 'Oh no, dear, *quite* unsuitable. It was good of Charles, but I don't think he knows the first thing about her. Of course, I was perfectly pleasant, and I won't have it said I didn't give her a fair chance, but…well…'

Eleanor carried on stuffing her envelopes. Felicity was embellishing the story of Lizzie's death in a breathless whisper. Eleanor folded the letters neatly, addressed the envelopes, and daydreamed about smacking Felicity around the head with the tea tray.

She thought of the black-eyed woman often, and always in moments like this. What couldn't she do, if the wishes did not come at such a high price! Eleanor would make Felicity grovel and beg for forgiveness. She'd make it so that Mr Pembroke would never touch another girl again. She would make herself an avenging angel, beautiful and terrible, and she would be glorious.

But if she did, someone would have to die.

Eleanor addressed another envelope. Felicity's voice carried through the dressing-room door. 'Oh *yes*, my dear. I wouldn't be at all surprised if she'd put the poor boy up to it...'

She'd been a fool to trust the black-eyed woman, Eleanor thought. Concealing the cost of the wishes was a betrayal, locking Eleanor into a deal she wanted nothing to do with. How many more lies would she uncover? What else was the black-eyed woman keeping from her?

But, Eleanor thought, if she'd lied about the cost of the wishes, how did she know that a death was really necessary to make them come true? The black-eyed woman had lied about everything else. She could be lying about this, too.

Could there be a way to make a wish without harming anyone?

Eleanor's heart began to race. She shouldn't do it, she shouldn't even think of it. It was far too dangerous. She couldn't risk losing her soul, let alone killing someone else. But if there was a way, she had to find it. Surely there was something she could wish for that would not result in murder. There was clearly a scale to the wishes; her wonderful shoes had only cost the life of Mr Pembroke's poor canary. If she asked for something that already had a good chance of happening, it might not need a death to usher it along.

She had to know.

The sight of Granborough House caught Eleanor by the throat. She slipped on the steps of the carriage and almost lost her footing in the rain. Felicity glared at her and waited for her to put up the umbrella.

It was just as Eleanor had remembered it as a child. All the windows shone like mirrors in the rain. The black railings stood out sharp against the freshly scrubbed stone, glowing gold in the light from the streetlamps. Any moment now the door would be opened by George, the second footman, who would smile and say 'Why, Miss Eleanor! Step in out of the rain...'

Felicity coughed. Eleanor came back to her senses, put up the umbrella and escorted her to the door. Close to, the paint on the window frames was starting to flake, and Eleanor could see patches of rust on the iron railings. George had been dismissed years ago; Mrs Banbury said he owned a public house in Brixton now. He'd married Janie last year – she, at least, had managed to find happiness after Mr Pembroke had tried to snatch it from her. With a pang, Eleanor prayed that the same would be true for Leah. She looked around the sodden street, and hoped Leah had somewhere to wait out the rain.

Felicity swept into the hall, the damp hem of her dress leaving a faint tinge of green on the marble. She was like a slug, Eleanor thought, leaving poisonous trails wherever she went. She'd have to warn Aoife and Daisy – that dress was Scheele's green, dyed with arsenic. Felicity was protected by her corset, chemise and petticoats, but it had given Eleanor a headache lacing it up.

Felicity waved a careless hand in Eleanor's direction and began to climb the stairs. 'Make yourself useful, Hartley. I don't want to see you at dinner. See if there's something you can do in the scullery.'

'Yes, miss,' Eleanor said, gritting her teeth. She was a lady's maid, a position on the same level as the housekeeper. A real lady would never ask her to scrub pans.

Eleanor went into the kitchen and found Aoife struggling to put on her dress uniform and keep out of Mrs Banbury's way. Aoife's eyes filled with tears when she saw Eleanor, and fear flooded through her.

'Let me help you,' Eleanor said. 'May we use your rooms, Mrs Fielding?'

Eleanor ushered Aoife into the housekeeper's rooms before Mrs Fielding could object and shut the door behind her.

'What's happened?'

'It's getting worse,' Aoife whispered, tears running down her cheeks. 'He keeps asking me all these questions – things no decent girl should talk about! He says if I were a good girl, I ought to do as he says because he's the master, but...'

Aoife dissolved into weeping. Eleanor put her arms around her and tried to keep her hands from balling into fists. *How dare he*, she thought, seething. Aoife was a child – how could he even think of such a thing?

'When are you coming back?' Aoife sniffed, wiping her eyes. 'It wasn't so bad before you went.'

'Not until the wedding. Only a few weeks now.'

'A few weeks!' Aoife wailed.

Eleanor smoothed Aoife's hair. 'Aoife, listen to me. Have you given him the laudanum?'

'Well, he's not always in the study, so I—'

'Then you must drug the other bottles. Mrs Banbury keeps it in the kitchen cupboard; if you're quick then—'

'But that's poisoning, Ella! If anyone caught me I'd be up before the magistrate, quick as winking! Can't you do it?'

'I'd never get into the dining room without them noticing

tonight. Next time, I promise. But until then you must get yourself a knife.'

Aoife went pale. 'A knife? Ella, I can't, I can't...'

Eleanor gripped Aoife's shoulders. 'You have to do something!'

'I'm just...' Aoife's bottom lip was trembling. 'I'm just so scared! I don't want it to be like this, Ella!'

Aoife sobbed onto Eleanor's chest like a baby. Eleanor stroked her hair, blinking back tears. She couldn't let Aoife see she was upset, it would make everything worse. Why hadn't she refused to go with Felicity on the spot? How had she let things get so bad?

'It's all right,' Eleanor said. 'I'll find a way. I promise.'

A fine rain of coal smuts drifted over the city, leaving smeary black marks against hats, coats, windows and painted carts. They freckled Eleanor's face and hands until she looked like a chimney sweep. Felicity liked to see her that way. When she complained about the state of Eleanor's appearance a smile twisted the corner of her mouth. While she glided through warm shops, running her fingers over silks and satins, she made Eleanor wait outside. Like a beggar's dog. Through the window panes, Eleanor watched Felicity talking, laughing, smiling, and as she shivered on the other side of the glass hatred blossomed in her like a flower.

Regent Street was mired in carriages. Felicity was safe inside the dressmaker's shop, at the final fitting of her wedding dress. Eleanor was left in a cloud of fog while cold, greasy coal smuts pressed against her cheeks. Felicity hadn't even let Eleanor wait inside her new coach – a gleaming black brougham that would be her wedding present to Charles. She'd told Eleanor it was to preserve her modesty, in a voice that suggested she did not have any. The coachman tried to catch her eye twice before he gave up and went to buy some lunch.

Match-girls called out in reedy voices. Omnibuses trundled past, and as they went the drivers shouted the names of the stops, or swore at the traffic. Shop-boys were everywhere, wheedling one moment, yelling across the street the next. But all Eleanor could see were shapes in the fog. Voices on every side, with not a face in sight. She shuddered.

The coachman sidled back into view, clutching a cone of newspaper. He held it out to Eleanor with a hopeful grin.

'D'you want a whelk?'

Eleanor peered into the paper. The whelks stank of vinegar and were grey from newsprint. Snails, if she was any judge.

'No, thank you.'

The coachman shrugged and climbed back into his seat. Eleanor wondered if she should tell him about the snails, and then saw him shovel a handful into his mouth. She shuddered.

A clergyman all in black walked past, glancing at her underneath his wide-brimmed hat. A little later he walked past her again, jingling the money in his pockets. If he came past her a third time she was going to knock that stupid hat right off his head. And if he said anything, she'd scream. If she didn't, no one would believe she was respectable. It was bad enough already. She was loitering outside a shop all by herself, a lady's maid with no lady in sight. Certain types of men would treat that as an invitation. Perhaps she should buy an umbrella, to have something to hit them with.

'Eleanor?'

Charles had materialized out of the fog and tipped his hat to her. Immaculate and shiny, safe from all the grime and dirt around him. Eleanor couldn't hold back a smile.

'Charles! I didn't expect to see you here.'

'Nor I you. Where is Miss Darling?'

Eleanor kept her smile in place. 'She's inside. Shall I fetch her for you?'

'Good,' he said, dropping his voice. 'I need to speak with you, Eleanor. How do you get those bruises?'

Eleanor started. He might as well have stepped out of her daydreams, if she hadn't been panicking. When she had imagined this moment she'd been graceful and dignified, poised despite her pain. But now, she felt as if she'd been set adrift, grasping at any word she could reach.

'Bruises? I don't—'

'I see. You'd have no objection to rolling up your sleeve, then?'

She blushed. 'In public?'

'Of course. Of course *not*, I meant to say. Forgive me, I wasn't thinking.'

When she looked up, he was blushing too. He held out his hand. She shook it, and he saw the strip of skin between her glove and her sleeve. Mottled green bruises peeked out from underneath her cuff.

'Oh, Eleanor. Why didn't you tell me?'

She took her hand away, ashamed.

'I would have believed you. Do you think I never look at you?'

Felicity was careful when she left her bruises. She planned ahead when she slapped Eleanor and kept her out of sight until the bruises faded; visible marks would only cause her problems. She made Eleanor roll up her sleeves, or gather her hair away from the nape of the neck.

Eleanor could barely meet his eyes.

'I'll speak to Felicity,' he sighed. 'I expected better of her.'

'You can't!' hissed Eleanor. 'You mustn't say a word!'

162

Charles rubbed his jaw. He did not seem so immaculate any more.

'I'm sorry, Eleanor. I never thought she would treat you like this. I don't seem to be much use at helping you.'

'Don't be silly, Charles.'

He smiled at her, but it did not reach his eyes. 'You don't think you'd be better off without me?'

The world seemed to shift. The street was unchanged: the match-girls still called out plaintively, the shop-boys still tried to coax in customers. Only now a strange kind of urgency mounted around her. How many more seconds would slip away before Felicity opened the door? She needed them all, and yet she could only let them pass. She wanted to run, to shout, to pull Charles towards her and whisper in his ear, but noise and movement were too sharp, too close. They would smash the fragile thing she wanted so much to build.

'No. Never.'

The words were raw. The moment she said them, she regretted them, and yet she had never said anything truer.

'Thank you, Eleanor. May I ask you one more thing?'

'Of course.'

'Do you think I made the right choice?'

They both knew the answer. But why ask her at all, if he already knew the truth?

'I don't know, sir,' she said. 'Do you love her?'

'That's a very personal question, Eleanor.'

'As was yours, sir.'

He gave a sad laugh. 'I seem to recall asking you not to call me "sir".'

'You did. Once more ought to do it.'

He laughed – a real laugh, this time, and the sound warmed Eleanor from the inside out.

Behind the window, Felicity was standing at the counter. Her wedding dress was neatly folded in a box. She sent the errand boy running with a clip round the ear and smirked. Charles saw, and his expression was something Eleanor never wanted to see again.

Eleanor laid the facts before her like a craftsman setting out his tools.

Felicity was going to dismiss her. She would not let Eleanor stay in Granborough House, even as a scullery maid: she wanted Eleanor gone. But Felicity would wait until after the wedding: she knew Charles and Eleanor were close, and she would not make such a risky move until her position was secure.

Mr Pembroke was getting worse. Aoife had cried like a child – she *was* a child, Eleanor thought, her temper flaring. She'd been terrified, and lonely, and too ashamed to even repeat the things he'd asked her. Eleanor could not leave her in Granborough House for a moment longer. She had to find a way back.

And then, there was Charles. Remembering the look on Charles's face as he watched his future wife swipe at shop-boys sent a strange mixture of guilt and anger crawling across her skin. Eleanor could not stand the thought of him pouring all his warmth and gentleness into Felicity's hands when it was only going to slip through her fingers.

It was time to make another wish.

Eleanor chose her words carefully, stitching them together with the same care that she would take over a piece of fine lace. Felicity had to go; with her as mistress of Granborough House

Charles would be miserable, Eleanor would be dismissed and there would be no one to stop Mr Pembroke from putting his hands on Aoife. Charles was already having doubts; she might not need to make a wish at all. Still, she could not wait for him to come to his senses when Aoife was in so much danger.

If she was careless, someone would die. There were countless reasons why people did not marry, and death was one of them. But it was a risk worth taking. The black-eyed woman had told her that the wishes needed a death to come true, but she had proven that Eleanor could not trust her. Why should Eleanor believe that, when so many other things the black-eyed woman had said had turned out false? If she phrased her wish so that Charles and Felicity would choose not to marry, no one might get hurt at all – or perhaps, if she was lucky enough, it would be only an animal…It was a gamble, but one she had to take.

Eleanor waited until Felicity was at another dinner, pacing beside the dark windows and watching the lights of the hansom judder out of sight. Then she locked the door and spoke into the empty hotel room.

'I wish that Charles Pembroke would choose not to wed Felicity Darling.'

Flames hung rigid in the fireplace. Raindrops froze on the window pane. For a moment Eleanor was lost in the stillness, her thoughts trickling through treacle. Then, crackling energy swept down her arms in a whole-body shiver.

She'd done it. She'd made the wish.

Felicity came home a few hours later, when Eleanor's head was drooping over her mending. The door slammed open and she jerked awake.

'Miss?'

Felicity's face was contorted with anger. 'What have you been saying to him?'

'Excuse me, miss, I'm not sure what you—'

'Deceitful little witch! You know full well what I mean. Charles was good enough to tell me he thinks I've been treating you unfairly! What have you been saying to him?'

Eleanor held out the half-finished handkerchief like a white flag. 'I've said nothing you've not heard, miss.'

'Liar,' Felicity spat. 'Your connection to the Bartram girl was bad enough, but this...'

Felicity's hands were clenching and unclenching. Her jaw was set. She ground her teeth, and a vein in her neck twitched. But she stood like a woman confined by a straitjacket, and Eleanor knew Felicity would not hit her.

Curious, she pushed a little further. 'I hope I have not caused any problems between you and Mr Pembroke, miss.'

Felicity's face twisted.

'Out. Out!'

She threw a pair of opera glasses at Eleanor's head. Eleanor ducked; they smashed against the wall. She darted into the dressing room, closed the door and rammed a chair underneath the handle. Felicity thrashed against it, kicking and yelling like a child, and it was only after she had screamed herself hoarse that Eleanor heard her crying.

She kept the door closed.

'Did it work?' she whispered, staring into the corners of the room.

There was no reply.

* * *

Autumn sunlight gilded Rotten Row. A haze of orange leaves shone overhead, glowing like the embers of a fire. Society filed past. Dukes and earls preened on horseback, riding boots glistening. Barouches trundled along sedately, filled with laughing women and attentive men. Ostrich feathers rustled; ribbons snapped in the breeze. It was like a field of pennants, Eleanor thought, the kind she'd read about at medieval tournaments. For a moment she imagined herself as a princess in a box, preparing to watch knights jousting in her honour. There were even spectators leaning on the iron railings that ran on either side of the track. They were here to see, not to be seen, but Eleanor watched them all the same.

Staring out of the window was much better than listening to the silence in the coach.

Felicity sat with her notebook unopened in her lap, glowering out of one window. Charles stared out of the other, sitting like a man on trial. They could have been strangers. Eleanor would have given anything to bury herself in a book, even if it was just something to hide behind.

She went back to watching the crowd. There were sailors on leave, guardsmen in scarlet jackets, nursemaids bouncing perambulators by their hips. They passed a young family: the father had a beard like W. G. Grace, the mother had a green feather in her hat and their pudgy little son was chasing after a hoop. He flailed after it with his stick, occasionally barrelling into the knees of passers-by, but no one seemed to mind. It was hard to be angry with a boy barely out of skirts.

The boy took a wild swipe at the hoop and it disappeared into the crowd. Eleanor smiled. She edged closer to the window and looked back. It was nice to see a child at play, instead of hanging around the costermongers' barrows, begging for scraps.

The hoop rolled through the iron railings and into the path of a carriage. The boy's mother looked around.

'Samuel?'

The little boy charged after the hoop.

'Sammy!'

The horse reared. The boy turned. His parents vaulted over the railings. Eleanor banged on the roof of the carriage.

'Stop!' she yelled. 'There's a—'

The horse's legs came crashing down. The family crumpled.

Then, there was nothing but screaming.

Eleanor leant out of the window and called up to the driver. 'There's been an accident behind us! We have to—'

Hooves. Screaming. A crunching sound she didn't want to think about. Eleanor turned, and saw the horse tearing towards them, dragging the carriage along with it. It crashed into a barouche, knocking it sideways. Riders tugged their horses out of its path.

Eleanor ducked back inside as the coachman tugged on the reins, swearing. Their horses snorted, stamping their feet, and the whole carriage lurched.

'Good Lord,' said Charles, reaching for her, 'are you—'

Something hit them. The carriage jerked forward. Felicity shrieked. The coachman swore, something cracked, and they all tilted sideways.

Unbalanced, Eleanor fell.

She staggered into the door. It burst open. She caught a glimpse of Felicity's wide eyes and Charles's reaching hand before she slammed into the dirt.

Screaming. So much screaming. And a rumbling worse than thunder that shook the ground and made her teeth rattle. The horses. She looked up and saw hooves, fetlocks and enormous wheels, flecked and splashed with blood. She threw herself out of the way, tumbling over dirt and gravel until she smacked into the iron railings.

She held tight to one of the railings and stared up at the sky, her head ringing.

'Miss! Miss, are you hurt?'

'You, boy! Fetch a doctor!'

Two sharp cracks rang out and Eleanor felt something slam against the ground. Someone held out a hand; she took it, and was hauled upright. Knees shaking, she slumped against the railing and stared out at the chaos.

Splintered wood. Shattered brass spokes. Blood splashed across the ground. Something was screaming, but she could not tell if it was a horse or human over the ringing in her ears. The horse that had bolted lay dead, bleeding from a shot to the eye. Riders had been thrown from their saddles, their feathered hats rolling in the dust. Horses stomped and shrieked, mouths flecked with foam. Carriages tangled together, lying on their side with dark shapes underneath the wheels. Eleanor was not the only one to have been thrown from a carriage. A young woman in green lay sprawled, her head at an unnatural angle. She wasn't moving.

Eleanor could not see the little boy.

Someone on horseback was yelling orders. The horses were led away, snapping at coachmen and straining at their bridles. A handful of guardsmen climbed over the railings to help. A horse kicked out at one of them and he fell back, blood twisting through the air.

169

Something warm trickled down her face. A nursemaid in the crowd saw it and gasped.

'She's bleeding! Miss, miss, you're bleeding!'

A man with dust in his whiskers took Eleanor by the shoulders. 'Miss? Can you hear me?'

'Where's the little boy?'

He frowned. 'A boy? Miss, please, you've hit your head—'

Eleanor shook him off. 'The child! The one that startled the horse! Where is he?'

The man's face paled. 'A child?'

A lump swelled in her throat. 'I...I saw him go under the carriage.'

The stranger ran towards the wreckage. The crowd poured after him. Flower-sellers let their trays swing around their necks as they went to the wounded. Soldiers and sailors strained to lift the shattered coach. Eleanor slumped against the barrier, retching at the smell of blood.

Gravel sprayed across her legs as someone skidded to a halt beside her.

'Eleanor? Eleanor, are you hurt? Did you – dear God...'

Charles was standing beside her. He was pale, his hair was mussed, and fear was scrawled across his face.

He scrabbled in his pocket for a handkerchief. 'Here. Does it hurt? Is it deep?'

She shook her head. He pressed the handkerchief against her cheek. She closed her eyes and leant into the warm weight of his hand.

'I'm sending you home,' he said. 'I want your word that you'll go straight to Mrs Banbury; she'll care for you. Tell Mrs Fielding I want Dr Macready sent for if...well. It won't come to that. But she's to send for him if it does. Do you understand?'

'What about Felicity?'

'Hang Felicity!' he snapped. 'Come along. Can you stand?'

There was a scream from the wreck of the carriage. It was thin and high, and she knew it belonged to a child. She lurched forward but Charles held her steady.

'What the Devil are you thinking? You're in no condition to—'

'The little boy! He's alive – oh *God*, Charles, he's still alive! I have to—'

He blocked her path. 'No,' he said. '*You* are bleeding from the head, Eleanor, and I insist you go home and get that cut seen to. I'll find the child. Go home. Please.'

Fear flickered in his eyes. Some part of her wanted to keep on arguing, if only to keep him with her, but she said nothing. Charles rolled up his sleeves like a workman and joined those trying to lift the wreckage. Eleanor waited until her head stopped spinning and followed him.

A woman staggered across her path, eyes unfocused. Eleanor put an arm around her shoulders and led her over to the railings, helping her to lean against them before she went back. An apprentice who'd been trying to calm a horse lurched backwards; it had kicked him in the arm and something had snapped. As his friends caught hold of the bridle and held it steady, Eleanor ripped the sleeve off his jacket and bound his arm in place. A girl of eight years old was wandering around, chewing on a finger as she looked tearfully for her mother. Eleanor found her and had her hand wrung by every member of the little girl's grateful, terrified family.

When they finally let her fingers go she turned back to look for Felicity's carriage. It was gone.

* * *

171

Eleanor hunched over the kitchen table at Granborough House, holding a damp cloth to her head. One side of her body throbbed and there were scrapes across the backs of her hands. Each twinge was a bright and bitter reminder: she was alive, and others were not.

Water dripped down her cuff. Dust coated her legs. Her dress crackled when she shifted, and shed red-brown flakes of blood. It wasn't hers. That was what she had to remember. Forget the screaming, forget the bodies, forget the smell of blood and sweat and God knew what else. Focus on the water in her sleeve, the rough wood under her elbows, and remember walking away.

The drawing-room bell rang, again. Eleanor got to her feet as Aoife put a cup of tea in front of her.

'Bloody hell,' said Daisy. 'Does she ever pack it in?'

Mrs Fielding gave her a stern look. 'You are speaking about the future mistress of this household, Daisy.'

'More's the pity,' Daisy muttered. Mrs Fielding opened her mouth to deliver a lecture on propriety and Eleanor left before she could get started.

Felicity was waiting in the drawing room. It was dark outside, but all the curtains were still wide open.

'Where've you been?' she snapped. 'I've been ringing for five minutes! Where's Charles? Have you had word?'

'No, miss.'

Felicity turned back to the window and watched the rain run down the glass. The dim outline of a lamplighter moved through a yellow haze. The streetlights flickered into life in his wake, fluttering in the cold like moths.

'Well?' said Felicity. 'Don't loiter; go and do something useful. And make yourself presentable. You're filthy.'

'I can't change, miss. All my things are at the Langham.'

172

Felicity snorted. 'Haven't you a uniform? Put it on. I can't stand the stench of you. Horses, dirt, and—'

'And blood,' Eleanor finished, temper flaring. 'Of course, miss. I should have considered your comfort. It's quite clear that you didn't care for the smell, because you did not come down from your carriage and help anyone.'

'How dare—'

'I doubt Master Charles cared for the smell either,' Eleanor went on, 'but he went to help the wounded just the same. Does he know you waited in your carriage, while all those people were bleeding?'

Felicity had gone pale. 'Don't be stupid,' she whispered. 'What good could I have done?'

'I don't know, miss. Nor does anyone, because you didn't do it.'

'Why, you little—'

Eleanor held up a hand. 'Call me what names you choose, miss. It shan't change what you did.'

Felicity's mask fell away. For the first time Eleanor saw her for what she really was: a lone woman bobbing in the water, snatching at anything that might keep her from drowning. Eleanor tried to feel sorry for her, and felt nothing.

A carriage pulled up to the front door. Moments later, Charles came into the drawing room. Exhausted, filthy, and pale, he could have passed for a man ten years his senior. He collapsed into the nearest chair with a groan. Felicity sprang up, panic flashing across her face.

'Charles, darling! Are you all right? Hartley, fetch him something to eat. And brandy. Be quick about it!'

He shook his head. 'No need to trouble yourselves. I couldn't eat a thing.'

He tried to smile. It came out more like a grimace. Felicity knelt beside him and took his hand.

'Really, dearest, you must at least try to...'

'No, I couldn't. I've...I've come from the hospital. They were quite overwhelmed when we arrived. Typhus, along with everything else.'

Felicity took her hand away. Charles didn't seem to notice.

'We were too late for most of them.'

'Sir,' said Eleanor, 'what happened to the little boy?'

Charles gave her a sad smile. 'He survived, but they had to amputate his leg. It couldn't be saved.'

Eleanor remembered the screaming – the hollow, *awful* screaming – and wanted to scrub it from her thoughts. The boy had been three years old. Three years old, and he'd lost his leg.

Charles turned to Felicity. 'I'm afraid his parents weren't so lucky. I've offered him a home with us, when he's recovered. I'm not sure how long that may take.'

Felicity straightened up.

'Excuse me?'

'Both his parents were killed, and he has no relatives who could afford to take him in—'

'You promised that urchin a *home*? Charles, you don't know the boy!'

'What other choice did I have?'

'He has relatives of his own, does he not? He can stay with them!'

'His relatives,' said Charles, sitting up straight and glaring at Felicity, 'are nine living in one room! They have seven children, all of them working, and they still cannot afford to

174

pay their rent, let alone for the medical care the child will need—'

'Oh, Charles, you're being ridiculous. They'll know how to make ends meet!'

'The child will starve!'

'Don't be silly! There's always the workhouse—'

'The workhouse? How can you even suggest that?'

'How can *you* make such an offer to a stranger? You know *nothing* about the boy! Who are his people? Has he been brought up in a decent Christian household? My God, Charles, he could be a savage for all you know!'

'He is a child. He has no one, no means of income, nothing! Without someone to take him in he shall be reduced to begging! I can give him a better life, Felicity!'

Felicity spun around and glared at Eleanor.

'Hartley, leave us!'

'Yes, miss,' Eleanor muttered, and ran from the room.

The front door slammed three times that night.

The first was not long after Eleanor had rushed back to the warmth of the kitchen. When Charles and Felicity took their argument into the hall, she could hear the shouting at the foot of the servants' staircase. Daisy climbed it, so she could listen better.

The second was almost two hours later. Eleanor sat at the kitchen table, worrying at the cuffs of her dress. It was past ten o'clock, and Felicity had not sent for her. Daisy and Aoife were rolling out their straw pallets and Mrs Banbury had already changed into her nightgown. Even Mrs Fielding had unpinned her hair. Eleanor was shocked to see how much grey there was in it.

'Do you think I ought to go back to the hotel?' Eleanor asked, plucking at her sleeve. 'Miss Darling might not manage without me.'

'If she wanted you, she would have sent for you,' Mrs Fielding said. 'Best if you stay here. You ought not to be out at this hour.'

Mrs Banbury patted her hand. 'She can unlace her own corsets tonight, Ella. You stop along with us.'

'May I remind you, Mary, that any talk about the corsets of the future mistress of this house is most—'

'Oh, give over, Bertha,' said Mrs Banbury, yawning. 'You can rap my knuckles in the morning.'

The door slammed. When they went up to look, Eleanor saw her suitcase dripping quietly on the marble floor. Mrs Fielding laid a hand on her shoulder.

'It's for the best, I'm sure,' she murmured.

And that was that. No more lady's maid. The only things Eleanor would miss would be the wages and the hotel dinners. At least now she could keep an eye on Aoife.

The third time the front door slammed was much later. Clean and dry, Eleanor lay in her bed and listened to the yelling coming from Mr Pembroke's study. When the door slammed this time, she had no idea if it had been Charles or his father who'd stormed into the rain.

The moment the house was quiet, Eleanor went down to the library. Every time she closed her eyes she saw the blood splashed across the dirt. She had to have something to chase out the screaming in her head.

She crept along the corridor on silent feet. A fairy tale was what she needed, something Mrs Pembroke might have read to her. She ached all over and her legs wouldn't stop shaking. Tonight, she would not sleep unless she believed that ugliness could be transformed into beauty with a magic word and that the good and kind would be rewarded. If her head was full of castles in the snow and under the sea, there would be no room for anything else.

Something cold knocked against her foot. Eleanor clapped a hand over her mouth to keep herself from shrieking. It bounced and rolled along the corridor and Eleanor chased after it. If Mrs Fielding heard the noise – or worse, Mr Pembroke...

She snatched it up and darted into the library to examine it properly.

It was a ring. Felicity's ring.

Eleanor stumbled backwards. The ring dropped to the floor and rolled away. Eleanor's candle fell too; it sputtered out on the way down and snapped in half when it hit the floor. Eleanor barely registered it. All she saw was the sudden darkness and the library walls pressing in on her.

Her wish had been granted, and it had taken the accident to make it come true.

All those people were dead because of her...

Eleanor's knees gave way. The moment of falling seemed to stretch, as though she were standing on the scaffold and the hangman had opened the trapdoor. When she hit the floor, she barely felt it.

All those people...

A strange noise was building in her chest. Half-whimper, half-wail, it sounded as if it could've come from a kicked dog. Eleanor pressed both hands over her mouth, desperate to keep it from escaping. She could feel her fingers shaking as she pressed them into her skin.

She hadn't just killed people. She'd mutilated them. The bones broken as passengers had been thrown from carriages, the limbs crushed under horses' hooves – *she* had done that. She had torn carriage wheels off their axles, sent drivers flying from their seats as they tried to hold back the horses, snapped the passengers' necks as they slammed into the dirt. She had done it with a word. It was all her fault.

All her fault. The woman had been telling the truth. All wishes came with a death. *Oh God,* Eleanor thought, why had she even tried? How could she have been so stupid?

The whimpering wail was still lodged in her throat. Eleanor pushed her hands down harder, desperate to keep her grief and horror from spilling out. Tears were pouring down her face. All the warmth and hope seemed to have bled out of her, her thoughts jumbled together in a desperate litany: *I'm sorry I'm sorry I didn't mean it I Oh God I didn't I don't want—*

'Ella?'

Someone was crouching in front of her; no, two people. They tried to help her up but she couldn't take her hands away from her mouth, she couldn't, because then they would hear and then they would know what she had done and then, God, what was she going to do...

'It's all right, Ella, it's all right. Up you get.'

Two pairs of hands grasped her elbows and hauled her upright. They guided her down the servants' staircase, and it was only when she had been put down on a straw pallet in the kitchen that she registered who they belonged to. Daisy and Aoife were crouched in front of her, looking very worried.

'Stove's still hot,' Daisy whispered, 'I can get some tea out of it.'

She got up and went to the range. Gently, Aoife lifted Eleanor's hands away from her face. The sudden absence of pressure made her skin throb.

'Jesus, but your hands are cold,' Aoife murmured.

Eleanor laid her head on Aoife's shoulder and sobbed.

Part Four

There would be no more wishes.

Eleanor had spent the night on the kitchen floor, perched on the edge of Aoife's straw mattress. By the time a cold, grey dawn slid its fingers through the greasy window pane, Eleanor had made up her mind. There was no way to cheat the black-eyed woman. Eleanor no longer wanted to try. She was not going to be the cause of any more bloodshed.

She would find her own way out of Granborough House.

Eleanor considered her choices as she got dressed. There was always marriage, but that would be hard to escape if it went wrong. She could set up a business – she could read and write people's letters for them, and she was a fair seamstress. But she'd need money for that, and she still hadn't been paid. Besides, she couldn't take Aoife or Daisy with her, and she wasn't going to leave either of them alone in Granborough House. She still felt a wrench at the thought of never being a real lady – Mrs Pembroke wouldn't have wanted her to give up – but it was better than never getting out at all.

Eleanor coaxed the range back into life and decided on a plan. She'd forge references for herself, Aoife and Daisy. It would be risky. She couldn't use the cheap paper Mrs Fielding kept in her rooms, grey and soft before it was even touched. She'd need the paper and envelopes from Mr Pembroke's study, and his India ink. She had no idea what to put in a letter of reference and she'd never seen Mr Pembroke's signature, but she had to try.

Aoife got up, hooking on her stays and tugging her uniform over her chemise as quietly as she could. She picked her way past Daisy, still sleeping, and laid a hand on Eleanor's shoulder.

'Are you well now, Ella?' she asked.

Aoife still looked pale and worried. Eleanor felt a rush of affection for her; even after everything Mr Pembroke had put her through Aoife still spared a thought for her.

Eleanor gave her a hug. 'Thank you, Aoife. I'm sorry about last night.'

It had cost her so much to get back to Granborough House so she could keep Aoife safe. Eleanor would be damned if she was going to leave her here to rot.

'Can you see anyone?'

'I don't think so.'

'Aoife, you have to be sure—'

'She said she didn't see anyone! What more do you want, Miss Eleanor?'

Eleanor pulled out three sheets of paper with shaking hands. She filled up the inkwell, gripping the bottle tightly. Aoife stood in the doorway, staring into the corridor. Daisy stood beside her, one hand resting on the small of Aoife's back.

'It was *this* afternoon he said he'd be out, wasn't it?' Aoife asked.

Eleanor's head snapped up. 'What? You said you were sure!'

'Pack that in,' Daisy hissed. 'I saw him go. Now would you get on and write those bloody letters.'

Eleanor bent over the desk and tried not to think about all the painted faces watching her. It was a bad idea. It was *illegal*. Anyone who'd seen Mr Pembroke's handwriting would know that he hadn't written these letters; her own hand was nothing like his.

Eleanor took a deep breath. It wouldn't matter that her handwriting didn't look like Mr Pembroke's, she told herself. If they applied to somewhere out of the neighbourhood, no one would know what Mr Pembroke's handwriting looked like. No one ever needed to find out that she'd been the one to write the references.

To whom it may concern, she wrote, *I write to recommend Miss Aoife Flaherty in her services as a housemaid...*

Eleanor hesitated. 'You're sure that no one's—'

'Yes!' snapped Daisy. 'Now will you get on with it!'

Eleanor had never even seen a letter of reference before. Doubt curled at the edges of her thoughts. What if the person reading it could tell? What if there was some secret phrase that she'd left out? Worse – what if the letters got back to Mr Pembroke?

Eleanor blotted the letters as quickly as she could, desperate to get them into envelopes and out of sight. She sealed them, put the desk back in order and handed one each to Aoife and Daisy.

'Here,' she whispered, 'I did the best I could. Don't go for anywhere nearby. My handwriting is nothing like Mr Pembroke's, so anyone who knows him will be able to tell.'

Daisy shoved hers inside her bodice immediately. Aoife looked doubtful. 'Isn't it dangerous?'

'Yes,' said Daisy, chucking Aoife under the chin, 'so be careful with it.'

Charles did not return for two days. Eleanor tried her best not to notice, but Granborough House seemed different without him. Every footstep sounded unbearably small in the silence, and the cobwebs clustered around the high ceilings like clouds heavy with rain. Eleanor chewed her bottom lip. Did he miss Felicity that much?

'He's gone after her,' said Aoife, as she fished out a clean rag. 'You mark my words. He'll have flowers, and chocolates, and a gypsy fiddler…'

Daisy smiled as she scrubbed out a pan. 'What kind of flowers?'

'*Sciolla earraigh*,' Aoife sighed. 'I've not seen them here. Blue as Irish eyes.'

'I'll find you some,' said Daisy, flicking suds across the floor. 'But he's not gone after her. Out drowning his sorrows if you ask me. He'll be back right enough, and stinking of gin—'

'Daisy!' Mrs Fielding snapped.

When Eleanor went up to clean Charles's surprisingly neat room, every souvenir carefully put in its place, she found an empty envelope addressed in Felicity's hand. There was no sign of the letter inside. She tucked it away where the other maids could not find it, guilt rolling over her in waves.

She only found out he had reappeared when she was up to her elbows in a bucket of soda and water, cleaning the cutlery, and Mrs Fielding laid a hand on her arm. 'Ella? You're wanted in the library.'

Eleanor dried off her stinging hands and went upstairs, as a convict ascends the scaffold. Had Mr Pembroke heard from

Felicity? Had she told him her suspicions about Eleanor? What would he do if she had? Eleanor remembered Leah again. *Don't let him touch you.* Her stomach twisted. Where *was* Leah?

But when she opened the library door, Charles was waiting for her.

He looked terrible. There was a thin layer of stubble across his face, shadows smudged under his eyes, and his hand was swathed in bandages.

'Your hand!'

'It's nothing to worry about,' he said, waving her towards a chair, 'it's entirely my own fault. I'm afraid I made a fool of myself, and must suffer the consequences.'

Eleanor sat down. 'What happened?'

'I can't remember,' he confessed. 'I bumped into some of the old Oxford fellows, and when they heard what happened they took it upon themselves to lift my spirits. I gather it involved rather too much brandy, no one's quite sure of the details. I'm afraid that this has left me somewhat incapacitated, and there's a lot of correspondence, now that...now that the wedding has been called off. It'll be dull work, and I'm afraid it will keep you from your other duties, but if you would assist me I'd be most grateful.'

Eleanor tried not to feel too pleased that she wouldn't be scrubbing floors all day. 'On one condition.'

'Name it.'

'You must tell me what you taught me to say in French when you were—'

Charles went scarlet. 'No. Absolutely not!'

Eleanor laughed. 'Oh, come now. Was it really that bad?'

'I was fifteen! I thought it would be amusing...'

187

'Then you're a scoundrel, Charles Pembroke.'

The corners of his mouth twitched. 'That sounds rather charming, coming from you.'

'Messrs Ashdown and Rowe, I am writing to request the cancellation of the Pembroke account with your establishment. Any purchases made after the fourth of October should be charged to Miss Felicity Darling at the following address...'

Charles was standing with his back to the fire, his hands clasped. As he recited Felicity's address the lines around his mouth tightened. Guilt pricked at Eleanor's thoughts. Had those lines been there before she'd wished away his engagement?

Eleanor finished the letter as neatly as she could and Charles sank into an armchair, one foot tapping restlessly against the floor.

'Are you quite all right?'

He tried to smile at her. 'I'm a little apprehensive this afternoon.' He rang the bell for tea and started fiddling with the button on his shirt cuff. 'I have to write to Felicity.'

Eleanor remembered the empty envelope she'd found in his room, almost a week ago. How many letters had he received since then? She imagined Felicity's parents coming to collect her from the Langham. What would they say when they saw her jewels, her silk and satin dresses, the gilt-framed mirrors on the walls? Eleanor's guilt spread like a blush. She would have written to Charles too, if she'd been in Felicity's place.

'It appears she's prepared to forgive me,' said Charles, standing up and gripping the back of his chair. 'She said the wedding could proceed as planned, on the condition that I send the boy to the workhouse.'

Would he do it? Had he seen the workhouse children, with their shorn heads and thin faces? Eleanor had. When she misbehaved, Mrs Fielding had taken her to the St George's Union and made Eleanor look at it. She'd point at the long, thin windows and hiss in Eleanor's ear: 'Keep on like that and the mistress will send you to the poorhouse. That's where you belong.'

Eleanor smoothed out her skirts. In front of Charles, it felt more like caressing her thighs. She clasped her hands, quickly. 'What will you say to Felicity?'

He sighed, still for a moment. 'I cannot marry her.'

It was what Eleanor had wished for. But she imagined how Felicity would feel when she received that letter, written in Eleanor's own handwriting, and something curled up inside her. Perhaps she'd been too hasty.

'A lady in her position would know little of these things. Perhaps if she understood what she was suggesting, she might be more forgiving.'

He smiled at her. 'You're so reluctant to speak ill of anyone, Eleanor. It's very gracious of you.'

'Thank you.'

'I must say, I wish you'd been less gracious about Felicity.'

'I'm sorry, I—'

'No, don't apologize. I barely knew her.'

'Would you be terribly upset if I asked how you met?'

He laughed, and sat back down. 'Of course not! You needn't worry about that!'

Mrs Fielding came in with a tea tray set for one. Eleanor poured him a cup, but when Mrs Fielding had left he passed it back.

'It was at a ball, in Paris,' he began, 'in the spring. Paris is

189

lovely in the spring, did you know that? Just to be there seemed like a gift; everywhere I looked I found something beautiful. But it isn't at all like London. It's charming, but it doesn't have the...the substance London has. Sometimes it felt like the whole city could blow away in the wind. It's difficult to explain...do you know what I mean?'

Eleanor shook her head. 'I've never been to Paris.'

Charles sprang up and went to the bookshelves, grabbing an illustrated account of travels through France with one hand. He sat next to Eleanor and opened the book, ignoring all the words she'd savoured and flipping straight to a drawing of Notre Dame.

He pointed, grinning at her. 'I stood in this exact spot,' he said. 'If you go down this street,' he indicated a narrow road, 'there's a restaurant that does the most marvellous *coq au vin*. Napoleon himself used to eat there, the proprietor told me. You *must* go, Eleanor. You'd have them all eating out of your hand in days.'

Eleanor smiled. 'Not the *coq au vin*, I hope. Isn't that a stew? I'd ruin my dress.'

'It'd be worth it, I assure you. And of course you must go to Versailles,' he said, flipping through the book until he found the picture. 'But only in spring. The smell of the gardens is wonderful...'

Despite her curiosity, Eleanor looked away. 'I suppose that is where you met Felicity?'

Charles blushed. 'Oh. Yes.' His leg started jittering again. 'Well, I was at a dance given by the Prussian ambassador, and I hadn't spoken to an Englishman in weeks. The French were perfectly friendly, but sometimes there seemed such a gulf between us that I felt quite stranded. That was where I met her.'

A sad smile crept across Charles's face. It tugged at her.

'She was the first Englishwoman I'd met in Paris,' he said, a faraway look in his eyes, 'and we spent half the night talking of home. She seemed so familiar that I thought I knew her far better than I did. Father had spoken about marriage before I left for the Continent, and after a certain amount of time these things become expected. Her family were considering taking her home and she grew quite frantic, so I proposed. It seemed like the gentlemanly thing to do. But I never knew anything of her real thoughts or opinions until we returned to England. Of course, Father didn't object; he was pleased I'd found an heiress...'

He trailed off. Eleanor set down the teacup and tried not to think about the morning room, mouldering under dust sheets; the coach house, its windows all smashed; the laundry room, deserted these past two years.

'You must forgive me, Eleanor,' he said. 'Once I saw how she treated you, I knew I could not marry her. She...she was not the person I hoped she might be.'

'There's nothing to forgive.'

'There is.' He took her hand. A muscle in his jaw twitched when he tried to move his bandaged fingers. Eleanor kept them still. She would hold his hand for hours if it meant she could keep the pain at bay.

'Eleanor, I cannot bear to disappoint you. My father failed to take care of you; Felicity failed to treat you kindly. But it was my choices that put you in their care, and the burden of your unhappiness is more than I can take. You deserve every joy in the world, and it shames me to think that I might have kept them from you. Say you'll forgive me, please.'

She stared into his eyes. They were bluer than the ocean, and just as full of promise.

'Of course I forgive you.'

'Thank you.'

Eleanor and Aoife spent the next few days preparing the old nursery. It had been shut up for years, and every time they lifted off another dust sheet they would descend into a fit of coughing and sneezing. They washed the floor, shook out the mattress, swept the spiders from every corner, and found a little rag rug to sit beside the bed.

But it was all for nothing, because the little boy died.

Charles broke the news as they finished. He stood in the doorway of the nursery, clutching a letter, his throat working frantically.

'If you'd like a moment to compose yourselves, I understand,' he said. 'I'm sure this has come as a shock.'

Aoife fled, running for the servants' staircase. Eleanor swayed against the bedpost and a fragment of an old memory resurfaced. She was sitting on the floor at the foot of her mother's bed, curled into a ball, her hands over her ears, wishing that the noise would stop...

'Good Lord,' Charles said, darting into the room, 'you've gone quite white.' He took her by the elbow and led her into the top-floor corridor. Eleanor leant against the door to the servants' bedrooms, her heart beating very fast.

'Take the rest of the afternoon off, Eleanor,' he said. 'I'll speak to Mrs Fielding. You shouldn't be working like this – none of you should. Father and I can fend for ourselves for an evening.'

Eleanor shook her head. She was tempted, but she could

not bear the thought of lying around and dwelling on what she'd done. 'I'll be all right, Charles.'

He fetched a chair from the nursery – one-handed, she noticed – and helped her into it. 'I shall be the judge of that, thank you.'

She gave him a weak smile. 'Perhaps you could do my scrubbing for me, then.'

She'd meant it as a joke, but he looked thoughtful. 'Perhaps I ought to ask Mrs Fielding if she has anything for me to do. Moving furniture, and so on. My bedroom window sticks, I could try and fix it.'

Eleanor stared at him. 'Do you know how?'

'Well, no,' said Charles, rubbing the back of his neck, 'but I'm sure I could learn. I feel awful lolling about all day while you're working so hard. I must have a purpose.'

She hesitated. 'If you don't mind me asking, Charles, what do you do all day?'

He went scarlet. 'There's the rub,' he mumbled. 'I keep asking Father, but he says if I want to help I should find myself another rich fiancée. He won't let me *do* anything.'

'You could always review the finances,' Eleanor suggested.

He looked away. 'I've never been much good with the account books. Not like Mother was. I can do it in my head, but when they're on paper the numbers jumble themselves up. It gives me a frightful headache. Father's sold off the last of our properties, so I can't go and visit those. And there's no point planning another trip, because Father wants to keep me here until—'

He fell silent. Eleanor knew what he was going to say: *until I find another wife*. The thought itched. To take her mind off it she asked, 'Do you really want to go away again?'

'Yes,' he said. He glanced at her, lightning-quick. 'And no.'

Eleanor could feel herself blushing. 'Well,' she said, 'I'm glad you're back, at least. It's been—' She broke off, wondering how much he knew about his father's behaviour. 'And you know, Charles, I can certainly find something for you to do. You can carry my coal scuttle for me, and move all the furniture so I can dust underneath it.'

He smiled. 'Then I am yours to command.'

Eleanor thought she could hear a music hall. She sat up in bed and listened. It was as close as she would ever get, if she wanted to stay respectable. All sorts of things went on in music halls. A few years ago, the cancan girls at one of the big halls had made such a spectacle of themselves that the whole theatre had been banned from having dancers. Had it been the Alhambra, or the Gaiety? She couldn't remember.

What she could remember was Leah, coming home flushed and giddy after she'd sneaked out one night. It was the happiest Eleanor had ever seen her. Leah had still been laughing as she took off her old bonnet and shook out her hair. It had taken weeks for her to stop humming 'Champagne Charlie'. Eleanor had remembered Mrs Pembroke then – always calm and serene – and wondered if ladies ever laughed so loud. Now, she could only think of Leah. Where *was* she?

Eleanor listened. She couldn't hear much. Distant rumbling could have been applause, or it could have been a cab. A cloud, stained orange by the streetlamps, drifted across the sky. Stars winked as it passed.

There could not have been a more perfect night for theft.

Eleanor crept down the servants' staircase and along the first-floor landing. She stood in the doorway and listened for any noises from the floors above. The silence made her hesitate. Was Mr Pembroke asleep, or sitting in his study, waiting for a footstep on the floor below?

She slipped into the morning room and closed the door behind her. The white dust sheets loomed out of the darkness like ghosts. Wincing at every creaking floorboard, Eleanor tiptoed over to the writing desk. There, she found what she was looking for: Mrs Pembroke's address book.

Eleanor's heart wrenched at the sight of the familiar flowing handwriting. The ink was still as black and sharp as if Mrs Pembroke had just laid down her pen. At the beginning of the book, in a slightly more careful hand, was her own mother's address, next to a note that read *Alice Hartley, née Waters*. It was the house her mother had died in. Eleanor clutched the little red book to her chest, feeling suddenly small.

Once she started going through the desk, she couldn't stop. She pored over old bills, the menus that Mrs Banbury still used, letters still in their envelopes. Eleanor found Charles's old school reports – he had tried hard but did not get far – a few references, a handful of love letters from Mr Pembroke which she shoved away at once, and, near the back, a letter about her. Her own name stood out sharp on the paper and she unfolded it at once.

Dear Mrs Pembroke, the letter ran, *following my examination of Miss Eleanor Hartley I am pleased to report that she shows no signs of consumption. However I judge it unlikely that the child will ever speak again. It is possible that her parents' deaths, in particular that of her mother, have addled her wits. Should you decide to offer her a permanent home I would recommend engaging the services of a nurse...*

Eleanor stared at the letter. It had been written by Dr

Macready, the Pembrokes' family physician. She couldn't remember not being able to speak. Eleanor felt a stab of indignation. *Addled her wits?* The man was clearly a quack.

She shoved the papers back into their drawer and went upstairs, picking her way around the squeaky floorboards. Some of the people in Mrs Pembroke's address book must remember her. If Eleanor wrote to them, they might help. She could remember some of Mrs Pembroke's friends – a few severe spinsters, a friendly Irish couple, a handful of distracted-looking mothers – and they'd all been kind. Surely they would help.

She tucked the address book underneath her mattress, the beginnings of a plan taking shape. 'Addled her wits,' she muttered, as she got into bed.

Granborough House had soaked up the rain like a sponge. It trickled through the floors of the maids' rooms and pooled in the ceilings below, blotching the walls like measles. The smell of damp crawled through the house, and Eleanor fretted about the library.

Mrs Fielding begged the money for repairs from Mr Pembroke, but until the workmen arrived the maids had to pin up sacking over the leaks in the attic rooms and hope that they would hold. It was unpleasant work. A chill rose off the damp walls and floor, the hem of Eleanor's skirts trailed through the puddles, and every so often a corner of wet sacking would drop, slapping her in the face or dragging itself wetly over Aoife's shoulder.

'I hate this,' Aoife grumbled.

'Well, think of something else,' Eleanor snapped, as water dripped onto her hair. 'Tell me a story. It'll take your mind off it.'

Aoife sulked for a moment, and then began telling a story about a dog whose master had been lost at sea. She had got to the part where the news of the shipwreck was about to be delivered when there was a knock at the door. Eleanor shrieked and dropped the sacking; Aoife laughed at her.

It was Mrs Fielding. 'Ella, the Inspector's here. He wants to see you.'

Eleanor rushed downstairs. The Inspector was waiting in the drawing room, clearly trying not to look at the cobwebs gathering in the corners the maids could not reach. Eleanor closed the door behind her.

'Good morning, Miss Hartley,' he said, flipping open his notebook, 'I wonder if I might trouble you for another account of the day of Miss Bartram's murder.'

Eleanor frowned. 'But why? I thought you had everything you needed from me. The butcher's boy—'

The Inspector held up a hand. 'I'm afraid that is no longer our main line of inquiry. He has proven he was nowhere near Granborough House on the night of the murder – he was with another young lady who has vouched for him. Is there anything else you can tell me about Miss Bartram's death?'

Eleanor sagged into a chair.

How could this be possible? The butcher's boy *had* to have killed Lizzie. Eleanor may have spoken Lizzie's death into being and the black-eyed woman may have granted her wish, but *he* had been the one to strike the killing blow. Lizzie's death could not be the result of pure magic – that would be a terrible and vicious thing, and Eleanor pushed the thought of that awful spectacle aside. But Lizzie had been stunned and drowned, cheaply and messily in the kitchen garden. What was magical about that?

The Inspector was watching her carefully. 'You advised me to find the other maids, Miss Hartley. My search has proven most interesting. I have discovered that Miss Leah Wallace was dismissed from Granborough House a few days before Miss Bartram's death. I believe you two were close.'

Eleanor couldn't grip the arms of her chair. She couldn't curl her hands into fists. She could only sit perfectly still, staring right into the Inspector's eyes, and force down every flicker of fear and anger that crackled under her skin. Surely he couldn't suspect Leah.

'Perhaps you could tell me a little more about her,' the Inspector said. 'Can you describe her relationship with Miss Bartram? Could you tell me more about the circumstances of her dismissal?'

Eleanor flattened her tone into shape. 'Leah was five months pregnant,' she said, and relished the sight of him flinching. 'She couldn't fasten her own corsets on the day she left. She would not be capable of something like that.'

A dull flush was creeping up the Inspector's neck. *Good*, Eleanor thought.

'I would advise you to discuss this with Miss Wallace, Inspector,' Eleanor said. 'I have not seen her since she left Granborough House. If you find her, I would be most grateful if you could give me her address. As you say, we were close.'

She got to her feet. The Inspector scrambled upright, still scribbling as he snatched up his hat. Vicious triumph lit Eleanor from within. It was so satisfying to put a dent in a man's composure.

'Allow me to show you out,' she said, leading him into the corridor.

'Ella!'

Mr Pembroke's voice cracked like a whip. Eleanor froze halfway down the passage. The Inspector turned, his eyes flickering between her and Mr Pembroke. A calm voice wormed its way through Eleanor's fear: *use this.*

She whimpered. It sounded a little forced to her ears, but the Inspector heard. He looked down at her and saw her eyes flash to Mr Pembroke.

Mr Pembroke's hand clamped around her upper arm. He stank of brandy. 'A word,' he hissed, hauling her back into the drawing room. 'Inspector!' he called. 'You're dismissed!'

The moment the door was closed he rounded on her. 'What did you say to him?'

Eleanor drew her shoulders back, refusing to be cowed. 'I was assisting with his inquiries.'

'Inquiries about what?'

'I think you'll find that's a police matter. *Sir.*'

Mr Pembroke took a deep breath and tried to smile. It looked like someone had dragged back the corners of his mouth with fish-hooks. 'Now, Ella, there's no reason why you can't tell me what you discussed. You ought not to keep secrets from your employer.'

'And you, sir, ought not to interfere with your maids.'

The words slipped out before she could stop them. For a moment, Eleanor was drenched in panic. But so, it seemed, was Mr Pembroke. His hands curled into fists, and his frog's eyes kept darting towards the door, the Inspector standing on the other side. Then he reached for his pocket-book and began counting through the notes. 'What would it take to make this go away?'

Eleanor summoned up all the hauteur she could muster. 'I want you to leave Aoife alone. Leave Daisy alone. Leave *me* alone. And if you lay a finger on any of us, ever again,' she said, 'I'll kill you in your sleep.'

Eleanor had given up on shivering in her room when the clock struck ten. Determined to find a book about somewhere hot and dry, she picked her way down the servants' staircase. Half an hour in the library was all she wanted. Thirty blessed minutes to bring the colour back to her thoughts.

She crept along the corridor. It had been so long since she'd had time to read. Without it her imagination had atrophied, like flowers wilting in a jar. Writing Charles's letters was not the same. She wanted to sink into words as rich and warm as velvet, not line them up like strings of rope.

The library door opened with a creak. Eleanor winced. She'd have to oil the hinges.

Gold titles winked at her from a hundred spines. The vanilla-smell of the binding was better than smelling salts; one breath and her mind came alive. Her gateway was open, and a hundred leather-bound keys waited for her. Where would she go? Who would she be?

Her eyes fell on *The Travels of Marco Polo*. What more could she ask for? The Tartar khan, in his Persian palace. The merchants of Tauris, surrounded by silk and gold. The story of the Old Man of the Mountain, and his secluded Eden. The first volume alone was near-bottomless in its riches, vaster than the khan's empire. Half an hour would never be enough.

She slid it off the shelf, and the door opened.

She froze.

There was nowhere she could hide. Candlelight illuminated the white of her nightdress, the yellow of her hair, the gold embossing of the book in her hand. It was half-off the shelf, and she could not have looked more guilty if she'd tried.

Fear flooded through her. This was it. This time she really would be dismissed. She was going to be thrown out in her nightdress, without a penny to her name, and there was nothing she could do about it. Would she have to make another wish? No, she couldn't. It would be murder. But *God*, where was she going to go?

'Eleanor?'

It was Charles, holding a candle in one hand and a poker in the other. She shoved the book back in place, thinking fast. Oh God, what was she going to tell him?

He smiled. 'I thought we were being robbed! Whatever are you doing here?'

She shuffled away from the shelf as he put down the poker. She could lie to him. But what would be the point? He'd already seen the book in her hand. And besides, she didn't like the thought of lying to Charles.

'I'm so sorry. I was only looking for something to read.'

He went over to the shelves. 'Marco Polo? A fine choice but somewhat out of date, I fear. I hadn't thought you cared for travel.'

'I haven't had the chance to try it. I've lived in London all my life.'

'Surely not! You must have left the capital, at least!'

She shook her head. 'I'd dearly like to, even if it was only as far as Bromley.'

He grimaced. 'I passed through on my way back from France. I would advise you to aim a little higher.' He waved her over to an armchair and sat down opposite her. 'Now. Where would you go?'

For a moment, Eleanor hesitated. She could never afford to go abroad, and spelling out her daydreams like this would be painful. Only ladies could afford to visit all the places she longed to see. Worst of all, twisting like a knife in her gut, she had the power to make her dreams come true, and she could not use it. But Charles's eyes were alight with interest, a smile was playing around his full-lipped mouth, and suddenly she could not think of a reason to keep all her hopes secret.

'Everywhere,' she said.

He smiled, the lines around his eyes crinkling. 'Pick somewhere to start, at least.'

Eleanor pulled an enormous atlas off a shelf. The book was as big as her torso; Charles sprang up to help her with it, pressing his lips together whenever it caught his bandaged fingers. They laid it carefully on the floor, and as they sat side by side, Eleanor opened the book to a map of Europe.

'I suppose it would be sensible to start in France and make my way around the Continent,' she said, tracing a path from Dover to Calais. 'Paris, of course. I've read about it so much it'd be strange not to go there. And then Orléans, Nantes, Bordeaux – oh, and Carcassonne. I'd love to see the old Cathar stronghold. And Nice, but I suppose while I'm in the southwest it would make more sense to cross the border into Spain and visit Nice after I'd made a circuit of the Iberian peninsula. Then I could – what is it?'

Charles wasn't looking at the map any more. He was smiling at her, his eyes soft. He started when he saw her looking at him. 'Nothing,' he said, putting down his candle so that she could see better. 'Please go on.'

'Well,' said Eleanor, suddenly aware that there were inches between them, 'then I'd cross the Alps, make a brief tour of

Switzerland and then on to Italy. I'd want to linger there, I think – certainly in Rome, Naples and Milan. And Florence. Oh, and Bologna. And Venice, of course – but you've been, haven't you?'

'I have,' he murmured, 'there's nowhere else like it. The whole city seems to be floating. It's astonishing; you'll turn a corner and an unassuming little church will have a Tintoretto or a Titian tucked away. I could live there for the rest of my days and never uncover all its secrets.'

Eleanor looked up at him. The candlelight shone on the planes of his cheekbones, illuminating a fine layer of golden stubble. If she moved her hand, Eleanor thought, her arm would brush against his, quite by accident. 'Does it really seem to float?'

'If you stand in the right spot,' he said. 'In the centre of the city it feels solid enough, but around the edges there's nothing on the horizon but the sky and the Adriatic. It's incredible. You can be walking along a busy street, buildings on every side, and then suddenly all you see is a vast expanse of blue.'

She was leaning towards him as though he was magnetic. 'Do they still have the Carnival?' she whispered.

'Eleanor,' he said, his blue eyes fixed on hers, 'they'd never let *you* hide away behind a mask.'

They were so close now. Eleanor could count every one of his eyelashes. She shifted closer, her face turned up to his – and suddenly, the light lurched as the candle fell over. She'd knocked the edge of the atlas without realizing.

Charles pushed her out of the way and snatched up the candle. The edges of the atlas were smouldering. He smothered the flames with the sleeve of his dressing gown before they could catch.

'Be careful!' Eleanor hissed. 'What about your hand?'

'Nothing to worry about,' he said, inspecting his cuffs. 'The material is a little singed, but that's all.'

Eleanor closed the atlas and stood up, wincing as she lifted it. 'You could've hurt yourself.'

Charles got up and helped her take the weight of the book. 'But *you* could've been hurt too, Eleanor,' he said, 'and what kind of man would I be if I allowed that to happen? I...I want you to be safe.'

He was blushing. Eleanor could feel the heat under her skin. 'Well...thank you, Charles. I – I suppose I'd better go to bed.'

'Of course. Of course,' he said, raking a hand through his hair. He opened the library door for her. 'Goodnight, Eleanor.'

'Good night.'

She lingered. Just for a second, she wondered what he would do if she reached out and pushed the library door shut, keeping them both inside. But she went through it as she knew she ought to. As she passed she saw Charles's hand twitch, as though he wanted to touch her, but had thought better of it.

The nights were drawing in, and Aoife claimed the evenings for her storytelling. She gathered Eleanor and Daisy around the kitchen range, and, eyes gleaming, told them tales of faceless ladies eternally searching for mirrors and headless horsemen who travellers would be lucky to escape with a blinding. Now that she was no longer afraid of Mr Pembroke, Aoife had made fear something to be played with.

Charles and his father were having dinner, and while the maids waited to clear the plates Mrs Banbury served up slices of ham pie and cold potatoes. Aoife was holding court at the end of the table, half a potato speared on her fork.

'But of course, he'd not set store by such things, for he was a gentleman and knew more than you or I. But the very next night—'

Daisy snorted. 'I'll tell you what gentlemen know all right.'

Mrs Banbury laughed. 'Don't let Bertha catch you saying that. You're lucky she's after another housemaid, she wouldn't be waiting at table otherwise.'

Aoife glared at them. 'The very next night, *I said*, the knocking came again, this time from right outside his bedroom door...'

Daisy rapped her knuckles on the kitchen table and winked at Aoife. Aoife blushed.

'So...from outside the door. The bedroom door. So. But he knew this could not be possible, for there was no one about and—'

There was another knocking sound. Aoife pointed her fork at Daisy. 'I know that's you.'

'It's not,' said Daisy, picking up her plate.

'It is!' Aoife insisted. 'Ella, tell her she's—'

The knocking came again. Daisy was carrying her plate, Eleanor was holding her knife and fork, Mrs Banbury froze halfway through pouring a glass of water. All of them looked at each other, dread uncurling in the pit of Eleanor's stomach.

Aoife laid down her fork. 'Did you—'

The knocking came again. Aoife shrieked. Eleanor started up, groping for a kitchen knife.

'It's the door, you pigeons!' snapped Mrs Banbury.

'I'm not answering it,' Aoife said in a rush. Mrs Banbury stared at Eleanor meaningfully until she went to the tradesmen's entrance. Eleanor's hand hesitated on the latch. Surely there wasn't anything to be frightened of.

It was Leah.

Eleanor could see the shape of her skull in Leah's heart-shaped face. She was wearing the same dress she'd left in, only now it was ragged and stained. It gaped around her shoulders and strained across her stomach. When she saw Eleanor, she smiled, and the flash of familiarity made Eleanor's stomach lurch.

'Little Nell,' she said, 'I was hoping it'd be you.'

'Leah!' Eleanor gasped. 'My God, I – come inside, come inside!'

Leah headed straight for the range. She let out a sob when she held her hands to the heat. Eleanor dragged out a chair. Leah sank into it.

'I'm sorry,' said Leah. 'I didn't know where else to go.'

Mrs Banbury started making up a plate. 'Don't apologize, pet. Wash your hands.'

Leah dunked her hands in the sink and grabbed the plate with dripping fingers. She made grunting noises as she ate, snatching the hot potatoes with her bare fingers, and sucked every last drop of jelly from under her fingernails. Eleanor had to look away. Leah had never used to eat like this.

'Have you been keeping well?' Eleanor asked, when Leah had finished.

Leah bristled. 'Well enough, thank you. I've been to my brother's.'

'And how is he?'

Leah's face grew dark. 'I didn't stop to find out.'

As she spoke, Eleanor noticed a faint smell coming from Leah's drying skirts. It was damp and chilly, with something of the sewer in it. Where Leah had been sleeping?

'Have another slice of pie,' said Mrs Banbury. 'How's the baby treating you?'

Leah put a hand to her stomach. 'It fidgets. Is that normal?'

'My mam always says so,' said Aoife, her eyes brimming with tears.

Eleanor put a hand on Leah's knee. Her dress was damp and sticky. 'Not that it isn't lovely to see you, Leah – we've all been terribly worried – but why have you come here?'

Leah set aside her plate. 'I want to see him upstairs. It's his child. He ought to do something for it.'

Aoife put her hands over her mouth; Daisy stopped halfway through scrubbing a plate. Mrs Banbury beckoned Aoife over.

'Fetch Lizzie's old things. Leah can have them if she wants.'

Aoife scuttled upstairs. Leah got up, massaging the small of her back. 'Won't Lizzie mind? Where is she?'

Silence swelled through the room. The sloshing water in the sink seemed to crash through the quiet like waves. Daisy yanked her hands out of the water, face ashen, and Eleanor remembered the cold, sickly smell drifting out of the water trough.

'Lizzie's dead,' Eleanor said.

The door opened. Mrs Fielding came in, closely followed by Aoife, clutching a moth-eaten carpetbag. Mrs Fielding's eyes narrowed when she saw Leah.

'Please—' Leah began.

'I made your position clear,' said Mrs Fielding.

'Please, I only want—'

Mrs Fielding turned to Aoife. 'Fetch the constable.'

Eleanor ran upstairs for her shawl. By the time she was in the kitchen again, Leah was already shuffling down the street, bent-backed and weeping. Eleanor burst through the back door and ran after her, snatching up the carpetbag as she went.

Eleanor shoved the shawl and the bag into Leah's hands.

'Here.' Then, before Leah could speak, she ran back towards the house.

October sent a chill creeping through the city. Damp oozed through the windows. Mould stretched its crawling fingers through the house and mottled everything black and green. In unused rooms, Eleanor could see her own breath misting in the air, like a housebound cloud. Her garret was so cold that she awoke sore from shivering. In the kitchen, they huddled beside the range like misers bent over jewels.

When Mrs Pembroke was alive, this would never have happened. She ordered her coal in the summer, when prices were cheaper. She had been ready when winter slid its fingers through the crack under the door. She commanded the maids to stoke up the fires and sent them scurrying across the house, armed with hot water and carbolic soap. But now Mrs Fielding had to beg the money from Mr Pembroke, who begrudged every penny that was not spent on brandy or the fees for his club. The house grew stiller and darker every day. The air tasted flat; it could have been abandoned already.

Mrs Fielding tried to keep the house in order. She had them all up before dawn, scrubbing, dusting and polishing, and still expected them to keep their hair tidy and their uniforms spotless. Hands raw, arms aching, Eleanor went to bed with polish under her fingernails and the biting smell of carbolic lodged in the back of her throat. But when the library bell rang, Eleanor could throw down her brushes, her rags, and her dusters, and retreat into a soft, warm room.

Charles insisted on having a fire. The lamps were always lit. The only sounds were the crackling of burning coals, the scratching of Eleanor's pen and Charles's low voice. The room shone. Anything seemed possible there. She'd even told Charles about Leah, and when he'd seen her trembling hands and heard the catch in her voice, he had promised to find her. Eleanor wasn't going to let anyone take that away from her.

The others would have tried, but none of them could read. Once, she'd gone downstairs and seen Aoife hunched over the *Illustrated London News*, tracing the words with a finger and frowning. Daisy had laughed when she'd seen her, and leant over to rub the crease between her brows.

'That'll leave a mark,' she said.

Aoife swatted her hands away. 'Your hands smell like onions.'

'You don't mind,' Daisy said, smiling.

Daisy saw Eleanor and jerked her hands away. Aoife scrambled for the newspaper and shoved it into a bucket, avoiding Eleanor's eyes.

'Eleanor! Your hands!'

Eleanor flinched and almost knocked over the inkwell. Charles had been standing behind her and he'd almost yelled in her ear. She blushed and hid her hands in her lap.

'It's nothing.'

Her hands were red, covered in a web of fine cuts and flaking skin. Knotted knuckles and corded veins only made it worse. They looked like boiled lobsters – damp, crustaceous creatures dredged up from the ocean floor.

'Will you let me see?'

'It's nothing to trouble yourself over.'

'Please?'

She hesitated, then offered him her hand. Shame crawled under her skin. Let him see she was no real lady in all the veiny detail. The trails of his touch burned.

'Does it hurt?'

'Sometimes. Three years of housework leaves a mark.'

Charles's face fell. 'I should have been here. Father never would have dared to put you into service if I hadn't been away.'

It was something she'd wondered at, in the dark of night, for years. She hesitated. 'Why didn't you come back, Charles?'

He gave her a sad smile. 'Father and I have never been easy. Without Mother...'

She squeezed his hand. 'Of course. Forgive me, I wasn't thinking.'

'Well,' said Charles, glancing at the clock, 'I must beg your permission to leave. I have a few business matters to attend to in town.'

Eleanor felt a pang of regret. She shouldn't have brought up Mrs Pembroke, it had only made him upset. He left before she could apologize again.

With Charles gone, it was back to work.

There were floors to scrub, tables to polish, carpets to beat and cushions to cudgel into plumpness. There were grates that needed black-leading, laundry to put away, dead mice to dispose of, their heads still in the traps. There were herbs to pick, boots to clean, coats that needed to be hung out to dry. And now, there were fires that needed to be lit, even though the sun had set and every part of her ached.

She went into Mr Pembroke's room and lit the fire, trying not to look at the empty birdcage looming ahead of her. The room was thick with his scent – brandy, stale sweat, and the tang of something that might have been old vomit – and she thought she might drown in her own disgust. She put his clothes back into the press without a twinge of fear. For once, Mr Pembroke had restrained himself; Aoife had not cried in weeks. He took his meals in silence whenever Eleanor waited at table, watching her pour every glass and serve every plate. Sometimes she would turn her back and stir his drink with a spoon, and watch the sweat bead across his forehead when she handed him his brandy with a smile. She never actually added anything, but seeing his eyes flicker from the glass to her hands lit her from within.

When she left, she caught a glimpse of several empty bottles clustered like flocks of pigeons. Laudanum, port, crystal decanters lying on their sides, and empty plates she could not remember being sent up to his room. Eleanor gave a vicious grin. He was avoiding her. *Good*, she thought. Let him see how it was to be afraid for once.

There was nothing like that in Charles's room. It was calm, quiet – and cold, because he always insisted on keeping his windows open during the day. His clothes had been neatly put away, and all the things on his washstand were lined up with military precision. He had a set of well-used clothes brushes and a neat square of cloth folded on top of the clothes press. Eleanor knew she shouldn't be surprised – he didn't have a valet to keep his clothes clean, of course he had to do it himself – but she hadn't known he'd made such a habit of it.

Eleanor knelt by the fireplace and stacked up the kindling. Her hands didn't look like they belonged to *her*. She imagined peeling them off to reveal a pair of neat lady's hands, plump and white and unscarred.

She struck a match. It guttered out.

It ought not to matter. Hands were hands. The most

important thing was that they worked. But that was it. They *worked*, and anyone could tell by looking.

She struck another match, which broke in half.

She was lucky that was all her hands gave away. By rights they should be twisted claws, thick with blood, or the haggard and veiny hands of a witch. She'd killed people with a word, and when she looked in the mirror there was no sign of it on her face.

She had taken so much from so many.

Eleanor tried to strike another match. She went too fast, and smacked her wrist on the iron grate.

So much had been taken from her, too. Her innocence, her future, her soul. What would she be without it – what if it was already gone, and the black-eyed woman had lied? Where did she even keep it? Eleanor had seen a few anatomical diagrams and knew that every organ had its function: the brain housed thoughts, the heart pumped blood, the lungs breathed air. None of the clever medical men who'd written finely illustrated books had ever found the thing that housed the soul. What if it was never there at all?

The door clicked open. 'Eleanor?'

She lurched to her feet, matches spiralling to the floor. Charles stood in the doorway, immaculate in snowy white and gleaming black. Everything about him seemed shiny and soft, and everything about her seemed shrivelled and shabby next to him.

She curtseyed, reflexively. 'I'm so sorry,' she said, 'I'll have the fire lit in a—'

'You're upset.'

'No, no, it's the smoke—'

'From an unlit fire? Come, now. What's troubling you?'

'Nothing.'

Charles shut the door behind him and set down his candle. He'd loosened his collar, and she could see the shape of his throat, the bulge of his Adam's apple.

'Do sit down, Eleanor. Let me light the fire.'

Even as she told herself not to, she was handing over the book of matches. Charles's hands were steady, and the fire was soon blazing.

'I haven't done that since school,' he said, straightening up, 'although we only ever set fires to burn away cigarette packets and punishment slips, beasts that we were. You're quite sure you're all right?'

For a moment, she considered explaining, but then she pictured the look on Charles's face and pushed the thought away at once. 'It'll pass.'

'Well, this may help to hurry it along. I have something for you. Close your eyes.'

She did, and a small metal disc was pressed into her hands. When she opened them again, she saw a small white tin, decorated with fine blue flowers clustered around the words 'Hyssop's Hygienic & Soothing Lotion, London'.

'It's for your hands,' Charles explained, a blush crawling up his neck. 'They always look so painful. Not that they aren't lovely hands, of course...' He blushed. 'But I thought...'

'Thank you.'

'It's the least I could do, after all you've done. You've been an angel.'

They were standing very close together. His candle was burning low, and the fire did little more than turn darkness to dimness. It made him shine. Polished buttons glinted. Pearlescent silk glowed. Even his bandages were the colour of a sunrise on snow. This close, she could see how the lines

213

around his mouth deepened when he smiled, and smell the last curling trail of cigar smoke caught in his clothes.

She wanted him to lean down and kiss her. She was terrified of what she would do if he did.

'I'd better go,' she said, her voice hoarse. 'Mrs Fielding will want her coal scuttle back.'

'Oh. Oh, yes. Of course.'

Still, she hesitated. Then she slipped the tin into her pocket and left, the empty coal scuttle bouncing on her arm.

She was silent as she put it away. She said nothing as Mrs Fielding locked the door and Daisy and Aoife unrolled their straw pallets. Aoife slowly unpinned her dark hair, and Eleanor saw the hungry way Daisy watched it fall across her shoulders. From the languorous movement of her hands, Aoife knew Daisy was watching.

Eleanor climbed the stairs, and remembered everything she touched. The warp of the old steps under her boots. Her fingers, curled in her skirts as she climbed. The way her corset shifted above her hips as she moved. The weight of the tin in her pocket, like a secret, or a hand. Alone in her room, it was worse. Undressing seemed indecent when she felt every pull and swish of the material sliding over her skin. Across her hips and down her arms, it felt like bandaged fingers.

She splashed her face with cold water before she could imagine anything else.

She got into bed. It was cold and lumpy, and she'd never been more grateful. A sliver of moonlight came through the window and turned the little pot silver in the palm of her hand. She hesitated, and opened it.

It was soft and slick, and it made her blush.

* * *

They squelched their way to church, picking through mud and puddles and the damp refuse of the pavements. The street was hidden beneath a forest of umbrellas, with only a hatless beggar visible every now and then through the black canopy. Charles would follow them in a hansom; he was still tearing through his clothes press, looking for a cravat, when they left.

At least, he said he had been.

Eleanor's mind was full. Every swish of her skirt over her hips felt like a caress. When she closed her eyes she could still see his face, made golden by the firelight. He hadn't looked at Mrs Fielding when he'd said he would follow them to church; was it Eleanor he was truly hoping to avoid? Was he thinking of her too?

And, when she finally succeeded in pushing all thoughts of Charles out of her head, she was faced with another puzzle.

Were souls real?

Thoughts buzzed around Eleanor's mind like flies. How did she know, truly, that she even had a soul? She'd always assumed she did. The part of her that lived behind her eyes, which felt the tug of strange new worlds whenever she opened a book – that *must* be the soul. What else could it be? But, Eleanor realized, thoughts and feelings came from the mind and from the heart – what did the soul have to do with it? What did the soul have to do at all?

Did she only think she had a soul because someone had told her she had one?

They reached the church before she knew it. The gravestones cast long shadows across the churchyard, reaching for Eleanor's feet. She stumbled over the wet path, mind still reeling. She felt as if she was viewing her own thoughts through a telescope. If souls were not real, what had she given to the black-eyed woman? And if it wasn't there, then what *was* she? Had Eleanor only been imagining her, all this time? She seemed so real.

Eleanor could not stand it. She seemed to be half-outside her own head, both detached and screaming at the detachment. She drifted over to the reverend, amazed that she was able to put one foot in front of the other.

'Might I have a word, Reverend?'

The reverend blew his nose. 'Now, Miss Hartley? The service is about to start.'

She ignored him. 'I wondered what you could tell me about the nature of souls.'

He gaped at her. 'I've not heard such a question since my university days! What interest could you possibly have in souls?'

Eleanor groped for an excuse. 'I...I am simply curious. I wish to better understand things...'

'Excessive curiosity in a young woman can be a dangerous thing, Miss Hartley. You must be careful not to overstimulate your mental faculties. It can lead to hysteria. You must think of your health.'

'But—'

The reverend looked stern. It was rather spoiled by his runny nose.

'Unless you are thinking of taking the veil, such topics are hardly appropriate for one such as yourself. You've not been reading again, I hope?'

'No,' Eleanor said, immediately.

'Then I would advise you to put the whole topic out of your mind. Really! My dear girl, what has come over you? A certain childlike curiosity is understandable, even appealing, in matters such as these, but if I hear any more from you on these subjects I shall have to speak to your guardian.'

Eleanor wondered what Mr Pembroke would have to say on the nature of souls, and realized it would not matter. He would seize on the excuse and have her carted off to Bedlam, safely out of the way. The thought came laced with panic. If souls were not real, and the black-eyed woman was not real, then perhaps Bedlam was where Eleanor belonged.

'Turn your mind to more agreeable things,' said the reverend, 'and now if you will excuse me, I must begin my sermon.'

The bandages around Charles's hand were shrinking.

Eleanor had been trying to ignore it for days. When the last of the bandages came off, the library door would be closed, and she would be shut out of its warmth forever. The thought was like a cold hand on the back of her neck.

They were alone in the library. The rain muffled everything but the scratch of her pen and Charles's low voice. Eleanor forced herself to push all thoughts of souls and Bedlam from her head. Of course she was not seeing things. Charles would not trust her to write his letters if he doubted her sanity. She ought to have as much faith in herself as he did, she told herself, and blushed when she wondered how much faith that was.

'...yours etc. I'm sure you know how to finish these things off, Eleanor. I leave myself in your capable hands.'

She signed the letter and addressed the envelope. 'Oh yes. I'll call him a wastrel on your behalf,' she teased.

He laughed and rang the bell for lunch. 'How are your hands?'

'Much improved, thank you.'

'Capital.'

Charles sprawled in an armchair and smiled at her. He was

always smiling at her. And when he wasn't smiling, he was looking at her. She sometimes caught him staring at her mouth, her hands. He turned away every time she noticed.

There was a knock on the door and they both flinched. Aoife came in, carrying Charles's lunch on a tray. She lingered by the fireplace as she set it down, and when she left she looked tired enough to cry.

Charles did not notice. He was beaming at his lunch. There was a steaming bowl of soup, bread, a plate piled with cold meats and cheeses, and three tiny fruit tarts, the jam gleaming like jewels. Eleanor had a hunk of bread and cheese waiting for her in the kitchen, if somebody hadn't already eaten it.

'Well,' she said, getting to her feet, 'if that'll be all...'

'Sit and eat with me.'

'Charles, I couldn't deprive you of your meal—'

'There's plenty here. I shan't let a lady go hungry.'

Eleanor caught the scent of marjoram. Mock turtle soup – one of Mrs Banbury's best. She'd watched her make it countless times, but had never tried it once.

'Well, if you insist.' She sat down beside him.

'Here,' he said, holding out a laden spoon.

'Charles, I am far too old to be spoon-fed.'

He smiled. 'What gentleman would allow a lady to lift a finger, let alone a spoon?'

The spoon clinked against her teeth as he put it in her mouth. The broth was buttery and rich, with a hint of rosemary-and-clove sharpness. She had never tasted anything like it.

There were inches between them. She could have reached out and stroked his silk cravat. Faint lines nestled at the corners of his eyes; she wanted to trace them. She licked her lips and his eyes darted to her tongue. She saw his Adam's apple bob as he swallowed, his eyes still on her mouth. This close, she could see a suggestion of pale stubble on his cheeks, and she remembered that night in the library. If she hadn't knocked the candle over, what would he have confessed in that soft, dark room, with Eleanor's dreams spread before them both?

He shifted in his chair and looked away, and they ate the rest of their meal in silence.

Charles's bandages came off the next day, and Eleanor spent it cleaning. Mrs Fielding insisted. Eleanor scrubbed, wiped, dusted and polished until her back was sore and her knees ached. The smell of carbolic soap and ground-in mould tangled in her hair.

'Best thing for you, Ella,' Mrs Fielding said. 'A girl like you needs to be put to work.'

By the end of the day Eleanor was a clammy, grey creature. More than anything she wanted to step into her ink-and-paper armour and leave Granborough House behind. How had she ever stood the stink of damp, and the feel of ground-in dirt under her nails? The mould had crawled under her skin, rotting all her veins from the inside. No matter how many times she lathered soap up and down her arms, or soused her hair with rosemary water, its cold fingers crept up her arms and down her neck. She'd never escape it.

There was a knock at her door. Eleanor kicked her dirty clothes under the bed and answered it. Charles was standing there, looking hopeful and holding a large bottle under his arm.

'I've brought you something. May I – good Lord! Is this where you sleep?'

'It has its merits, I suppose. I'd rather not sleep on the kitchen floor.'

'Oh, no, I didn't mean...I'm sorry, that was dreadfully rude of me. I'm sure your room is lovely.'

Eleanor raised her eyebrows. He blushed.

'We could go somewhere warmer, if you prefer.'

'Go and...?'

'Celebrate, of course!' he said, waggling the bottle at her. 'I can't think of a better way to thank you for all your help. Will you come downstairs?'

She hesitated. 'If Mrs Fielding found out...'

'She's a good old stick, she shan't mind.'

'She shan't mind if you do it. I daresay things are a little different for me.'

'Of course. Silly of me.'

He looked crestfallen. The last of her self-control melted. 'We'll have to be discreet.'

He grinned at her. They crept down the servants' staircase and sneaked into the drawing room. Charles locked the door behind them and Eleanor huddled by the fire, trying to stir some life into the coals.

There was a pop. Eleanor flinched so hard she almost dropped the poker.

'What was that?'

'Just the champagne,' he said, pouring her a glass, 'nothing to worry about.'

'I hope you didn't go to any trouble to get it.'

'Frankly, I can't think of a better use for my hand than

opening champagne.' He handed her the glass. 'Here's to an excellent scribe!'

Eleanor almost choked on her champagne. The bubbles prickled across her tongue.

'Do you like it?' he asked, his face hopeful.

Eleanor nodded, her eyes watering. She wasn't sure she did, but with something this expensive she decided she'd better. Charles beamed and topped up her glass. His was already empty.

'Have as much as you like,' he said, 'there's no point opening a bottle of champagne unless you finish it. We got through the stuff like water back at Oxford.'

She took another sip. 'And we all thought you were so hard at work.'

'The amount we drank was hard work, I assure you!'

She laughed. 'I don't believe you. This doesn't taste like hard work at all.'

He topped up her glass again. 'With you, nothing ever is.'

She drank, if only to hide her blushing. Now that she was used to the bubbles, she was starting to enjoy it. She took another sip, and was shocked to find her glass was empty. But not for long; Charles was already pouring her another.

'Do sit down if you like.'

'I'll stay here, thank you. I'm a little cold.'

He set down his glass at once and shrugged off his jacket. 'How remiss of me! I do apologize. Here, take – no, I insist, Eleanor.'

He draped the jacket over her shoulders. It was warm, and smelled of cigar smoke and something slightly spiced. He smoothed the sleeves down her arms, and even through the fabric Eleanor shivered.

Then, they heard a creak.

'Hide!'

Eleanor darted behind the sofa as Charles unlocked the door. 'I say, who's – oh, Mrs Fielding. I didn't think you were still up.'

Eleanor tried to make herself smaller. If Mrs Fielding saw her now – hiding behind a chair, wearing her nightdress and Charles's jacket – she would be dismissed. She should be afraid, but with champagne crackling through her veins all she wanted to do was laugh.

'Master Charles! Was that you I heard earlier? I thought we'd be murdered in our beds!'

He laughed. 'Nothing so dramatic! I was only having a drink. I do hope I didn't alarm you.'

'You can always ring if you need any—'

'At this time of night? I wouldn't dream of it! Do go back to sleep, Mrs F. I'll be quite all right up here.'

'Well...all right. Goodnight, sir.'

'Goodnight.'

Eleanor heard the door shut. There were a few seconds of silence, and then she heard a distant door close. She uncurled herself like a woodlouse and bit back the urge to laugh.

Charles helped her out from behind the sofa, his eyes twinkling. 'Another drink?'

All Hallows' Eve drew closer, and brought darkness rolling in with it. Aoife said the two were linked. She crossed herself, even though Mrs Fielding scolded her for it, and put her stockings on inside-out on purpose. For luck, she said. So far, all she'd got were blisters, and a lot of teasing from Daisy.

Eleanor wasn't sure what to make of all Aoife's superstitions.

It was difficult to imagine ghouls and ghosts could be real when she was scrubbing a floor. But Granborough House was so cold, and so dark. Sometimes the air was so still and damp it tasted dead. Sometimes, Eleanor would linger in the kitchen as the maids got ready for bed, and listen to Aoife whisper about the *sluagh* – a horde of soul-eating revenants that flew on dark wings – and then Eleanor would run upstairs, two at a time, and flinch at every pigeon flapping outside.

Mrs Fielding tried to scrub it out of existence.

The carpets were not beaten, but thrashed. Fresh coal was ordered in and every spare bit of paper went for kindling. The walls were cleaned, the hallway was mopped, and every inanimate object in the house was dusted and polished to Mrs Fielding's satisfaction. With all the work it was easy for Eleanor to ignore her fears. But when it stopped, she and Daisy would huddle by the range and listen to Aoife's stories. No matter how many times she told herself she was jumping at shadows, Eleanor kept expecting Aoife's next tale to be about a woman with all-black eyes.

Eleanor shifted closer.

'You've to be careful by windows facing west,' Aoife whispered, 'that's where they come in. Don't open them.'

Eleanor glanced up at the kitchen window. It was already dark outside.

'You're not serious, Aoife,' said Daisy, with a smile. 'Besides, who's going to open a window in this weather?'

'You're not to open them,' Aoife repeated. 'You'll invite them in, and it's bad luck besides. The good Lord knows we've had enough of that.'

Something flashed past the window. Eleanor flinched back

before she realized it was only a rat. Aoife started away from the range with a shriek and Daisy laughed.

'The pair of you!' Daisy said, getting to her feet and stretching. 'Take it from someone older and wiser: there's no such thing.'

'You're only nineteen,' Aoife snapped. 'Besides, everyone's scared of *something*.'

'My pa's a sailor,' said Daisy, brushing her fingers against Aoife's hair as she passed. 'I know a tall tale when I hear it.'

Eleanor shifted closer to the range. 'I'm sure Daisy's right. Besides, the *sluagh* wouldn't come after us, would they?'

Daisy shook out the straw pallets and laid them on the floor. She laid them very close together. Aoife watched her work.

'They come for sinners,' Aoife said, a strange look on her face.

Eleanor saw her expression, and the two pallets laid so close together, and understood. She remembered Daisy watching Aoife's hair and felt the weight of her loneliness anew. Aoife and Daisy had a secret they would never tell her, but it was one they made together. Eleanor's secret was too great, too terrible to be shared.

On All Hallows' Eve, London was a haze of fog. When Eleanor left Granborough House she stepped into a grey void. Walk through it, and the street revealed itself in flashes: horses, coffee-sellers, pamphlets thrust at her by disembodied hands, a fur trader who she was sure was selling gloves lined with cat. Eleanor shuffled along, her arms full of bed-hangings. The costermongers' unseen cries sounded like ghosts calling through the mist. She shouldn't have listened to Aoife's stories. Granborough House had enough ghosts of its own.

By the time Eleanor got back she was cold, muddy and had a fine layer of moisture coating her dress, slightly black and sticky from the coal smuts. She spread out the hangings to air over an upstairs banister and crept into the library. The cold had oozed into her. Snatching up a travelogue of Asia – she was rarely in the mood for fairy tales now, and all their hateful wishes – she crouched beside the fire and began to read, desperate to try and imagine herself warm. By the time she gave up it was dark outside, and the chink of knives and forks echoed along empty corridors. She shoved the book back and snatched up the bed-hangings, trying to think of sunlight on the steppe as she shuffled upstairs to Charles's room.

Boots and apron off, Eleanor knelt on Charles's bed. The hangings might have been dredged up from the river, they were so heavy. Hoisting the material above her head, Eleanor tried to slip another eye onto the nearest hook. It was like trying to hang water.

Her candle flickered. Too late, she remembered Aoife's tales of the *sluagh*. It was only a story, she knew – but wouldn't they come at a moment like this, when she was alone in the dark with her back to the door?

'Eleanor?'

Eleanor yelped and sprang off the bed. She whirled around and saw Charles, blinking at her from the doorway. She sagged against the bedpost.

'I'm so sorry,' she said, 'I thought you'd be at dinner.'

'Let me help.'

'I couldn't. Mrs Fielding would—'

He smiled. 'I shan't breathe a word.'

Eleanor gave in and showed him the row of hooks that ran

along the inside of the canopy. She climbed back onto the bed and started hanging the material up again; Charles followed suit. Eleanor concentrated on slotting the rings onto the hooks. She had to. Her hair was coming loose. Every movement made it sag a fraction further down her neck. What would Charles say, if he saw it all spilling across her shoulders?

Concentrate, she thought.

A shock of white out of the corner of her eye. Charles's shirtsleeve, immaculate in the candlelight. When had he taken off his jacket? She couldn't remember. Had she ever seen him in his shirtsleeves before? She must have done, but not when it had mattered. What would it be like, to watch him remove his starched and proper armour piece by piece?

Concentrate.

The mattress shifted when he moved, and therefore so did she. They might have been adrift on a raft in some great expanse of ocean, just the two of them. She could hear the swish of linen on silk as he lifted his arms.

Concentrate.

Their hands were moving closer together. She should have thought of this; she should have known. Their hands would meet, and in the darkness and the quiet it would not be like all the times their hands had met before.

Concen—

Charles's hand brushed against hers. He did not take it away.

They'd buttoned themselves into their own little box of darkness. Cold, damp, hunger – they were all things that belonged on the other side of the curtain. Eleanor could not bring herself to let them in. It would be safer if she did. She had her reputation to think of. Eleanor would not be an exception; she'd be treated as Leah had been, and all the girls before. But for once Eleanor wanted to act as if cold, hunger and the threat of dismissal were not things she had to consider.

'Eleanor?'

'Yes?'

'May I ask you something?'

'Of course.'

She felt him shift. Was that how it was for wives, when their husbands shifted in bed beside them?

'Do you think me wicked?'

'No. Why do you ask?'

He cleared his throat. 'Since the wedding was cancelled, I've been told so many times that I must be distraught. But I've not shed a tear for Felicity and I'm not sure if I ever shall. What kind of a man does that make me? What kind of—'

She reached out. Her fingers found his cheek. The beginnings of stubble rasped across her palm. His breath caught in his throat. She thought of all the kindness he had shown her, of all that they had lost and shared, and knew there was only one thing she could say.

'Charles,' she whispered, 'you are not wicked.'

His lips on her hand. Her fingers in his hair. His arm slid around her waist, her hands glided over his silk waistcoat. She was giddy with fear and terrified by the force of her own longing, but when their mouths met she knew she could never walk away.

It was three o'clock in the morning. The house creaked and clicked around them, and in his sleep Charles pulled Eleanor closer. After years of negotiating a mattress like a patch of cobblestones, she couldn't sleep on something as insubstantial as Charles's feather bed. Every time she closed her eyes she thought she might drift away.

She stared up at the canopy.

She had fallen, as Eve had before her. She was officially ruined.

It hadn't felt like being ruined. Being 'ruined' sounded painful, or as if it was something to cry over. But it had been neither. If anything it had been a strange kind of relief to put away her cares and sink into his arms.

Eleanor knew she ought to be ashamed. She ought to place a dramatic hand to her forehead, lament prettily, and then throw herself off a bridge like all the girls in the penny bloods. But she could only make herself feel ashamed when she pictured Mrs Fielding ripping open the curtains and shrieking her out of bed, and what were the chances of that?

Charles murmured into his pillow. The curve of his shoulder was just visible in the gloom.

And why should she be ashamed? Even the Prince of Wales had his mistresses, and some of them were titled ladies. Three years below stairs had made Eleanor well aware of what went on between men and women. In the early days there'd been footmen who sneaked off to the coach house with giggling maids. Later, there'd been shop-boys who waited by the back gate clutching fistfuls of flowers. Some of them had married the maids; some of them had not, and no one seemed to mind.

Of course, Mrs Fielding had found out, but only when Nature had made it impossible to hide. Then it was instant dismissal, without a reference. Eleanor was far more worried about that. Her face burned as she remembered the way Mrs Fielding spoke about Leah. She remembered her friend's worn face, the smell coming off her skirts. Her family clearly hadn't taken her in – Leah had spoken of them once, and her Evangelical brother had not sounded forgiving. God only knew where she was sleeping, or how she put a roof over her head.

What if Eleanor ended up like her?

For a moment, she closed her eyes and let herself savour the softness, the warmth. Then she peeled Charles's arm away and began to dress.

'Eleanor?'

He pulled aside the curtain as she was pulling on her stockings. 'I'm sorry. I didn't mean to wake you.'

'Come back to bed.'

She shook her head. 'I can't. I must go.'

His face paled. 'Did I hurt you?'

'No.'

'Good,' he said, with feeling. 'But don't go, Eleanor. Let me hold you a little longer.'

'Charles, do you know what would happen if anyone should discover us? Or if I should carry a child? Better for the both of us if this never happens again.'

He leant forward and took her hand. 'I'd never let anything happen to you.'

'So you'd marry me?'

'Sometimes I wish we could.'

For a second Eleanor thought she saw the shape of the black-eyed woman in the corner of the room. She looked closer, and saw only darkness.

'If the worst should happen,' Charles continued, 'I will take care of you, I promise.'

'And your father? What will you do if he finds out?'

Fear flashed across Charles's face. It was gone in an instant, but Eleanor could not forget it. 'I *will* take care of you,' he said again.

Eleanor nodded. It was too much of a risk. She took her hand away and went back to her cold, empty room. As she walked she remembered Charles's warm bed, and the gentle light from his fire. The way he'd smiled and sighed. All the things he'd whispered to her.

She would have to forget them.

As the days curled up on themselves, the fogs grew thicker, and Eleanor cursed herself for giving her shawl away. She had nothing else. She shoved newspapers down her bodice and slept in all her clothes, but no matter what she did she awoke sore from shivering. Fog leached all the colour and heat out of her until she felt like a damp mushroom. Dark spots appeared on all the mirrors in the house, as if her reflection had been put in a drawer and left to moulder.

Sometimes, she saw the black-eyed woman there.

No one else saw her, even in the mirror. When Aoife bustled in with arms full of laundry, or when Daisy called up the stairs, the black-eyed woman would vanish. Eleanor wondered if anyone else had *ever* seen her, or even heard the echo of her voice. Surely someone must have heard her whispered promises.

Surely she must really be there.

Eleanor wanted to make a wish so badly. She wanted warm clothes, hot food, a roof that did not leak. She wanted jewels, furs, flowers, fresh oranges in midwinter, all delivered by cavalry officers on white horses who would make Charles jealous. She wanted the smell of carbolic soap and vinegar out from under her fingernails. But who would have to die to give her what she wanted?

So she scrubbed, and polished, and kept her eyes demurely lowered, and tried not to think about how much she hated chilly, stern virtue.

'What,' hissed Mrs Fielding, 'is the meaning of this?'

The rain spattered against the basement window of the kitchen. Eleanor, Aoife and Daisy were lined up while Mrs Fielding paced in front of them, holding a letter. Aoife's forged reference.

Eleanor stared straight ahead, every trace of expression wiped off her face, hands squeezed together behind her back. Next to her, Aoife was crying, a red mark on her cheek. Aoife had been down to the Servants' Registry Office on her afternoon off, looking for another position. She hadn't gone far enough afield. When she'd handed over her reference letter, the clerk had realized it was not in Mr Pembroke's handwriting.

Eleanor's palms were slippery with sweat. Forging a reference was a criminal offence. She was the only housemaid who could read and write. Mrs Fielding stalked up and down the line, the letter crumpled in her hand, staring into each frightened face. Eleanor's heart was pounding. Soon, the housekeeper would realize what Eleanor had done.

Mrs Fielding stopped in front of Aoife. 'I ought to dismiss you on the spot,' she spat.

'I...' Aoife was crying too hard to speak. Mrs Fielding slapped her again and she stumbled back.

'Stop that this instant!' the housekeeper snapped. 'I ought to send for the magistrate right now—'

'It's not her fault!' Daisy yelled.

Eleanor's head snapped around to look at her. Daisy was

flushed, her fists clenched. She had a forged reference of her own, surely she wouldn't tell...

Mrs Fielding rounded on her. 'And why's that?'

Eleanor willed Daisy not to look at her. There was a moment's silence.

'Aoife can't read,' Daisy said. 'How was she to know the letter wasn't from the master?'

'Perhaps,' Mrs Fielding said, her voice icy, 'because I did not give it to her. Where did you get this letter, Aoife?'

'I...I found it,' Aoife gulped, 'in the study, when I was cleaning.'

'You found it,' Mrs Fielding repeated.

'Yes, and I knew it was for me because it had my name on the front and I don't know my letters but I do know those ones, and what else would the master be writing to *me* for?' Aoife said, in a rush.

Mrs Fielding thrust the letter under Aoife's nose. 'Show me.'

Eleanor held her breath, praying that Aoife hadn't been lying.

'Those ones,' said Aoife.

Mrs Fielding sniffed, but said nothing. Eleanor heard Daisy sigh. A lump of coal shifted behind the range's vast doors and all three of them flinched.

'I've seen this hand before,' said Mrs Fielding, slowly.

Eleanor felt like she was falling. *Charles's letters.* Mrs Fielding must have seen them when Eleanor was writing them for him. She knew, dear God, *she knew.*

The housekeeper walked towards her. Each step rang through the kitchen. Eleanor stared at the spot above the kitchen door and fought to keep the fear from showing on her face.

'Upstairs,' said Mrs Fielding. 'Now.'

Mrs Fielding marched her out of the kitchen and up the servants' staircase. Before she knew it Eleanor was outside the study door and a voice was calling 'Enter!'

Charles was behind his father's desk, staring at a large pile of account books with his head in his hands. He jumped to his feet when Eleanor came in, his eyes flickering between her and the housekeeper. All the colour drained from his face.

'What's happened?' he asked.

Mrs Fielding held out the forged reference. 'I wonder, sir, if you recognize this handwriting.'

Charles took the envelope and scanned through the letter. For the first time Eleanor noticed how slowly he read. He was frowning, lips moving as he worked down the page. Eleanor wanted to snatch the letter out of his hands and throw it on the fire.

At last, he looked up. He glanced at the paper, then at Eleanor, and back to the letter again.

'I'm afraid not.'

Relief flooded through Eleanor. It took everything she had to stop her knees from sagging. Aoife was safe.

'Are you sure, sir?' asked Mrs Fielding. 'Would you stand a little closer to the light?'

Charles gave Mrs Fielding his most charming smile. 'Mrs F, I know I'm not the most academically minded young man but I do hope you think me capable of recognizing a familiar hand.'

Eleanor could feel Mrs Fielding looking at her. Eleanor didn't say anything. She didn't even move. She just stared straight ahead and tried to prop up her self-control.

'Perhaps I'd better speak with your father instead,' said Mrs Fielding.

Charles slipped the letter into his jacket pocket. 'Allow me. Father has many demands on his time and this is clearly a delicate subject. I think it best if you don't make any changes to the household staff until we've got to the bottom of this.'

Mrs Fielding pressed her lips into a thin line. 'Very good, sir. Come along, Ella.'

Mrs Fielding swept out of the study. Before Eleanor followed her, Charles gave a small smile and threw the letter on the fire.

All Eleanor could see were packages, and they were slipping out of her hands. She'd crammed what she could into the basket, but it wasn't big enough. Two parcels of laundry were wedged under one arm, and the third was clutched in her damp hand. She forced her way through the crowds, hating them all. To think that less than a week ago, she had been in Charles's bed – but no. She gave herself a shake. She couldn't think about that.

'Songbirds! Lovely songbirds, beautiful tunes—'

'Old clo'! Old clo'!'

'Pigeon pie! Hot pigeon pie, nice and – oi! You put that back, you thieving bugger!'

They called out on all sides, lost in a brown fog that choked the afternoon light. Shapes in the mist dissolved into passers-by as she drew closer. Eleanor kept to the pavement, listening for the rumble of carts and omnibuses. There was a yelp from somewhere in the road and a burst of swearing; someone, or something, hadn't moved out of the way of the traffic in time. Someone barged into her shoulder and a package flew out of her grip. Before she could reach it a child darted out of the fog and snatched it.

'Stop! Stop!'

He stuck his tongue out and ran off. Eleanor beckoned to a boy in a threadbare jacket.

'You, boy! Get that package back and you'll have a sixpence!'

He looked her up and down with a calculating eye. 'You ain't got sixpence, missus!'

'You shall have it! Just run and fetch it, quickly!'

'I ain't no fool! You ain't got sixpence for a shawl, you ain't got one for me!'

He sauntered off. Eleanor stared around desperately, but the thief had vanished into the fog. No constable in sight. No aimless young men susceptible to tearful blondes. No trail to follow, because six feet in front of her he'd vanished. There was nothing she could do but go home and explain herself. It'd come out of her wages. Depending on what was in the parcel, that might not be the end of it. She'd just have to hope it was the maids' aprons and not Mr Pembroke's silk cravats.

Mrs Fielding cuffed her round the head when Eleanor told her what had happened. She took the laundry parcels into the housekeeper's rooms and made Eleanor wait in the dark corridor while she picked them apart.

Mrs Fielding opened the door. 'Cuffs and collars,' she said. 'You're lucky it wasn't the cravats. Go on up to the study and explain yourself.'

'But—'

'It's not for me to choose your punishment now. Go on. Upstairs with you.'

Aoife shot her a sympathetic look as Eleanor climbed the stairs. Her heart sank. What was she going to do? She could threaten Mr Pembroke with the Inspector, but she'd already done that once before. Would it work again?

The door to the second-floor landing creaked open. Light pooled at the foot of the study door, the only spot of colour in the gloomy corridor. He was waiting for her.

What would he do when she told him? Would he stay slumped across the desk, glassy-eyed and silent – or would he reach for her instead?

The door loomed in front of her.

Could she turn back? No – he'd notice his clothes had gone missing. Or would he? Mr Pembroke was either drunk or hungover, and the laudanum only made it worse. Did he pay attention to the contents of his wardrobe? Or worse – what if the cuffs and collars had been a present from Mrs Pembroke, the last thing she made before she died?

Her hand rattled on the doorknob.

Eleanor took a deep breath, desperate for a plan. She could lie, she could snatch up the poker, she could pour him another drugged drink, she could flirt – no, she thought, she couldn't do that. Was this how it had started for Leah?

She opened the door.

Charles was sitting at his father's desk, ledgers spread in front of him. He sprang up, his chair clattering away.

'Eleanor! I – please, sit down! Sit down, do. Can I...can I get you a drink?'

She shook her head. 'There's something I must tell you.'

He blanched. 'Oh God. You aren't...you're not...'

'I've lost some of your laundry, sir. I'm so sorry. It was snatched on the street and I—'

Charles sagged with relief. 'Is that all? I thought you were going to tell me something else entirely!'

'Oh? I – *oh*. No.'

He poured himself a glass of brandy, smiling. Eleanor remembered the laudanum; guilt twisted as she watched the amber liquid splash into the glass.

'Aren't you angry?'

'Goodness, no! It's only laundry. You do look frightened.'

'I thought I'd find your father here. You won't tell him, will you?'

'I wouldn't dream of it, if it would inconvenience you. No need to disturb him when he's at his club.'

Relief flooded through her. She shifted closer to the fire.

'You look quite frozen,' Charles said. 'You haven't been out in this awful weather, have you?'

'It's not as bad as it looks. I've yet to find a new shawl, so it seems worse than it is.'

'A new shawl?'

She told him about giving her shawl to Leah. All the lines around his eyes crinkled when he smiled. He'd been close enough for her to trace every single one, that night, and the thought made her voice catch halfway through a sentence. His smile would melt her self-control, if she was not careful.

'Well,' he said, when she had finished, 'you must stay and warm yourself by the fire. I should be glad of your company.'

The fire crackled in the quiet, just as it had when they'd made love. She'd only picked out the sounds when Charles had rolled away from her, panting. He'd pulled her to his side and fallen asleep, and she'd wondered if this was how it had been for men and women in ancient times, before starch and corsets cajoled them into behaving.

She wanted to stay. She wanted to take Charles's hand and run into the fog, where no one could see where they went.

But then she remembered the fear in his eyes when she'd asked what they'd do if his father found out. She'd made her choice and she would stick to it, no matter how much it hurt. 'I don't think that would be wise, sir.'

He blushed. 'Perhaps not.'

She curtseyed, and saw him wince. She turned away from the heat and light.

'Eleanor? Please don't call me "sir". Not after everything.'

She nodded, and stepped back into the cold.

The next day, there was a parcel outside her door. Eleanor found it when she went up to bed. It sagged when she picked it up, brown paper crackling under her fingers.

She opened it, and colour spilled into her lap. Rich red, with gossamer-fine patterns in white and yellow. Fluid and soft, it slipped through her fingers, but when she put it around her shoulders she felt warmer than she had in days. She might have been wearing a sunset.

There was no note.

Charles had chosen well. It was lightweight, warm, and large enough to cocoon herself in. Wearing it, she would not look like a servant, and no one would ever tell if she also used it for a blanket. It was the softest, prettiest thing she owned. And he'd left no note. He hadn't even handed it to her himself, or lingered to watch her unwrap it.

It was the only spot of colour in her room. Everything else had faded through endless washing or the slow march of damp. Her curtains had once been red. Now they were rust-brown and plastered to the grimy glass, slick with condensation. Even as the colours burned, she knew that if she left the shawl here it, too, would fade.

So would she.

All the colour and softness would be leached out of her. It had already started. Wasn't she always tired, always sore, always cold? How long had it been since she'd crept down to the library and let her imagination carry her away? What if she forgot how to do it – what if one day she would never be able to escape, not even into her own head? Soon, she would be as cold and colourless as all the other empty things in Granborough House, and she wouldn't even notice what she'd lost.

No. She wouldn't let that happen. She *couldn't*. She would not move through life like an automaton running on its groove.

She stood up. The shawl fell away.

She ran.

When she knocked on his door, Charles opened it at once.

'Eleanor! What are you—'

She grabbed him by the lapels and kissed him. For a moment he was frozen, but then he pulled her close, winding his arms around her waist. He shut the door behind them, and the cold and the dark ceased to matter.

When the sun was up, Eleanor had to be perfectly respectable. If Mrs Fielding caught the slightest hint of any impropriety between Eleanor and Charles, she would be dismissed. He lingered in the rooms she cleaned, pretending he'd offered to move furniture or steady a stepladder if anyone came close. Eleanor kept her eyes downcast and pretended to be out of his reach. Sometimes, she'd catch his eye while she did it, and watch his Adam's apple bob as he swallowed.

They had to be careful. On her afternoon off she walked

to Chelsea to find a sympathetic apothecary, looking every inch the lady's maid. She'd made delicate enquiries on behalf of a fictional mistress and had been supplied with a small bag of herbs. She had a quiet word with Charles, and now he was careful too.

He was always careful with her. There was always food and drink in his room, the fire was always lit. He made sure she never got too cold, and always had a hot bath waiting if she wanted one. On the nights when Mr Pembroke was out she would read aloud, and Charles would stroke her skin and sink into the sound of her voice. When Mr Pembroke was home, they crept into distant rooms, locking the doors behind them, and stopped each other's mouths with kisses. The thought of not seeing each other did not even occur to them. The cold was driven away and the dark grew brighter every minute she was with Charles. How could she ever stay away, when he brought so much warmth and light?

But at four o'clock in the morning, she would have to leave. It was Eleanor's job to clean and light the range first thing in the morning. She could not be late; the others would come looking for her.

Charles pulled her close, burying his face in her hair. His mouth found her neck.

'Stay here today,' he murmured, 'that's an order from your employer.'

She gave him a playful shove. 'You know I mustn't.'

'I know you want to.'

His hand was sliding across her skin. 'Yes.'

'Tell them you're sick. They won't suspect.'

'And if they send for the doctor?'

He grinned. 'Then I shall nurse you back to health myself.'

His hands were everywhere. He kissed her, reaching for her again – and the front door slammed. Unsteady footsteps rang through the house. Someone was coming up the front stairs. Charles swore, and blushed.

'Eleanor, I'm so sorry—'

She shushed him. 'It's your father.' She crept out of bed and shoved her clothes back on. Her dress was crumpled, her hair was a mess. One look at her and anyone would know what she had been doing.

Charles was struggling into a dressing gown and trying to flatten his hair. 'Let me go first. I'll help him to his room and then you can slip away.'

He left. Eleanor could hear them talking on the floor below. She shook out the creases in her skirts, waiting. When it was quiet, she opened the door and crept out, her hair sagging down the back of her neck.

She'd almost made it to the servants' staircase when Mr Pembroke lurched up the stairs. He was still in his evening things, but they were damp, crumpled and stinking. Charles was behind him, his face white.

Mr Pembroke stared at her, eyes unfocused, and she took her chance.

Eleanor bobbed a curtsey. 'Excuse me, sir,' she said, and left. She heard him retching, and wondered if he would remember.

Later, Eleanor was scrubbing the mould off a windowsill in the library and struggling to keep her eyes open.

Her nights with Charles were bliss, but they took their toll. All her bones were lead and her eyes ached to close. The rocking-chair squeak of the cleaning rag on wet wood. The undulating rumble of wheels over cobblestones. The spitting and sputtering of chestnuts roasting in the street. It was no lullaby, but her eyes were closing nevertheless.

'Eleanor!'

Her eyes flew open at the sound of Charles's voice. He strode across the room and knelt beside her.

'Are you quite well?'

'I'm just a little tired.'

Guilt flickered across his face. 'I should never have kept you up all night.'

Eleanor resisted the urge to make a joke. 'Please, darling, don't worry.'

'Mrs F really ought to take on some more girls,' he said, as he led her to a chair. 'It's cruel that the burden should fall on your shoulders.'

'Do you think she will?'

He grimaced. 'She's spoken to Father, but we can't take on more staff until the roof is repaired. The workmen have been rather unhelpful about Father's credit.'

Someone coughed.

'Master Charles,' said Mrs Fielding, 'what are you doing?'

Eleanor stood up at once, smoothing her hair with an unsteady hand. How much had Mrs Fielding heard?

Charles straightened up, already smiling. 'Nothing to worry about, Mrs F. Eleanor was feeling a little unwell.'

'*Ella* has duties to attend to,' said Mrs Fielding, her eyes flickering between them.

'I'm sorry, Mrs Fielding,' said Eleanor. 'I'm feeling quite myself again now.'

'I'm sure you are.'

Charles stiffened, his voice suddenly hard. 'What do you mean by that, Mrs Fielding?'

242

Eleanor started back; he sounded just like his father. Mrs Fielding stared at the floor and dropped a curtsey. 'I meant no harm, Master Charles. I only wish to see that Ella does not shirk her duties.'

Charles gave her a starched smile. 'I'm sure you needn't worry about that.'

Mrs Fielding left. Charles turned back to Eleanor, grinning, but she held up a hand. The floorboards creaked; Mrs Fielding was still outside the door, listening.

'Will that be all, Master Charles?' Eleanor said, loudly and clearly.

He winked at her. 'For the present.'

The floorboards creaked again as Mrs Fielding moved away. Eleanor closed the door as quietly as she could.

'What are we going to do if she finds out?' she whispered.

Charles caressed her cheek. 'I told you I won't let anything happen to you, Eleanor.'

She leant into his hand. 'We need a plan.'

'I couldn't do without you,' Charles murmured, pressing a kiss on her forehead. 'If she finds out, we'll run away.'

'Do you mean it?'

'Of course I do! But we'll need a little time. I'll have to get some money together, and find lodgings – and of course, we'll need tickets to Gretna Green.'

Eleanor felt as if she had been bathed in light. Her heart seemed too full of life and love to be contained. She beamed at him, hardly daring to believe what he'd said.

'Gretna Green?'

Charles kissed her. 'You don't think I'd spirit you away and then not marry you? And from there – anywhere you like. It'll be just like we planned, that night in the library.' He tucked a stray curl behind her ear. 'I'd take you to the stars themselves, if you asked.'

In that moment, wings could have sprouted from her back and she would not have questioned it; she could have done anything.

Mrs Fielding was watching Eleanor. Sometimes, when Eleanor was scrubbing the floors or sweeping up ash, she would catch a glimpse of the housekeeper – a reflection in wet marble, or a shadow moving by the grate. Sometimes, Eleanor saw the black-eyed woman too. Her empty eyes might have been following Eleanor, or they might not. It was impossible to say. In the shadows, she seemed to see her everywhere. Eleanor shook the visions away, never sure if they were really there.

Granborough House was full of shadows now. December shrouded the house in darkness. Fog choked the stuttering lamps. Fires spat and coughed like dying men. Street-mud froze to the hall floor and oozed across the marble when it thawed. Not even the hulking kitchen range could banish the mauso-leum chill in the air. Daisy and Aoife pushed their straw pallets right up against the oven door, and when Eleanor came down-stairs she saw them tangled in each other's arms. For warmth, they said, when they sat up, blushing.

Her warmth was Charles.

Eleanor came alive under his hands. One touch could make her skin sing. One look could make her feel like her whole body was blushing. He did not even need to be there – some-times, the memory of their last night together thawed her from the inside out. Every smuggled glass of port, every hidden tray of tarts lit a candle inside her and now, she was glowing. She was always tired, these days – but it was a luxurious, languorous tiredness, like a cat stretching in front of a fire. Her hair was glossy, she did not ache, and the sharpness of her ribs was beginning to fade. Love suited her.

Now, she lounged on Charles's bed like Cleopatra, their legs tangled together. They'd been together for hours, but so far he'd only said her name. He stared up at the canopy while she watched the rise and fall of his chest, the flutter of his eyelashes when he blinked. There was a small mole underneath his ear she'd never noticed before.

She kissed it. 'Is something the matter? You've hardly said a word.'

'Just something Father said. It's nothing.'

Eleanor sat up, clutching the sheets. 'You don't think he suspects anything?'

'Good Lord, no! No, I'm sure he doesn't.'

'Then what's troubling you?'

'Our finances. I'm afraid they are...not as secure as I would like them to be.'

Eleanor was not surprised. Mould on the windowsills and damp on the walls were hardly the marks of a prosperous house. A hasty marriage to an heiress might have fixed all that, but she had prevented it. Eleanor was the cause of Aoife's chilblains, the ice on the attic windows and Mrs Banbury's swollen joints. Eleanor pushed back her guilt. If Charles had married, they never could have been together.

'Father won't allow me any extra funds. I'm afraid it may take longer than I'd hoped to raise the money we may need for Gretna Green. We'll need to stay there for three weeks before we can be married. And then there's the honeymoon. We'll visit the Highlands, and see lochs as blue as your eyes.'

She smiled. 'How shall you manage it?'

He sighed. 'Sell something, I suppose.' He pulled her closer.

'I don't understand,' said Eleanor. 'You must have an income. Aren't there lands, titles, shares?'

He stroked her arm. 'Father sold them off. Even lands that had been ours for centuries. Not that I know when they first came into the family. There's all sorts of stories.'

The air shifted. Eleanor could have sworn she felt a hand on her shoulder. 'Oh?'

'My ancestor, Jacoby Pembroke. Made his fortune in the Civil War, came out of nowhere. There were all sorts of rumours. Blackmail, piracy, witchcraft.'

Eleanor thought of the black book, waiting on a library shelf. How long had it been in the Pembroke family? How many other desperate people had seen the scribbled-out creature on the frontispiece, and looked into a pair of fathomless eyes?

Charles grinned at her. 'He died in 1666, you know. They say he was so wicked the Devil came to collect him himself. And,' he said, his hands moving slowly downwards, 'he had a terrible weakness for girls with golden hair...'

'You're a beast!'

'Oh, yes. I get it from wicked old Jacoby.'

Relief flooded through Eleanor. It could not be a coincidence; Charles's ancestor had made the family fortune with the black-eyed woman's help. Eleanor hadn't imagined her.

He kissed her. They said nothing more until the morning.

The next day Eleanor was hunched over the front steps, scrubbing. The street was silver with frost and the iron railings glittered with every passing lantern. It was too dark to tell if the steps were properly clean and they would freeze over when she was done. But Mrs Fielding had insisted. Clean steps were respectable, so clean steps were what they must have.

Horses snorted as their hooves skittered on the ice. Children slid past like ice-skaters, shrieking and laughing. A costermonger's boy sidled up to her, a man's jacket flapping around his knees, glancing nervously at the long windows of the tall Mayfair houses.

'Hot coffee, missus? Only a penny from Pa's barrow.'

'No, thank you.'

When she had finished her hands looked like lobster claws, and all the bones in her back clicked when she stood up. She hurried down to the kitchen and hunched over the range, trying to ignore the fug of Mrs Banbury's onion soup, which smelled a lot like sweat. It was not usually so bad; she must have changed the recipe.

Mrs Fielding waved her over. 'Ella? A word, if you please.'

Charles, Eleanor thought, dread swelling up like a balloon.

Mrs Fielding led her down the corridor and into the housekeeper's rooms. The parlour was small and brown, made hot and damp from the heat of the range. There was a table and chair and a door leading to Mrs Fielding's bedroom, and not much else. Mottled dark patches spread across every surface, giving Eleanor the uncomfortable sensation of being enveloped in the paws of a great lynx.

Mrs Fielding's eyes flicked to Eleanor's stomach. 'Sit down.'

Eleanor obeyed. She sat up straight, making sure that Mrs Fielding could see there was no curve to her belly. Mrs Fielding stood by the table, giving her a searching look.

Eventually she said, 'Have you given any thought to your future, Ella?'

Eleanor was taken aback. She'd given plenty of thought to

her future – to the wishes, and to her and Charles's plan to elope to Gretna Green. If she could not be rid of the wishes, Eleanor would be watching her language for the rest of her life: speaking an idle fancy aloud could kill someone. That shadow would hang over her until the day she died – but that might be easier to bear when she and Charles were married. She'd have to forge another reference for Aoife before they went to Scotland. Eleanor's threats against Mr Pembroke had worked, but they only worked because Eleanor was still here. If she left, she would take his self-restraint with her.

Out loud, she said, 'No, Mrs Fielding.'

Mrs Fielding pursed her lips. 'I find that most unlikely. You're seventeen years old. That's the age a girl starts to wonder what the future may hold. Husbands, and so on.'

Eleanor went still. Husbands? Did she know about Charles? She must have seen something. Had she heard footsteps along the corridors after the servants had gone to bed, and crept up the stairs to see?

'But, Ella, these things are not as simple as they seem. You must keep your wits about you. Gentlemen will say all sorts of things to turn a girl's head. I know that you were close with Leah and I must warn you not to follow such a poor example. The virtuous thing is not to listen, but to hold true.'

Eleanor kept her face blank. It was something she had become very good at, after three years of service. But she knew that Mrs Fielding, who had been managing housemaids for decades, could see the shutters coming down behind her eyes.

'I don't know what you mean.'

Mrs Fielding rubbed the scar on her neck. It was a wobbly curve about two inches long, wider at each end, and with intermittent pits and ridges running along its length.

Teeth marks.

But it couldn't be *her* teeth marks, no matter what Lizzie had said. Even as a child Eleanor never would've dared to bite the housekeeper, and if she had she'd certainly remember doing it. Mrs Fielding's hand flattened against the scar. She twisted slightly, as if she was ready to back away.

Eleanor looked away. No. It wasn't true. It couldn't be true. She hadn't done it.

'We were speaking of your future,' Mrs Fielding said. Her voice was too loud.

'As I've said, Mrs Fielding, I'm afraid I haven't—'

Mrs Fielding held up a hand. 'I know this is not what you wanted. You've made no secret of that. Had Miss Darling been a better fit, things might have turned out very differently, and not a one of us would have begrudged you for it. You've never been happy here, have you?'

Eleanor squirmed.

'But…you're young, Ella. You've yet to learn the value of patience. And Master Charles…he's a good boy, but with his mother gone he has only his father's example to follow. He's four years older than you, and has seen a good deal more of the world – and all the worldly things in it.'

'Mrs Fielding, I—'

'Did he buy you that shawl?'

Eleanor swallowed. 'He gave me a small sum as a token of his appreciation after I helped him with his letters. I got it second-hand, with my wages from Miss Darling.'

Mrs Fielding pursed her lips again and fell quiet. As soon as Eleanor opened the package she'd known she would need an excuse. Charles *had* been favouring her, anyone could tell.

Eleanor leant forward. 'Mrs Fielding, I shall certainly think

249

on what you've said. But I would like to reassure you that Master Charles has never behaved improperly with me, nor I with him.'

Relief swept over Mrs Fielding's face. 'You may go.'

Eleanor stood up. She couldn't seem guilty. After all, she'd done nothing wrong. She hadn't bitten Mrs Fielding and her relationship with Charles would soon be thoroughly above board. No one would care how they met when they were married.

Eleanor left the housekeeper's rooms, knowing that Mrs Fielding was watching her go. She kept her back straight and forced herself not to falter. How much did Mrs Fielding know?

The church had been cold enough to make Eleanor's breath mist in the air, but outside was worse. For once, the maids were left alone: Mrs Kettering's son had returned from India with his new wife, and half the parishioners were interrogating the poor woman. Charles fended off the rest of the congregation – gossips and eager mothers with blushing daughters in tow. Watching Charles be introduced to girls bundled up in sleek furs and velvet capes made Eleanor more conscious than ever of her rough hands and darned clothes. Would he really marry her, when London was full of so many pretty girls?

'Come along,' Mrs Fielding said, when he was still failing to extricate himself from a knot of parishioners, 'the Sunday dinner must be prepared.'

They went home, shivering through the streets. Eleanor ached all over and there was so much ice underfoot that she slid along the pavements. She saw her own reflection staring out of a sheet of brown ice and wondered, blushing, if this meant the man behind her could see up her skirts. He'd be disappointed. She was wearing so many layers he'd be lucky if he saw the tip of her boot. When she looked up, she realized she'd lost the others – she'd been going so slowly that she hadn't noticed how far ahead they'd gone.

A fug of coffee, soup and smoke hung in the air and made her gag. Horses steamed in the street and beggars sidled up to them for warmth. She saw a chimney sweep and envied his coating of soot – there was so much of it, it looked as if it kept out the chill.

She was about to head back when she heard a voice.

'Ella?'

The woman standing in front of her was distorted. Every spare ounce of flesh had been scraped away by hunger, apart from her belly, which was so swollen and distended it looked as if she'd overbalance. Her bones strained through her skin. Eyes large, lips cracked and white, she could have been a ghost from one of Aoife's stories. It was only when she noticed the tartan shawl – sparkling with frost, now – that Eleanor, horrified, recognized her.

'Leah! Good God, I—'

Leah's hand clutched at her arm. A cold sore oozed at the corner of her mouth. 'Give us a penny. Enough for a cup of hot soup, that's all I ask.'

'I don't have any money. It's all at the house.'

Leah gave her a rictus grin. 'You must have something. Anything. Just enough for a night in the flophouse. Please.'

Eleanor led Leah over to the nearest soup stall. 'I really don't have any money,' she said, as the stall-holder waved them away. 'Leah, where are you sleeping?'

Leah didn't answer. They stopped in front of another coster-monger's cart. A pot of soup was bubbling there, and the smell of the onions made Eleanor feel sick. The stall-holder, a middle-aged Indian woman wrapped in shawls, gave them both an appraising look.

'Madam,' Eleanor said, 'will you feed this poor woman a bowl of soup a day, please? She's a good girl, but fallen on hard times.'

The stall-holder looked at Eleanor critically, her eyes flicking between her dress and her much finer shawl. 'It's a shilling a week.'

Eleanor thought of Mr Pembroke, drunk and stinking in his bed, and hatred sparked through her like lightning. *He* would never have to worry about where his next meal came from.

'You may send the bill to Granborough House,' she snapped. 'It *will* be paid.'

The costermonger sighed. 'I might've known. All right, love. Come back same time tomorrow. I don't want you hanging about the stall, mind. You'll put off my regulars.'

Leah grabbed the cup of soup the woman handed her. She gulped it down, snorting and lapping like an animal, and sucked the splashes off her filthy fingers. Anger and shame roiling in the pit of her stomach, Eleanor turned away.

Daisy was in disgrace. She had persuaded Mrs Banbury to let her try and make an oyster pie. 'Family recipe,' she'd said. 'Gran used to make it all the time.'

Eleanor hunched over the chamber pot and retched. *Family recipe*, she thought, bitterly.

At least she was not the only one, Eleanor consoled herself. Aoife was outside, hurling into the rose bushes; Mrs Fielding was in her rooms insisting that she had 'a slight headache'; Mrs Banbury was swearing listlessly at Daisy in between bouts of vomiting. Mr Pembroke had taken one look at the pale, sweaty faces of his maidservants and left for his club.

'I'm sorry!' Daisy wailed. 'There must've been a dodgy one!'

Mrs Banbury let out a bark of mirthless laughter.

The others were better in a few days, but Eleanor found it harder to shake the illness off. She never felt as though she had finished being sick. It was worse in the mornings, and when she caught a whiff of a strong smell. No matter what she did it was always in the background, like the stench of the Thames on a hot day.

Charles doted on her. His father's absence had let him rifle through all the rooms and make several trips to the pawnbroker's, but he regarded this as taking advantage of Eleanor's illness. To make up for it he fed her morsels of crystallized ginger, and bought her tonics and tinctures which, he said, had been guaranteed to work. Eleanor tried a few; most of them were sugar water. She drank them anyway, because Charles had tried.

After that, she had the best Christmas she could remember.

She threw up six times and her dress uniform was too tight, but that did not matter. When the maids were home from church, they all filed into the drawing room and received presents from the family. They all got the same thing: enough cloth to make a new uniform and a handshake from Charles while Mr Pembroke snored in the corner.

Mrs Banbury and Daisy – relegated, now, to chopping vegetables – created a feast. Roast goose, vast tureens of potatoes, Palestine soup, chestnuts, sausage meat, pickled walnuts and a plum pudding smothered in brandy butter. It was far too much for Mr Pembroke and Charles to eat themselves, so when they sent down their leftovers the maids fell upon them, gorging themselves on fluffy roast potatoes and crackling golden goose-skin.

Eleanor stole away when Aoife and Daisy were still groaning. Charles was waiting for her upstairs.

He gave her a present – dove-grey kid gloves, soft and supple as silk. She handed over hers – a book of sonnets – and it felt cheap by comparison. It was so small, and the blue dye was coming away on her fingertips. But when Charles read the inscription – 'for C, with love' – he beamed, and all her shabbiness was forgotten. His smile mended all her faults, and when he kissed her, she was made new.

January dragged its freezing fingers through the house. Water pooled on windowsills and made the curtains sag. The smell of damp forced its way into Eleanor's mouth and made her stomach roil. She retched into a chamber pot and cursed all oysters. She was never eating anything that came out of the sea again. It was the servants' diet; she didn't have the strength to fight off illnesses now. When she was a girl she had eaten what she liked, and she'd never been sick until her first bleed.

Eleanor wiped her mouth and straightened up. The truth dawned.

She was tired. She was sore. Her dresses were growing tighter. Smells choked her, she'd been throwing up every morning and she could not remember when she had last bled.

But that could mean anything. There were lots of things she couldn't remember; she'd learned not to rely on her memory. Her monthly bleeds had never been monthly. Her dresses were growing tighter because Charles was smuggling her half his dinner. And everyone had got sick from those oysters – was it really surprising she'd caught something she couldn't quite shake off?

That was it. That *had* to be it.

Her hands slipped down to her stomach. She pressed down, hard. She couldn't feel anything. But that meant nothing. There were things you couldn't always see and feel, but they were there all the same. Eleanor couldn't always see the black-eyed woman, and yet she was still there.

Of all people – of all things – she would know.

Eleanor cleared her throat. 'I'd like to talk to you. Can you come out?'

The shadows shifted, and the black-eyed woman was there. 'Of course.'

'I...I need to ask you something. If I do, will you answer me truthfully?'

She smiled. 'I always do, dear heart.'

Eleanor closed her eyes. 'Am I with child?'

'I believe you know the answer to that.'

Nausea swirled through Eleanor. Her stomach twitched – was that *it*, making itself known? It couldn't be. She wasn't ready. She'd thought about children, but in the same vague way she wondered what she might look like if she had red hair. Perhaps in ten years, she might have liked some, once she was married to Charles and had seen the world twice over. Not when she was unmarried, not in the depths of winter, not before she got her next wage packet. Not now – oh God, *oh God*, not now.

'That's no answer,' Eleanor said. 'I thought you were supposed to know these things!'

'I do.'

'Then tell me!'

The woman's eyes flickered. 'I can tell you this. It will be a boy. He will be born in July; not too far from your own birthday, I believe. He will be a healthy child when he comes into the world. After that I cannot say.'

'What? Why?'

'That depends on you.'

Eleanor sank down onto the bed, her head in her hands. All her grand plans were splintering – France, Italy, the lingering tour of Europe she'd dreamed of. Her stomach had opened up into a yawning pit. 'How could this have happened? I've been so careful!'

'Not careful enough, it would seem.'

Eleanor sneaked into Charles's room the first chance she got. He was sitting on the edge of his bed, brushing his jacket clean, and he beamed when he saw her.

'Eleanor? This is an unexpected – good Lord. Are you quite well?'

There were two glasses on his bedside table, sticky and purple with last night's dried port. Eleanor picked one up and rolled the stem between her fingers, her throat suddenly too tight to speak. Sunlight caught all the facets of the crystal as it turned, the light leaving each piece as quickly as it came. A new fear was gnawing at her. Was all they shared just as insubstantial – nothing more than a flash of light in the dark?

'Charles, I am with child.'

She rolled the glass again, and watched the light flicker. Charles closed his bedroom door and locked it. Never had the click and grind of the lock seemed so loud. Was he locking her in, or locking the rest of the world out?

'What are we going to do?' she asked.

'Pack your things. We're going to Gretna Green.'

Charles lifted up a corner of his mattress and rummaged around. He pulled out a train timetable and read it, running a hand through his hair.

'We'll get the express tomorrow morning,' he said. 'I have a few things to attend to before we leave, but they won't take long. We'll need money, and clothes – is that all you have? That won't do for Scotland, you must keep warm. Oh Lord. Where's my trunk?'

'But what about all our plans?' she whispered. 'What about all those places we were going to see together?'

'Oh, Eleanor,' he murmured. 'We don't have to have grand adventures to be happy.' He drew her close and tilted her chin up to his. 'I could live in a little village for the rest of my days and count myself a lucky man, with you beside me.'

Eleanor tried to smile. 'But…but it won't be like we planned.'

'It'll be better than we planned,' he assured her. 'A little slower, perhaps, but that's nothing to fear. And we can still travel, once the baby is old enough. We'll only have to wait a little while. Right now, all I want to do is to protect you and our child, and give you both the best I can.' He beamed at her. 'Our child. Doesn't that sound wonderful?'

He kissed her. Eleanor knew she ought to be pleased. Charles was going to keep his promise and marry her. They would be starting a new life together, far from the smoke and the city and all the things she'd done. She probably would be happy with a life like that, but it would be a happiness she would have to settle into. And for all that Charles said they could still go away together, Eleanor was not so sure. She saw her dreams become smoke. How old would she be – and how many more children would she have to worry about – when she finally saw all the things she'd dreamed of? Would she never get a chance to dance in the shoes she'd wished for? How many nights would she lie awake, thinking of all she had given up?

'I'll have a cab waiting at three o'clock in the morning,' Charles said. 'You'll be careful, until then?'

'I shall be the soul of discretion.'

He laid a hand on her stomach, very gently. 'That's not what I meant. No heavy lifting. And you must take care with what you eat – oh Lord, what *are* you supposed to eat?'

Eleanor smiled at him, her eyes brimming with tears. 'It'll be in a book somewhere.'

He kissed her again. 'Three o'clock. Don't be late.'

Shouting rang through the house. Full of trepidation, Eleanor went to the dining room under the pretence of cleaning. From there, she could hear something of what was being said.

The smell of Mr Pembroke's dinner – old mutton and onion gravy – crawled its way into her mouth and made her gag. She had to breathe into the tin of polish to stop her stomach heaving. When her nausea subsided, she realized the argument had stopped. All she could hear now were unsteady footsteps, and the faint hush of people listening.

The voices belonged to Charles and his father. Eleanor crept over to the fireplace and picked up the poker. Whatever Mr Pembroke did now, she wasn't going to let him find her unprepared.

The door clattered open. Mr Pembroke staggered into the room.

'So,' he seethed, 'you've sunk your claws into my son.'

He kicked the door shut and slumped into the nearest chair, head in his hands. Eleanor pointed the poker at him. She wasn't going to let him get close.

'Put that damn thing down,' he said, voice hoarse. 'You'll mark my jacket.'

Eleanor's lip curled. 'There are worse things I could do.'

He glared at her. 'Like marry my boy.'

Her temper flared. She was a respectable girl from a good family. There was no reason why she shouldn't marry Charles, but Mr Pembroke was speaking about her as if she were a common whore.

'How did you find out?' she asked, keeping her voice level.

Mr Pembroke's face twisted. 'I caught him in his mother's room,' he spat, 'rifling through her jewels! He had her ring in his hand! To think he would bestow Emmeline's ring on such a worthless, ill-bred—'

'That's enough,' Eleanor said. To her surprise, he stopped.

'I won't have you for a daughter-in-law,' Mr Pembroke muttered. 'Do you hear me? I will see this place burned to the ground before I let you anywhere near my son.'

'So burn it,' Eleanor hissed. 'He loves me. You can't keep him away.'

Mr Pembroke sprang to his feet. Eleanor pointed the poker at him like a sword. For a long moment they glared at each other. Then Mr Pembroke loped over to the sideboard and poured himself a brandy.

'Have you put anything in this one?'

Eleanor did not answer. Did he know about the laudanum, or was he just goading her after all the times she'd stirred his drink with a spoon and watched his face grow pale?

'I ought to have you dismissed,' he muttered, slumping back into his chair. 'I ought to have you brought before the magistrate. And that boy ought to see a doctor! Gretna Green...'

'You know that would never work,' Eleanor said. 'Charles is of age, he may marry who he likes. And you couldn't get a doctor to believe there's anything wrong with him. I am not without my charms.'

'If you so much as look at my son again,' he muttered, 'I will *ruin* you. I'll call back that constable and tell him you killed Lizzie. With my word against yours, you'll be hanged before summer.'

Eleanor kept her voice level. 'And if you do that, your son will never see you again.'

Mr Pembroke's jaw clenched. 'What will it take to keep you away from him?'

Eleanor pulled out a chair and sat down, thinking fast. Mr Pembroke had a point. Without another suspect, if Mr Pembroke accused her of killing Lizzie she would be arrested; he was a gentleman, he would be listened to. She wanted to marry Charles, to go where Mr Pembroke could never find them. She wanted it so much she could feel it tugging at every part of her. But she could not have that, and asking for it again would put it forever out of reach.

But there were other things she could do.

'I know you do not want me to be a part of your family,' she said. 'Charles does. This does not have to be an insurmountable problem. Secure me a house and set aside an allowance for me, to be paid into my account every month. You'll have to set one up for me, of course. I'll tell you my preferred bank.'

He sat up straighter, staring at her as if he'd never seen her before. His mouth fell slightly open and for one horrible moment, he looked like Charles. Eleanor shook her unease away. She could not afford to hesitate now.

'How dare—'

'I am not finished. Along with that you shall find me a maid and pay her wages – the little Irish girl will do,' Eleanor said, trying to sound careless. 'Let me see out my confinement as a respectable lady and I will not come here again.'

'Mercenary whore,' he muttered. 'How much d'you want?'

'Enough to cover rent, a maid's wages and the costs of feeding and clothing myself and a child. Perhaps three hundred pounds a year, to be paid in monthly instalments. I don't intend to go back to work once your grandson is born.'

Mr Pembroke snorted. 'The Devil take your three hundred pounds! I ought to throw you out in the clothes you stand up in!'

Eleanor gave him the nastiest smile she could muster. 'But you won't. You remember the Inspector? He was quite taken with me.'

All the colour drained out of Mr Pembroke's face. There was a fine sheen of sweat coating his skin and a tremor in his hands. Good, Eleanor thought. Let him be frightened. He deserved it.

'All right,' he muttered, 'all right. I'll give you what you asked for – but on one condition.'

'What is it?'

'Get rid of it.'

Eleanor froze. She'd wondered if he might ask her that but somehow, hearing him ask out loud was a knife in her ribs.

'You'll get your house, and your maid, and your damn three hundred pounds,' Mr Pembroke spat, 'if you get rid of the thing. My son *will* marry an heiress, and *you* will have no claim on him. I won't have him paying for this mistake for the rest of his life.'

Eleanor tightened her grip on the poker. 'I am not a mistake!'

'I beg to differ. Are we agreed?'

Eleanor knew she had only one real choice. If she refused, Mr Pembroke could ruin her. If he told Mrs Fielding, Eleanor would be thrown out with no wages, no reference and nowhere to sleep. She'd end up like Leah, freezing in shop doorways as her baby kicked inside her and all her friends turned their backs on her.

But if she took Mr Pembroke's deal, she would have a roof over her head, an income, and, best of all, Aoife would be out of Mr Pembroke's reach.

There was only one thing she could say. She thought of Charles, the way that he had held her and smiled at her, and it was only then that it hurt.

'I want it in writing,' she said. 'Not the parts about the baby, of course – just a signed agreement that you will allow me three hundred pounds a year as long as I...remain unmarried. I'm sure you have a lawyer who could oblige.'

His face twisted, and she had no idea if he was trying to smile or grimace. 'You'll have the agreement by this evening.'

She stood up. 'I'll take care of the rest.'

Turpentine. The herbs. Pennyroyal. Tansy. A box of 'Dr Merryweather's Female Pills', which rattled as she walked. Eleanor had taken everything she could find, and thrown it all up again behind the apothecary's shop. Her throat still burned from the turpentine. Now her room smelled of mildew and vomit, and the combination made her feel sick all over again. There was no point taking any more pills. She'd only bring them back up.

The house was quiet. She'd told the others she'd eaten a bad whelk and so far, they believed her. But tomorrow she'd be sick again, and they'd seen girls like her often enough to know the signs.

When she'd arrived back from the apothecary, throat still burning from the turpentine, she'd found a piece of paper slid underneath her bedroom door. It was Mr Pembroke's signed agreement. She'd crammed it into her case along with Mrs Pembroke's address book. The silver shoes winked up at her, and in that moment she wanted to tear them into pieces. She knocked on Charles's door, but when she went inside his room was empty.

She still didn't know where he was. His things were strewn about his room, Mrs Pembroke's ring forgotten on the floor. Eleanor remembered what Mr Pembroke had said – *that boy ought to see a doctor* – and shuddered to think of where he might be now.

She went back to her room and sat on the edge of her bed with her head in her hands, feeling as though all the warmth and colour had been wrung from her. If she and Charles had got away in time, it would not have been perfect. She would have never been a lady, never seen the world, but they would have had each other. But now, she did not even have that. Once again, Mr Pembroke had ripped the future she wanted from her fingers. How much more was he going to take from her? Was her self made up of component parts that could be snatched away or bartered off? Would she ever be whole, and happy?

She had to take Mr Pembroke's deal. A baby was not

something that she could hide. Without any money, she and her baby would be cold, hungry, dirty. There would be nowhere for them but the workhouse, and even there they would be separated if the child was a boy. It'd be her name that was passed around in whispers outside the church, her example mothers would use to warn their daughters. And even if she passed herself off as a respectable young widow, how could she bring Charles's baby into the world without him beside her? How could she bear to see his eyes, his smile, in a face that was not his own?

Eleanor shivered. She wasn't sure if she could look after another person who depended on her so completely. She had tried with her mother, all those years before. While Alice Hartley had lain in her bed, coughing up blood, Eleanor had tried to wash the bedsheets, clean the house, cook the dinner. But the laundry copper had burned her fingers and the stick was too heavy; she couldn't carry enough buckets of water to mop the floor; she couldn't light the kitchen range properly and had to stand on a chair to reach the stove. At first Eleanor cried and asked her neighbours for help, but she stopped when no one came.

Panic flooded her body at the thought of the burden, the weight.

She couldn't do it. She wouldn't. She wasn't going to put herself through that again. She'd wear herself down to nothing if she tried. At least if she took Mr Pembroke's deal, she could start again, unencumbered. No one need ever know what she'd done or who she'd been.

She was going to make a wish.

The black-eyed woman had been at the back of her mind all day, like a shape moving below the surface of the water.

Her empty eyes glittered in every puddle, in every half-glimpsed reflection. When she called her, Eleanor knew that she would be smiling.

It was dark outside. The snows had melted in a fine hiss of rain. It oozed down her window pane like tears. Later, she would cry again, but now there was no time.

'Hello? Are you there?'

The voice, when it spoke, came from somewhere over her shoulder. Eleanor turned, and the black-eyed woman was standing by the head of her bed.

'I am always here, dearest.'

'I would like to make a wish.'

The black-eyed woman's smile widened. 'I take it you've changed your mind about our arrangement?'

Eleanor nodded. Her knuckles had gone white. When she took her hands away from her stomach, the fabric of her dress had left ridges on the palms of her hands.

The woman's eyes shone like oil. 'I know what you want me to do, but I cannot do it unless you make the wish.'

A few months ago Eleanor had been sure she would never call on the black-eyed woman again, but now all her firmness had melted away. People would die. She could too.

'If...if I do this, will anyone else be hurt?'

Eleanor thought she saw a flash of pity in the woman's eyes. 'No,' she said. 'No one else.'

The black-eyed woman's shadow flickered on the wall. For a second it could have been anything – a man in a tall hat, a twisting vine, a boneless thing oozing out of a bulbous cocoon. In that moment, with the woman's wine-dark eyes so flat and calm, anything might have been possible. Eleanor caught a glimpse of her own reflection in the window behind the black-eyed woman's head. She'd been terrified her own eyes would look empty and dark, but they were blue as a summer sky.

Eleanor made the wish.

There were a few things that Eleanor was certain of.

The first: she was lying on the floor. Her bed was lumpier and smelled different. She was reasonably sure she was lying in something unpleasant, because there was a stench so hot and thick it forced its way into her mouth like a warden prising open an inmate's jaws.

She was also certain that she was not properly dressed. She was far too hot. Had she put on all her clothes at once? It was the wrong kind of heat for that – it was a lush, prickling heat that wound around her like a snake. It curled in her abdomen, uncoiling its lazy tendrils all through her body.

It *hurt*.

The things she was not certain of were more complicated. She was not entirely sure how she had ended up on the floor, or where the smell had come from, or where she was. When she'd last checked it had been January, chilly and damp. But it clearly was not January, because January was never quite this humid. Also, she was not sure what the voices were talking about.

'Oh God, oh please, please, *please*...'

'...and I came to fetch her like you said, and then—'

'You silly girl. Oh, Ella, you poor, silly girl...'

She knew those voices. They washed over her like waves, and with every ebb and flow she began to realize that something was wrong. She had to get up.

She tried.

There was a shriek, a brief glimpse of blurred faces and a bright flash of pain that lanced across her abdomen. She fell back, senseless.

Eleanor had strange dreams.

Her stomach had been replaced by a pit of snakes; they moved inside her arms and legs like a hand inside a glove. She bobbed on the surface of a vast ocean; something huge and dark thrashed in the water beneath her, and in forcing it back under the waves her hands and dress were soaked. A long line of children shuffled up to her and placed large, smooth rocks in the palm of her hand; they would not stop, even when all her fingers were crushed.

When she came to, it was to see Charles sitting by her bedside.

He had evidently been there for some time. The beginnings of a beard stretched across his pale face. His eyes might have been bruised. His shirt was unbuttoned at the collar and cuffs, his waistcoat flapping open, his cravat dangling over the back of a chair. It was unsettling. She'd seen him naked, but he had never seemed so vulnerable then.

She reached for his hand. It seemed to take an age. When had her fingers become so thin? When had her arms become so heavy? If she put a hand to her head, would all the strands of her hair be white?

She took his hand. Charles flinched, and burst into tears.

Eleanor was not supposed to have visitors, but Charles never left her side. Cocooned in morphine, she did not remember much, but he was always there. Charles's hand, pressing a cold flannel to her face. Charles's voice, soft and slow as he read from the book of sonnets. Charles's white-shirted back, hunched over the washstand or bending over the fire.

He did not want to tell her what had happened.

What she knew for certain was this: the black-eyed woman had granted her wish. It had left her in a lot of pain and a lot of blood, among other things. Charles had found her and sent for Dr Macready, who had supplied her with all the morphine. It was not enough. Her abdomen still hurt; the morphine only softened the edges.

Eleanor only regretted what she'd done when she saw Charles's face. He tried to smile and keep his voice light, but the mask kept slipping. He looked old, and sad. Sometimes he would press his lips to her hand and whisper 'I'm so sorry' against her fingers. It felt like a prayer. Then, she thought about the life they might have had if they hadn't been discovered; softer and slower than the future she'd dreamed of, but still happy.

There was no point in pining after what might have been, because what might have been was not what had happened.

Eventually her strength started to return and the morphine began to fade. Still, Charles hovered at her side, fussing with her pillows and lifting tumblers of gruel out of Eleanor's hands the moment she'd finished eating. He seemed to find it hard to meet her eyes, but even when she reached to take his hand he sprang closer at once, afraid that one wrong twist would break her apart.

'This is not your fault, Charles,' Eleanor said.

He shook his head. 'I never should have tried to take Mother's ring. We never would've been discovered if I hadn't been so stupid!'

She leant forward and grabbed the scruff of his neck, forcing him to look at her. 'You are the last person to blame.'

'It's my fault,' he said. 'If you hadn't had such a shock – if I'd been here when Father spoke to you…but he told me if I didn't return the things I'd pawned he'd press charges and I didn't want to leave you, Eleanor, to r-raise our child while I…'

His eyes gleamed with tears. She brushed them away, and yearned to ease his burden as simply as that. For all that she told him it was not his fault, he would always blame himself. He thought of her the way he always had done: a poor, sweet girl deceived by the brutal world around her. Innocent.

She was tempted to tell him everything. He thought she'd lost the baby; he didn't know what she had done. The secret weighed on her like manacles. And not just that. She'd told no one about the black-eyed woman who stole through every shadow. No one knew about the terrible things the black-eyed woman had done – no one had even seen her. If Eleanor told him, there would be no more barriers between them. At last, she could share that burden, and Charles would truly know Eleanor when he looked at her.

The thought was terrifying.

How could she do it? It would be like cutting open her chest and peeling back her ribs to show him the pulsing mess beneath. And what if he turned away? What if he, of all people, looked at her with horror and disgust as she told him what she'd done?

He would think her mad. Worse, he would believe her, and think her a murderess. Shock, disbelief, fear, maybe even hate – she could never allow him to feel such things about her. She was a good person in every other aspect; let him see those parts of her instead. The black-eyed woman had killed all those people, and she knew that Eleanor did not want her to do it. Eleanor was still the friend who had fed and clothed Leah when she was starving, the girl who had tried her best to protect Aoife, and the woman who loved Charles.

Eleanor knew she was not a murderess, but she did not want Charles to see her that way.

So she said nothing. She smoothed his hair, placed a hand against his cheek, watched him close his eyes. He needed her so much it made her heart soar.

'I love you,' she said.

He gathered her into his arms and placed her in his lap, as if she were a little girl. She buried her face in his chest, and felt his tears drip onto her forehead when he kissed her hair.

'I love you too,' he said, his voice thick. Guilt burned in the pit of her stomach. She was glad she could not see his face.

Charles sagged in his chair, head lolling on his shoulder. The fire smoked and spat in the fog seeping down the chimney, but it was not enough to wake him. Now that he was asleep, Eleanor could see where the new lines on his face had settled, and the way his shirt hung where it had once fitted. He wouldn't hear of sleeping in his own bed. It was all she could do to persuade him to eat, and even then he had his meals sent up to her room.

The peace would not last.

For now, she was safe. She was still recovering, and until she was out of bed Charles would be by her side. But when she was well enough to leave, she would be sent away. On her only visit, Mrs Fielding had looked Eleanor in the eye and placed her case at the foot of the bed. Aoife had sneaked up after the housekeeper had left, red-eyed and pale.

'Oh, Ella,' she'd whispered, as Charles slept in the chair by the bed, 'I'll miss you something fierce.'

Eleanor took Aoife's hand. 'You won't. You're coming with me.'

Disbelief swept across Aoife's face. 'What? But I – what about Micheál? I've to pay for his medicines, I can't leave this place.'

'They're putting me up in a house somewhere. They're giving me a maid. I've asked for you. You'll still get your wages and you'll be away from all of this.'

Aoife's eyes were alight. 'Can Daisy come too?'

'I can't take both of you. I'm sorry.'

Aoife took her hand away. She pressed her lips together as though she was trying not to cry.

'Daisy will be all right,' Eleanor soothed, 'she's a strong girl. Mrs Banbury will keep her in the kitchen as much as she can, and she's still got that reference. She'll manage.'

Even as she tried to sound comforting, Eleanor could feel the lies swirling underneath her words. It would be cruel to leave any girl alone in Granborough House. But Eleanor could only take one maid with her, and Daisy – who was sharp, and watchful, and cynical – stood a far better chance of surviving Granborough House than Aoife.

Aoife nodded to Charles. 'Did you get all that because of him, then?'

Eleanor looked away, blushing. Aoife would never understand the truth.

'He was really going to marry you, wasn't he?'

Eleanor looked at Charles. His head was slumped onto his chest; his neck would ache when he awoke. The thought put an unexpected lump in her throat. Such a little thing to cry over.

271

'I thought we were being robbed when he came back,' whispered Aoife. 'We was all in our nightgowns and the front door comes crashing open and there's steps on the servants' stairs. Daisy and me thought it was – well, they're saying it wasn't that lad from the butcher's now, aren't they, but I never liked him. Anyway, we went upstairs and there he was, with…'

She trailed off.

'He locked himself in with you after the doctor went,' she said. 'Yelling through the door at the master when he tried to have you sent away. D'you think you'll get to see him, once you've left?'

The weight of the bargain Eleanor had made seemed to smother her. 'No. I don't suppose I shall.'

Aoife glanced over her shoulder. 'Well…if I'm coming with you, I'd come back and visit Daisy on occasion. If you wanted to write to him, I could bring the letters with me.'

Eleanor snatched up Aoife's hands, hope fluttering like a caged bird. 'You would? Really?'

Aoife smiled. 'Surely I would! You've read so many letters for me, I daresay I'd post a few for you.'

As her strength returned, Eleanor tried to be cheerful. Mr Pembroke's agreement was in Eleanor's case and soon she would be leaving Granborough House behind. Aoife would be coming with her and, best of all, she had promised to help Eleanor communicate with Charles. And, of course, Eleanor's latest wish had shown that there was a way to bring the wishes back under her control. The black-eyed woman would have to take a life, but Eleanor could hold her back from wholesale destruction.

She was not foolish enough to think that made her safe.

The black-eyed woman was in the shadows at the corner of the room. Eleanor had thought it was empty, but the crumpled dust sheets had become the shape of her skirts, the legs of the washstand became the folds of her dress. She saw Eleanor watching, and winked.

The door swung open.

'So,' Mr Pembroke slurred, 'you did it, then.'

He slumped against the doorframe, his clothes half-undone and reeking of brandy. Eleanor glanced towards the black-eyed woman, still waiting in the shadows, but her smile only widened. Mr Pembroke stumbled into the room without seeing her.

'As you see,' Eleanor said.

Mr Pembroke fumbled in his jacket pocket and threw a wad of papers at her – the deeds to her house and the first instalment of her allowance. She felt a pang as she riffled through them. She'd gambled for such a little thing.

He plopped down on the foot of her bed. 'You don't regret it.'

'Do you?'

He glanced at Charles, still slumped in his chair. Even in sleep, dark circles sprawled under his eyes. Eleanor shifted. It was only when she looked at Charles – drowning under the weight of guilt and sorrow – that she wished she hadn't taken Mr Pembroke's deal.

'You set the terms of the agreement,' she said. 'I would have had the child.'

He shot her a sharp look. 'And tied yourself to my son forever. I did what was best for him and, in time, he will thank me for it.'

The black-eyed woman still stood in the corner of the room,

smiling. Mr Pembroke had walked right past her. Eleanor had realized months before that the black-eyed woman had taken a shape from her own imagination. Was that the only place that she existed? When Eleanor took the woman's hand, did she feel the clasp of her cold fingers only because Eleanor imagined she ought to feel something? Was she even there at all?

Eleanor gathered up her papers and put them in order, forcing her wayward thoughts back into line. Of course the black-eyed woman was there. Eleanor's wishes had come true, what else could be happening if the black-eyed woman was not granting them? She had *chosen* to appear only to Eleanor. It was another trick of hers, meant to put doubts in Eleanor's head.

'Are you going to tell him?'

Mr Pembroke fell silent. They both looked at Charles again, the lines on his face thrown into sharp relief by the guttering candle.

'Don't breathe a word of this to him,' Mr Pembroke muttered. 'It would destroy him, if he found out.'

'I won't,' Eleanor agreed. 'You'd break his heart.'

The black-eyed woman melted back into the shadows. The last thing to go was her grin.

PART FIVE

When Eleanor opened her eyes, she realized she was not in Granborough House. There was a faded yellow quilt on the bed instead of crisp white sheets. Pale green curtains let in a wash of pond-like light. The floorboards were bare, there was a smell of new plaster, and Charles was gone.

Eleanor pushed herself upright and morphine swirled around her. The colours twisted, sharpened, melted under her gaze. She lurched over to the window and looked onto an unfamiliar street. She was surrounded by neat rows of houses, each one two storeys tall and barely stained by smoke. Carts rattled along the street, and from somewhere close by came the shriek of a train whistle.

Eleanor clung to the curtain. Where were the parks? Where were the spires of Westminster Abbey, slicing through the fog? Where were the music halls, bleary and quiet in the morning light? A church bell rang, tolling ten o'clock, and Eleanor flinched. It sounded so *wrong*.

She was not in Mayfair any more.

Her case was at the foot of her bed. On top of her neatly folded things was a letter. She recognized Charles's rounded hand and a lump came into her throat.

She pulled on her shawl and went downstairs.

The house smelled of display: polish, plaster and paint. Upstairs were two bedrooms, hers and a smaller one. Downstairs was a tiled hall, a drawing room at the front and a dining room at the back, both cheaply papered. Further back was a kitchen, filled with clattering pans and the hiss of boiling water.

A short, dark-haired woman a few years older than Eleanor was standing by the stove. She grinned when she saw Eleanor.

'Hallo, miss! Cuppa tea?'

Eleanor clung to the doorframe. 'Where am I?'

The woman nodded. 'They said you wasn't well. It's your new place, and I'm your new maid. Bessie Banbury.'

The room tilted. 'I...what? Where's Aoife?'

'Who?'

Bessie took her arm and steered her into a drawing-room chair. Apart from a limp sofa and an empty bookcase the room was bare, like set-dressing in an unfamiliar play. Any minute now, a wall would roll back on its casters and Eleanor would be staring at the audience, listening to them laugh.

Bessie came in with a cup of tea and thrust it at Eleanor. It slopped over Eleanor's lap.

'Are we in London?'

Bessie pulled a face. 'Peckham,' she said. 'Not too far from the station, though.'

'How long have I been asleep?'

Bessie shrugged. 'Not sure. You slept all the way here. Auntie Mary said you'd been told.'

Eleanor set down her cup with a rattle, seething. No one had told her anything. Mr Pembroke had drugged her, bundled her up like old rags and shut her out of sight.

'He can't do this!'

Bessie raised her eyebrows. 'Can't give you a nice place out in the country? Dunno about that.'

Eleanor slapped the arm of her chair, slopping tea everywhere. 'You don't understand. They never told me I was coming here! I'll have him up before the magistrate on a charge of kidnap! He can't *do* this!'

'Kidnap, miss? It ain't kidnap. You've a nice little home, with a hard-working and well-appointed servant, if I do say so myself. No point going to a magistrate. He'll only laugh.'

Eleanor sat back in her chair, still woozy, still seething. Bessie patted her knee.

'Cheer up, miss. It'll all seem better in a day or so.'

Eleanor screamed in frustration, and Bessie ignored her.

It took Eleanor a long time to read Charles's letter. At first all the words bled together, twisting around each other like black ivy. It was only when she started shivering and sweating that she recognized the last vestiges of the morphine. Bessie left her to sleep it off, layering her with blankets.

When Eleanor woke, it was with a pounding headache and a dull fury throbbing in her veins. Mr Pembroke had drugged her to avoid a scene when she left. Granborough House was falling apart and half the maids had been interfered with, but still, *she* was the centre of the scandal. She had to be discreetly sent away, while Mr Pembroke drank away his son's prospects and assaulted any maid who got close. Worst of all, he'd kept Aoife with him – oh God, what would Aoife think when she found that Eleanor had gone without her? Fear gripped Eleanor in its talons. What would Mr Pembroke do, now that Eleanor had let him know that she cared about Aoife?

Eleanor wanted to go back. But her arms shook when she tried to sit upright and the bones in her legs might have been replaced with string, they felt so weak. How could she make it to Mayfair and back?

Eleanor wiped her eyes. Slowly, she drew out the letter. The paper fluttered as she unfolded it.

Dearest Eleanor,

I write these few lines in the little time I have, and I know they shall never be enough. My love, I have grave news. I have persuaded Father to arrange a comfortable living for you, but in exchange, he demands that I never see you again. How could I ever choose anything but your comfort and security?

Had I known that Father arranged your departure for tonight I would have rained flowers in your lap and covered you in jewels. But the memory of our time together, however brief, was brighter than any diamond.

The knowledge that you shall be safe and well cared for is the best balm a man could ask for. My darling girl, I shall think of you always, but I beg you, do not think of me. I would not have you shed a tear for this lovesick fool.

Your ever loving,
Charles

Confined to her bed, Eleanor seethed.

Bessie fed her on an invalid's diet: gruel, chicken broth and beef tea – the food Eleanor had once tried to make for her mother, while she lay coughing in her bed. The smell sent Eleanor back to the age of nine, when she'd stood on a chair to reach the stove-top and wasn't strong enough to lift the pan off the heat. Eleanor still wanted to throw it at the wall.

The worst part was that she needed it.

The morphine was all at Granborough House. Without it, she realized how weak she'd become. Even as January melted into February, goosebumps still prickled along her arms and her pulse fluttered like a caged bird. She begged Bessie for magazines, newspapers, penny bloods, forcing herself to focus on the exploits of Spring-heeled Jack and Dick Turpin while she turned the pages with shaking, sweating fingers. No matter how cheap and flimsy it was, she needed her shield.

If she didn't have that, she'd only read Charles's letter again.

Tears had only been the beginning. When she'd reread it, she'd been so furious that she'd nearly torn it to pieces. Mr Pembroke had lied to his son. He'd allowed Charles to believe that Eleanor's house had been his own idea, and made Charles promise his happiness away in exchange. It was bad enough that she'd bartered her own.

Eleanor tried to calm herself down. She was not above breaking a promise. A couple of months to make Mr Pembroke think it had all been forgotten, and then she'd find Charles again. Until then, she'd make herself a lady.

It was harder than she thought. Eleanor's eyes sprang open at five o'clock every morning, and she felt strangely guilty for sitting in a chair. But now that her food was not being snatched out of her hands, and she was no longer fetching and carrying, all the graces Mrs Pembroke had taught her came flooding back. She had the manners of a lady already; all she needed now was the money.

Mr Pembroke's three hundred pounds would cover rent and basic necessities, but it would not last. The workmen had refused his credit to fix the roof of Granborough House; if knowledge of his debts had spread to tradesmen, they must be substantial. The next month's allowance might never arrive, and Eleanor could not help Aoife leave Granborough House without money. She had to find another source of income.

For that, she turned to Mrs Pembroke's address book.

She wrote to every name that sounded familiar. Eleanor did not directly ask for money – that would've seemed cheap – but she hoped that she might have the pleasure of renewing their acquaintance a dozen times over, and in her best hand-writing. They were crawling, spineless letters, and she hated herself for writing them. But Eleanor would need to match Aoife's wages to buy her way out of Granborough House, and there was no respectable way Eleanor could earn that much. Only a wealthy patron could provide the funds, and Eleanor would only meet such people if she grovelled in pen and ink, pretended she'd never even seen the inside of a coal scuttle and smoothed down all her sharpness. She would become the pretty, perfect thing she had no choice but to be.

She would not make a wish. The black-eyed woman would get no more blood from her.

Of course, finding a patron might be easier if her neighbours visited. But Eleanor could not remember the last time she'd spoken to someone who wasn't a servant or a shopkeeper. Bessie was hardly a companion: she went out at every oppor-tunity, and when she was in the house she was working. Eleanor didn't even get any letters; she had only Charles to write to her, and his father had forbidden it.

She missed the way Charles's eyes softened when he looked at her, the way he murmured her name, all his secret smiles.

Sometimes she dreamed they had run off together, and he sat beside her while their child grew, and when she awoke her grief throbbed like an old wound.

The back door opened. Bessie had come home.

Eleanor got up, desperate for company that would take her mind off Charles. Bessie shut the door behind her, humming, and took a few steps down the hall. Then, she stopped, and Eleanor heard the rustling of paper. *No*, Eleanor thought, her temper rising. Bessie wouldn't dare.

Eleanor burst out of the drawing room. Bessie had her hand in the letter basket. She flinched, turned, and knocked the letters all over the hallway floor.

'What do you think you are doing, Bessie?' Eleanor snapped.

Bessie still had her shawl on. She folded it neatly over her arm as she spoke. 'Checking through your letters, miss.'

Eleanor flinched. 'You admit you're going through my correspondence?'

''Course I am,' said Bessie, without a trace of guilt. 'It's what I'm paid for.'

'It is *not* what you are paid for,' Eleanor snapped, 'you are my maid! You are here to cook, and clean, and that is all! How *dare* you speak to your employer this way?'

Bessie grinned. 'Ain't you who pays my wages, miss.'

She winked at Eleanor and strolled back into the kitchen.

The next day, Eleanor waited in line at the duty sergeant's desk, praying that nobody had recognized her when she came in. After weeks away from the press and clamour of London, it seemed louder than ever. Noise pressed in on every side. Constables trooped in and out, rattling keys, whistling, calling for telegraph boys. A woman in a threadbare dress trudged past, her shawl draped over her hands; Eleanor caught the jingle of handcuffs as she passed. From a distant corridor came the sounds of the cells – drunken singing, crying, a truncheon clattering against the bars. The station was not far from Mayfair; Charles might have seen her go inside, and what would he think then? Eleanor forced her shoulders down and kept her head held high, determined not to seem furtive. She had done nothing wrong.

She reached the sergeant's desk and asked to see Inspector Hatchett. She was shown into his office and the Inspector stood up at once, stooping a little.

'Miss Hartley! This is a surprise. How can I assist you?'

Eleanor sat down. 'You once told me, Inspector, that if any of the maids at Granborough House should find themselves in trouble I should come to you.'

The Inspector snatched up his notebook, his face dark.

'One of the maids is in particular danger,' Eleanor said, relief flooding through her as he scribbled her words down. 'A young woman named Aoife Flaherty, fifteen years old. I saw Mr Pembroke conversing with her in a corridor. He means her harm, I know it!'

'Miss Hartley, conversing in a corridor is hardly a criminal offence.'

'You didn't hear him!' Eleanor snapped. 'He was...insinuating things. And whenever she had to be alone with him she always came back in tears! She was so frightened – she's fifteen, Inspector!'

The Inspector laid his pen aside. He rubbed his eyes, letting out a long sigh.

'Miss Hartley,' he said, 'I am aware of the kind of man that Mr Pembroke is. I do not doubt it when you say that your friend is in danger. But what do you expect me to do? I need more evidence to pursue this further.'

Eleanor felt sick with disbelief. 'Will you wait until she is attacked?'

The Inspector's jaw tightened. 'I cannot pursue this case without evidence. My hands are tied.'

Eleanor stood up. The Inspector had offered to help her, but she may as well have been screaming into the void for all the good he'd done her.

'Then you will excuse me, Inspector,' she said, desperately trying to rein in her temper. 'I do not have time to wait for Justice to remove her blindfold.'

Eleanor wrote letter after letter until her shoulders ached and her hands began to cramp. It was the only way she could think of to help Aoife. Eleanor seethed as she wrote. The Inspector had been worse than useless, she thought. Why would no one help her? Inspector Hatchett, Mr Pembroke, Mrs Fielding, even Lizzie – all of them were supposed to have had the maids' best interests at heart, and all of them had let her down. Now, Eleanor was reduced to begging from strangers, calling on connections she could barely remember because they could not be trusted. It made her want to spit.

Among all her letter-writing, Eleanor often thought of Leah, too. It was hard not to. If things had been different it might have been Eleanor scrabbling in the street, and Leah tucked up in a warm, clean bed. But Leah, she realized, would be easier to help than Aoife. Eleanor could find Leah without Mr Pembroke breathing down her neck.

Not that she would use a wish. There were far too few of them for that – only three left now, and that included the one she must never use. She wrote to the workhouses instead. Leah must have given birth by now and with a child to think of, surely she would have to go there. Eleanor's heart twisted to think of Leah in such a place.

Eleanor pinched the bridge of her nose. It felt odd. She'd lathered her hands in bear's grease to try and make them soft and supple, but she'd used so much that her fingers kept slipping in and out of her gloves. Move too quickly and she'd end up with a greasy wodge of material in the palm of her hand.

There was a knock at the front door.

Charles! He'd come at last. She never should have doubted him. St Valentine's Day was only a few days away, of course he would be thinking of her. She glanced down at her dress – why, *why* hadn't she put on something better – and slapped her skirts into submission, tugging the folds back into place. She ripped off her gloves, shoving them under a cushion – she couldn't be seen to wear gloves indoors, what would he think? – and wiped the grease off her hands. What was she going to say? What was he going to do?

Bessie opened the door, her nose in the air. 'Mrs Flora Cleary.'

All her hopes wilted. He hadn't come.

Eleanor kept the disappointment from showing and rifled through her memories at speed. After a moment's horrible blankness, she remembered – she'd found Mrs Cleary's name in Mrs Pembroke's address book, and best of all, she lived nearby. At once, Eleanor's nerves exploded into life. Here was her chance to help Aoife leave Granborough House; she could not afford any blunders.

Mrs Cleary was a rounded, shiny woman with grey hair

and a mass of lines on her face, leaning on a silver-topped cane. She was dressed in a black going-out dress trimmed with fur *and* feathers, which rather spoiled the effect of her widow's weeds. Eleanor tried desperately to remember something about her, and came up with nothing.

'Come here, Miss Hartley,' Mrs Cleary drawled. 'Let me look at you.'

Eleanor recognized the accent at once. Irish. A feeble memory twitched – Eleanor was sitting beside Mrs Pembroke while she poured the tea. Eleanor watched Mrs Pembroke, staring at the sapphire ring winking on her finger, waiting for the moment when Mrs Pembroke would ask her to hand Mrs Cleary her cup.

Smiling, Eleanor came closer. 'Such a pleasure to see you again, Mrs Cleary—'

'Yes, yes. Let me look at you, girl!'

Eleanor closed her mouth as Mrs Cleary swept an appraising eye across her face and dress. She hadn't remembered this.

'Well,' said Mrs Cleary at last, 'I can't say I'm surprised. I always knew you were going to be a beauty. Of course, that comes with its own problems, but I'm glad to see you've not had ideas above your station.'

Mrs Cleary looked at her expectantly. Eleanor jolted into life.

'I'm glad to hear you think so,' Eleanor said, waving Mrs Cleary into her best chair. 'Incidentally, Mrs Cleary, allow me to offer you my condolences. Had I known you were in mourning...'

Mrs Cleary gave her a stately nod. 'That is kind of you, Miss Hartley, if somewhat delayed. My Alfred passed over two years ago.'

Eleanor flushed. 'I am very sorry to hear it. Mrs Pembroke always spoke so highly of him,' she said, remembering nothing about Mr Cleary.

'Dear Emmeline,' said Mrs Cleary, her face softening. 'She was such a kind woman. She would not have taken you in, otherwise. You were very…difficult. Used to scamper about the house screeching and snapping at the servants, the first year I knew you. And you wouldn't say a word, even when you were spoken to.'

Eleanor could hardly believe what she was hearing. She had never behaved so poorly. She gave a demure cough. 'Well, I…I apologize for my past behaviour. I must confess, I don't remember it.'

Mrs Cleary sniffed. 'I daresay that's for the best. Emmeline taught you your manners eventually, and I must say that she did a sterling job. Nobody who met you now could ever believe you were such a terror.'

Mrs Cleary, smiling, appeared to think she had genuinely given Eleanor a compliment. Eleanor fought to keep the disbelief from showing on her face. But then, Mrs Cleary's smile slipped. Eleanor could see the memories settling on her like fallen leaves. Eleanor pounced.

'I daresay she did,' Eleanor said. 'I've so longed for her guidance these past few months. She was quite a mother to me…' She let her words trail off and looked away, knowing Mrs Cleary was watching. 'I miss her terribly.'

'Of course you do. Anyone who knew Emmeline would,' said Mrs Cleary, blinking fast. 'Well, Miss Hartley, if you require guidance you must write to me. I shall be more than happy to oblige.'

Eleanor blinked as if she was holding back tears, and

288

wondered if it was too much. 'Why, Mrs Cleary, how kind of you to offer! Oh, that *shall* be a comfort to me.'

Eleanor took in the sable trim on Mrs Cleary's dress, and the diamond pins in her hair, and was charming and attentive all afternoon.

The train into London rattled past long rows of terraced houses, huddling together under a haze of smoke. Here and there Eleanor could see a thin slice of brown – a damp street, or the slick bark of a bare tree. A brief flash of colour as the train passed a market, a flat spread of mossy green as they trundled past a park and then, at last, the slug-like back of the Thames, oozing beneath them as they rattled over the bridge and into Victoria Station.

Enormous iron arches vaulted over her head, lost in a haze of steam. A pall of smoke lay over the platforms, thick and dark. Whistles shrieked. Suitcases caught against her dress. Someone trod on her skirts. Eleanor kept her composure and fought her way over to the exit. Granborough House was not far; half an hour's walk at most. It might be pleasant if she kept alongside the parks, but she needed her wits about her. If she took a wrong turn off Piccadilly in her fine shawl, she'd be lucky if she was only robbed. Still, she had to try. If she was careful, she might see Charles or Aoife, or find out if Leah had tried to visit again.

From the square opposite, Granborough House looked shabby and damp. It hunkered over the street like an enormous toadstool, water stains weeping from every window. Fog curled around the railings like a cloud of spores.

If Eleanor hadn't known better it might have been shut up for the winter. All the windows were dark and the front steps were grimy. The coach house brooded next to it, a squat, dark shape in the fog. Now and then a hansom would pass by, and the light from its lamps would glitter over the smashed windows like broken teeth.

It should have looked like a castle in a fairy tale. That would make her feel better about all the years she had spent cooped up in her garret. But there was no romance in the flaking shutters, no hint of Gothic mystery in the warped and swollen window frames. It was a sponge of a house, soaking up rainwater and grime, and seeing it clearly was disappointing.

Eleanor watched the coach house.

It was easy to tell when it was occupied. Everything inside had been sold or stolen long ago – start a fire inside and the flames would cast orange light through every broken window. But Eleanor saw nothing; Leah was not there. Disappointment washed over her. Despite the shelter the coach house provided against the clammy February fogs – and the friends who might help Leah if she stayed near to Granborough House – it was too much of a risk. Still, she waited, half-hidden behind a damp plane tree. Leah might not be there, but she might catch a glimpse of Aoife, or Charles.

Out of the corner of her eye she saw a quick flurry of curtains in the window of Granborough House. Was it Charles? Aoife? She went back to her spot in the square and waited, staring up at the dirty glass.

That Sunday, Eleanor saw Mrs Cleary's coach and four as she went to church, rolling through crowds of churchgoers heading in the opposite direction. Mrs Cleary was not inside. Standing in the cold and surrounded by her whispering neighbours,

Eleanor was riddled with envy. Bessie had been gossiping with the neighbours, and Eleanor brought silence and a flurry of whispering in her wake whenever *she* set foot in church, even though she'd been in Peckham for nearly two months. But not only did Mrs Cleary not have to put up with Eleanor's fellow worshippers – Mrs Cleary's coach was trundling in the direction of the Catholic church – she didn't even have to leave her home. Sending the coach on her behalf was enough of a gesture to keep people satisfied, whereas Eleanor had to sit up straight and look devoutly attentive while everyone whispered behind her back.

The moment she got home, Eleanor wrote another letter to Mrs Cleary, asking for advice she did not need. When she finally secured an invitation to dinner, it took everything Eleanor had not to dance around her drawing room. This was her chance.

Mr Pembroke's money was going to run out, and soon. Eleanor was not a lady in the real sense yet: she didn't have to work and she had the right manners, but without the money that meant nothing. She couldn't afford to dress the part, to buy first-class train tickets, to be seen at the right places in the right company. She couldn't afford to search for Leah properly, or to search for Aoife one day. She needed a wealthy benefactor. That would be Mrs Cleary.

Of course, Eleanor could always marry. She had not heard from Charles, after all, and his father would be pushing him at the nearest heiress the moment the Season started. Why should she wait for him, when he would not be allowed to wait for her? But the thought left smeary fingerprints over all her daydreams. Standing by the altar with a faceless stranger would be a betrayal. Still, it might not be so bad. Her neighbours were all avoiding her, apart from Mrs Cleary, and if Eleanor married at least she'd have someone to talk to.

But she *did* have someone to talk to – albeit someone she neither trusted nor understood. It was Bessie's afternoon off and the house was quiet, but still, Eleanor shut the drawing-room door before she spoke.

'Can you come out? I'd like to talk with you, if I may.'

Sparks spat out of the grate as a piece of coal shifted. Eleanor stared around, looking for the black-eyed woman. She faded into view, the pattern of the sofa slowly bleeding into her printed calico dress, all the colours blurring together. She smiled at Eleanor.

'Hello, dear,' she said. She looked around the drawing room. 'You *are* moving up in the world, it seems.'

Eleanor blushed. 'All thanks to you, of course.'

The black-eyed woman inclined her head.

'Although I must admit,' Eleanor probed, 'I'm not quite sure why you'd go to all this trouble on my account.'

'We struck a bargain. I am bound to keep it, by laws greater than us both.'

'But...why did you appear to *me*? I cannot have been the only one in Granborough House to have read from that book.'

The black-eyed woman smiled and took Eleanor's hand. 'It is not enough to read from the book. I require something a little stronger.' She traced a line across one of Eleanor's gloved fingertips. 'This was where the mark was made. Don't you remember?'

Eleanor shook her head. The woman's smile widened.

'Of course. There are so many things that you do not remember.'

Her tone was like fingers on Eleanor's neck. Unbidden,

Eleanor remembered Lizzie, screaming at her that she'd bitten Mrs Fielding. Lizzie had been lying, of course. She smoothed out her skirts as an excuse to take her hand away.

'I wonder if I might ask you something.'

'Ask away, my dear.'

Eleanor fixed her eyes on a seam running down her skirt. 'Why did you ask for my soul? What will you do with it?'

'I shall treasure it,' the black-eyed woman said, her voice carefully light. 'I shall string it on a silken cord and wear it around my neck.'

'But surely you must have a reason to want it.'

'Indeed I do.'

'Won't you tell me?'

There was a sudden rattle in the fireplace. Eleanor flinched, but it was nothing; a piece of coal had rolled into the grate. When she looked back the black-eyed woman was still there. Her face was set and she remained motionless, but the light seemed dimmer and something cold prickled the back of Eleanor's neck. Beyond the shriek of train whistles and the rattle of hansoms and carts, Eleanor could have sworn that she heard a low, soft rumbling.

The black-eyed woman leant forward. As she moved, all the shadows shifted. Strange shapes contorted on the walls. Sinuous darkness pooled behind the black-eyed woman's skirts, crawled across the wallpaper, and curled around her feet.

She gave a grin. It had far too many teeth.

'No,' she said.

A door creaked – Bessie had come home. Suddenly, the black-eyed woman was gone. Eleanor was left sweating on the edge of her seat, her heart rattling as she stared at the empty sofa. The cushions were plump and unmarked. There was no sign that the woman had ever been there, apart from a lingering darkness at the corners of the room.

For a moment Eleanor stared into the shadows, half-wondering if she had imagined it. Then she, too, left the room, squeezing her hands very tightly to stop them from shaking.

When Eleanor first saw Mrs Cleary's house she wondered if she had taken a wrong turn. With its wrought-iron gates, wide, sweeping walls and carefully laid-out garden she might have been back in Mayfair, or at one of the smaller railway termini. As Eleanor strode up the path, Bessie bobbing along behind her, the sound of the rain on leaves was something like applause. Bessie was eyeing the front door with undisguised greed. Panic jolted through Eleanor. The damage that Bessie could do if she were to talk to Mrs Cleary...

'Why don't you take the evening off?' Eleanor said, trying to sound nonchalant.

'Don't need to tell me twice,' said Bessie, taking off with the umbrella.

A footman answered the door and took Eleanor's cloak. The butler showed her into the drawing room and Eleanor's mouth nearly fell open.

She'd read about the palaces of Egyptian pashas, and all the glittering spoils they sent back to the courts of their sultans. It seemed as though they had all come here instead. Swathes of red velvet, glittering glass and gold, and gleaming porcelain. Slim dark tables, overstuffed sofas and knee-high ottomans crowded together like courtiers vying for a king's attention. Ferns made green fans in all the corners, flowers spilled out of every vase and a large ornamental fish tank sprawled across the mantelpiece.

Mrs Cleary was waiting for her, sitting in a chair and leaning on her silver-topped cane. She was resplendent in a black silk evening dress and glittering with jet, one large black feather tucked into her grey hair. She extended a hand when she saw Eleanor, but did not get up.

'Good evening, Mrs Cleary,' said Eleanor, smiling at full capacity. 'Thank you so much for the invitation, it is very kind of you to—'

Mrs Cleary waved Eleanor's thanks away. 'No need.'

'Will we be a large party?' Eleanor asked, trying not to look at the plain blue skirts of her best dress.

'Just you and I. My companion, Miss Hill, is indisposed this evening.' Mrs Cleary leant forward and patted Eleanor's hand. 'There's no need to worry about your appearance, Miss Hartley. In a person of your age and class, simplicity of dress is entirely proper.'

Eleanor papered over the cracks in her smile. 'I'm glad to hear you think so,' she managed.

The butler materialized at the drawing-room door. Mrs Cleary looked expectantly at Eleanor, who helped her hostess out of her chair at once. 'In the absence of any gentlemen, you will escort me into dinner,' Mrs Cleary said, and Eleanor offered her arm. She wondered if this was how Charles felt, and missed him more than ever.

Eleanor led Mrs Cleary into the dining room. A constellation of candles made the regimented lines of cutlery sparkle, bathing the flowers on the table in golden light. Eleanor sat down, and tried to remember if Mrs Pembroke had said anything about using a fish-slice.

The food was so good it almost brought her to tears. There was oxtail soup, boiled haddock, roast mutton, pigeon pie, and several tureens of vegetables, all followed by rhubarb tart, a rainbow of moulded jellies and an enormous, cream-laden pudding that Eleanor wanted to jump into. She tried to eat carefully – there were so many things to try – but, surrounded by clouds of fragrant steam, glistening meats and vast bowls of cream waiting for a spoon, it was all she could do not to lick the plate.

Mrs Cleary laid aside her cutlery. At once, a footman appeared behind her chair, ready to pull it back. 'Send some coffee through to the drawing room, Watkins, and do pass along my compliments to Mrs Allesley.'

'Very good, ma'am.'

The footman pulled back Mrs Cleary's chair and Eleanor started as another one did the same for her. He'd been so quiet, she hadn't heard him approach. She offered her arm to Mrs Cleary, noting the glint of approval in the old woman's eye, and led her back into the drawing room. A silver coffee pot and two china cups were already waiting there. Eleanor helped Mrs Cleary into a chair and poured her a cup of coffee.

'I must say, Miss Hartley, you are not at all what I expected,' said Mrs Cleary, fixing Eleanor with a look that pinned her to her chair. 'There have been all kinds of rumours flying around about you.'

Eleanor almost choked on her coffee. 'There have?'

'Of course there have!' said Mrs Cleary. 'You all but vanished after dear Emmeline died. People are saying you went into *service.*'

Eleanor thought fast. She couldn't tell an outright lie; if Mrs Cleary had heard rumours about her, she could still find out the truth. But the tone was clear: a former housemaid was not suitable company for the illustrious Mrs Cleary.

'I can see how people might have thought that,' Eleanor mused, keeping her expression neutral, 'but that's not strictly true. My circumstances were reduced, but not quite so much. Mr Pembroke allowed me to continue my studies on the understanding that I would become a governess.'

Mrs Cleary nodded. 'Of course I knew such a thing could not be true. You have the manners of a lady; those would not last below stairs!'

Eleanor breathed a sigh of relief. People rarely asked after governesses; they were far too respectable to be interesting.

'But you must tell me how you came to this neighbourhood, alone?' Mrs Cleary continued, the gleam coming back into her eyes. 'I had heard there was a young man...'

Eleanor thought of Charles and felt herself going scarlet. 'Goodness,' she said, making sure she was sitting up straight, so that Mrs Cleary could see she was not carrying a child. 'Why should anyone think that?'

She could not tell if the old woman was relieved or disappointed. Either way she leant forward and patted Eleanor on the knee. 'Miss Hartley, such rumours will always follow a pretty young girl. You must pay them no mind. Comport yourself with dignity and modesty and everyone will see that they are not true.'

Eleanor put on her best relieved face. 'Thank you, Mrs Cleary. I must say, I sorely feel the need for guidance. I'm quite terrified of making a misstep, now that I no longer have Mrs Pembroke's example to follow. I don't suppose you have any daughters that I might write to, so that I may ask their advice?'

Mrs Cleary gave her a tight little smile. 'I'm afraid I have no children living.'

'I'm so sorry,' Eleanor said, laying down her china cup.

'But if you require any advice, Miss Hartley, you must come to me. I can see that you would benefit from the counsel of a woman of my experience.'

Triumph burned in Eleanor's chest. This was exactly what she had been hoping for. 'That is most kind of you, Mrs Cleary,' she said, an angelic smile on her face.

March brought out the street-sellers like spring birds. Under watery sunlight, they trundled hot-potato carts down the street, lugged buckets of milk onto doorsteps and brandished posies at passers-by. They crowded around the entrance to Victoria Station, snatching at Eleanor's elbow as she passed. A ticket-seller tried to persuade her to take a box at the Variety for a week. A pockmarked boy of thirteen offered to take her on a tour of the sights of London, stuttering and blushing as he spoke. A man with a flower tucked into his buttonhole attempted to steer her into a side-street; Eleanor stamped on his foot and marched off towards Mayfair, seething with her head held high.

In a certain light Eleanor could see Granborough House the way it had once been. A spring wind twitched apart the clouds, and when the light fell on its walls she might have been thrown back into the past. The stone gleamed, the railings shone. She allowed herself to imagine a liveried footman opening the door and calling her 'Miss Eleanor' as he welcomed her home. But after the first flash of light the water-marks at every window looked like tear-tracks and all the sooty marks stood sharp against the pale stone.

Charles was not there.

Eleanor had circled the house until she was in front of his window, careful to keep a safe distance from the doors. It was closed, and so she knew he could not be there; he always had his window open during the day. Where was he? Had he been sent away? He must have been. Mr Pembroke had already tried it once before.

Thinking of Charles was like standing in the eye of a storm; staying perfectly still and calm was the only way to avoid being torn apart. She missed him so much that she could only think of him at a distance. Move closer – allow herself to remember the blue of his eyes, the feel of his arms around her, the way he held her hand – and all the things she had lost would crowd around her, doubt shredding all her hopes. She had loved him so much – she still did, even though it hurt to admit it. Surely he had not forgotten her.

She stalked back to the front of the house again, peering up at the drawing room, the library, the dining room. Their windows were dark. Perhaps she should leave some sign, to let him know that she had been there when he returned – her shawl, tied to the branch of a tree? No. It was the first thing he had ever given her; she could not part with it.

She made herself look for Leah instead. She'd paid for the train fare, she may as well use the time. And perhaps when she was done, Charles would have returned.

Eleanor found the soup-seller, but she hadn't seen Leah since the New Year. Next, Eleanor called at every shop with a description of Leah, and asked if they'd seen her begging or sleeping in their doorway. None of the assistants remembered her. Eleanor swallowed her pride and visited the tradesmen's entrance of every residence on the street. No luck there. The other servants recognized her as Granborough House's latest disgrace, and shut the door in her face.

The sun was nearly setting. She'd spent the whole day

surveying the street, and what did she have to show for it? Sore feet, a filthy hem, and disappointment that hung on her like Marley's chains.

When Eleanor visited Mrs Cleary now, the coach and four was sent to collect her. At the first snap of the whip the children next door would shriek and rush to the window, and the sound of running feet was as good as any doorbell. Eleanor was ready when the coachman knocked, head held high as her neighbours stared. The coach sailed down the street like Cleopatra's barge and she sat with her shoulders thrown back, fierce and proud.

She was careful not to let it show when she arrived.

Every time she saw the gleaming walls of Mrs Cleary's home she thought of Aoife. A fraction of Mrs Cleary's fortune would cover Aoife's wages. Bessie barely spoke to her; Charles had been sent away; she had not found Leah. Without Mrs Cleary she had no one. Eleanor could not lose her favour. If she did, there would be no hope of getting Aoife out of Granborough House.

Eleanor laughed at Mrs Cleary's jokes, and asked her to explain things she already understood. She complimented Mrs Cleary's dresses and was demure and blushing whenever the old lady asked her about husbands. She met Mrs Cleary's companion – a tall, poised Black woman named Miss Hill who was also in mourning – and tried her best to emulate the easy way Miss Hill shrugged off Mrs Cleary's barbs. She even wore green on St Patrick's Day, just to be polite, and fretted about it for days when Mrs Cleary didn't mention it. Eleanor was pious, she was shy, she was kind, she was admiring, and Mrs Cleary never noticed when Eleanor slipped off one mask and put on another. But Mrs Cleary never mentioned anything about an allowance, and at the end of every evening Eleanor was left staring at the bare walls of her shabby little room, listening to the clock ticking slowly towards midnight.

Now, Eleanor was drinking a cup of coffee and trying not to wince. It was Turkish, and probably expensive, so she was determined to enjoy it no matter how long that would take. Mrs Cleary was finishing a monologue about the latest fashions, all of which she followed despite being in mourning, while Miss Hill nodded along politely. Eleanor had not met many widows, but she was sure they were not supposed to glitter.

'...and of course, it is always pleasing to see a return of the fashions of one's youth,' Mrs Cleary concluded. 'I suppose that is why they suit me so well. A young lady should never be *too* interested in fashion, but now I may be daring.'

Eleanor, who had been coveting the dramatic swoop of the overskirts on Mrs Cleary's dress, nodded. 'Your gown really does look lovely,' she said.

Miss Hill cleared her throat. 'But you dress very well too, Miss Hartley. I can see you have quite a way with the needle; such fine work on the—'

'No,' said Mrs Cleary, eyeing Eleanor up and down. 'No, Miss Hartley, you really ought to have something better to wear. Come with me.'

She held out her hands. Miss Hill helped her off the sofa while Eleanor fetched Mrs Cleary's silver-topped cane. Mrs Cleary stumped into the hallway and up a wide, sweeping staircase. She led them both into a gargantuan bedroom, dominated by a four-poster bed with blue brocade curtains. Mrs Cleary's face was flushed.

'Miss Hill,' she said, 'would you bring through my old walking dress? The green and white – and perhaps the burgundy, too. I find myself a little overtired.'

Miss Hill disappeared into a dressing room while Eleanor helped Mrs Cleary into a chair. 'Mrs Cleary, this is too generous—'

'Nonsense! My dear Miss Hartley, I shall be in mourning for the rest of my life, I shan't wear them again. Besides, I may wish for your company in public, and you could never be seen with me wearing *that*,' she said, nodding to Eleanor's sweet blue dress.

'You are too kind, Mrs Cleary,' Eleanor said, swallowing her pride. 'I wonder, could I ask you some advice this moment?'

'Ask away.'

Eleanor licked her lips, suddenly nervous. 'I would like to try and find an old friend, but I believe she may have fallen on hard times.'

'If she's got herself in the family way, you must wash your hands of her,' Mrs Cleary said, sharply.

'Oh, Leah would never do that,' Eleanor said, the truth tangling itself under her skin.

Mrs Cleary nodded. 'In that case, I can offer you the services of one of my grooms. He will accompany you, should you wish to visit anywhere less respectable. Although I must say, Miss Hartley, that you would do better not to be seen in such places at all. Barnes is perfectly capable of enquiring on your behalf.'

Barnes arrived the next day, hulking on Eleanor's doorstep. He was a middle-aged man who looked as if he had been welded together in a shipyard, and he had clearly been told to treat Eleanor like a lady. He took off his hat when he spoke to her and barged a path through the crowds on Oxford Street so that she could walk through undisturbed. Eleanor was touched; Mrs Cleary must have told him to look after her.

She would need him.

Churches, charities, boarding-houses, workhouses, agencies and registry offices: Eleanor had visited them all, and found nothing of Leah. She'd been along every respectable street and knocked at every clean door. The people living in those neat, well-kept houses either hadn't seen Leah or had moved her along. But London had plenty of places to hide. Cramped courts where narrow houses clustered together for a scrap of daylight. Fetid cellar rooms where sewage seeped through the walls. The reeking, crowded rookeries, where corpses lay stinking because no one could afford to call an undertaker. If Eleanor visited any of those places alone, it would be a miracle if she came out unscathed.

The first such street on her list was St Christopher's Place. It sat between Oxford Street and Wigmore Street like a gap in a smile. It looked like a wet mouth, brown and stinking and ready to swallow her whole. A thick layer of tamped-down sludge coated the pavements and something grimy oozed down a wall. Strings of filthy laundry sagged between the upper windows. A legless beggar slumped against a wall, and Eleanor could not tell if he was drunk or dead.

It wasn't a long street. In theory, she could be through to Oxford Street in less than five minutes. But the once-grand houses had been built to last, with thick walls and boarded-up windows. Inside one of those tall, dark houses, no one would hear her scream.

'Well,' she said, gathering her skirts out of the filth, 'I suppose we'd better begin.'

They went to the nearest door and knocked. No one answered. Barnes took a long look at the grimy shutters and pushed it open. He held Eleanor back for a few moments before they went inside.

All the floorboards had been ripped up to show the dirt beneath. Limp curtains divided the room into quarters and caught the smell of smoke and damp. Barnes strode across the room and yanked the nearest one back, sending something scuttling into a corner. There was a shriek and Eleanor found herself staring at a terrified Jewish family, clutching at each other and pleading in a language she could not understand.

'Do you know what they're saying?' she asked.

Barnes shook his head.

The next house was little better. In the garret was an old, one-legged soldier whose room was full of twittering songbirds, on the middle floor was a nine-year-old girl dosing a dozen babies with gin, and on the ground floor was a hive of curtained cells, each one with a narrow bed and a few tired-looking women. Next to that was a vast laundry filled with clanking copper drums and shuddering pipes. Then a room where a hobbled old woman boiled vats of oranges and a gambling den blue with smoke. Eleanor longed for the little slice of daylight at the other end of the street. The strings of laundry over her head felt like a descending net.

Barnes had pulled a cosh from his jacket and hammered with it on every door. It was a talisman, she realized. The sound of leather on wood would be enough to tell that he was armed. A group of sailors lurched into the second house and, too late, Eleanor understood what it was. Something sloshed out of a window; Barnes yanked her out of the way. A child laughed, then there was the sound of a smack.

Grimy children, club-footed beggars, hollow-eyed men made thin in the Crimea, women with too many babies and not enough money. Eleanor could feel their desperate eyes on her face and wanted Charles more than ever. How easy it would be to retreat into his soft, warm world, where other people cooked his food and washed his clothes. There she could be laughing, pretty, intriguing, but what was she here? A victim? A threat? How many of these people thought her some kind of inspector, sent to take their children away?

At last they reached the other side. The cosh vanished back into Barnes's jacket. Eleanor stood in the bright March morning, shaking. Her dress was filthy, she felt clammy all over, and she was still no closer to finding Leah.

She fumbled in her purse and pressed a coin into Barnes's hand. 'Thank you, Barnes. If you'll excuse me, I have some business to attend to.'

She should not have done it. It would only make it worse. But still she went to Granborough House and stared at the unlit windows.

Eleanor sat on an overstuffed chair in Mrs Cleary's dressmaker's, fighting the urge to pinch the bridge of her nose. The shop was crammed full of beautiful brocades, rows and rows of ribbons, and counters laden with silks and satins dyed to suit the latest trends. Mrs Cleary was standing at one of the counters examining samples of black silk so rich they almost seemed to glow. Even though no one was watching her, Eleanor was careful not to let her tiredness show. Her face hurt from smiling. She had been patient, tactful, and enthusiastic all morning, and behaving so impeccably was exhausting. Still, it was necessary. Only the wealthy could afford to be rude, she thought, staring at Mrs Cleary.

It was a long way from the muck of St Christopher's Place. Eleanor had spent the whole of the Easter weekend scrubbing it off her skin. She shuddered. She ought to be glad that Leah was not there, but she could not be. St Christopher's Place was not bad enough to make it into the papers. There were far worse places Leah could be.

A rustling of skirts nearby made Eleanor start. Miss Hill was standing in front of her.

'Are you well, Miss Hartley?' she asked. 'If you'll pardon me for saying so, you look a little pale.'

'I'm simply distracted,' Eleanor said, keeping one eye on Mrs Cleary. 'The search for my friend is not going well.'

Miss Hill sat gracefully beside her. 'I'm sorry to hear that.'

Eleanor stared into her hands. 'Have you ever tried to find an old friend before?'

Miss Hill gave Eleanor a sad smile. 'Yes. I found him, too, but I'm afraid the reunion came far too late. Before I came to Mrs Cleary I volunteered as a nurse in the Crimea, and—' She broke off.

'I'm so sorry,' Eleanor said.

'Please don't trouble yourself, Miss Hartley. It was sad, of course, but now I find I have little to be sorry for. Mrs Cleary has accepted me in a way that not many other ladies would have done. She can be…particular,' she said, a knowing look in her eye, 'but she is very generous.'

Mrs Cleary stumped over to them, her silver-topped cane muffled by the thick carpets. 'Look at the two of you, gossiping like old hens,' she said. 'Now, Miss Hartley, come here. There is a polonaise here that would do for you.'

Her most blinding smile back in place, Eleanor allowed Mrs Cleary to lead her over to a display. She had to fight the urge to look over her shoulder. *Particular, but generous*, she thought. Why had Miss Hill chosen those words? Could she tell that Eleanor was only tolerating Mrs Cleary for the sake of her money? Even halfway across the shop, Eleanor could feel Miss Hill watching her carefully.

What had Miss Hill heard about her?

Eleanor was always mindful not to let Mrs Cleary find out about her past, but it was an increasingly easy occupation. Mrs Cleary had been widowed almost two and a half years ago, and had retired from Society as was correct – adding to which the fact that she was a Catholic, and therefore not welcome in all corners of high society, meant Mrs Cleary had heard hardly a thing about what really occurred in her old friend's home.

Each time a new invitation came, Eleanor floated on relief. She was going to make sure Mrs Cleary adored her, and nothing was going to get in her way. Eleanor dismissed Bessie at the door with strict instructions to return at ten; she could not let her talk to Mrs Cleary's servants. She made sure to wear the dresses Mrs Cleary had given her at every dinner, altered to fit the older woman's own ideas of what was appropriate for young ladies. Mrs Cleary gave Eleanor advice which she sometimes wrote down, if she thought that Mrs Cleary suspected she was not sufficiently grateful; by the first week of April Eleanor had filled a notebook. Eleanor escorted Mrs Cleary into dinner, helped her in and out of chairs, and made sure to smile while she did it. She insisted on helping Miss Hill, too, and knew that Mrs Cleary's companion was grateful for the respite. Eleanor was dutiful, innocent, and attentive: in short, the perfect daughter.

But it was all for nothing, because when she left the drawing room at ten o'clock one night she saw Miss Hill and Bessie standing together, whispering. They fell silent when they saw her.

The moment the front door had closed behind them Eleanor rounded on Bessie. 'What did you say to her?'

Bessie smirked. 'Nothing, miss.'

When she called at Mrs Cleary's house the next day, there was no answer. She tried again the next day, and the next, and it was only when the footman told her to clear off that the truth finally sank in.

Bessie had told Miss Hill about Granborough House, and Miss Hill had told Mrs Cleary.

Mrs Cleary knew Eleanor had lied. Well, not lied – all right, she hadn't been perfectly honest, but she'd only embellished a little. Bessie was the liar. God only knew *what* she'd told Miss Hill. Surely the truth wasn't enough to make Mrs Cleary cut her off like this – no, she had to have lied. Two whole months of nodding and smiling and listening to advice she didn't need – *wasted*.

Eleanor marched home, veins alight with fury. She'd lost the best chance she had of finding Leah and getting Aoife out of Granborough House, and it was all Bessie's fault. From the moment they'd met Bessie had dripped poison into the neighbours' ears. Now Eleanor was without friends, without a benefactor, without anything to show for herself. Well, that was *fine*. No more nodding and smiling and shaping her personality like dough. What did she need Mrs Cleary for, when Eleanor could wear her independence like a fur coat?

Eleanor would find Leah herself – she had her own two

legs, there was no reason why she couldn't. And she'd get Aoife out of Granborough House too, without anyone else's help. Let Mrs Cleary sit and rot in her overstuffed house. Eleanor didn't need her.

Eleanor's temper was still churning through her when she reached Granborough House, sharpening the edges of all her thoughts. Every passer-by who trod on her skirts or knocked her elbow was slighting her, every costermonger calling to her had mockery in their voice. Her forearms ached from clenching her fists; she longed to draw them back and punch something.

'Ella?'

Aoife was walking towards her, shadows pooling underneath her green eyes. Eleanor beamed at her – it was so good to see her again – but then she noticed Aoife's expression. Her face seemed about to fold in on itself, she looked so tired.

Aoife was carrying a large parcel, wrapped up in brown paper and string. 'Lord above, what are you doing here?'

'Aoife! How is Charles? How are *you*? What's been happening here? For God's sake, Aoife, tell me! I've heard nothing for months!'

Aoife looked over her shoulder. 'You'd better go. If Mrs Fielding finds out we spoke...'

Eleanor blocked her path and snatched the parcel out of her hands.

'Give that here!'

Eleanor darted out of reach. 'You shan't have it until you've answered me.'

'Keep on like that and I'll fetch a constable!'

'Please do. I'll tell him it's *my* parcel, and we'll see who he believes.'

309

'You...you wouldn't. Ella, you wouldn't!'

Shame crawled across Eleanor's skin, but she did not give back the parcel.

Aoife glanced at Eleanor's well-cut dress and her shoulders slumped. 'You won't tell anyone I saw you?'

Eleanor shook her head.

'Master Charles was sent away. None of us knows where he's gone. He's coming back for the Season, though. The master says he'll have him married before the year is out.'

Eleanor felt a lump in her throat. 'Do you think he'll go through with it?'

Aoife shrugged. 'I don't see how he has any choice.'

Eleanor scrubbed at her eyes. Aoife had the decency to look away.

'And how are you, Aoife? You haven't been...'

Aoife shushed her, her face flushing. 'I'll not discuss such things out of doors, Ella!'

'But you are safe, aren't you?'

'I...most of the time. He knows about the laudanum but he doesn't care – he has me mix it into all his drinks now. And he kept all your morphine, so half the time he can't see straight. But...'

Eleanor led Aoife out of the earshot of a fruit-seller. 'But what?'

'He keeps making me do all the syringes for him. I hate them! I keep thinking he'll go for me with one of them and I – I think he's thinking that too. The way he looks at me... sometimes he'll...'

Aoife put a hand to her mouth, tears pouring down her cheeks. Eleanor put an arm around her shoulders.

'I've not had it as bad as Leah,' Aoife whimpered, 'but it's not because he doesn't have it in him. It's just because he doesn't want to yet.'

A cold, creeping fear rippled through Eleanor. Aoife was weeping into her shoulder, clinging to Eleanor's clothes like a child. The top of her head barely came up to Eleanor's chin. How could anyone stand to make Aoife cry like this?

'I won't let anything happen to you,' Eleanor muttered. 'I'll find a way to—'

Aoife pulled away from her, snatching the parcel back as she did so. 'How?' she wailed. 'You aren't here!'

Eleanor slammed her front door, still shaking with anger. She'd tried to find Leah and she'd tried to help Aoife but nothing had come of it. Weeks of searching, all that simpering at Mrs Cleary and she had nothing to show for it. Aoife was still in danger, Leah was – God knew where she was! Eleanor had tried and tried and it had all come to nothing. Nothing!

Eleanor kicked the umbrella stand, sending a patched umbrella rolling across the floor. It wasn't enough. She wanted to break something.

Bessie was out. She was *always* out. Sooner or later she'd be out for good, because she liked being a servant about as much as she liked her mistress. And then where would that leave Eleanor? Scrubbing an empty house, yet again.

The children next door were playing as their father tried to shepherd them to bed. Eleanor's house echoed with the sounds of running feet and screaming. The last few dairymaids and coffee-sellers called out, dust-carts rattled down the street, and train whistles shrieked in the distance. Life pressed against her door, hot and sharp, but no matter how she tried, nothing she did could touch it. She might have been a doll trapped inside its box.

She needed money to make a difference. As a rich woman she could buy Aoife's way out of Granborough House, or employ a proper detective to find Leah. If Eleanor had been rich, when her mother had taken ill her father could have paid for a doctor or a nurse, instead of leaving his daughter to tend a dying woman when she was too small to lift a coal scuttle. What could she do without money? Last month's allowance was two weeks late, Mrs Cleary had cut her off and getting a job would never provide the kind of funds she needed. Seamstresses and washerwomen were paid in shillings, Eleanor needed guineas. She was sick of watching her bank account waste away and knowing she could do nothing about it.

Unless she made a wish.

The sun had started to set, staining the sky a dirty orange. Next door's children had stopped playing. The carts and coster-mongers moved further down the street. Eleanor was left in a bubble of quiet, and inside it, something was waiting.

No. She couldn't. Someone would die if she did. It wasn't like before; she wasn't making a wish that would work only on her. If she made the wish, someone else would die. Someone who was more than a nudge in her abdomen – a person, a *real* person, with hopes and dreams and a family.

Eleanor looked around. Her curtains needed mending. The chairs would need replacing. More coal would need to be ordered, more polish would need to be bought, more rags would need to be scrubbed out and re-used. How could she find Leah and rescue Aoife when the shabby house ate everything she had?

If she made a wish, someone else would die. But if she did not make a wish, Aoife would be assaulted, Leah would die in a damp and stinking gutter, and Eleanor would wear herself down to the bone trying to keep the threads of her life from fraying.

It would take her one step closer to losing her soul. But perhaps her soul was already gone – perhaps she'd never even had one in the first place. Losing her virtue had not made her feel any less virtuous; perhaps losing her soul only mattered because someone had once told her it should. If it was even there, if the woman was even real, if she wasn't going mad. How could she put her faith in wishes, when she didn't even know if she'd dreamed them up?

Eleanor took a deep breath and wrestled her doubts back into place. Fretting over whether the black-eyed woman was real or not was not going to help Eleanor save Aoife or find Leah. She had to put her faith in something; it might as well be herself.

She would need to be careful. Whether souls were real or not, Eleanor did not want to risk making the final wish. Every instinct in her body screamed that it would be a bad idea.

A golden realization dawned.

Perhaps there was a way to solve both her problems with one wish.

The first problem: she needed money. However, she was still under the age of twenty-one: until then, all her money would be controlled by her legal guardian, Mr Pembroke. The second problem: Mr Pembroke was going to assault Aoife and throw her on the streets once he'd had enough.

If she wished for money, Mr Pembroke would have to die for her to get it.

Even though she hated him, the thought chilled her. It would not be like all the times she'd made a wish before. She would know exactly who was going to die when she spoke the death into being. She may as well slit his throat herself.

Could she do it?

Eleanor sank into a chair, her mind reeling. She tried to imagine holding a knife to Mr Pembroke's throat, watching the fear in his eyes, and every part of her shrank from the thought. She couldn't do it. He'd already made her into so many things she didn't want to be: a housemaid, a disgrace, a blackmailer, a keeper of shameful secrets. She would not let him add murderess to that list.

But it wasn't as if *she* would be killing someone. The black-eyed woman did that, and she knew that Eleanor did not want her to. Eleanor only made the wishes because she had to. And she wasn't even wishing for Mr Pembroke's death, not really. She was only wishing for money, and thousands of people made that wish every day. She wasn't asking the black-eyed woman to kill Mr Pembroke – that would simply be an unfortunate by-product of the wish.

It was not her fault.

'I wish to have enough money to see the things I dreamed of and keep those I care for from harm.'

Dust hung in the air. Blood rushed in her ears; her own breathing was all she could hear. Something else was listening.

Eleanor woke up in her own bed. Her feet hurt. Her arms hurt. In fact, everything hurt. She heaved herself upright and felt immediately sick.

There was blood on her bedsheets.

Her hands shook, just as they did every time she awoke to

find her bleed had come in the night. An old fear crept through her thoughts, and she hated herself for it. She was seventeen, she was old enough to know better. But every time she saw it she remembered the bitter sick-room smell, saw her mother pale as the sheets around her, blood bubbling up from between her lips and oozing down her chin...

Eleanor ripped off the covers. The bottoms of her feet were scratched and bloodied. Eleanor was surprised. Had she gone out last night? She must have done. There were bruises, too; purple marks across her arms and abdomen. Had she been fighting? She checked her face in the mirror. It looked pale, but unharmed. Her hands were fine, and her hair was tangled, but hadn't been pulled. She must have gone out for some night air and stumbled into something.

She cleaned the cuts and covered the bloodstains before asking Bessie to help her dress for church. There was no need for Bessie to know what had happened. Eleanor tried to remember, and came up with nothing. The last thing she remembered was making the wish.

She went downstairs and checked her letters. No enormous postal order that would solve all her problems. No black-bordered letter informing her of the tragic death of her guardian. But then, it was Sunday. Perhaps she wouldn't find out how Mr Pembroke had died until tomorrow, when the post came. How long would it take for the wish to come true? She put on her hat and shawl and tried not to think about how Charles would take the news of his father's death. A ripple of guilt spread through her just thinking about it.

There was the shriek of a police whistle.

She stopped. Through the window Eleanor could see people running. She drifted closer, and heard screams. Across the street, the black-eyed woman stood perfectly still, smiling. No one else saw her.

Eleanor went to look.

The street was full of running people: tartan-clad church-goers, children clutching nursemaids' hands, workmen with caps in hands. Horses stamped and snorted, their eyes rolling. Eleanor followed the sound of the screaming.

It was coming from Mrs Cleary's house.

There was a crowd clustered about the gates. A housemaid was hunched away from them, throwing up at the foot of the wrought-iron gates. A man with thick, dark whiskers tried to propel Eleanor back. 'Best go home, miss.'

She shook him off. He grabbed her and now she could see the policemen, filing out of the house, holding up shaking servants. Eleanor caught a glimpse of Miss Hill, her face ashen.

Eleanor yanked her arm away. 'Let me through!'

'For God's sake, miss, come away—'

She pushed forward. Someone caught her around the waist and tried to turn her back; she pushed him off. A hand closed around her arm. Another came down on her shoulder. She pulled away and stumbled forward. Mrs Cleary's house was bone-white in the morning light.

'Miss!'

Her cheeks were wet. Had a burglar been in the night? No. It was worse than that. She could feel it in every hand pushing her back, see it in every pair of hollow eyes. Then, the smell hit her. Blood. Reeking waves of it rolled over the crowd, forcing its way into her throat. Worse, there was something horribly sweet beneath it. Dread swelled around her. She knew that smell, had known it since she was nine years old.

She burst through the crowd, bruised and aching. The house

loomed up ahead of her. She already knew what she would find inside. Grey faces, policemen, that smell – but it couldn't be true. Any minute now Mrs Cleary would emerge from the shadowy hallway, ushering her inside, forgiven. It wasn't true. It couldn't be true.

A policeman stepped forward. 'Go home now, miss.'

Through the open doorway, she saw the big, dark stain on the hall floor. Her stomach lurched.

'No,' she whispered. 'No, no, it can't be true...'

A pair of hands came to rest on her shoulders. A man's voice came from a long way off. At the other end of the darkened hall, a door opened. A policeman shuffled out, carrying one end of a large bundle, wrapped in cloth. The fabric was stained red.

The black-eyed woman flickered in and out of focus. Each time she appeared, her smile grew wider.

'Come away now, miss. Don't look.'

She had already seen.

Swaddled in her quilt, Eleanor sat in her drawing room and tried to listen to the police constable. There were footsteps in the hall, squeaking floorboards as policemen paced, creaking doors as Bessie cracked them open. People tapped on her windows, newspaper boys yelled in the street, carts rumbled past. Eleanor wondered which one of them was the police cart, come to take Mrs Cleary away.

Someone forced a hot mug into her hands. She wasn't quick enough; it spilled all down her skirts. A tawny stain seeped across her legs. Brandy. The smell made her stomach lurch. She'd been given the same drink after she'd found Lizzie. How alike the two days were, Eleanor thought. Her dress was even

317

damp, now, as it had been on the morning after Lizzie had been drowned.

The constable squatted in front of her.

'Think back, miss.'

What did he want her to remember? There were so many gaps. The feel of cobbles under her boots, the fingerprint bruises on her arms, the press and noise of the crowd – these things were real. She could still feel every line of the cobblestones on her bruised feet, still smell the hot, close mix of sweat and drying blood. But could she give him the date that she had last seen Mrs Cleary alive? She couldn't remember.

'When did you last—'

The black-eyed woman.

She'd killed Mrs Cleary. *She* had done it.

It wasn't *fair*. Eleanor had worked out how to solve two problems with one wish, so the black-eyed woman had killed Mrs Cleary to spite her, and let her see the body. This teeming, stinking city was filled with people. Why couldn't she have chosen someone else?

Eleanor put her head in her hands.

'Miss?'

When would it ever stop? She'd thought that facing death would become easier as she got older. Instead, it was like returning to a vast ocean, at a different place every time. No matter how often she saw it, she would never understand its depths. All she could do was stand on the shore and scream.

She wanted them back. She wanted them all back; not just Mrs Cleary, but all the people at the accident, even Lizzie. Mrs Pembroke. Her mother. She would have waded into the water and pulled them all out, one by one, if it had only been that simple.

'Sarge, could you...'

'Miss? Come now, miss, listen to me...'

Something aged her every time she saw another body, but she still felt like a child. She wanted Charles to come back and find her, she wanted the policemen to stand guard outside her door; she wanted open skies, empty fields, to shout and scream where no one could hear her. Cold, hot, old, young, lonely and desperate to be alone. She was untethered. Bobbing aimlessly in dark waters, where the creature that wore the black-eyed woman's face was stirring beneath her.

The sergeant crouched in front of her and took her hands. A row of silver buttons sparkled down his chest, winking like shined shillings. Her father had had buttons like that, once. He'd let her play with them when they'd fallen off his jacket.

'Now, miss, I know you're upset, but we do need to talk to you. Is there someone who could come and calm you down?'

Her eyes were hot with tears. 'I want Papa.'

'Now that's better. Constable, run and fetch the young lady's father. Miss, could you give us his address?'

'He's dead,' she sobbed, 'he's dead.'

Eventually, Eleanor told the police about her last dinner with Mrs Cleary, leaving out the details of their estrangement. She wanted her last memories of her to be happy.

For once, Bessie had acted like a proper maid and put Eleanor to bed, dosing her with Godfrey's cordial as if she were a baby. The sickly-sweet syrup, heavy with laudanum, had sent Eleanor dreams full of claws, hacking and slashing and tearing, and she had awoken in a cold sweat.

Dressing and coming downstairs had made her feel better, even though she still ached. Eleanor went through her letters in the drawing room. When she found a thick, creamy envelope her busy hands stilled.

The paper was thick and weighty. She could feel the delicate warp and weft beneath her fingers. A legal address was written on the back flap. Condolences came on black-edged paper. The workhouses could never afford paper like this. The realization sank through her, dragging her down. There was only one thing it could be. For a moment, the black-eyed woman's face wavered in her inkwell. It was, as ever, smiling.

She opened the letter.

Miss Hartley, she read, *it is my duty to inform you that you are the sole beneficiary of the estate of Mrs Flora Cleary. Please find enclosed a full list of property and accounts, which will pass to you as heir to the estate...*

She pulled out another wad of paper. It fluttered as she read.

Mrs Cleary had left her everything. Property in London, Manchester and Liverpool. A stake in her husband's old shipping business. Deeds, stocks, bonds, shares. She could travel the world with money like that, and, unbidden, the words of the wish came back to her.

Tears stung the corners of Eleanor's eyes. This was her salvation – and not just hers. She could find Leah, she could rescue Aoife, she could marry Charles. It had been a high price to pay – Mrs Cleary had been her only friend – but now there were no more obstacles in her way.

She read the letter again, to make sure.

...which will pass to you as heir to the estate. Owing to your tender years, the estate shall be held in trust until your marriage or until you reach the age of twenty-one; until such time it shall be administered by your legal guardian, Mr Frederick Pembroke...

The paper crumpled under Eleanor's hands.

No. He had to be dead! She'd wished for money, and it couldn't be hers until Mr Pembroke was out of the way. She tore through the pile of letters, looking for something with a black border. Bills, a reply from the workhouse, a sympathetic note from the reverend – nothing bringing news of Mr Pembroke's death.

Eleanor stormed upstairs and slammed her bedroom door behind her.

'I need to talk to you.'

The black-eyed woman did not appear from the shadows this time. Eleanor blinked and she was there, sitting at her dressing table and drowned in pale green light. The woman's black eyes made her look like a sea creature.

Eleanor brandished the letter at her. 'Is Mr Pembroke still alive?'

The black-eyed woman smoothed out her skirts. For the first time Eleanor realized that they were not floral, but patterned with something very like flowers. She tried to focus on the design, but it made her head hurt.

'You seem upset,' the woman said. 'Why? I granted your wish.'

'No, you didn't!' Eleanor hissed. 'I asked for money, and—'

'And you have it – legally, even if you cannot access it. But my dear, wishes can only take you so far. Seventeen-year-old girls do not have access to their money in *this* day and age. Did you really expect me to change English law overnight? Your faith in me *is* sweet.'

Eleanor slammed the letter down on the dressing table. 'I expected you to kill him! You cheated me!'

The black-eyed woman gave her a smile. It was an empty, dead thing.

321

'If you want something, my dear, you must ask for it. Do not talk to me of cheating; you knew what you really wanted when you wished for money. You wanted him dead, but you could not bring yourself to slide in the knife. I may not have given you what you wanted, but I did give you what you asked for.'

Eleanor seethed. The black-eyed woman was right. She should've known better than to trust in the wishes. They were poison.

'Couldn't you have chosen someone else?'

'You make the wishes. I carry them out. Do you have any idea what that means? Do you know how hard it is to look into the morass of the future and shape it to your demands? By all means, give me your suggestions; perhaps I can improve upon my method!'

In the soft, green light the black-eyed woman looked embalmed. She was motionless. When she took a step forward, Eleanor flinched.

'If you want him dead,' the black-eyed woman said, silkily, 'make another wish. Speak the words aloud. I will kill him, if you ask me to. I will even let you witness the granting of your next wish. I know how you hate him, my dear. Should you like that?'

'No, thank you,' Eleanor whispered.

'Then do not question my methods, child. I granted your wish; ask no more of me.'

She vanished. Eleanor was left staring at an empty chair and her tangled bedsheets. She slumped onto the bed and put her head in her hands. They were soft and white now, thanks to diligent work with bear's grease and lemon juice. Lady's hands. Not the hands of a murderer.

She had not killed Mrs Cleary. The black-eyed woman had

done that, and Eleanor had had no say in the matter. How could that make her a murderess? She hadn't wanted Mrs Cleary to die. Mrs Cleary had cut Eleanor off, true, but she would have come around eventually. She wouldn't have left Eleanor all her money if she'd truly wanted nothing more to do with her. Eleanor hadn't even asked for Mr Pembroke's death – all right, she'd wanted it, but she'd been wanting it for years and that hadn't made her a murderess.

She was not the same as the black-eyed woman, Eleanor told herself. They were entirely different kinds of being: one human, one very much not. Why was Eleanor surprised that her wish had been misinterpreted?

Besides, she thought, as she got to her feet, what else was she supposed to do? The world around her was a sharp and vicious thing. Beggars died drunk in the gutter, children contorted themselves sweeping chimneys and froze selling matches, maids were raped by their masters and thrown out on the streets. Eleanor had been granted the power to change those things. One word and the beggar would find a home, the child could go to school and not to work, the maid could have vengeance on the master. Was she really supposed to sit around and watch that happen to her friends when she had the power to save them? Surely it would be another kind of murder to do nothing, knowing what horrors they would face. And at least now she had the power to help without resorting to a wish – or would, once Mr Pembroke was dead.

Eleanor had smoothed down her bedsheets before she realized she was not supposed to make beds any more. Still, it had helped her put her thoughts in order. Now, at last, she knew what she had to do. The only question that remained was whether she was brave enough to do it.

PART SIX

If Eleanor wanted to go into mourning for Mrs Cleary, she would have to write to Mr Pembroke and ask him to release the funds. The realization made her feel sick. Eleanor made herself a black armband instead, and felt ashamed every time she tied it on. The black-eyed woman had used Eleanor's wish to kill Mrs Cleary, and Eleanor couldn't even mourn her properly.

There was a knock at the door. Eleanor didn't bother getting up from her writing desk. It would only be another ghoulish visitor hunting for gory details. She'd told Bessie to turn all callers away.

The drawing-room door opened and Bessie walked in, her eyes gleaming. 'Inspector Hatchett, miss.'

Eleanor got to her feet as the Inspector ducked through the door. Why was he here? What could he want? She plastered on a smile and tried to keep her nervousness from showing.

'Inspector! Do sit down. Bessie, I shan't be needing you any further.'

Bessie slammed the door behind her as the Inspector sat down. Eleanor had no doubt that her maid was eavesdropping.

'Miss Hartley. You *are* still Miss Hartley, I presume?'

His eyes flickered to her hand. She was still wearing her

327

gloves, fingers slathered in bear's grease. He wasn't to know she had no ring. It might be easier to lie, but God only knew what she would do if the Inspector asked to speak to her imaginary husband.

'For the present,' she said, blushing. 'How may I help you?'

'I've come to offer my condolences,' he said, nodding to her armband. 'When I heard you had discovered another body, I was most concerned for your well-being.'

There was a curiously flat tone to his words. With a sudden stab of fear, Eleanor wondered how many times he had rehearsed them.

'That's very kind of you,' she said. She shifted her chair into the light, making sure he could see how pale her face was, and all the shadows pooled under her eyes.

'You seem to have very bad luck indeed. Two murders in such a short amount of time.'

Eleanor folded her hands in her lap. She was sure he was watching them, waiting to see if they twitched.

'But, happily, you have not been left out in the cold. I understand Mrs Cleary left you everything. How good of her to think of you.'

His voice was utterly empty, his dark eyes fixed on her face. Eleanor forced herself to look at him. If she looked away, if she shifted in her chair, she would seem suspicious. She must keep her face smooth and blank, or he would pounce.

'It was good of her,' she agreed, letting her voice catch in her throat. It was not hard. Whenever she thought about Mrs Cleary, grief, guilt and anger threatened to choke her. Mrs Cleary had *tried* to be kind, even if she hadn't succeeded. 'I don't suppose you've heard anything about the investigation? The local police haven't told me anything.'

'Nor should they,' said the Inspector. 'It would not do to make such details public.'

Eleanor's hands were sweating. Could he tell?

'Could you shed any light on the matter?'

'I could not.'

Her insides were squirming. To think that he considered her capable of committing those murders – to think that she knew the real culprit, and could not tell! Eleanor stared into the corners of the room, and saw the black-eyed woman staring back. She was standing like an attentive maid, and her smile slid across her face like a knife. The Inspector said nothing, and Eleanor knew he could not see her.

He hadn't taken his eyes off Eleanor's face once. He was waiting for her to make a mistake, she realized, with the same quiet confidence of a hunter stalking his prey. Anger flickered beneath the fear. She'd had enough of being hunted.

'Perhaps you ought to offer the local police your services,' she said, trying to smile. 'It is a pity this case is left to them, rather than coming under your jurisdiction. I feel sure that *you*, with all your experience, could bring the murderer to justice.'

A muscle in the Inspector's jaw twitched. Eleanor had to fight back a grin.

'An excellent notion, Miss Hartley. Perhaps I shall.'

'I hope so,' said Eleanor. 'I shall never forget the way you offered me your help at Granborough House. Such a shame you were not able to give it, when I asked.'

The Inspector flushed. 'That was not by choice, as well you know.'

Eleanor got to her feet, willing her knees not to shake. 'I find there are few situations in which one really has no choice, Inspector. There is always something that can be done.'

She went to the door and held it open for him. He got up, but did not follow her.

'No matter how unpleasant?' he asked.

'I don't know what you mean.'

The Inspector picked up his hat and went to the door. 'I think, perhaps, you do.'

Eleanor tore through every paper she could get her hands on over the next few days. They were all filled with the grisly details of Mrs Cleary's murder. She combed through the finer points of the investigation. Someone had to have killed Mrs Cleary; surely the black-eyed woman's magic could not slit throats without a hand to wield the knife. But while there were plenty of outraged letters in the papers, and plenty of constables standing outside the doors to Mrs Cleary's old house, Eleanor heard nothing about a suspect.

It unsettled her. Whenever Eleanor walked past a constable she felt their eyes on the back of her head. She seemed to be watched wherever she went: in church, at the post office, behind the glass of her drawing-room window. Her neighbours had always whispered about her but now they did not even bother to lower their voices.

Eleanor made sure they saw her grieving.

She worked up her old dress uniform into a mourning dress – with a few alterations and her armband, she did not look like a lady's maid. She sewed black borders onto all her handkerchiefs, and used them extravagantly in church. She placed advertisements in the papers, asking for information and promising a reward – although how she was going to pay it, she didn't pretend to know. In her black dress, Eleanor felt like a macabre magnet, but it was enough to turn the worst of the rumours away.

The performance of grief was stifling. Eleanor hated having to trim everything she owned with scraps of black to dull the sharpened glances of people who hated her. If there was any justice in the world she would be allowed to mourn Mrs Cleary in a way that suited her. But until a suspect was named in the papers, anything but extravagantly public weeping would mark her out as a killer.

Every day she went to the post office to ask for the responses to her advertisement. Usually, there was nothing but a smattering of badly spelled lies. But on one April morning, a damp spring fog clinging to the hem of her black dress, Eleanor received a telegram containing nothing but the address of a church in Pimlico and the words *most important that we meet*.

Excitement rushed through her. At last, something promising. All she would need to do was let the details slip to Bessie and Eleanor's innocence would be proclaimed from the rooftops by lunchtime. Eleanor got on the next train to Victoria, elbowed her way through the crowds and was soon stepping into the whitewashed halls of the church.

It was quiet. Eleanor's feet rang out over the scuffed flagstones as she passed rows of shiny pews. A vast organ hulked over one end of the church, and a musicians' gallery ran along the west wall. Eleanor looked around. A woman was praying in one of the pews and the reverend was speaking in a low, earnest voice to a blushing young couple. There didn't seem to be anyone waiting for her.

A soft knock came from the gallery. The reverend looked up, then turned back to the couple. Eleanor hurried over to the stairs and climbed to the gallery. Of course the informant would not want to be seen, she chided herself.

Waiting at the top of the gallery stairs was Charles.

She froze, one foot on the final step. The world seemed to shrink down to a point. Eleanor forgot Mrs Cleary, the rumours swirling around her, the Inspector's growing suspicion. In that moment there was only the fresh spring sunlight gilding Charles's hair, the gentle brush of his fingers on her cheek, and his smile, brimming over with joy.

He cupped her face in his hands. 'Eleanor,' he murmured, 'it's you.'

Tears sparkled in his eyes. How could she have ever forgotten how blue they were? Memory could never do justice to that shade.

Someone coughed in the church below. Charles cast a furtive glance over the edge of the gallery, shuffled two steps to the left, and kissed Eleanor hungrily. Out of sight, he wrapped his hands around her waist and pulled her closer. She tugged on the lapels of his jacket, kissing him fiercely. She never wanted to let him go.

They broke apart, breathless. Charles seized her hand, kissed it, and led her away from the stairs.

'What are you doing here?' she whispered.

'Father called me back for the Season,' he explained. 'He's trying to arrange my marriage.'

Eleanor pulled her hand away, her pride smarting. 'Then you shouldn't even be here.'

'On the contrary. This is exactly where I should be.'

She blushed. Charles grinned at her, and took her hand again.

'I knew I could put the roses back in your cheeks. But you look pale, Eleanor. I read about that awful business with Mrs Cleary and I had to see you. You must be distraught.'

It was hard to feel distraught with Charles holding her hand.

With him by her side, she doubted she would ever feel unhappy again. She told him what had happened since they parted, and as she spoke she could not take her eyes from his face. She wanted to commit every detail to memory.

'I never should have let Father send me away,' he muttered. 'I only agreed because I thought it would be best for you. To think you've had to bear such burdens alone!'

'And I shall keep on bearing them alone, if you are married.'

She tried to pull her hands away, but Charles held them fast. 'Father can make what plans he likes. I shan't marry anyone but you, Eleanor. I see no reason why we can't go to Gretna Green as we planned. Only this time, I shall be far more careful.'

Eleanor could barely believe it. After all her months of longing Charles was back, holding her hands and saying everything she'd dreamed he would. His words had set something in her alight; she could feel it glowing under her skin.

'We'll have to be discreet,' Charles was saying. 'Father mustn't suspect a thing. When I have the money I'll tell him I'm visiting a friend; you must follow. He needn't know anything about it until we return as man and wife.'

Even as she smiled – *man and wife* – doubt dimmed her joy. Mr Pembroke could still have the marriage annulled; he was her guardian, and she would need his permission for the marriage to be valid. Worse, he could have Charles declared mad and thrown into the asylum. It happened in novels all the time. And even if he didn't separate them, could she really move back into Granborough House? Watching Mr Pembroke spend her money would be bad enough. Could she really go back into that house, and put her neck into that noose once again?

'I must go,' Charles whispered, 'but I'll be back soon. Very soon, Eleanor.'

He kissed her again, and left. Eleanor watched him go, and prayed that he was right to be so hopeful.

Eleanor paced around her drawing room, her mind writhing with plans.

She'd been through everything she owned, looking for things to sell. The fine dresses Mrs Cleary had given her would fetch a good price, but she could not sell them all: no one would believe she was Charles's wife if she dressed like a housemaid. The furniture technically belonged to Mr Pembroke – if he realized she'd sold it he could charge her with theft. Everything Mrs Cleary had left her was technically under Mr Pembroke's guardianship; if Eleanor sold anything, he could contest it. That left nothing but a few odds and ends: a collection of hatpins, a few books, and an old hat she thought might go for a shilling with a few trimmings added to it. Not nearly enough for a train ticket to Gretna Green, and the three weeks they would need to stay there before they married.

Eleanor slumped into a chair. It was galling that she was an heiress and could not touch her own money. She'd been to the bank and they'd told her that if she wanted to withdraw money, she'd have to present proof of her guardian's permission. Then the clerk had patted her hand and told her not to fret; money would spoil her, and her guardian was acting in her best interests. Eleanor left with her hands balled into fists.

Once again, Mr Pembroke was standing in her way.

In truth, she did not want to go to Gretna Green. Why should she and Charles run off into the night as if their marriage was something shameful? Only because Mr Pembroke thought it was. *I won't have you for a daughter-in-law*, he'd said. Even the memory made Eleanor's lip curl.

That was not freedom. Even though they would be running away, Mr Pembroke would still dictate the terms of their marriage. He was a vile puppetmaster, and the only way to be free of him was to cut the strings.

Eleanor remembered the black-eyed woman. *If you want something, my dear, you must ask for it*. She shivered.

There was a gentle tap at her front door. Eleanor sat up at once. Charles? But no, it couldn't be. Surely he wouldn't be so careless as to come to her house, when Bessie reported everything she did to Mr Pembroke.

Bessie barged into the drawing room. 'It's Miss Hill,' she said, and stomped back to the kitchen. Miss Hill gave the maid a brief nod as she left, and Eleanor felt a prickle of fear. What had Bessie told her?

'Good morning, Miss Hartley,' said Miss Hill. 'I hope I'm not disturbing you.'

Eleanor put on her most brilliant smile. 'Not at all! It's such a pleasure to see you again. Will you sit down?'

'You're very kind.'

Miss Hill's dress had been recently mended and as she sat Eleanor glimpsed a pair of scuffed boots. She was not the only one observing. Miss Hill's dark eyes darted to the bare walls, Eleanor's black dress, the empty coal scuttle. Throughout it all her face retained the same expression of reserved interest, and Eleanor sat up straighter. She was clearly dealing with an expert.

'Please accept my condolences,' said Miss Hill. 'I know you were close to Mrs Cleary. I would have come earlier, had circumstances allowed.'

Eleanor tried to look suitably distressed. 'Yes, I – I miss her terribly, of course. Such a shock. You must be quite bereft.'

'I'm sure she would have been proud to see you coping with such grace.'

Proud? Why had she said proud? Eleanor remembered her last dinner with Mrs Cleary. She certainly hadn't been proud of her connection to Eleanor after that. Why would Miss Hill bring back such unpleasant memories? What did she want?

'Thank you. Now, to what do I owe the pleasure of your company?'

Miss Hill's fingers pinched the cuffs of her dress. Her face was still polite and calm, but Eleanor felt a vicious thrill. She'd given herself away. She was nervous.

'Would you be so good as to write me a character reference? I hoped you might oblige, as you have observed me in my role as Mrs Cleary's companion. Without one, I should have to go into service, and as a young lady yourself I'm sure you can understand my trepidation.'

Eleanor relaxed. Miss Hill was not going to demand a share of Mrs Cleary's money or a house in the country. If a new position was all Miss Hill wanted, Eleanor would have nothing to worry about.

Eleanor went to her writing desk and pulled out pen and paper. She was dipping her pen into the inkwell when a thought occurred to her that sent cold fear crawling through her veins.

Miss Hill had told Mrs Cleary about Eleanor's past. What would Eleanor do if she also told the police? Miss Hill knew that Eleanor had lied to get close to Mrs Cleary. What would the Inspector make of such information?

Eleanor's hands began to sweat. Giving Miss Hill what she

wanted would be like loosing an arrow into the dark; she would not know where it would land. She had to keep Miss Hill in her debt, so that she would never think of going to the police.

'I'd be very happy to oblige you, Miss Hill.'

Eleanor penned a glowing recommendation, knowing that Miss Hill could see the paper from her seat. Shame crawled across Eleanor's skin. Then, she tucked it into a drawer.

She turned to Miss Hill, who was pinching the cuffs of her dress again. 'There,' Eleanor said, smiling. 'When you find your next position, give me the address and I shall send it along myself.'

A muscle flickered in Miss Hill's jaw. 'That would be most disruptive for you, Miss Hartley. I should hate to cause you any trouble. If I could take it now...'

Eleanor laughed, cringing at the sound. Miss Hill had hinted it had been difficult for her to find the position with Mrs Cleary. And yet Eleanor had no choice; she could not let Miss Hill talk. 'That is sweet of you! Please don't worry about causing me any trouble. I should be glad to help you.' Eleanor smiled. 'You have only to ask.'

For a second, Miss Hill was motionless. Her face, at last, was blank. Then, she rose to her feet and assumed her expression of polite detachment once again. 'Thank you, Miss Hartley. Incidentally, on a more sombre note I should be grateful if you would inform me when Mrs Cleary's funeral will be held.'

Eleanor stiffened. She'd been so distracted she'd all but forgotten the funeral. Mrs Cleary had made her own arrangements before she died, and when the police had released the body it had been shipped back to Ireland as she'd wanted. Eleanor had put the undertaker's bill in a drawer, and hadn't thought of it since.

'Of course,' Eleanor lied. 'Yes, I shall – yes. I will write and inform you of the details. Good morning, Miss Hill.'

Eleanor turned away, shame curdling in the pit of her stomach. She caught a glimpse of her reflection in the inkwell as Miss Hill left, and started back. The pupils of Eleanor's reflected eyes were enormous yawning pits.

Eleanor and Charles met in another church, this time on the edge of Soho. Under the cover of the choir, they whispered their plans to each other. They tried to act like strangers, but behind the high backs of the pews, they were holding hands.

Charles ran a thumb across the back of Eleanor's hand. 'It won't be long now,' he promised. 'A few more weeks – a month, at most. I can't bear to be apart from you any longer.'

Eleanor pressed her knee against his. 'When we're in Scotland, it'll be three weeks before we can marry. You'll have to wait a little.'

'It'll be different then,' he whispered. 'You'll be near me. We can take our meals together, stroll around the village, visit churches and ruins – anything!' He gave her a sheepish smile. 'Do you know how long I've wanted to show you off?'

She shifted closer, looking up at him through her lashes. 'Won't you miss keeping me all to yourself?' she said, her voice low.

He slid an arm around her waist. 'Eleanor,' he murmured, pulling her close, 'I have missed you every day—'

A cough echoed through the church. They flinched and broke apart.

'I must go,' Charles hissed, giving her hand one last squeeze. 'I'll write again soon.'

He left. Eleanor waited, pretending to pray. Her mind was teeming.

One wish would solve all her problems. Mr Pembroke was controlling access to her money. Mr Pembroke was preventing her marriage to Charles. Mr Pembroke was abusing Aoife. Eleanor wanted him dead.

All it would take was a word.

She lined the sentence up in her head. *I wish that Mr Frederick Pembroke was dead.* Even thinking the words made her feel powerful. There'd be nothing he could do to stop her. He could grovel and cry and fight and nothing he did would stop the black-eyed woman from coming for him, like an avenging angel. She'd see him *beg*.

Eleanor recoiled from her own anticipation. What was she doing? When had she learned to relish the prospect of death and violence? This wasn't who she wanted to be. She wanted to keep her friends safe, she wanted to marry Charles, but surely this was not the only way to do it.

Surely she didn't have to make herself into a monster.

Eleanor stared up at the stained-glass window. Saints wept and angels sang as Jesus suffered in brilliant colours. All their eyes seemed to be fixed on her. A better woman than she would have trusted in God, or Fate, or whatever it was that was supposed to reward the good and punish the wicked. Once upon a time, she would have done so. But now she had seen what life could do to people who trusted in a vague and benevolent higher power and nothing else. Perhaps such things were only there because other people believed them to be. Perhaps they weren't there at all, and it was only the sheer force of millions of people desperately wanting something to be true that gave them the signs they were looking for. Perhaps that was all she could feel, prickling at the back of her neck.

Perhaps it was only because she wanted the black-eyed woman to be there that Eleanor saw her at all.

Eleanor shook the thought away. She'd gone to the inspector for help. She'd tried to take Aoife out of harm's way with a deal of her own. She'd tried to get Mrs Cleary to give her the money to find Leah and buy Aoife's way out of Granborough House. It had all come to nothing. Things had only ever got better when Eleanor took matters into her own hands.

She'd already done so many things she'd never imagined she would do. She had lain with a man outside of wedlock, threatened her employer, got rid of a child she had not wanted. How many of those things were truly evil? She and Charles were in love, threatening Mr Pembroke had got him to leave Aoife alone, and surely it was better not to have a child at all than to bring one into the world when she could not care for it.

Would killing Mr Pembroke really be a bad thing?

Eleanor gave herself a little shake and stood up. Fresh air would clear her head.

A fine haze of dirty rain drifted over the city. This close to Soho, Eleanor's plain dress seemed fine among the patched and worn clothes of the crowds around her. Little girls selling watercress grown on dirty flannels trudged from door to door, their hair limp in the rain, while chimney sweeps hacked and spat into the gutter. Eleanor walked quickly, heading for the larger, cleaner streets. A woman in a fraying shawl started following her as she passed. It would not do to linger here.

Eleanor forced her way through the crowds, past brightly

lit shop windows, painted Highlanders outside tobacconists' and men wearing sandwich-boards advertising everything from shoes to sealing-wax. Booksellers scrambled to cover their wares in the rain; colourfully dressed women mended wicker chairs on the back steps of fine houses; a boy with hastily applied clown makeup handed out grubby leaflets for a passing circus. Eleanor drifted through the press and swell of the crowds and wondered what they might have wished for, or what they would say if they knew what she had done.

Before she knew it she was outside Granborough House.

It took her a moment to recognize it, because the house was all but crumbling. Tiles had fallen off the roof and smashed in the street below. A thick layer of grime coated every window and damp stains oozed down every wall. The drawing-room was shuttered, along with half the bedrooms, and one of the chimneys was not working properly, the smoke coming out of a long crack running down the side. The front steps, however, were still clean, and Eleanor felt a strange lump in her throat at the sight.

Behind the garden wall, Eleanor heard the back door open. Moments later, Aoife came through the gate, a large basket hung over one arm. Eleanor darted forward at once.

'Aoife!'

Aoife's hand clamped down on the handle of her basket the moment she saw Eleanor. She hurried away, but Eleanor was too quick.

'Aoife, wait! I only want to talk to you!'

Aoife wouldn't meet her eyes. 'The master said we're not to talk to you.'

'Of course he did,' Eleanor snapped. 'When did that ever matter? We're friends, aren't we?'

'The master said we're not to talk to you,' Aoife repeated.

Eleanor stopped. Aoife was wearing a new dress of fine merino wool. There was lace at her collar and cuffs. And still, she would not look at Eleanor. Fear reared its head.

'Aoife,' Eleanor said quietly, 'what have you done?'

At last Aoife raised her head. Her eyes were burning. 'I've done nothing! Don't you dare—'

'Then where'd you get your new dress?'

'He's come into some money,' Aoife muttered. 'He says we'll all get them. He only gave me mine first because...'

Eleanor laid a hand on Aoife's arm, feeling horribly sick. 'You don't have to say it. I know you don't like talking about these things.'

'You don't understand, Ella!' Aoife said in a rush. 'I've a family to think of! Micheál's worse by the day and the master says if I do as I'm bid he'll give me a little extra for the medicines and it'd be better, wouldn't it, than just waiting for him to...to...'

No, Eleanor thought, *not Aoife, please, not Aoife...*

'You haven't—'

Aoife glanced over her shoulder. 'Not yet,' she hissed, 'but I'm going to. Don't you dare try and give me a talking to, Ella, I've enough of that from Daisy!'

Eleanor gripped Aoife's arm, digging her nails in. She remembered Leah's bruises and horror and revulsion crashed through her in waves.

'Aoife, you don't have to do this,' Eleanor hissed. 'I'll find a way to get you out, I promise—'

Aoife tugged her arm away. 'You said that before,' she said, 'and I'm still here. By all that's holy, Ella! I'll not sit around and wait for you to come up with another stupid plan. I've made my choice.'

Aoife stalked off. Eleanor did not try to follow her. She did not think she could. All her bones seemed hollowed out, frail as porcelain. One wrong move and she would shatter.

She turned.

Mr Pembroke was standing at the window of Granborough House. He was watching Eleanor, and he was smiling.

The rain had curdled into a fog that pressed up against the windows, greasy and black. It had grown dark long before the sun had set. A feeble streetlamp tried to penetrate the gloom, but all Eleanor could see from her window was a slightly lighter patch of darkness.

Eleanor remembered every detail of her journey back from Granborough House. She had stared at the vast iron beams of Victoria Station, the rough wooden seats in the third-class train carriage, the cobbles under her feet. She had crammed all her horror and disgust and fury into a tight, pulsing little box to let herself get home safely. When she'd pushed open her front door, she had gone straight up and lain on her bed, fully dressed, staring at the ceiling until she heard Bessie go upstairs for the night.

The clock chimed midnight. The old memory rose to the surface, as it always did – the foot of the iron bedstead at Eleanor's back, her own hands pressing against her ears. The bed had shaken with her mother's every cough, springs creaking, and the metal had knocked into Eleanor's spine. If she had gone to her mother, she might have been able to soothe her, but instead she'd curled up into a ball, wishing that the noise would stop – until suddenly, it did.

She'd done nothing, then. She'd been too young, too scared. But she knew what she had to do now.

Streetlamps glowed dimly outside her window. There were no sounds coming from the street outside. It wasn't like Mayfair; when this street closed its doors, everything slept. Eleanor lit a candle and crept into the kitchen.

She uncorked a bottle of brandy.

The smell made her eyes water. The taste would be worse. She slopped some into a glass. For a moment she felt guilty – it was expensive, she should save it – but she ignored it. It was *her* damn brandy.

No. It was Mr Pembroke's brandy.

She'd bought it with his money; therefore, it was his. It was his house too. Never mind that she actually lived there, and had done her best to make it a home – it was still his house. Had she ever had anything that was truly hers? Even if she made her dresses herself, she'd never bought the cloth. It always came from someone else. And someone else could always take it away.

She gulped down the brandy. It burned; she spluttered, and made it worse.

She'd had enough. How long had she put up with that man plunging his fingers into every corner of her life? There was nothing he wouldn't take from her. Even Aoife – poor, sweet Aoife. He'd smiled to see the despair on Eleanor's face when Aoife had walked away. He wanted Eleanor to know that he could take her friends and crush them.

Eleanor topped up her glass. She knew she shouldn't. She knew she shouldn't make the wish, either. This, more than anything she had done before, would make her a murderess. But if she waited any longer, knowing what would happen, what would *that* make her? She might be making herself a monster, but even in all her nightmares, she could never be as monstrous as him.

She drank again.

And after he had finished with Aoife, what then? Would Eleanor have to simper and smile at him in order to get her allowance? No. For years she'd been what she needed to be: a dutiful daughter, an obedient maid. They were masks. She had put them on and taken them off for as long as she could remember. Did she even have a face beneath them?

She would not do it any more. Not for him.

This time, she drank straight from the bottle.

How many more girls was she going to watch him ruin? It wouldn't stop at Aoife. There were always maids who didn't listen to the rumours. And he, with his well-shined shoes and well-cut clothes, would always be safe, cosseted and ignorant behind piles of sovereigns and shillings.

She drank again. Better to put him out of his misery, if he was going to spread it around.

Eleanor was sick of it. She was sick of watching the parade of bruises and tear-stained faces and swollen bellies and knowing that she couldn't do a damn thing about it. And not just that. She was sick of her bare floorboards, sick of being snubbed by all her neighbours, sick of this choking, stained city. She'd never seen a horizon and when she stared into the sky it was depthless, like the lid of a box.

It was all Mr Pembroke's fault. He bruised everything he touched and her future was no exception. She took another swig.

Well, she'd put a stop to that. She'd have Charles for her husband and get Aoife out of Granborough House, and all it would take was a word. Just a few little words. After that Eleanor could remake the world as she wished it, with all her money. She could mend all the things Mr Pembroke had broken, see all the places he'd kept her away from. All that she'd dreamed of was within her grasp, if she only had the courage to remove this last obstacle from her path.

She put the bottle down. It was empty, and she hadn't noticed.

If you want something, my dear, you must ask for it.

She knew what she wanted. She had always known. Now, she would take it.

'I wish that Mr Frederick Pembroke would die before the sun comes up.'

The world went still. Moonlight gleamed on glass. A mouse watched her, motionless underneath the dresser. Every grain in the wood stood out sharp. The briefest pressure settled on her shoulders, like a mother's loving hands.

Eleanor woke up the next morning in her own bed. Everything ached. Sunlight streamed through her curtains, staining the room jade green. Train whistles shrieked, carts rattled past her windows and a few streets away, the church bells chimed ten.

She sat up. Her stomach lurched, and the inside of her mouth tasted foul. Her head ached, too, the way it always did after she'd been crying.

She splashed cold water on her face. Her dress was dumped on the floor, crusted with mud and still damp. Had it been like that yesterday, when she'd come back from Granborough House? She couldn't remember. She checked her purse; she was short four shillings. Surely she hadn't been stupid enough to take a hansom all the way back to Peckham – but, no, she'd taken the train, hadn't she? Eleanor felt the brandy boiling at the back of her throat and retched into the bowl on her washstand. She vowed never to touch alcohol again.

She looked up, and met the eyes of her pale reflection. She wouldn't need any more brandy. She'd never have to make a wish like that again. There was nothing in her way now. She felt the knowledge settle on her like stones in her pockets, and retched again.

She pulled on her shawl and went downstairs. Bessie was in the kitchen, singing tunelessly as she went through the cupboards. She smirked when she saw Eleanor.

'Good night, was it?'

'I beg your pardon?'

Bessie slapped a couple of onions on the kitchen table and began to peel them, flicking onion skin and clods of earth across the floor.

'Bessie, what do you mean?' Eleanor asked.

'Heard you come in, didn't I? At an hour that decent folk is all in their beds. Not surprised you don't remember. You was lolloping up the stairs worse'n a sailor.'

Eleanor flushed. 'I don't know what you mean.'

Bessie gave her a knowing smile and went back to her onions. The knife flashed in her hand. Bessie couldn't know about Mr Pembroke, or she wouldn't be smiling like that.

'Did...did I have any callers after I stepped out? Or letters, perhaps?'

'Now why're you asking about that, miss?'

'I...I don't...'

Bessie set down the knife and grinned at her. 'You think I don't know you've been slipping off to see your fella, and what you got up to the last time round? Bet that's why you was asking about callers. Afraid you'd missed a fare?'

'How dare you. How *dare* you! Get out of my house. I never want to see you again!'

347

Bessie laughed. 'You can't dismiss me, *miss*. You ain't the one who pays me.'

It had been two days since Eleanor had made her wish. Rain slapped against the windows. Wind bellowed down her chimney and made the fires flicker. The snap of harnesses and the trundle of wheels hid in the howl of the storm. With all the noise of the street lost, every creaking floorboard might have been someone approaching her door. Setting her hairpins on her dresser sounded like a key clicking in the lock. The slightest noise sent her rushing to the nearest window, heart hammering, but there was never anyone there.

She knew that Mr Pembroke was dead. She could feel it. But until she had the news, she could not stop flinching at shadows.

A lamplighter shuffled down the street, bent in the wind. The pole wobbled in his hands, and the gaslamps flickered like pale yellow butterflies as he passed.

Eleanor tried to regret the wish, but felt nothing. She had done the right thing. Mr Pembroke was the last obstacle to her happiness and now he had been removed. Aoife would be safe, Eleanor and Charles would be married, and her money would be her own. All she would have to worry about now was the final wish. The black-eyed woman would be waiting for Eleanor to make it for the rest of her life.

The black-eyed woman saw everything that Eleanor did. She could never get away from her. In church, at Mrs Cleary's, with Charles – dear God, she'd seen her *with Charles*. If Eleanor never made the last wish, all the most intimate moments of her life would have an audience. The exact spot in her drawer where she'd hidden her savings, the red-haired guardsman who'd winked at her when she was fourteen, her one and only attempt to write poetry. Once she'd clutched these secrets to her chest, and if she'd known she'd never have privacy again she would have held on so much tighter.

Eleanor stared at the edges of her reflection, looking for movement in the shadows.

Secrets were not all the black-eyed woman saw. She'd seen that Eleanor's baby would have been a boy. She had seen something of Mrs Pembroke and Eleanor's mother, and they had been dead for years. Eleanor wondered how the black-eyed woman saw time. Did the past and the future echo back to the present? When she was not there, was the black-eyed woman hovering above them all, in some place where time and form and distance did not matter?

The wind wailed. Eleanor looked into reflected darkness and saw nothing. She was not foolish enough to think that meant there was nothing there.

There was a knock at the door.

Eleanor leapt up and sprinted to the window. It was too dark to see; the lamps had gone out in the wind. Close to the glass, she could feel the chill of the wind, every spatter of rain, but there was something else there – a strange, magnetic feeling that made the hairs on her arms stand up. She tugged on her shawl and picked up the candle, heading for the stairs. It guttered in the draught, throwing twisted shadows on the walls.

The knock came again.

Bessie stumbled out of her bedroom. 'For God's sake,' she muttered. 'This had better not be one of your bloody callers.'

Eleanor ignored her and went downstairs. Whoever was on the other side of the door had been brought here by the wish.

She knew that they would tell her that Mr Pembroke was dead, with a certainty that was as cold and final as death itself.

She needed to hear the words. A strange longing pulsed under her skin. When she heard those words her future would unfurl before her, a shining path with nothing in her way.

Bessie hurried after her. 'Come away! Don't play the fool on a night like this!'

Something was wrong. Instinct picked out all the colours in the darkness and made every bump in the floor sharp beneath her feet. Cold air rushed around her ankles. On the other side of the door, someone was rattling the doorknob.

'Miss!' Bessie hissed. 'I was only fooling. Of course you don't have callers. For God's sake don't let in a stranger! No one'll hear us in this weather!'

Eleanor hesitated. There was always something. She had done what the black-eyed woman asked for and told her what she wanted, but Eleanor knew that would not be rewarded. What sharp and nasty thing would be coiled around her wish?

She set down her candle and snatched up an umbrella. Holding it like a club, she yanked the door open.

Charles stood on the doorstep. He was drenched, his lips pale. Stubble sprawled across his cheeks, and shadows lingered under his eyes. He reached towards her with shaking fingers. From the look on his face, he expected his hand to pass right through her.

His cold, wet hand brushed her cheek, burning like ice.

'Eleanor,' he whispered.

The umbrella slipped out of her hand. He clung to her, sobbing.

'It's Father. He's dead.'

* * *

Eleanor did her best.

She hung up Charles's clothes to steam in front of the fire. She sent Bessie out for tarts and gilded gingerbread with a few precious shillings. She held his hand. All the while, hot lumps of guilt burned in the pit of her stomach. She'd killed Mr Pembroke, and Charles was holding her as if she could save him from drowning.

It shocked her to see him this upset. There was nothing in their way now; they could finally be together. Surely he would see that, soon. She stroked his hair, and said nothing. In time, he would realize what a blessing Mr Pembroke's death had been.

Charles returned the next day, armed with roses. Next to his drawn face, they looked garish, insincere. She arranged them in a battered jug and told herself to be patient. He'd come around soon enough.

'Eleanor,' he said, 'I want to thank you. The comfort you have brought me…I…'

He was crying. Eleanor kissed him on the cheek.

'I'm sorry. Damned childish behaviour.'

She pushed him into a chair. 'You've every right to be upset.'

'There's no use mewling about it. There's so much to be done. The expense, the inquest, and then there's the house, and the servants, and the will, and – God! Oh God!'

He buried his head in his hands. Eleanor slid an arm across his shoulders.

'You don't have to bear this alone. Let me share your burden. You know how I love you. Let me help you.'

Charles seized her hand and pressed it to his lips. Tears slid across her fingers.

'Leave everything to me,' she murmured. 'There's no need

to concern yourself with the details, not when you've so much to bear already. This...this inquest...'

'You're an angel.'

They sat together for a while, Charles staring into the fire while Eleanor stroked his hair, the word 'inquest' rattling around her head. She asked, but Charles would not discuss it. Later, she began planning the funeral. She wrote letters to undertakers, to the rector, to mourning warehouses. She ordered black-edged writing paper and material for armbands. She made enquiries about horse-drawn carriages, undertakers' mutes, and plumes for the horses, and cringed at the cost. With each scratch of the pen, she buried Mr Pembroke. She imagined shovelling ink-black soil onto his coffin, and felt nothing.

PART SEVEN

When Charles and Eleanor sat beside the fire and worked together, they might have been man and wife. While Eleanor reviewed the undertaker's bill, and Charles looked at the cartoons in *Punch*, nothing could touch them.

Charles turned a page and snorted with laughter. 'Good show! Eleanor, look here.'

He held out the magazine. Eleanor leant over to look at the cartoon as someone knocked at the door. From the kitchen, Bessie swore and clanged some pans together. Moments later, she yanked open the drawing-room door and cleared her throat. It sounded phlegmy. 'Inspector Hatchett, miss.'

Eleanor almost dropped the undertaker's bill. The Inspector? What could he want? She glanced at Charles and to her surprise, saw that he had gone pale. Something prickled on the back of Eleanor's neck. What had Charles said about an inquest?

Inspector Hatchett ducked through the door. Shoulders hunched, he looked like a bird of prey. Eleanor stood up and smiled, every inch the perfect hostess.

'Inspector! What an unexpected pleasure. As you can see, I have company, so perhaps we could conduct our interview in the dining room? It's down the hall.'

'Thank you, Miss Hartley, but this is not a social call. I need to speak with you both as a matter of urgency.'

Eleanor's smile slipped. The word 'inquest' rattled around her head. 'Is everything all right?'

The Inspector pulled out his notebook. 'I should prefer to speak to you both separately. If you could give us the room, Miss Hartley—'

Charles's foot started jittering against the floor. 'Is it really necessary to bring her into this?'

The Inspector fixed Eleanor with a long, hard look. 'I believe it is.'

Eleanor could feel her own pulse fluttering in her throat. Could the Inspector see it twitching beneath the high collar of her dress? Even when she looked away she could feel his eyes on her face. They taught policemen how to look for all the signs of guilt. Had she already given herself away, and not known it yet?

Charles took her hand and spoke to the Inspector. 'I want to be present for Miss Hartley's interview. I won't have you frightening her.'

Eleanor stared at Charles's pale face, heart rattling against her ribs. 'Is there a reason for me to be frightened, Charles?'

'I – well—'

'Mr Pembroke,' said the Inspector, and Eleanor flinched to hear him address Charles that way, 'this is ridiculous. I would have thought you would take the investigation into your father's murder a little more seriously.'

The words dropped into Eleanor's mind like leaden weights. It couldn't be murder. Mr Pembroke was old, he drank, he took morphine. The Inspector must have been mistaken. His heart had given out, or he'd put the needle in the wrong place, or he'd—

'Murder?' she whispered.

Panic flashed across Charles's face. The Inspector was scribbling furiously.

'Charles, your father…your father was—'

'I thought you knew!' Charles cried. 'It's been in the papers!'

Eleanor flushed. She wasn't used to having a fortune; she could walk past a hundred paperboys and not think to spend the money. She frowned. 'Why didn't you tell me?'

'Do you mean to say, Miss Hartley,' said the Inspector, disbelief laced through every syllable, 'that you did not know that Mr Frederick Pembroke had been murdered?'

Eleanor put a hand over her eyes and sank into a chair. *Murder.* Another act of spite from the black-eyed woman. She ought to have realized, Eleanor thought bitterly. The black-eyed woman was perfectly capable of stopping Mr Pembroke's heart, or allowing one of his needles to slip. Instead, she had made someone murder him – *please God*, Eleanor thought, *not Aoife* – because that death would snap and claw at Eleanor's heels, dragging her closer to the Inspector and the final, forbidden wish.

Charles dropped to his knees beside her. 'Eleanor, I'm sorry, I should have—'

She got up, knees shaking. 'Please forgive the delay, Inspector,' she rasped, 'but would you postpone my interview? I find myself somewhat indisposed.'

The Inspector was watching her, his brow furrowed. His eyes moved from her pale face to her black dress. He closed his notebook, still watching her.

'Of course, Miss Hartley,' he said. 'I will call again when you have recovered.'

*   *   *

When Charles and the Inspector had gone, Eleanor resolved to find out the truth. She picked through the household waste until she found an old newspaper, crumpled and stained by raw mutton.

Mr Pembroke had been stabbed in the night. The papers suspected he'd been drugged: there were no signs of a struggle. Someone had simply crept in, killed him, and slipped away. Two maids had gone missing, along with a large amount of money. Eleanor remembered Daisy watching Aoife's hair spill across her shoulders, and hoped they were safe, and together.

Perhaps it had been Daisy or Aoife who wielded the knife. Perhaps it had been someone else – Leah, maybe, or some other poor girl just like her. Eleanor could think of a long list of girls who would've been happy to see him die, and Eleanor would be lying if she didn't add her own name to the list.

She had done what they'd all been dreaming of. She had sent the black-eyed woman after him like an avenging angel, and the world was a better place because she'd done it.

But now, she had the Inspector to contend with.

Eleanor prepared for his visit carefully. Everything he saw would end up in his little notebook; therefore, perfection was the only thing she could let him see. She had Bessie scrub the house from top to bottom and then sent her out for the day; Bessie had done enough damage with Mrs Cleary. Eleanor brushed her black dress to a shine and covered her only mirror with a scrap of dark cloth. The May sunshine streamed through the drawing-room window, baking the air inside; Eleanor angled her chair carefully so that the light would catch her hair, but keep her from sweating in the sun.

When he arrived, Eleanor showed him in herself, like a girl greeting her father at the door instead of an heiress who could buy him ten times over. She went to the carefully placed chair, leaving the Inspector squinting into the sunlight, and started sewing a black border on a handkerchief. Better to keep her hands busy, in case they gave her away.

He sat down. With his long limbs bunched beneath him, he looked as if he'd been badly folded in half.

'Miss Hartley, before we attend to the matter at hand I must apologize. I had assumed that you were aware of the nature of Mr Pembroke's death. I hope I did not distress you on my last visit.'

'Not at all, Inspector. I quite understand. It must be so difficult to deal with such tragic circumstances.'

He opened his notebook. 'And now, if you please, I should like an account of your whereabouts on the twenty-seventh to the twenty-eighth of April.'

The twenty-seventh was the day that she'd been to the church in Soho: the night she'd made her sixth wish. Eleanor was ready. She had practised in front of the mirror at her dressing table, smoothing her voice and her face into blandness as she'd spoken.

'Well,' Eleanor began, 'I got up at about eight, attended to some business matters and household tasks in the morning, and then went into town in the afternoon. I came back at about six o'clock but went straight to bed, not feeling well. The next day was much the same, only I didn't go into town.'

The Inspector was still writing it down. 'And can anyone confirm your movements?'

Too late, Eleanor remembered Bessie. She'd heard Eleanor coming back home in the middle of the night. Where had she been? Eleanor couldn't remember. There'd been money missing from her purse – had she taken a cab, or a train? Had she been robbed? Eleanor fought to keep her face blank. Why couldn't she remember?

'I still have the ticket stubs upstairs, if you'd like to see them,' Eleanor said.

'What about your maid?'

'I'm afraid she's out. I can send her down to the station when she returns, she'll find her way.'

The Inspector looked at her for a long time. There was a flash of grey at his temples, his face half-hidden in a mass of lines. His expression was unreadable.

'Forgive me, Miss Hartley,' he said, 'but I am surprised that you have gone into mourning for Mr Pembroke. To be blunt, I had not thought you cared for him.'

Eleanor hesitated, and realized that in hesitating, she had given him all the answer that he needed. She blushed.

'I care for Charles,' she said. 'I mourn for his sake.'

'That is one benefit to this sad affair. I understand you were planning to elope; now you may be married without opposition.'

Each word was empty of insinuation, placed with all the care of a chess master lining up his pawns. He was not writing now, just watching her, and as he did so the black-eyed woman materialized behind his chair. She peered over his shoulder and read the notebook, then looked up at Eleanor and tutted.

The Inspector followed her eyes. He turned and looked right at the black-eyed woman – no, right through her, because he was looking around the room for the thing that had caught her eye.

Eleanor gave herself a little shake and forced herself to ignore the black-eyed woman. He'd think Eleanor was mad, if he saw her jumping and starting at nothing.

'It is very kind of you to see the good in this, Inspector,' Eleanor said. 'I shall take comfort from it.'

He made another note, and said nothing.

Charles returned a few days later, with armfuls of roses. With clouds of colour around his face, petals drifting gently downwards, he looked like a tree shedding brightly coloured leaves. Still smarting from the news about Mr Pembroke, Eleanor stared resolutely at the dress she was mending.

'I've brought you flowers,' Charles said.

She kept her eyes on her sewing and a hold on her temper. 'So I see.'

'There's red ones, for passion. White is for innocence, or perhaps charm. Pink is...grace, I believe? And there are others, too. When one puts them together, they mean "you are everything to me".'

Eleanor did not look up. 'Is there anything in there that would do for an apology?'

He shifted. 'That's hyacinths. I...I thought that might look odd.'

She went back to her sewing.

'Eleanor, I—'

'Were you ever going to tell me what happened to your father?'

The flowers drooped. She wanted to smack them out of his hands.

There was a tightness in his voice when he spoke. 'I know I should have told you. I'm sorry.'

Eleanor sighed and laid aside her sewing. 'I hope you don't intend to make a habit of this. I don't care to find out all your news from a police officer.'

'I imagine not. Was he civil to you, when you met?'

'Civil enough. He's rather stern, isn't he?'

He gave her a small smile. 'Good Lord, yes.' Charles set down his flowers on a table and perched on the edge of the sofa. 'I really am sorry, Eleanor,' he said again.

She felt a twinge of pity and kissed his pale cheek. 'I know.'

'I have something else for you,' he said, putting his hand into his pocket. 'The Inspector asked about you and when I mentioned our plans to elope it occurred to me how silly they were.'

He drew out a small box. There was a sapphire ring inside: Mrs Pembroke's ring. Charles had risked so much for this ring – Mr Pembroke had all but thrown him out when he'd first tried to take it. Now, it was finally Eleanor's. It had been a long and bloody journey but, at last, she had carved out a place at his side.

Charles slid it onto her finger. 'Much better to do it properly,' he said. 'You've been such a comfort to me, Eleanor – the one constant thing in this horrible affair. You deserve something better than an elopement.'

Her hands must have been unbalanced before; the weight of Charles's ring on one hand made them feel so right. Warmth spread through Eleanor like a sunrise. Finally, she could set her past behind her. There would be no more wishes. She already had everything she needed. Now she could start to put things right. With Charles by her side, there would be nothing she could not accomplish.

She kissed him, happiness burning through her like wildfire.

Charles's ring transformed her from a friendless waif to a girl who was going to be a princess.

All the doors had flown open. Her neighbours finally came to see her, with brittle smiles and evaluating eyes. Charles had secured her an invitation to a friend's ball and Eleanor laboured over her thank-you note, etiquette books spread in front of her. It had to be perfect; Charles was going to present her there as his fiancée.

She did not think about what she had done to get there. Eleanor only regretted killing Mr Pembroke when she saw the shadows under Charles's eyes, and then she buried her guilt under silk and satin dresses and drowned it in champagne. Nor did she feel guilty about Mrs Cleary's death – Eleanor mourned her, of course, but she hadn't asked for Mrs Cleary to die. The black-eyed woman had killed Mrs Cleary to upset Eleanor, and the best way of honouring Mrs Cleary's legacy was to enjoy it. Eleanor had inherited her money in unfortunate circumstances, but that did not make it any less *hers*.

She had such plans. She'd written to Aoife's family, promising to arrange a doctor to treat her brother. She'd thought about trying to find Aoife, too, but thought better of it. If the black-eyed woman had used Aoife to strike the killing blow, Eleanor should not draw attention to her. For now, Eleanor busied herself with making enquiries for a house of her own: she never wanted to set foot in Granborough House again. But that could wait until after the honeymoon. Charles had brought the atlases from Granborough House – mildewed, now – and they'd planned it out together, just as they had done that night in the library. They would go all around Europe, and they would do it in style.

For the first time in her life, she felt like she could do anything.

Her stomach was not growling. Her shoulders were not slumped forward. There was no pain in her back, no twinges in her knees. She soared above the dirt and the cold where no one could touch her. At long last, her rightful place in the world would be acknowledged, and no one could take it away from her.

Nothing would ever touch her now. She was immune to poverty, hunger and cold. There would never be another night spent shivering in a garret, or curled up against the foot of her mother's bed, waiting for the coughing to stop even though she knew what that meant. What did it matter that when she asked for help, no one had come? Now, if she wanted help she could pay for it, and people would come running. Eleanor would float above it all and watch other people scurry around, carrying out her orders, and every single one of them would thank her for the privilege of serving her. After all, why should she spoil her lily-white hands, when she'd worked so hard for them?

She flicked through her letters. Invitations, enquiries, bills of sale – and something written on soft, cheap paper. She opened it, ink smudging her fingers.

Dear Miss Hartley, she read, *thank you most kindly for condessending to inquire about a certain Miss Leah Wallace. It is with the uttmost joy that I humbly beg to inform you that the said Miss Wallace is currently residing in our humble institushion. Miss Wallace & her child, a boy named Josiah, are receiveing every care & attenshon a busy poorhouse may provide...*

Leah was alive. Her child was alive. How? The winter had been so cold, and Leah had been so thin. But they were alive, thank God, they were alive.

364

Eleanor clutched the letter, certain that she had made the right choice.

The cab sat in Hanover Square, outside the St George's Union. The shadow of the workhouse spilled across the street. Yesterday's letter crouched in her purse like a spider. Eleanor stared at her gloves, her dress, and the inside of the cab, but she could still feel the long windows of the poorhouse watching her.

Her parents could be in a pauper's grave behind those walls. She'd never found out where they'd been buried. She might have been told, right after it had happened, but after the bed had stopped shaking and Alice Hartley had breathed her last, all Eleanor could remember was the wait for someone to find her, and the smell.

Charles helped her down from the cab. 'It does look severe. Do you think it shall be safe?'

It would be safe, for him. Anyone could tell. He had never worn through his shoes, or eaten his dinner fast enough to prevent other people snatching it. Eleanor had grown plump. Her hair was glossy. Her shoes did not pinch, her dress was neatly fitted, and her gloves were brand new and thin enough to tear. But stepping into the shadow of the workhouse, Eleanor became acutely aware of how fragile such things were. A harsh winter or a bad investment would take them away from her, like leaves being snapped off the stem of a rose.

She took a deep breath. Even in May the air still tasted of smoke. She stared up at the long, thin windows and felt them staring back. She took Charles's arm. The last thing she wanted was to step into that place alone.

'Miss Hartley?'

Eleanor looked up at the sound of an unfamiliar voice and saw the workhouse matron. She was an unremarkable woman, tired and stout with jangling keys at her hip. The building seemed to dwarf her.

'Do come this way,' the matron said.

Eleanor glanced at the workhouse. There were faces at the windows, dark smears against soot and bird droppings. The front door was taller than it needed to be and under an arch on the brink of collapse. It shrank her down. Had Leah felt so small, when she'd stood outside the workhouse, or had she only been relieved to be behind dry walls?

She followed the matron inside, into a cheaply tiled hall where every footstep rang down the corridor. Eleanor's dark green dress looked unnatural against all the shades of brown and grey. She'd thought it demure and perhaps it was, outside. In here it was as vivid as a fresh bruise.

The matron led them to a small room with bare floorboards and whitewashed walls. In front of them was another long, dirty window, looking onto the women's yard. To Eleanor's right, the matron was fumbling with her keys and standing by a small door. On her left was a much larger door, secured by bolts at the top and bottom, leading to the men's block. Eleanor could not see the graves, and was not sure if she wanted to.

The matron unlocked the door. Eleanor flinched at the sound.

'Wait a moment,' the matron said, and went inside. Eleanor heard yelling – 'All right, into the yard, the lot of you!' – before the door closed.

Eleanor clutched Charles's arm tighter. He gave her hand a squeeze.

The matron came back when the shuffling had stopped on the other side of the door. 'Just through here, sir. Miss.'

She held open the door. Eleanor walked into a larger room – still barren, still cold. One framed sampler hung on the wall, and standing in the middle of the room was a young woman with dark hair and naked hope scrawled across her face.

Leah. She was alive. She was safe. After all this time, Eleanor had found her.

Leah was thin, but not as thin as she had been. There were new lines on her face and a permanent droop to her shoulders. But it was Leah, just older and sharper. Eleanor felt the weight of all her new clothes and shame curled itself around her.

'Little Nell,' said Leah, softly, 'look at you.'

The familiar nickname brought a lump to Eleanor's throat. 'Leah. You look...' The word 'well' shrivelled on Eleanor's tongue. 'How are you?'

Leah glanced at the matron, who was carefully saying nothing. 'Oh, very well, thank you.'

'And your boy?'

Leah's face softened. 'Growing so fast I can scarcely credit it. Of course,' she said, not looking at the matron, 'that's to be expected, now he's getting decent food.'

A rat scuttled across the room. The matron stamped her foot and it darted away. Eleanor flinched; so did Leah. She could feel the bolted door in the corridor behind her, like a hand on her shoulder.

'Leah,' Eleanor blurted out, 'how would you like to come and live with me?'

'Are you...'

'Bring Josiah. I've a house in Peckham with a garden. I shall be married soon, and the house will be yours if you want it.'

The matron coughed. 'Say thank you to the lady, Wallace.'

Leah had put a hand to her mouth. Her eyes were shiny with tears. 'D'you mean it?'

Eleanor took Leah's hands. They were stained, the nails split; they must have her picking coir, like a prisoner. Eleanor held them tight and thought of all the things that Leah must have gone through, in all the time it had taken Eleanor to find her.

Leah would never have to think of such things again. Eleanor could give her a home, an income, a profession, if she wanted. Mr Pembroke had taken Leah's future from her – Eleanor could give it back. How could she ever regret selling her soul, when it had given her the power to do this?

'Of course I mean it,' Eleanor said.

Leah was crying. 'Bless you,' she kept saying, 'bless you, bless you.'

Charles took her arm. 'Let me take care of the paperwork, dear,' he murmured. 'Why don't you go and wait in the cab?'

Eleanor nodded. Before she left the room she hesitated, wondering whether to ask the matron where the paupers were buried. But there would be no point – without a headstone she wouldn't know if, when she stood at the graveside, it was really her parents rotting beneath her feet. Better to leave them behind, as she had left everything else.

Eleanor stumbled into the cab, shaken. She was out. Warm sunshine, birdsong, the smell of baking apples – each one was a sharp and shining thing. Heat, music, scent, snorting horses, stray cats, church bells ringing in the distance: she wanted to fold them all up inside a handkerchief and clutch it to her chest.

But she had done it. She had brought Leah home.

* * *

Bessie had objected to the idea of a workhouse girl coming to live with them. They were, she'd said, respectable people; why invite trouble into their home? The neighbours would talk, the child would cry at all hours of the night and Leah would tell all the criminal types she knew about the foolish little rich girl and her unguarded house.

Eleanor dismissed Bessie the next morning. Perhaps Eleanor was foolish, but Bessie should have remembered that she was not a little girl.

Bessie also should have remembered to ask for a written reference, but Eleanor wasn't going to tell her that. What did it matter if Bessie couldn't get another position? She hadn't been a very good maid.

Eleanor went upstairs and made up the empty bed, just this once. There was a chest of drawers beside it; the bottom one would do for the baby. Then Eleanor went downstairs to make tea. It took longer than she'd thought and came out far too weak. She'd lost her touch. All those weeks remembering to be ladylike had clearly paid off. It wasn't just her hands that had changed. Suddenly it seemed that all the colour and strength had been leached out of her until she was as soft and white as her fingers. Pretty. Pliable.

What else had she lost? When was the last time she'd read a book – a good book, one that wasn't filled with dastardly counts and young women dying prettily in white dresses? Once, Eleanor had coiled words around her like vines. She'd felt the strength of them as if they'd had their roots in earth. Now they were more like bracelets: shiny, shallow things to be slipped on and off as she pleased. Until now, she hadn't noticed how they'd changed. What else was she missing?

Had she really done the right thing?

She dropped a few more tea leaves in her cup. She was being silly. She hadn't lost anything, she'd merely changed – and it was natural to worry about change because soon her life would be very different. But at last, it would be what she made it. She could bring order to chaos, light into the darkness. How could she ever doubt that?

And, of course, there were the wishes. Those *had* changed her. Hot fear and constricting guilt had burned away her regrets and made her into something hard and brilliant. Now, she was diamond.

Leah arrived the next day, clutching her baby. The workhouse had taken back her uniform and she was wearing Eleanor's shawl and the dress she'd left Granborough House in. They had been cleaned, and stank of carbolic soap, but they were stained and crumpled from months in storage.

Leah took one look at Eleanor, waiting on the front step, and burst into tears.

Eleanor led her inside and made a pot of watery tea. She showed Leah around the house like a child might have done, chattering non-stop and pointing out inconsequential things. Leah cried through it all, eventually just sitting down on the stairs and howling into her baby's shoulder. Eleanor put her to bed, still giddy from her triumph.

Next, she would find Aoife.

The next morning Leah was calmer. Her eyes were red but she was smiling, and together they went down to the dining room, baby Josiah drooling onto Leah's shoulder. He was a still, quiet child, with eyes too large for his face, and he did not look five months old. Eleanor would have to make sure that Leah had the money to feed him up.

Leah took Eleanor's hand as they ate breakfast. 'I can't tell you how much this means to me,' she said, her voice thick. 'I'll never be able to repay you.'

'I don't want you to,' said Eleanor, smiling. 'I might need a little help until the wedding, but I'd be happy to pay you for it.'

Leah shook her head, grinning. 'This place is payment enough. Look at this! A dining table of my own! I could lie right across it!'

'Let me finish my breakfast first.'

Leah laughed. It seemed quieter than Eleanor remembered, and she felt a twist of sadness at the sound. But Leah was laughing, and she was here, and Mr Pembroke could never touch her again. The hungry creature Leah had been was gone. Eleanor had brought the real Leah back.

The atlases were spread across the dining-room table and at the sight of them, Eleanor seemed to float. She was looking at her honeymoon. First Paris, then Vienna, and from there Rome, or perhaps Constantinople. She could feel the pull of distant horizons, buried in her chest.

Leah edged into the room. 'Someone's here to see you.'

'Who is it?'

'It's a policeman,' Leah hissed. 'I swear I ain't done nothing wrong. Haven't I been good to you? Don't send me back there, *please...*'

She was crying again. Eleanor soothed her. 'Calm yourself, Leah. I shan't send you anywhere. Tell him I'm indisposed.'

Leah shook her head. 'He says it's important.'

'Bring him a cup of tea, then. I'll be through directly.'

Inspector Hatchett was waiting in the drawing room and clutching his hat, a fly among all her flowers. What did he want? Why was he here? His eyes widened when he saw her. Her mourning period for Mrs Cleary was over and, oh Lord, she'd told him she'd put on mourning for Mr Pembroke. He'd expect her to be in black for at least a year and now, thanks to her green and white dress, he'd caught her in a lie before she'd even opened her mouth. How could she have been so stupid? Why hadn't she been ready?

She put on her perfect-hostess smile. 'Inspector! This is an unexpected pleasure. How do you do?'

'Good morning, Miss Hartley. I've come to speak with your maid.'

Eleanor drew back her shoulders. 'Leah has done nothing wrong.'

'Not her. Your other maid – Bessie, I believe.'

'Oh! I see,' said Eleanor, relaxing. 'I'm afraid you've had a wasted journey, Inspector. She no longer works for me.'

'That's most unfortunate, Miss Hartley,' he said, reaching for his notebook, 'because I hoped that she could confirm your whereabouts on the night of Mr Pembroke's death. A woman matching your description was seen in the vicinity of Granborough House close to the hour of the murder. Naturally, I want to find her.'

Eleanor felt the mask descend. Behind it, she was screaming. A woman matching her description? But that made no sense, she'd been nowhere near Granborough House on the night of the murder. Or had she? The last thing she remembered was making the wish in her own kitchen, and then she'd woken up in her own bed with money missing from her purse – no. *No.* Of course it hadn't been her! She'd just had a touch too much to drink, gone out for some night air and lost a few shillings in the process. That was it. That *had* to be it.

'Matching my description?' Eleanor asked, in a carefully curated tone.

'Fair-haired, in a dark dress.'

Some of the tension eased out of Eleanor's shoulders. 'I'm not sure I'd say that matches *my* description, Inspector. Indeed, it could match anybody's.'

He made a note. 'Regardless, I should like to confirm *your* whereabouts, and your former maid is the only person who can do that. Could you supply me with her address?'

'I'm afraid I don't know it.'

'Do you have any idea where she might have gone? Had she any relatives?'

Eleanor thought fast. She couldn't let him know Bessie was Mrs Banbury's niece: he'd go straight to Granborough House, find the cook, and then he'd find Bessie. She couldn't let him talk to her. She had to get him out of the way.

'I believe she said something about looking for factory work,' Eleanor lied, 'somewhere in the north. I understand the wages are better.'

Dissatisfied, the Inspector put his notebook away. 'Have you no further information you can give me, Miss Hartley? Not even a previous reference for the girl?'

'I'm afraid not,' said Eleanor, relief flooding through her. 'I was not the one who engaged her services. If there's nothing else I can help you with…'

'No, thank you. Good morning, Miss Hartley.'

He left. Eleanor watched him go from the drawing-room window, picking his way past ribbon-sellers and flower-girls and sweating dairymaids. How long was he going to keep watching her? Would he stalk through the edges of her life forever, waiting for her to make a mistake?

The woman materialized beside her, her eyes as fathomless as ever. No shine, no glimmer of moisture – nothing but blackness, as if someone had cut the eyes out of a photograph and held it above the void.

'Such a nuisance,' the black-eyed woman said, softly. 'You could be rid of him so easily.'

Eleanor stiffened. If she made the final wish, she'd lose her soul. Ever since she'd made the deal, she'd wondered what she would be without it.

Perhaps it was time to find out.

On a bright and perfect morning, Eleanor inspected her hands. Clean, soft, largely unblemished – no one would be able to tell that six months ago she had been scrubbing floors. Tonight she would announce her engagement at Lady Winstanleigh's ball, and in her silk gloves, her past would be invisible.

Eleanor spent the day making herself perfect. She avoided the late May sunshine all day, in case she burned. Her gloves were pressed, her jewels were polished, her dress had the creases smoothed out. She lined up all the forks she had and tried to remember which one was which. By evening she was a soft, scented creature, girded with whalebone and armoured in silk and lace. No one could tell she was nervous with diamonds and sapphires at her throat. The quicksilver shoes she'd wished for clung to her feet, soft and shiny satin hidden under layers of petticoats and tulle. It felt so right to slip them on; even all those months ago, she had been on her true path. At last, the mirror reflected the person she'd always wanted to be: bright, beautiful, a queen surveying her subjects.

There was a knock at the door and Eleanor rushed to the window. A cab was waiting outside.

'Is it him? Leah, go and see who it is. Is it Charles? Quick, answer the door!'

Eleanor grabbed a blue velvet cloak and glided down the stairs, trying to think dignified thoughts and not trip over all her rustling skirts. No more walking with her head down. Tonight, she would survey high society like an Olympian goddess.

Charles was waiting in the drawing room, impeccable in black and white. When he saw her, his face lit up.

'Good God, Eleanor. You're an angel.'

He helped her into a waiting cab and held her hand when Eleanor started picking at her gloves. They passed over the glittering Thames, the streets widened, and soon the shape of a white stone mansion, turning copper in the evening sun, came up ahead. It was then that Eleanor noticed the strange sweetness in the air. She shoved away the thoughts of her mother before they could take root.

'Charles,' she began, 'perhaps I am imagining it, but is there a certain…'

He nodded, pulling a face. 'It's the old churchyard, Fortescue warned me. They're clearing out the land for a park – you know, digging things up and so forth. I'm sure it will be a lovely spot, but I can't imagine what idiot decided to start at the height of the Season. Lady Winstanleigh was furious.'

Suddenly, the smell seemed thick enough to choke on. 'Do you mean to say that…that that smell is coming from…'

Charles took her hands. 'They've all been cleared away, Eleanor, darling. There's nothing there any more, it's just a big pit. Anyway, we shan't go near the blasted place. Don't be upset.'

'This wasn't in my books! Oh, what if I should make a fool of you?'

He gave her a quick kiss. 'I don't believe you could. If you're your usual charming self, they'll all be half in love with you by the end of the night. I should know.'

The cab came to a halt and Charles helped her down. The old churchyard was closer than she'd thought. Wooden barriers closed off the entrance to the third street on the left. Beyond them was a low brick wall, and dark heaps of earth and stone.

But then she saw the house, and the sweeping staircase leading up to the gleaming black doors. All the brasswork glinted rose-gold in the evening light, the white stone stained amber, pink and saffron. A liveried doorman was checking invitations, footmen were waiting inside and a butler announced the guests, voice ringing through the hall. One look at her and they'd be able to tell what she'd been. Servants always recognized each other. Oh, God, what if she'd met one of them before and not realized it?

'There's so many people here,' she whispered. 'You will take care of me, won't you?'

He handed their invitations to the doorman and gave her gloved hand a kiss. 'Always.'

Until she stepped into the ballroom, Eleanor had thought the Pembrokes had been rich.

High, arched windows drenched the guests in amber light. Double doors led into a courtyard filled with fountains and flowers. A chandelier sparkled overhead and a wide mirror hung above an enormous fireplace on the far wall. Whirling dancers made strange patterns of light and shade on the polished floor. Jewels and pocket watches flashed, sending refracted light sparking across the room. Gold glowed, silver shimmered. Bright flowers sprawled in the empty fireplace.

Colours flashed as the dancers spun – turquoise, indigo, scarlet. Silent servants slipped through the crowds, trays balanced on gloved fingertips. A waltz wound through the room, curling around the dancers, and suddenly Eleanor's corset was too tight and her shoes were pinching and her sapphires felt like a collar around her neck. There was wealth, and then there was this.

A middle-aged woman swept towards them. She had a mass of brown hair and a wide smile, her amber-coloured dress fiery in the setting sun. She wore her jewels as if she'd been born in them.

'Dear Charles!' she said. 'I was so hoping you'd come. How are you, dear boy?'

'Very well, thank you, Lady Winstanleigh. May I introduce you to my fiancée, Miss Eleanor Hartley.'

The woman turned on Eleanor. 'Your fiancée? Well, I'd heard rumours…'

Eleanor flushed. She curtseyed, and tried not to wobble. 'How do you do?'

Lady Winstanleigh's eyes flickered towards Eleanor's stomach. She'd let Eleanor see it; no real lady would have made that mistake. Eleanor kept her smile in place, and studied Lady Winstanleigh's hair. Parts of it were darker than others; she had clearly been using hairpieces.

Lady Winstanleigh's laugh sounded like broken glass. 'Why, Charles, she's such a charming creature! Wherever did you find this little treasure? Now, come with me, there's *so* many people who want to see you again…'

'After the first dance, Lady Winstanleigh, I should be glad to join you.'

'Of course. And afterwards, Miss Hartley, you *must* tell me how you met. William tells me you were some sort of governess?'

The muscles in Charles's arm stiffened. Eleanor laughed. 'Why, Lady Winstanleigh, that sounds rather like *Jane Eyre*!'

The waltz came to a close, there was a smattering of applause, and Charles led her onto the dance floor. 'I'm so sorry,' he whispered, as they took their places, 'I'm afraid she's always been like that. You aren't upset?'

A soft chord swelled up from the violins. Charles placed a hand on Eleanor's waist.

'No.'

The music began to play.

How could she be upset with her hand in his? People would talk. They were already staring. But Charles was still here, smiling, his eyes soft. The other dancers were whirls of colour and flashes of black; formless shapes compared to his steady, solid presence. Cocooned by the sound of violins, she could not hear the whispers. With that expression on his face, would she ever notice someone else hissing in a neighbour's ear? They didn't matter. She was safe.

Soon, she would be the mistress of Granborough House. Orange blossoms and a white dress held no thrills for her: why should her life come to its peak with a quick kiss in a church? No more creeping through a forest of smoke and chimneys. As Mrs Pembroke, it would be horizons all the way. And such horizons! Vienna. Strasbourg. Paris. Rome. Petersburg. And why not further? Why not run at life with her arms outstretched?

She stared into Charles's face. His full lips were smiling, his blue eyes locked on hers as if she were the only person in the room. But the first threads of grey hair clustered at his temples, and there were new lines around his eyes. Grief had run its fingers across his face, but it made him hold her tighter. When he looked at her now, she knew how much she meant to him. When he promised to keep her safe, she believed him.

The waltz ended. Charles held out his arm. 'Are you ready?'
She took it. 'Yes.'

'Miss Hartley, if you are not otherwise engaged...'
'...all alone? How perfectly dreadful! And she left you everything?'
'Are you familiar with the work of the Pre-Raphaelite Brotherhood, Miss Hartley? You could have stepped straight off the canvas...'
Eleanor waded through a sea of insincere smiles. Dance cards were pushed underneath her nose. Champagne flutes were pressed into her hands. Flowers were plucked from buttonholes and vases and tucked behind her ears. Beckoned, waved to, admired and wanted, Eleanor felt magnetic.
She caught snatches of conversation as she passed.
'American, if ever I saw one...'
'...you know he jilted his first fiancée? Poor girl joined a convent, Millicent tells me, but you know how she...'
'...not even that! A *housemaid*. Imagine!'
Let them say what they liked. Jealousy would not stop her jewels from sparkling. Besides, her third glass of champagne had dulled their knives.
Charles pushed his way over to her, holding another two glasses. He pressed one into her hand as Eleanor's empty stomach growled.
'Is there somewhere we might take refreshments?' she asked. 'I was too nervous to have supper before we came.'

379

'You must think me an ogre! We must find you something to eat.' Arm in arm, they strolled along the edges of the ball-room, past dowagers and gouty old men and those not asked to dance. 'We can always creep down to the kitchens and see what we can find.'

She grinned at him. 'I believe I saw a hot-potato cart on our way here. Perhaps we could send a footman out for one.'

'And a pint of ale to wash it down.'

'And jellied eels. Or whelks. No – pigs' trotters.'

'*Trotters?* But how on Earth would you—'

Eleanor laughed. 'I'm sure Lady Winstanleigh could provide you with the appropriate fork.'

'Stop your teasing, you minx!'

She pouted. 'But I do it so well.'

'You *do*. How much longer do you want to stay? Perhaps we could have supper somewhere more private.'

'You're a beast! We can't leave now, we've only just arrived. Her ladyship would be desolate without us.'

'Heartless thing. Oh, that reminds me. There was someone Lady Winstanleigh wanted you to meet.'

'Why didn't you say so? I hope we haven't kept them waiting.'

'Nonsense. I'm sure he—'

Charles broke off. They had shuffled around the edges of the ballroom and were coming close to the hall doors. Lady Winstanleigh was waiting beside them, standing next to the tall, black-clad figure of Inspector Hatchett. Fear punctured Eleanor's bubble.

'Quick,' Eleanor hissed, 'if we turn back now—'

'Charles! *There* you are.'

Lady Winstanleigh was already sweeping towards them. Her

eyes flashed towards Eleanor, sharp and fast. 'I wonder if I might borrow you for a moment. Come and speak to Edgar about your Oxford days. He's considering Cambridge; you simply *must* talk him out of it.'

Eleanor laid her free hand on Charles's arm. 'Actually, Lady Winstanleigh, I'm afraid we were just about to leave.'

'I simply *won't* hear of it. This gentleman says he knows you, Miss Hartley. I'm sure you would not be so rude as to deny him the pleasure of a dance while I steal Charles away.'

The Inspector watched them steadily, a still, dark spot in a writhing sea, ready to wreck ships and drown sailors.

'I couldn't possibly. I've lost my dance card.'

Lady Winstanleigh laughed. 'My dear girl, that happens all the time! We would never ban young ladies from the ballroom for something so small!'

A muscle worked in Charles's jaw. 'I won't allow it.'

Lady Winstanleigh's eyes gleamed. In his work suit, Inspector Hatchett was a cuckoo among the ravens, shabby next to the gleaming blacks of the gentlemen. His hands were rough, his face was lined. And here he was, asking for Eleanor in her pretty ballgown and sparkling jewels. Whatever story Lady Winstanleigh ended up telling was sure to be salacious. Better to soften the blow.

Eleanor disentangled herself from Charles's arm and gave his hand a quick squeeze. 'It's all right, Charles. Lady Winstanleigh is quite correct. When I become a hostess, I shall always remember her civility towards *all* her guests.'

Lady Winstanleigh flushed. Charles didn't let go of her fingers. 'You're sure?'

'Of course. Go on.'

Charles let himself be led away. The Inspector stared at her, eyes burning, and held out an arm. She took it, and they walked onto the dance floor amid a flurry of whispering. Eleanor held the Inspector at arm's length, his hands like manacles.

The music began to play.

He danced like a soldier. Back and forward with mechanical precision, heels brought sharply together, jaw set. His spins were more like about turns. He was making her look foolish, dragging her all over the dance floor. Why was he here? What had he found out?

'Well, Inspector, this is—'

'I know what you've done.'

Eleanor stumbled on her backwards step. The black-eyed woman. Had she appeared to him too? Given Eleanor away? No, she couldn't have – the black-eyed woman never showed herself to anyone but Eleanor. The black-eyed woman had been standing right next to him and he hadn't noticed. He couldn't have seen her.

'Forgive me, but I don't know what you mean.'

'Yes, you do,' he hissed. 'Turn yourself in. Don't keep up this farce any longer.'

'What are you implying?'

He leant forward and whispered in her ear. 'I am not implying anything, Miss Hartley. I am accusing you of murder.'

She froze. The dance moved on without her. The Inspector dragged her along and she stumbled forward, chest suddenly tight.

'What?'

'Lizzie Bartram. Flora Cleary. Frederick Pembroke. All dead by your hands.'

Eleanor flinched. The black-eyed woman. *She'd* been the one who'd killed them while Eleanor had been...where *had* she been? Asleep. Of course, she'd been asleep.

She forced a smile. 'Come now, Inspector. I am seventeen years old. A young girl like me could never be capable of—'

'Yes, you could.'

Could she? No, of course she couldn't. If she'd killed them, she would have remembered. But she'd been – asleep, she must've been asleep.

'And what evidence do you have for such an accusation?'

'Miss Hartley, less than a year ago you were a servant in disgrace. These doors should be closed to you – they were, just weeks ago! And yet here you stand, with a gentleman fiancé and enough money to fix all his problems. How convenient.'

'I'd hardly call that evidence, Inspector. It is not my fault if Fate has been kind to me.'

His face twisted. 'Fate is not at work here! You murdered for money and social standing, and now you intend to reap the rewards.'

Eleanor forced her hand not to tighten on the Inspector's shoulder. It wasn't true. It wasn't murder. Her feet tangled in her underskirts; why had she had so much to drink?

'What on Earth makes you think that?'

'People you dislike have an unfortunate tendency to die.'

'Perhaps you ought to act like more of a gentleman, then.'

'Is that a threat? Or should I take that as your confession?'

'Neither. There's nothing to your ridiculous theory. What could I have possibly gained from killing my friends and guardian?'

The music swelled. With her head spinning, it pressed against her ears. The Inspector gave a tight, humourless smile.

'An end to Miss Bartram's torments? Mrs Cleary's considerable wealth? Freedom from the unwanted attentions of your guardian? Your treasures lie before you, Miss Hartley, and I know what you have done to get them.'

'And what was that?'

'You killed Miss Bartram. I spoke to the staff at Granborough House; they all knew how she hated you. For a time you were our prime suspect, until you conveniently remembered Miss Bartram's argument with the butcher's boy.'

'How dare you!'

'You then began an illicit relationship with Mr Charles Pembroke, which became public knowledge after you miscarried his child, and Mr Frederick Pembroke sent you away in disgrace.'

'Inspector, really, I—'

'You were determined to become a rich woman,' the Inspector continued, 'and so you set out to ingratiate yourself with your wealthy neighbour. But when she found out the truth about your past, you killed her before she could write you out of her will. Miss Hill tells me you didn't even pretend to mourn.'

'How can you even think such things!'

'But that still wasn't enough,' the Inspector hissed, 'because your guardian, Mr Pembroke, controlled all your money. You knew he would spend it, you knew he could stop you from marrying his son, and so you killed him.'

'Don't,' Eleanor spat, blood rushing in her ears, 'don't you dare...'

'You're a murderess, Miss Hartley,' the Inspector continued. 'The blood of three people is on your hands.'

Suddenly, the black-eyed woman was visible through the

dancers. She smiled, far too wide. *Such a nuisance*, Eleanor remembered.

Eleanor's fingers were crushed inside the Inspector's hand. 'I would never—'

'Then who did?'

'How should I know? *You* are the policeman!'

'All the evidence points to you. You are the only one who stood to gain from their deaths!'

They were spinning far too fast. 'Evidence? You *have* no evidence!'

'I do. Adelaide Hill has confirmed you lied to Mrs Cleary and withheld her reference. Bessie Banbury saw blood on your bedsheets the day after Mrs Cleary was discovered, and heard you come home in the middle of the night on the day Mr Pembroke was murdered. I'm surprised at you, Miss Hartley. I would've thought you, of all people, should know better than to underestimate a servant.'

Her head swam. A red dress flashed past; a sharp splash of blood on the ballroom floor. She flinched at the sight of it. The black-eyed woman reappeared, closer now, her smile even wider.

If you want something, my dear, you must ask for it.

Eleanor was so close now. She had money, she would be married, she could make a difference in the world. She was on the brink of leaving her past behind her and here he was, trying to drag her back towards it.

'I never killed those people!'

She couldn't let him do it.

'Liar,' he spat, 'I know what you did. You drowned the maid—'

She wouldn't let him take everything that mattered from her.

'You cut Mrs Cleary's throat—'

Time for the final wish.

'And you slaughtered Mr Pembroke in his—'

'I wish to be beyond the reach of law!'

There was a brief moment of stillness. Then, Eleanor's feet tangled together, she staggered backwards and tore herself away. She gathered up her skirts and ran into the courtyard, shaking.

Eleanor sat on the edge of a fountain with her head in her hands. The taste of champagne had soured in her mouth. The courtyard was empty, but she still felt as if she was being watched.

She'd made the final wish.

The shadows shifted. Eleanor looked up into the triumphant face of the black-eyed woman. Panic rose like bile at the back of her throat.

'So,' Eleanor said, with a calm she did not feel, 'this is it, then.'

The black-eyed woman smiled – had she always had so many long, thin teeth? – and the shadows curled around her. 'Yes. It is.'

'There must be something else you want. Here.' Eleanor fumbled with the necklace at her throat. 'Take this.'

A long, shadowy tendril lashed out. Eleanor jumped back, dropping the necklace.

'Do you think your soul can be bought with a few baubles?'

'My house, then. My clothes. My—'

The black-eyed woman held up a hand. The words died on Eleanor's lips. Her tongue sat on the floor of her mouth, a useless slab of meat.

'Your soul is worth far less, child. There is nothing you have done that I have not seen, no thought which was not laid bare before me. I know you better than you know yourself, and you are *deeply* disappointing.'

She advanced. Her shadow blossomed behind her, now squat, now clawed, now writhing.

'Did you really think you would not make the last wish? Oh, my dear. Countless others tried before you, and none succeeded. A truly good person is a rare and glittering thing – and you, dear girl, are by no means saintly.'

She laid her fingers on Eleanor's temple. They were so cold she flinched.

'So many excuses,' the woman continued. 'I believe that's all there is to you. You were poor, you were lonely, you were in love. So many people were cruel to you, weren't they, my dear? Excuses will not wipe the blood from your hands.'

The black-eyed woman leant forward. Her shadow spread across the courtyard behind her.

'But it is not love you crave, nor wealth, nor all your pretty dresses. It is power. *Destruction.* To hold a human being's life in your hands – and then squeeze. How many times did you imagine throwing something at your vile guardian's head? Did you ever picture how it would break his skin, and send the blood running down his cheeks? I know you did. I gave you the greatest gift you will ever receive, my dear. The power to make *all* your dreams come true. Even the ones you buried.'

Eleanor opened her mouth. She wanted to scream, to beg, to plead, but no sound came out. The black-eyed woman's fingertips bored into her temple, and Eleanor was sure that if she kept pushing, her skull would crack.

'Such a shame you don't remember. Do you know, my dear, I don't believe I've ever seen you so – well, happy is not quite the word. *Fulfilled.* You had such purpose.'

Eleanor shook her head, hard. She couldn't mean – no. It couldn't be true, it couldn't. Her cheeks were wet with tears. The black-eyed woman sighed.

'Still crying, after all I have done for you?'

Eleanor found her voice. 'You can't take my soul. You haven't granted my final wish.'

'Is that all?' The black-eyed woman raised her hand, her unnaturally long fingers ready to snap. 'That is easily remedied.'

'Wait!'

'It's far too late for that, my dear. You have made your wish. You cannot take it back.'

'There must be something,' Eleanor pleaded. 'You like making bargains, don't you? Make another. I'll do it. Whatever it is, I'll do it!'

The black-eyed woman considered her, hand still raised. Then, she lowered it. 'Very well. I am not unreasonable. You thought that you could outwit me; I think that we have both acknowledged that as an impossibility. But perhaps you can outrun me.'

The black-eyed woman took her arm and led her to another part of the courtyard. From that angle, Eleanor could see the barriers around the partially excavated churchyard.

'Did you see that charming churchyard as you came in, dear?'

Eleanor nodded, her heart pounding.

'Well, let's have a little race, shall we? If you can get to holy ground before the final stroke of midnight I shall release you from our bargain.'

388

Eleanor started towards it. The black-eyed woman's hand clamped around her arm, cold as stone.

'Not so fast, dearest. It would be too easy if you were to start now. No, our race will begin in the ballroom, at the moment the clock strikes twelve. If you can reach holy ground before the last bell tolls, then I will forfeit any claim I have on you and leave you in peace.'

Eleanor found her voice. 'And if I fail?'

The black-eyed woman smiled again. This time, Eleanor saw her teeth clearly in the light of the ballroom. Rows and rows of them, bone-yellow and thin as needles.

'I believe you know what will happen then.' She held out her hand. 'Do we have a deal?'

Without hesitation, Eleanor shook her hand. The black-eyed woman vanished.

Church bells rang in the distance. Eleanor whirled around. Was it midnight? No – the bells were chiming the quarter hour, she still had time. She'd head inside and position herself by the ballroom doors. That would give her the best start when the first bell tolled. Then along the hall, down the front steps, along the street until the third turning on the left, past the barriers and down the road to the old churchyard. Would it still count as holy ground if it had been dug up? It had to.

'There you are!'

Charles was striding across the courtyard, fury scrawled across his face. He faltered when he saw her.

'What time is it?' she asked.

'A quarter past eleven. Oh, darling. Have you been crying?'

Eleanor's hand flew to her face. 'Is it obvious?'

Charles took her hands and they sat down on the edge of

the fountain. 'Why are you hiding out here in the dark? You should've come straight to me.'

'I'm sorry. I wasn't – you know what happened, then?'

He handed her a handkerchief, the muscle in his jaw twitching again. 'Yes. I confess I lost my temper when I found out. But don't fret. Lady Winstanleigh has asked him to leave; we shan't be seeing him again.'

Eleanor crumpled the handkerchief into a ball. 'You don't... you don't believe—'

'Of course not! How could you even ask such a thing?'

Moonlight sharpened the lines on his face and turned his hair to silver. A lump swelled in Eleanor's throat. Was this how he would look in twenty, thirty years? Even now, he did not look like his father. Would she live long enough to see his features shift, until a dead man was staring back at her?

'We can leave, if you feel that would be best,' he said, rubbing the back of his neck. 'I...I'm sorry. You were so looking forward to tonight and I've completely disgraced you...'

Eleanor burst into tears. She buried her face in his handkerchief and sobbed. He laid a tentative hand on her shoulder.

'Eleanor...'

She wished she had more time. She wished she'd been able to tell him the truth and know that he would accept it. She wished she'd never made the deal, never been to Granborough House, never remembered the foot of the iron bed when she woke, sweating, in the dead of night. But wishing would not save her. It never had.

Charles pulled her close. 'Hush now, darling. I shall make it right, you'll see.'

There was a part of her she was too afraid to touch, because

390

its walls were eggshell-thin. Now, she could feel the cracks. Perhaps the black-eyed woman forced them open. Perhaps they'd always been there. Either way, Eleanor was terrified of what dark and nebulous thing would come slithering out.

She pulled off her gloves and pressed the heels of her hands under her eyes. It was going to be all right. All she had to do was survive the next forty-five minutes.

Charles still had his arm around her waist. 'Let me take you home, Eleanor. You've had a shock; you need your rest.'

She blew her nose and dabbed cold water under her eyes. 'No. No, I...I don't want them to say the Inspector chased me away.'

'You're sure?'

She nodded, and pinched some colour into her cheeks. 'Does it show?'

'Only a little. Stay out here for a moment longer. The cool air will do you good.'

She leant forward and kissed him. When midnight came, she wanted to feel his kiss still on her lips.

Eleanor sat on a chaise longue in the ballroom, right beside the doors. Thirty-three minutes to midnight. The ballroom was beginning to empty. Those that were left were slumped in their chairs, dozing, or still whirling across the dance floor, cheeks too flushed and eyes too bright.

She drummed her heels against the floor and stared out of the window. Sodium-yellow streetlamps burned like fireflies suspended in amber. She could just make out the shape of the barriers blocking the road to the old churchyard. There was a flash of yellow out of the corner of her eye; she ignored it.

It wouldn't take her long. Out of the ballroom doors, turn

left in the hall and head for the front doors. Then down the stairs – would it be quicker if she vaulted straight over them? No, she didn't want to risk a broken ankle. So, down the steps – the right set was closer – and then onto the street. Along for a good few yards, and then the third turning on the left, where the smell would be strongest. Over the barriers, and then—

A white shape moved outside the window.

Eleanor leant forward. Was it her reflection? No. This thing, whatever it was, was moving. She tried to put it out of her mind. It was probably just a child, or some drunk hoping to cadge scraps from the kitchen staff. Over the barriers, and then—

It lifted its head.

It was Lizzie. Her frizzy hair tangled. Thin face bloated and grey, lips blue. Hands still twisted up like snarled roots, and water dripping from her mouth.

Eleanor jerked backwards, gasping. It couldn't be her. Lizzie was dead! Eleanor had seen her herself, face-down in the water and struggling. Struggling? No, she hadn't been struggling, she'd been dead, and Eleanor hadn't seen her hands freeze halfway through their scrabbling. She was imagining things. No. It was the black-eyed woman, putting thoughts in her head to try and frighten her away.

Eleanor looked back. Lizzie was gone. Eleanor remembered the flash of yellow and thought of the little canary, shuddering.

Twenty-nine minutes to midnight.

Twenty-one minutes to midnight. Eleanor sat ramrod-straight on the chaise longue, digging her toes deeper into her satin slippers. She'd complained of the heat to get the footmen to leave the doors propped open. Opening them would take up valuable time.

Charles appeared out of the crowd carrying a plate of tarts. He pushed them into her hands.

'I smuggled these out of the kitchens for you. You look terribly pale. Are you sure you wouldn't like to go home?'

Eleanor nodded and picked up an apricot tart. It was too sweet, and the pastry crumbled like ash in her mouth. She ate it anyway. She'd need her strength.

'Will you join me for a dance?' Charles asked.

Eleanor glanced at the clock. Nineteen minutes to midnight. She might have enough time, but she needed to be ready.

'I'd rather sit here a little longer. Don't you want to enjoy the spoils of war?'

She held out the plate. Charles took a tart, grinning guiltily. 'This would be my third, I'm afraid. Oh, Ponsonby! Leaving so soon?'

A young man with receding hair was heading for the doors. Charles strode over and the two of them went into the hall, talking together. Eleanor watched them go, mechanically eating another tart. The young man's carriage was already waiting outside.

He climbed inside and Charles waved him off from the steps. The driver snapped his whip and suddenly, the horse bolted. The carriage careened forward, the horse's lips white with foam, and the screaming was—

Charles came back inside. 'I do apologize, Eleanor. Ponsonby is a dear – good Lord. Are you all right?'

Eleanor glanced back at the window. The young man's carriage was trundling off into the night, the horse serene and quiet. There hadn't been an accident.

393

'Perfectly, thank you.'

'You look as if you've seen a ghost. Let me get you a glass of something.'

'Charles, really, I'm—'

He was already gone. Eleanor ate another tart. Sixteen minutes left, and her stomach felt cavernous. Would she be able to run when she'd had nothing but champagne all night?

She reached down for another tart and saw a large red stain on her skirts. At first, she wondered if it was her monthly curse – in front of everyone, on tonight of all nights – but then she tasted turpentine.

Charles came back holding a glass of sherry. He didn't appear to notice the blood across her skirts. It was the black-eyed woman, toying with her again.

Thirteen minutes to midnight. With shaking hands, Eleanor drained her glass.

Six minutes to midnight.

Champagne crackled down her throat, sherry burned across her tongue. The tarts were sitting in a leaden ball halfway down her chest. Out of the doors, left along the hall, through the front door. Down the right set of steps, along the street until she saw the barriers. Then left, then—

A hand closed over hers. 'Eleanor?'

She flinched. It was only Charles.

'It's getting late,' he said, gently. 'I think we ought to say our farewells. Really, my dear, you do not look well.'

Eleanor pressed a hand to her cheek. She felt hot and cold all at once. She'd drunk too much. Would she have time to make herself sick? Would it help?

An empty chair sat across the ballroom. Eleanor knew what

was coming next. She blinked, and out of the corner of her eyes saw a dark shape. Blood dripped onto the floor. She could hear it, even over the music and all the passing footsteps.

She wasn't going to look at it. She knew what she was going to see. White sheets, red blood, or worse, the wound itself, ragged and weeping. Eleanor gave herself a shake. She hadn't been there, she hadn't seen what was under that sheet. The black-eyed woman was putting thoughts in her head. She didn't need to show Eleanor the visions now. Her tendrils were coiled around Eleanor's mind.

Charles was watching her. His eyes were kind and his touch was gentle. She loved him more than ever, but in this moment he would only get in her way.

'I think you're right,' she said. 'Will you give me ten minutes to compose myself?'

He let out a sigh of relief and kissed her hand. 'Whatever you need, darling. Ten minutes, and then we can put this evening behind us.'

'Will you make my apologies to Lady Winstanleigh? I don't think I could face her.'

'Of course. I shall take care of everything, don't fret.'

Behind Charles, an old major sat slumped in a chair. His head lolled onto his chest and suddenly his hair was dark, his face was wasted and there was blood pouring all down his white shirt-front. A silver watch chain glistened in his pocket, and as he raised his head to look at her, she saw the dark red line where his throat had been opened.

Eleanor closed her eyes. It wasn't real. When she opened them again, the major was back in his chair, snoring.

Charles got up. Eleanor didn't let go of his hand.

She opened her mouth. What would she say? Should she

ask him to remember her fondly? Should she warn him not to believe the things he would hear? This could be their last moment together. Or it could be the first moment of a life that was truly hers – free from secrets, free from hunger, free from a pair of flat black eyes that looked into all her thoughts. Where would she be, on the other side of this moment?

She could tell him the truth, or part of it. Lies were easier; she was good at them. She'd hacked his life apart and put the pieces back together in a way that suited her. It was kinder to let him believe that she'd saved him, and that he'd saved her.

If there was one thing she wanted, it was for Charles to remember her with kindness.

'You know I love you, Charles.'

He smiled. 'Of course I know. I love you too, Eleanor.'

She let go of his hand and he walked into the crowd.

The clock struck.

Midnight.

Eleanor sprang to her feet and sprinted for the doors. Whispers tugged at her like long grass.

'Eleanor?'

She skidded into the hall and hurtled towards the front doors. Closed. A footman stumbled into the hall, his wig askew.

'How may I—'

The second bell tolled. Charles was still calling her. God, she wanted to go back. She wanted to cling to him and never let go. She couldn't. She'd already left it far too late.

Eleanor wrenched the doors open. A *bang* from somewhere behind her – she looked over her shoulder and saw Charles staggering into the hall, catching his hip on a table.

'Eleanor! Wait!'

The third bell rang. She darted through the doors.

Cold air bit at her cheeks. Panting, she ran down the stairs, her corset cutting into her ribs. Her feet slid inside her satin slippers. She clattered down the last few steps as the fourth bell tolled.

A dark mass of carriages cluttered the street outside; the coachmen called down to her and the horses stamped their feet, their mad eyes rolling.

'Mind out, miss!'

'Need a lift?'

The fifth bell rang. Eleanor tore past the coaches, her feet slipping in her flimsy shoes. Something caught at the heel of her right foot and Eleanor was almost thrown backwards. Panic burst like a firework. She kicked off the shoes and carried on running in her stockinged feet, holding fistfuls of her enormous skirts out of her way. Behind her, Charles burst through the front doors.

'Eleanor! Eleanor, wait!'

The sixth bell rang.

Eleanor darted between the carriages, narrowly missing the hooves of a huge black horse. She pulled her skirts aside and kept running. A dark mass of people moved at the other end of the street.

'Stop! In the name of the law!'

Eleanor turned her head; the seventh bell rang. Inspector Hatchett was close behind, followed by constables with truncheons and a Black Maria waiting. She heard Charles shouting; it did not matter. The barriers were in sight. She was close.

The eighth bell rang.

Down the street, second – no, third turning on the left. Her feet were pounding into the cobbles. Every breath was a slice.

God, if only she could tear off her skirts and corset and run naked into the night, swift and sure-footed...

The ninth bell rang. Eleanor skidded to a halt by the barriers and clambered over.

'Eleanor! Eleanor, wait!'

'For pity's sake, can none of you outrun a debutante? After her!'

She was past the barriers now and the smell was choking her. Where was the churchyard? She hadn't been able to see this far down the street, how would she know where to find it?

The tenth bell tolled, she panicked, and ran. Her feet skittered over cobbles slippery with horse dung and mud. But there, at the far end of the street was a pile of broken gravestones. The churchyard. She'd made it, she was going to make it...

'Useless idiots! Fetch the horses! She can't outrun a charger—'

'Eleanor!'

The eleventh bell rang. Eleanor hurtled down the street, feet catching on rubble. Something caught at her skirts; they tore. So close now, so close. Footsteps behind her. Did they see which road she'd taken? Was a hand about to drag her back?

'Eleanor!'

Her stockings had worn through. Her feet were bleeding. But the entrance to the old churchyard was yards away. She tore forward, reached out a hand, and—

The final bell tolled.

Eleanor's fingers snatched at empty air. She skidded to a halt in front of the churchyard, legs raw, feet bleeding.

Beyond the iron railings was a churned-up pit. Moonlight glistened on a forgotten sliver of bone. Heaps of spoil stood like low, flat mushrooms and rubbish was scattered across the earth. There was no holy ground for her to stand on.

She had been tricked.

The black-eyed woman was waiting for her.

She walked out of the darkness, on the darkness, her shadow-limbs unfurling into the earth and sky. The figure in the calico dress rippled. Undulating shadows burst out of its skin. It stretched out a hand, and the fingers went on stretching.

'Come away with me, dearest.'

Eleanor couldn't move. Her trembling legs felt boneless, weak. There was nowhere to run. But fury boiled beneath her fear. The black-eyed woman had set her up to fail. Eleanor never would have survived their bargain unscathed. The black-eyed woman hadn't even granted Eleanor's final wish.

The black-eyed woman drifted forward. Shadows slithered under her skin. Her mouth was crammed with knitting-needle teeth, her jaw distended.

Eleanor clung to the lychgate. She didn't deserve this. She'd done nothing wrong. All she'd done was try and make a better life for herself. The black-eyed woman was drifting towards her, body twitching and cracking as the shadows finally burst free, and Eleanor didn't deserve to see it, she didn't deserve this horror.

And still, *still*, her final wish had not been granted. The black-eyed woman was coming for her, and Eleanor still didn't have what she wished for. She was not above the law; she could hear the policemen searching for her.

'You...you haven't granted my final wish,' Eleanor whimpered.

The black-eyed woman laughed. It sounded like cracking bone.

It wasn't fair. It wasn't *fair*, Eleanor thought. She'd risked everything she had to try and drag herself out of poverty. She'd done what other people only dreamed of. Why should she be punished? Wasn't she better than that? There was a reason the black-eyed woman had come for Eleanor, and no one else. Hers was a soul *worth* taking.

Eleanor was going to keep it. It was *hers*. The black-eyed woman could do what she liked. Whatever it took, Eleanor was going to put herself beyond her reach...

Eleanor stopped. Her breath caught.

She had wished to be beyond the reach of law. The black-eyed woman had said that she was bound to Eleanor by a law bigger than them both. Had Eleanor's final wish put her out of the reach of the black-eyed woman?

The black-eyed woman hung limp in the air. Darkness billowed around her. All her bones seemed to have vanished. Her arms hung like empty stockings and still, she raised a hand.

'You tricked me,' Eleanor hissed.

'You lost,' the woman rasped. Her mouth gaped open as she spoke. 'It is time to honour your bargain.'

Eleanor let go of the lychgate. She ground her aching feet into the dirt. She'd been tricked. She'd been lied to. The deal had been tilted against her from the very beginning. Why should she honour such a bargain? Why, *why*, had Eleanor thrown her trust away on this puppet? The only person worth putting her faith in was herself.

Eleanor had hauled herself out of poverty. Eleanor had made her dreams come true. Eleanor's life was what she made it: *she* had made the wishes. The black-eyed woman had only ever tried to drag her down.

It wasn't fair. Eleanor would *make* it fair. She would be

beyond the reach of law. *All* laws. Even those that governed the black-eyed woman.

Eleanor's heart beat so fast it hurt. Hope and fear and pride churned through her. Her hands balled into fists. She wasn't going to let the black-eyed woman take anything else from her.

The black-eyed woman was coiled in shadow. Something dragged her head upright, tugged her maw into a grin. Darkness snagged itself on her teeth.

Eleanor almost ran. Her heart was hammering. Her limbs were shaking. But the time for running was over. It was time to make her final gamble.

Breathing hard, Eleanor looked up at the grinning thing that had turned her dreams against her. She gritted her teeth. Her soul was hers. She was going to fight for it.

'I am tired of bargains,' Eleanor said.

She hurled herself at the woman, and into the darkness.

EPILOGUE

In the street outside a search was in progress. Moments before, there had been an enormous crack of thunder and the downpour began, but that did not stop the searchers. Wet constables swarmed over alleyways and knocked on doors, looking for a young girl in a blue ballgown. They checked the quiet street by the empty churchyard, and saw nothing but a deeper patch of darkness.

Outside the mansion, the guests huddled around the steps under umbrellas, whispering to each other. None of them left until the sun had started to rise. They could not; the Inspector insisted on interviewing each and every one, asking if they had seen or spoken to a young girl in a blue ballgown. He would not find her.

A young man had joined the search, even though they'd tried to stop him. His greying hair was soaked and there were early lines on his face. There would be more by the time the night was over. He would not find her either.

As the sun began to rise, the guests went home. The constables called in the day shift and trooped back to the station. The Inspector spoke to them all before they left, and wrote down the name of every street that had been searched. Charles Pembroke sat on the steps, limbs heavy.

Something winked at him from the cobblestones.

He lurched forward for a better look. It was a dainty little shoe; a delicate silver satin slipper still wet with rain. In the light from the ballroom it sparkled, like glass.

Charles reached out to it with trembling fingers. His fingers closed around the heel, and he held tight to all that could be found of Eleanor Rose Hartley.

Acknowledgements

You know that saying, it takes a village to raise a child? I've got no idea if that's true, but I can tell you that it definitely takes a village to make a book. *The Shadow in the Glass* has been twelve years in the making (and honestly, who gave time permission to do that) and a large part of that has been due to the following people.

First of all, I've got to thank my preliminary readers: Rosie, Jess, Georgie and Wei. I pestered them with endless drafts of this book and I am forever grateful for their thoughtful feedback and bottomless reserves of patience. Without their advice, I would never have got this far. I've still got the paper drafts and I will treasure them forever, especially the ones with the little faces drawn on them.

My wonderful agent, Chloe Seager, also deserves a huge thank you. Her advice and support have been invaluable on every level and I owe her at least one *massive* cocktail. Thanks also to everyone at Madeleine Milburn and Northbank; it's been fantastic to work with such dedicated and lovely people.

Speaking of, it's time for me to thank everyone at Harper Voyager! I could not ask for a nicer team to publish my first novel. Natasha Bardon and Vicky Leech – thank you both so much for all the fantastic editorial advice, for indulging my tendency to go off on historical tangents in the notes, and for letting me be as spooky as I like. Thank you also to the insanely talented Caroline Young for the gorgeous cover; it looks so nice I cried. I'm also very grateful to Rebecca Bryant, Jeannelle Brew and Robyn Watts for all their hard work on promoting and producing this book. If I've missed anyone at Voyager I'm very sorry and will buy you a drink; you are awesome.

The writing process can be really hard work; it was made so much easier through the support of my friends. A really special thank you goes out to my housemates, Cath and Claire, for keeping me supplied with endless cups of tea, indulging my mid-cooking writing rants, and for reminding me that I am a human being who needs to go to bed occasionally instead of an unstoppable word machine. (Although give it time, I'll get there.) Thank you also to Susie, Ellie and Catherine for letting me bounce ideas off you, for listening to me and for all your help and encouragement. You're the best, why do we not all have matching jackets already.

I have, of course, saved the best for last. I never would have been able to do this if it wasn't for the constant love and support from my family. Lucy: thank you so much for all your advice, for letting me rant at you even when it's all nonsense, and for taking my author photo much better than I ever could. Mum: thank you for supporting me, for believing in me, and for telling literally everyone that you meet that your daughter is an author now. Dad: thank you for going on that walk with me when I was seventeen and letting me explain the plot of the novel – your reaction was what let me know that I had something worth writing about. I love you all very much and I could never have done this without you.

– JJA Harwood, August 2020